What is addiction? Who is an addict, and why? Are we only addicted to substances, or also to patterns of thought: self-loathing, doubt, obsessive thinking, and perhaps even silence? *Subtle Gravity*, like Praeg's first novel, *Imitation*, departs from the assumption that we are all addicts. We all struggle with being alone. Taking as a point of departure an extreme form of addiction – a commitment to the silence we know precedes the violence that language imposes on us – *Subtle Gravity* maps a possible way back from addiction through a playful engagement with Buddhism, Christian mysticism and, of course, *Star Wars*.

Leonhard Praeg is Extraordinary Professor in the Department of Philosophy at Stellenbosch University, South Africa. He lives with his wife and daughter in Makhanda in the Eastern Cape, from where he works as a freelance researcher, editor, writer and yoga nidra teacher.

'*Subtle Gravity* is a complex interplay between philosophy and fiction, at once a novel and philosophical meditation on the "self", madness and hallucination in both Eastern and Western philosophies. What is real? What is a fake? Who, and what, is an Imposter? In a subtle and compelling way, *Subtle Gravity* delves into the political history and subconscious of white South Africa and privilege through a beguiling and whimsical interplay of texts, philosophies and films that range from Buddhism, Christian mysticism and quantum mechanics to Wim Wenders' *Wings of Desire*, Quentin Tarantino, *Star Wars*, Sigourney Weaver, and *film noir*. The result is fascinating, wonderful, astute, and masterly – and even better than the stunning and compelling *Imitation*.'
— JOAN HAMBIDGE, Hofmeyr Chair for Afrikaans and Netherlandic Studies, University of Cape Town

'Praeg's work belongs to a lineage of novelistic thought that challenges philosophy and/or science's self-proclaimed monopolies on thought. *Subtle Gravity* is a wonderful "novel of thought", which, through Praeg's vast intertextuality, extends our appreciation of how to think as only a novel can. In an ingenious melange of Buddhist notions of "rebirth" and Origen's doctrine of pre-existing souls that enter the world in search of redemption, characters are "reborn" into *Subtle Gravity*; into new worlds and novel situations in a way that illuminates with provocative clarity what Milan Kundera has called the "universe of the novel". In this sense, *Subtle Gravity* cannot fully escape the sense that Kundera has been "reborn" in South Africa. It is a brilliant novel, even better than the excellent *Imitation*, which restores dignity to thinking in a way only the novel can.'
— JASON M. WIRTH, Department of Philosophy, Seattle University, and author of *Commiserating with Devastated Things: Milan Kundera and the Entitlements of Thinking*

Also by Leonhard Praeg

Imitation (2017)

'*Imitation* is a strikingly original work of great subtlety, complexity, imagination, originality, and a clear homage to Milan Kundera's *Immortality*. It is a daringly original "variation of a theme" that illuminates aspects of South Africa and Côte d'Ivoire's colonial and post-colonial legacy. What is the real power of a work when it is not a mad plea for immortality? What is the fragile power of thoughts and works and lives that do not run from this question? Praeg transforms into an African post-colonial context themes we find in the stories of Goethe and Hemingway and their legacy in *Immortality*. He does so in ways that are both unmistakably "Kunderan" yet highly imaginative and original, thereby letting us appreciate Kundera in a new way while allowing Kundera to help us appreciate Africa's post-coloniality. I have never read a novel quite like this.'
— JASON M. WIRTH, author of *Commiserating with Devastated Things: Milan Kundera and the Entitlements of Thinking*

'*Imitation* is challenging, ambitious and intelligent. It is a fascinating and adventurous parallel to *Immortality* that is intriguingly and playfully managed; an impressive and carefully considered novel, which takes some of Milan Kundera's most enigmatic thoughts and modernises them.'
— ANDREW BROWN, 2006 recipient of the Sunday Times Fiction Prize for *Coldsleep Lullaby*

'In *Imitation* architecture is both a feature of form and content. It is a meditation on power, agency, free will, the existential fear of the void and our obsession with plenitude that shifts abruptly, but appropriately, from the Karoo, to Yamoussoukro, to ancient Rome, to Paris in the 1980s, to rural Switzerland and back to the Karoo. With stylistic virtuosity, Praeg successfully enacts the tempestuous relationship between philosophy and fiction while elegantly and eloquently exploring the relationship between coloniser and colonised subjects. It is a brilliant, sparkling novel that heralds a very thoughtful, new voice on the South African literary scene.'
— SAM NAIDU, Associate Professor of Literary Theory, World Literatures and English Literature, Rhodes University

'Argentine writer Jorge Luis Borges (1899–1986) did it. Italian philosopher Umberto Eco (1932–2016) did it. And now, there's South African philosopher Leonhard Praeg with his debut novel weaving together a tale of self-reflection and intrigue; philosophy, politics and coincidence, to say nothing of love and tragedy in a way that will grab you by the mind and spirit and not let go, even after you've finished reading it. *Imitation* is an extremely lucid narrative which doffs a hat to Czech writer Milan Kundera (b. 1929) as it plays intelligently and curiously with all the possibilities of what storytelling can be. It is a yarn of such noble and internal proportions that one is left sleepless; a very powerful read which is elegantly structured and beautifully told.'

— ROBYN SASSEN, Arts writer, reviewer, academic

'Like Kundera before him, Praeg has written a novel capable of showing us possibilities never seen before in the novel. *Imitation* not only offers us a reflection on the role played by imitation in history and our personal stories, but also on the human need to create. Praeg and Kundera continue a conversation about man, history and existence through which the two works illuminate each other with a respect, subtlety and humour comparable to the conniving gaze between two long-time friends.'

— FLORIAN BEAUVALLET, Department of English,
Université de Rouen

Subtle Gravity

Leonhard Praeg

UNIVERSITY OF KWAZULU-NATAL PRESS

Published in 2021 by University of KwaZulu-Natal Press
Private Bag X01
Scottsville, 3201
Pietermaritzburg
South Africa
Email: books@ukzn.ac.za
Website: www.ukznpress.co.za

© 2021 Leonard Praeg

All rights reserved. No part of this publication may be reproduced or transmitted in any form or by electrical or mechanical means, including information storage and retrieval systems, without prior permission in writing from the publishers.

ISBN: 978 1 86914 476 0
e-ISBN: 978 1 86914 477 7

Managing editor: Sally Hines
Editor: Alison Lockhart
Layout: Patricia Comrie
Proofreader: Catherine Munro
Cover design: Marise Bauer, M Design
Cover artwork: Mural by Ernest Zacharevic, Dubai, 2018

Printed and bound in South Africa by XMD Books (Pty) Ltd

Vir Ina, Margaret en Mrs Cowley

It isn't just ghost electrons that Bohr conjures out of the quantum equations, but ghost realities, ghost *worlds* that only exist when we are not looking at them.
— John Gribbin, *In Search of Schrödinger's Cat*

It is better to keep silence and to be, than to talk and not to be. — Ignatius of Antioch

Obedience to the force of gravity. The greatest sin.
— Simone Weil, *Gravity and Grace*

Contents

Part I: Waking

The Imposter   3

Schrödinger's Cat   39

The Finger   52

The Mystic's Curse   61

Part II: Arrival

First Session with the Emperor   72

Short History of a Long Fable I   83

Short History of a Long Fable II   90

Luc Falls through His Own Arsehole   104

Harvesters I   109

Luc's Scrotum   120

Part III: Detachment

Harvesters II   139

Second Session with the Emperor   154

Luc Has a Gut Feeling   163

Harvesters III   174

Luc's Heart Goes Out   180

Part IV: Attachment

Harvesters IV   193

Third Session with the Emperor,
in which Luc Makes a Demand   199

Luc Crosses Over   206

Harvesters V   213

My Iridescence   281

Author's Note

Our everyday understanding of karma is still trying to escape from the long shadow cast over Western history by the colourful, tie-dye sarong of the sixties when karma was reduced to the kind of vengeful moralism of 'what comes around, goes around' or, even worse, 'Don't worry about revenge, my love; he'll get what's coming to him in his next life.' The origins of this simplistic understanding of karma and the history of the complicity of intellectuals, scholars and 'gurus' in perpetuating it would doubtless fill an entire bookshelf. Suffice it to say that, rightly understood, the logic of karmic action is more suggestive of the kind of interrelatedness captured by Lorenzo's famous butterfly effect than it is the linear punish-and-reward system of the hippie imagination. The real logic of karma is at work when you find yourself in a certain place at a certain time, aware of the demons you are fighting, the shadows that haunt you and the promise of clarity, even redemption, that seduces you. To be *aware* simply means that you recognise your place in a karmic network of people, places and actions. When you are aware, you *will* meet the people who can and will help you to surface the clarity you seek.

This novel is only a tangible point or node in such a network of karmic actions. It could not have been written in any other place or at any other time. It could also not have come about in the absence of a number of relationships and incidents that all triggered butterfly actions I tried to chase down, understand and contain. A number of people have to be acknowledged for the place they occupy in this network: Juanita and Maria, for encouraging me to accept an opportunity that afforded me the freedom to explore that time and place; Maxi Schoeman, for initiating a leap that was such a singular combination of blessings and curses that I can only make sense of it in karmic terms; Amanda Oelofse, who kept me sane as I briefly contemplated offering my job to Luc; the reviewers of the manuscript who understood what I was trying to do when I thought nobody except my friends would: Dan Coughlan, Stacy Hardy, Michelle Keen, Steve Molyneux, Nigel Mullins, Susan van Zyl, Minka Woermann, Jason Day of the Third Way, and Linda Erasmus and Andrew Mason who, way back and 'for no apparent reason', sent me the image of the mural in Dubai by street artist Ernest Zacharevic, which I instantly recognised as the future cover of what was to become *Subtle Gravity*.

Then, as always, much gratitude to my editor Alison Lockhart, whose gentle clarity and keen eye endlessly reverberates through my writing actions. Last, but not least, to my friend Hermann Niebuhr, who made such beautiful sketches for *Imitation*, but somehow never managed to provide me with the sketches I commissioned from him for this novel – all I can say is, 'Pray the hippies got it wrong.'

There is one short extract from *Imitation*, which appears in double quotation marks.

Part I

Waking

The Imposter

1

As usual, I got up at 6.00 this morning. I had set the alarm for 5.40 to allow myself two ten-minute snoozes before I got up. This routine is a relatively recent development. I used to be much more of a disciplinarian about waking up. I would always set my alarm for the exact time I needed to get up and, when it went off, I would immediately sit up and let it ring for a couple of seconds to make sure I was awake. Only then would I switch it off and get out of bed. For as long as I can remember, the initial act of obeying the command of the alarm clock was followed by a series of other acts of discipline, all designed to ensure that I would arrive in the world as soon as possible, without bringing with me any of the nostalgia, melancholy or longing for forgetfulness to which I was so prone, and which made it so tempting to turn over and go back to sleep again. These acts were lined up in the same order every morning – like good little soldiers, who would take turns to salute the courage in my waking up with such clear determination. I would splash my face with cold water, rubbing it over my closely shaved head; next, cupping my hand, I would gulp several large mouthfuls of water before eliminating the remaining taste of decay with mouthwash. After relieving myself, I would walk back into my bedroom, pull the curtains aside and open the windows to let in the fresh morning air. Then I would shake out the duvet, fluff my pillows and make the bed, after which I would go to the kitchen to make coffee. For many years this was the discipline of my morning routine and for many years it worked perfectly well. By the time I had switched on the coffee machine and tamped the ground espresso coffee into the basket, I was not only awake, but felt as if I had successfully managed to step into the daily river, as if I had done so voluntarily and started the day because I wanted to and not only because I had found myself waking up in it. Yes, that is what my little parade of soldiers allowed me to believe: I chose to be here and consequently it would make little sense to regret being here. The result of this brave morning parade was that for a long time I was always the first person at the office.

But then things changed. I started to set my alarm ten minutes earlier than I needed to, so that I could have one snooze before I got up. But it did not take me long to arrive at the conclusion that one snooze was more like the continuation of deep sleep and I soon became annoyed because, instead of going through the irritation of waking up once, I now went through the same irritation twice. Rather than reverting to military discipline, I decided that a better solution would be to set my alarm twenty minutes earlier than necessary, so that I could have two snoozes. That made all the difference. While the first snooze still basically meant that I just went back to sleep again (for what felt like two seconds), the second snooze was always more superficial. I did not just plummet back into dark forgetfulness, but somehow stayed slightly aware of myself, of the fact that I was snoozing, never quite forgetting that the alarm would soon go off again. This state of slight self-awareness, of being half awake and half asleep, fascinated me. Once I got used to it, the recurring impression that danced through my waking consciousness was of midsummer sunlight falling through a leafy poplar tree in a peaceful, green park. The play of light and shadows on the small patch of grass under the tree was never constant; patterns of sunlight and shadow flickered playfully, so that a little island of light could turn into solid shadow in an instant and then back again. For the duration of that second snooze, my mind was the patch of grass where daylight flickered into night and back again, awareness into forgetfulness, presence into nothingness. I started to look forward to that second snooze even as I got into bed at night. Sometimes I was so excited by the prospect of experiencing that flickering light of awareness that I feared my excitement would get the better of me and I would struggle to fall asleep, or fall asleep very late, and as a consequence wake up tired and grumpy when the alarm went off. But, somehow, this never happened. The excitement seemed to comfort me and the prospect of flickering into wakefulness the next morning made me fall into a deep, relaxing sleep.

The first sound of the alarm annoys me into wakefulness, something that is soon forgotten as I sink back into sleep. But then, when the alarm goes off a second time and I hit the snooze button, things are usually (though not always) very different: the flickering of awareness never quite recedes; the shadows never completely reclaim the patch of grass. How I came to relish that second snooze! Even though it took me quite a while – three months, if I remember correctly – to work out exactly why I came to love it so much, I eventually realised that it was not only because during the second snooze my mind felt like a small patch of grass where wakefulness and forgetfulness playfully figured it out. The reason the flicker came to intrigue me so much was because it afforded me a daily glimpse into the birth of intention. The play of light and shade was the exact moment when my intention to live the day was born again every morning. *Where does intention go when we sleep?* I dreamily wondered one morning. But the question was quickly pushed aside by the sheer pleasure of experiencing how wonderful it was to witness the reincarnation of intention in my mind.

Along with the realisation that consciousness reincarnated in me every morning, and that it could be deeply pleasurable to witness this process of rebirth, came a whole different set of little rituals. After the second snooze, I now sit up and reach for the bottle of water I always place on the nightstand before I go to bed. I drink the whole bottle, my body soaking up the water faster than I can swallow. Who would have thought that drinking a whole bottle of water could be so invigorating for the sleepy body? The effect is not unlike the rush I will get from the cup of coffee I have a little while later while I prepare breakfast, with the important difference that while a bottle of water seems to wake up my entire body, a cup of coffee just seems to shake the mind awake – a bit like a wet dog after an unexpected shampoo. After relieving myself, I now slip back into bed and enjoy the erotic pleasure of wrapping the down duvet around my naked body as I prop myself up against the headboard.

I gave up on being the first person at the office. Instead, I now use the time to plug in my earphones and select one of the guided meditations from my playlist. Sometimes I fall asleep again – in fact, this used to happen a lot in the beginning, mainly because I initially made the mistake of lying down again. Then I worked out that I would be less likely to fall asleep if I sat propped half upright against the headboard. Now, when my head drops or my body leans to one side as I start drifting off, it is more a matter of falling awake than falling asleep again. Still, sometimes I do drift in and out of wakefulness, the soothing voice of the teacher first lulling me into sleepy comfort before welcoming me back to her generous world. I suppose what I discovered was simply how to nurture my wakening intention into something more than a struggling flicker, or how to prolong that moment until the sun breaks through the trees to chase the shadows away, until much later in the day when they will reclaim their rightful place on that same little patch of lawn that I call 'my consciousness'. After a couple of weeks of witnessing my own awakening in this way, the experience of observing intention flickering into existence suggested a second image: the morning meditation kindles my consciousness into life; a small flame is cupped between trusting hands and nurtured into existence from the embers of sleep, lifted higher, closer to the moment when I will know that I am fully awake.

'What brought about such a fundamental change in my waking ritual?' one may well ask. To go from a ritual structured as a military parade to one of generous sensuality suggests that somewhere along the line something important had happened, something pretty fundamental. What was it? A fair question. We all change constantly (sometimes less than we would like and more than a lover wants, or the other way around). Our likes and dislikes also change. What we once thought were routines that defined us may fade away and be replaced by new routines. We change our eating habits – we stop eating meat, for instance, and become vegetarian or vegan – and we mostly know why. Even if there is no clearly defined reason, we can at least refer to a sense of discomfort or a longing for a better life as having motivated the change. 'It was after the results of the last cholesterol test came in,' we say. Or when we turned 40 or 50 or 60 and decided it was time to quit smoking or drink less alcohol, to exercise more or spend less time at the office. The only thing more important than a fundamental change is knowing why the change came about. I knew with absolutely certainty what had brought about the change in my waking routine. It was an encounter with the Imposter.

2

My encounter with the Imposter was the indirect result of an uncanny experience I had one Friday afternoon when, on my way home from work, I stopped at the shopping centre two blocks from my apartment. It is a small centre, but it has everything I need to enable me to effectively contain my city life within the radius of a small village. There is a passably good restaurant where, mainly because of its proximity to all the embassies in my suburb, rather than its food, diplomatic staff – including ambassadors and ministers – languish deep into the night over cocktails, shared platters and scandalously expensive whisky; a coffee shop, where I sometimes stop for a glass of vegetable juice on my way home; a curio shop; two or three ridiculously overpriced men's boutiques; a massage parlour; a supermarket; a barber; a postal service and a bar called Harvesters, where I sometimes go for a drink on a Friday or Saturday evening. They often invite blues bands to perform there on

Fridays and for me it is the perfect solution to what may otherwise become a long, lonely evening. I walk down to Harvesters for a couple of drinks, have superficial conversations with one or two strangers until I eventually get bored and walk the two blocks back to my apartment.

On that particular Friday, I had stopped at the centre on my way home after work because I wanted to buy a birthday present for my favourite niece, Grace, who was turning twelve. I had been invited to attend her birthday party that evening. I had hoped to find something suitable for her at the curio shop, even though they mostly stock the kind of chic Afro-kitsch that foreign tourists love to buy. Every day, tourists visit the Union Buildings, three blocks from my apartment, where they walk around the beautifully kept gardens, admire the view and take selfies in front of the huge Nelson Mandela statue, with their arms stretched out in imitation of his gesture of welcoming forgiveness. Then they pile back into the bus and, on their way to the next attraction, all the buses (or so it seems to me) stop at my little centre, where the tourists have pancakes at the coffee shop. While they wait for their orders, many of them quickly go into the curio shop next door and invariably emerge with a more expensive curio than they would have been able to buy from the makeshift tables of the hawkers who trade in front of the Union Buildings. They buy large woven baskets, tall Giacometti-style carved wooden figures, nifty articles of wire work (animals, men, women, children on bicycles), tambourines made of Coke bottle tops, dyed cloth, aprons with wild animals on them – everything neatly categorisable into one of the three stereotypes that Africans cannot escape, just as a field mouse cannot escape an eagle swooping down on it: wild animals, writing in the childlike font of the illiterate and the joyful abundance of colours that seem to celebrate the blissful *hakuna matata* existence of a people who have never had a conception of the future.

I walked into the shop, confident that if I spent enough time looking around I would certainly find something there for Grace.

I hoped that, since she was only turning twelve, she would as yet be ignorant of what life in Africa meant, ignorant of the existence of kitsch and the terrible combination of the two that occurs so frequently. After spending considerable time procrastinating over what she would prefer, I settled on a beautifully carved wooden jewellery box, cheerfully labelled 'The Little Five', on which was depicted a happy carnival of elephant shrews, buffalo weavers, leopard tortoises, antlions and rhinoceros beetles. Pleased with my success, I walked over to where the cashier was sitting on a high stool behind the counter. I placed the jewellery box on the counter and started to rummage around in my rucksack for my wallet.

I had often seen this man sitting behind his counter as I went about my business in the centre. Mid-forties, slightly bald, always looking peculiarly content even when there was nobody in the shop and he was just sitting there, rearranging items on the counter in front of him or unpacking new merchandise from a box at his feet onto one of the shelves. *What does he do all day?* I have often wondered. Say, on an average day, three buses stop and a total of twenty people go into his shop, of whom thirteen or fourteen buy things. Given the prices of some of the items, I can well imagine that his business would be financially viable, but how does he survive it? How does he do it, day in and day out? And yet, he always looks perfectly content and friendly and often nods a greeting at me as I pass his shop.

That Friday was no different. While he lifted the wooden box up to look at the price on the bottom, I placed my wallet on the counter and waited for him to ring up the sale.

'It's a birthday present,' I said. 'I'd be grateful if you could wrap it nicely.'

'Sure,' he said, as he carefully removed the price tag without tearing it.

I pulled out my credit card and watched him ring up the sale. I handed over my card and he processed the payment. Then I placed the card back in my wallet and returned it to the secure inside pocket of my bag while I watched him carefully wrap the box, first in a thin sheet of crackling white paper and then in bright green gift wrap.

'Has it been a busy day?' I asked, trying to avoid what somehow suddenly felt like an awkward silence between us.

'No more than usual,' he said, as he tied a red ribbon around the gift.

'Do you ever get bored when it's quiet?' It slipped out before I could stop myself.

He just smiled and said nothing. He pulled a last bit of tape from the dispenser and secured the ribbon to the paper. Then, turning away from me to reach under the counter for a gift bag to put it in, he said, 'What are you unwilling to feel?'

I looked around to see if there was somebody behind me to which the question may have been addressed, but it was still just us.

'Excuse me?' I said incredulously.

He turned back to me and placed the gift bag in front of me on the counter with the same mysteriously timeless smile I always see on his face when he greets me.

'What did you just say?' I asked.

'I said I hope your niece enjoys the present.'

'How did you know . . .' I started and stopped. For a moment I could not remember if I had mentioned my niece. Then I remembered that I definitely had not. All I had said was that it was a birthday present. 'Did I mention my niece?'

'You didn't need to,' he said and started to arrange things in a box next to the cash register, making it clear that as far as he was concerned our interaction was over. But there was too much that was strange about this encounter for me to just turn around and walk away.

'And what did you mean when you said, "What are you unwilling to feel?" That is what you said, wasn't it?'

He looked at me with a mixture of bemusement and politeness. 'I'm sorry. I don't know what you are referring to.'

'You said, "What are you unwilling to feel?"'

He somehow managed to frown and smile at the same time. 'I'm sorry, Sir,' he replied politely. 'I think you misheard what I said.'

The thought *This could go on forever* flashed through my mind. If I asked him what he said, in order to see if he could come up with a phrase that sounded just like 'What are you unwilling to feel?' he would simply find another way to recede even further behind that mysterious smile. There was nothing left to do or say. And yet, I was 100 per cent certain that I had not mentioned my niece and that he had indeed asked me what I was unwilling to feel. Besides, the phrase is just too singular for me to have imagined it. The atmosphere between us now felt even more awkward, a discomfort I did not want to prolong by standing there while I placed the gift in my rucksack. So, I took the gift and, mumbling something I resentfully hoped only sounded like 'Well, have a nice day', walked out the door.

'You too, Sir.'

Outside the shop I placed the rucksack on my bicycle seat, opened it and slipped the gift inside. Then, as I slung the bag over my shoulder and turned the bicycle in the direction of the parking lot exit, I looked back in his direction. He was still rearranging the items in the container next to the cash register, that mysterious smile visible even from where I was standing. I shook my head, as if that would clear the confusion, got on my bicycle and started the uphill journey home.

I was suddenly overwhelmed by the feeling that I inhabited two worlds. In one world, I had just stopped to buy my niece a birthday present at the local curio shop. After settling on a beautiful jewellery box, I left the shop and got back on my bicycle. In the other world, a mysteriously ordinary man behind a counter in an ordinary curio shop seemed to know things about my personal life that I had not told him. And he had just asked me a question that unsettled me deeply – only then to deny having asked the question at all.

At the first crossing, I got off my bicycle and waited for the traffic light to turn green. As this happened, I felt so disoriented that I realised I may be a danger to myself and the responsible thing to do would be to push the bicycle across the busy intersection, where taxi drivers often jump the red light. Midway across the road, a memory inadvertently came to mind: Seinfeld had bought a big arcade-size version of *Frogger*, a video game in which the player must make a frog cross a series of perilous, crocodile-infested rivers all the way from the bottom of the screen to the top. Seinfeld's journey across the busy New York street is filmed from above, so that he looks like, well, a frog crossing a crocodile-infested river.

My feeling of estrangement was not so much the result of experiencing two worlds at the same time as it was because of being alienated from both. It was as if my encounter with the strangely content man had opened a doorway to another world, which exists even though, as a rule, we are not aware of it; a world that runs parallel or perhaps perpendicular to ours, inhabited by people who look and speak just like us and know things about us that they cannot possibly know – such as who our family is, or whose birthday it is – people who understand our deepest fears and yet somehow manage to contain all that knowledge without having the slightest desire to interfere in our lives in order to make life easier.

What are you unwilling to feel?

3

I pushed my bicycle through the gate, closed it, unlocked the door to my patio and leaned the bicycle against the wooden slats that separate my patio from the neighbour's garage. I unlocked my door and went inside, switched off the burglar alarm and casually dropped my rucksack on the couch. It was a hot day and I would not have been surprised if there had been a quick downpour – one of those short bursts of late afternoon rain I have often heard people in Pretoria (or is it Tshwane?) refer to as 'civil servant' storms. I have come across two different explanations for this name. According to the first, they are called civil servant storms because they only work for fifteen minutes, from 4.00 to 4.15 p.m. According to the second version, they are called that because they usually start around 4.00, just as all the civil servants head home. Somehow, the two explanations did not seem mutually exclusive to me and I am sure that if I put my mind to it, I would be able to come up with an explanation that accommodates both versions. That I have not as yet devised a Unified Theory of Civil Servant Storms is in part because I have not yet been sufficiently intrigued to try, but also because another part of me does not want to reconcile the two versions because it would resolve a slight tension between them that I find quite intriguing.

Having pushed my bicycle uphill for two blocks, I was not going to wait and see whether there would be a downpour. I still felt alienated from both my worlds and knew that only doing something physical would make the feeling go away. So, I stripped down to my shorts, put the kettle on to make tea and walked back onto the patio, where I unwound the garden hose, opened the tap and gently showered all the pot plants with a spray of cool water. Then, I pulled my shorts off and, holding the hose that was still set to shower mode above my head, allowed the water to run down over my whole body. This was one of my favourite things in the world and I always quietly blessed the landlord for having installed the retractable canvas cover over the patio, which afforded me the privacy to have these naked showers outside in broad daylight without having to worry about the upstairs neighbours looking down on me. Generally, I leave the canvas extended, not only for privacy, but also because it is quite tricky to retract. The elaborate rope pulley system is easy enough to operate, but there is a serrated edge where the canvas meets the wooden panelling that could be quite dangerous. One could quite easily get one's hand caught in it and sustain a deep cut – which, in fact, happened to me once shortly after I had moved in. And then, of course, there is the added security benefit of preventing any potential burglar who has made it over the neighbour's garage wall from getting onto my patio.

I aimed the hose's shower head under my armpits, then at my face, down my body, under the soles of my feet, massaging my toes one by one under the pressure of the water. Then I got down on my haunches and gave myself what I call the 'chakra rinse' – starting with the perineum, moving up to the general pelvic area, letting the water hit my solar plexus full force, moving up to my heart, rubbing my chest vigorously, followed by another blast at my neck, face and forehead and ending by holding the shower head high above my head, like an ordinary shower. This, I have discovered, is the best way to wash away the residue of the day and by the time I had wrapped the towel around my waist, turned off the tap and wound the hose back onto its wheel, I could hear the unmistakable sound of the kettle whistling for attention. Before I walked across the small lounge area back into the kitchen, I unwrapped the towel and paused for a couple of seconds to dry my legs and feet, so as not to walk too much water into the apartment. I switched the kettle off and poured water into the cup I had placed next to it. While the tea steeped, I walked outside again, hung the towel on the washing line and put my shorts on again. My world had been unified and I was back in it again. By the time I had completed my little homecoming routine and was sitting with my feet stretched out on the patio table sipping my tea, there was only about half an hour before I had to leave for Grace's birthday party.

I was not particularly close to either of my brothers or their families, but for some or other reason my oldest brother's youngest daughter Grace and I have always had a special relationship. Not that we have spent a lot of time together – on the contrary. But we both vividly recall every moment we have spent together and often remind each other of fun things we have done or of silly moments that have had us both in stitches with laughter. Grace's favourite memory is of a day I visited them when she was six or seven (possibly eight). We had been playing in the pool and were sitting next to each other on the patio sipping lemonade. We chatted about interesting and boring school subjects, friends and our favourite games when I suddenly had an uncontrollable urge to fart. I held my finger to my lips. 'Shh! Did you hear that?'

Grace stopped talking and, without turning her head, looked around, her eyeballs rolling in all directions. She seemed to clutch the glass of lemonade just a little bit firmer between her hands. 'What?' she whispered.

'*That!*' I whispered back and farted loudly.

She was shocked, horrified and delighted at the same time. We laughed and laughed, cheerfully clinking our glasses together and taking turns to imitate the sound of the fart, each imitation getting more and more exaggerated until our verbal farts sounded more like rolls of thunder than farts. Then, as the silly hysteria settled down into that strange quiet that always lingers after the secret celebration of shared mischief, Grace looked at me, an unexpectedly serious expression on her face.

'Uncle Dodo . . .' (Neither of us can remember where she got that name from nor why it stuck. Not remembering seemed part of our secret bond and therefore we never tried to remember.)

'Yes, my love?'

'I just want to say something . . .'

Her face became more serious; solemn, even.

'I'm all ears.'

She appeared to be thinking deeply for a couple of seconds as if she had difficulty finding the right words. Then she said '*That*!', lifted one bum cheek and farted. The sombre spell of a secret mischief whose attraction was briefly exhausted by its exposure to the light of laughter was broken and we laughed all over again, doubling up, imitating the sound of her little fart until it, too, assumed the ambition of rolling thunder, laughing and laughing, as if we were the first people in the history of the world to fart a conversation.

My most vivid memory of time spent with her is a bit less humorous, but I suppose it stuck in my mind because it explained why, despite our closeness, I did not spend more time at their place or visit them more regularly. I had gone to stay with them one Saturday night and late on the Sunday afternoon, Grace and I found ourselves idling around the house, slightly bored. My brother and his wife had gone grocery shopping and neither of us felt like watching TV. We had already spent considerable time in the swimming pool and played various board games. Eventually I said to her, 'I have an idea. Bring a towel.'

We went outside and I said, 'Today I am going to introduce you to yoga.'

'What is yoga?' she asked, picking up a towel and skipping ahead of me onto the lawn.

I stopped for a second or, to be honest, for a second I was stopped in my tracks by the question. I had no ready-made answer for an eight-year-old. 'Um,' I said eventually, 'think of it as teaching the body how to pray.'

'We go to church every Sunday to pray,' she said, as she stopped and turned around, waiting for me to catch up with her.

'I know. And you have to sit still the whole time, don't you?'

'Not always,' she said. 'Sometimes we stand up to pray. I like that.'

'Standing and praying?'

'No, getting up and sitting down. Up and down, up and down,' she said, with exaggerated up-and-down movements of her head. 'Then it's not so boring.'

'Well, then you're going to love yoga,' I said.

We had reached a patch of grass under a mulberry tree. It was edging towards late afternoon and sunlight was playing lightly through the leaves, making patterns of light and shadow on the grass that shifted and danced, almost as if to dare the eyes: *See me if you can!*

I spread out my towel on the grass and instructed Grace to do the same. Then I stood solemnly at the end of my towel, folded my hands in a gesture of prayer and said, 'Well, what makes yoga cool is that you get to move all the time while you pray. You never have to stand or sit still for very long.'

Grace had imitated me and, with her hands folded in a gesture of prayer, was looking at me out the corner of her eye.

'So, this is it,' I said. 'The body has seven motors called chakras.'

'Motors? Like a motor car?'

'No, more like an aeroplane. Think of them as seven propellers that all have to work in order for us to fly. And these seven motors have to be synchronised, otherwise the aero . . .'

'What is simchronised?'

'They must be clean, well oiled . . . And they must all work at the same time, otherwise our aeroplane goes flying off skew to the one side or lopsided . . .' and with that I threw my arms wide open. 'Like this . . . whooooosh.'

'And then it crashes like this!'

She imitated a crashing plane and fell on the lawn.

'Yes, but we don't want that to happen. So, we have to constantly clean our propellers and yoga helps us do that.'

Grace had got up again and was standing at the end of her towel. She seemed unsure of herself, waiting for me to do something new. I said, 'Each of the aeroplane's propellers has a different job. I'll show you where they all are and tell you what their job is. The first chakra is here,' and I pointed to my bum, 'where farts come out when we have a farting conversation.' She grinned widely, wringing her hands a little, as if she were unsure what to make of this lesson about farting aeroplanes. 'When the first chakra is well oiled and working properly, you know you have a right to exist.' Seeing the sceptical look in her eyes, I quickly continued. 'The second chakra is here,' and I vaguely indicated the genital area, 'and its job is to make sure you can feel emotions and enjoy pleasure. The third chakra is here,' and I pointed to my solar plexus, 'and here a wonderful thing happens. . .'

Her eyes widened. 'To everyone?' she asked, 'or only those whose propellers work?'

'Potentially everyone,' I said. 'Potentially, everyone's propellers can work. It's just that we sometimes forget to maintain them properly. They break and we don't fix them . . .'

'And then the the the airplane goes all skew-whiff again and flies with one engine and everyone gets scared and and and and . . .' She was nearly exhausted by the power of the analogy, '. . . then the pilot has to make an urgency landing on a highway and and and . . .'

'Yeah, yeah, yeah,' I said. 'I get it. But yes, you're right. The plane can crash if the propellers don't work properly. That's why this one – and I pointed to my solar plexus – is so important because when it works well, my intention will coincide with God's will and I will understand the reason why things happen in my life.' I could see this confused her.

'So, this is God's exercises? I thought you said . . .'

'I know what I said,' I interrupted her, sensing immense complications gathering on the horizon. 'The body must learn to pray. But who or what it prays to is up to you. It can be God or just . . .' I stopped, at a loss for words.

'Sandy's mom goes to the gym every morning. It's on the way to school, so Sandy has to sit and wait in the car for her mom to finish.'

'Well,' I said, 'maybe you can show Sandy some of these propeller exercises and then she can do them in the park or somewhere while she waits for her mother. Anyway, on to the fourth one, which is right . . . here.' I held my hand on my heart. 'This propeller is all about love. Loving yourself and the world you live in.'

'Daddy says Jesus died because he loved us so much,' she said and I could tell from the way she was fidgeting and pulling at her clothes that she was getting restless.

'Well, that just goes to show that Jesus's heart propeller worked very well.'

'His heart propeller! Ha ha ha!' she laughed. 'And what about his bum propeller?'

'You know what? Never mind all that. Just do what I do. Follow the leader.'

We had done about five asanas when she lost interest. 'What does all this have to do with the propellers? This is boring. You made it sound like much more fun.'

And so our first yoga class came to an inglorious end.

After dinner that evening, my brother John took me aside. His wife Cath and Grace were doing the dishes and my brother steered me out onto the patio, each of us with a glass of wine in hand.

'Grace told me about the yoga this morning.'

'Yes, was fun,' I said, 'if unexpectedly brief.'

'We don't approve of yoga,' he said. 'From a Christian perspective, it's a form of devil worship. I know you won't agree, but it's not up for discussion. We've been warned about this by the *dominee*. All this New Age stuff – it's just another way the devil is trying to find his way into people's hearts. People are so confused, they'll try anything that makes them feel good.'

Makes them feel good, I thought in the Uber on my way home that evening. *And still the original sin lingers.*

My reverie about the rest of that Uber trip home was interrupted by the ringing of my cell phone. It was John. 'You still coming, or what?'

'Yeah, of course,' I said. 'You said 6.00.'

'I know. Relax. Just checking if you can stop and get some more buns on the way. It's hot dog central here.'

'Of course. I'll be there shortly. Looking forward to the ketchup.'

This is how my brother and I have resolved the fact that we live in parallel universes. We let the buns and the ketchup do the real work. Or most of it, anyway.

4

'What an odd thing to say. Are you sure that's what he said, that he didn't perhaps say something that just sounded like "What are you unwilling to feel"?'

'You mean something like . . .'

'I don't know. What are you . . . unwilling, unwitting, un-milling . . .'

'To eal, peal, shmeal,' I added. 'Right. I tried everything I could think of. That is definitely what he said and then he was all mysterious and coy about it.'

'He denied it altogether?'

'Yip. He just looked at me with that mysterious face and said he hoped my niece liked the present.'

'Even though you hadn't mentioned it was for your niece?'

'Precisely.'

'That is just weird,' my brother said. He turned away from me and leaned with both elbows on the balcony, beer in hand. We were standing on the first floor of their home and for a while neither of us said anything. We watched the kids playing on the lawn, running in and out of the house. *An awkward age, twelve,* I thought. *In the middle of nowhere. No longer a child whose idea of a party is to run around the house chasing one another or playing hide-and-seek, but not yet old enough to just sit and make conversation.* And yet, there they were – some of them running around, the rest huddled around the big flat screen TV playing video games.

I had arrived at the house just after 6.00 p.m. with a big bag of buns in one hand and a bottle of wine in the other. Immediately, as I got out of the Uber, my world mysteriously split in two again. The strange experience of two worlds that exist side by side and, along with that, the fog of alienation that comes from recognising that I belong to neither, returned. The philosopher in me took a desperate stab at defusing the discomfort. I rang the doorbell and while waiting for someone to open the front door, I told myself that in order to feel estranged from two worlds at the same time I must be occupying a third position of sorts and this third position is what we know as 'awareness'. All that is going on, I comforted myself, is that I have become aware of the multiple worlds we all inhabit every day. So, I am not worldless. It is just that the experience in the curio shop had temporarily made me conscious of my otherwise ordinary world. I felt alienated from my existence precisely because the encounter with the man in the shop opened up another world and from the perspective of that other world I somehow felt compelled to question the fundamentals of my everyday world. But to question the world's fundamentals does not amount to abandoning them. I just needed time to think through what had happened and to discover what would no doubt be a perfectly good explanation for the man's odd behaviour. Once I could do that, the fundamentals of my ordinary world would be restored, along with my sense of feeling safe in the world.

But do I ever feel safe in the world? The thought shook my entire being. It popped up unexpectedly and with brutal clarity. But before I could domesticate it, I heard the safety chain drop and the door opened. I entered the house, greeted John and Cath and gave Grace a long, warm hug. 'Here you go, Didi,' I said, letting go of her and handing her the gift bag. (We also do not know when or why I started to call her Didi. My guess would be that it was sometime soon after I became Dodo.)

'Thank you, Dodo,' she cheekily replied, took the bag from me and placed it on a table where there were other gifts. She turned away and joined her friends again. I had hoped that two glasses of wine and the comfort of being with family and children would have the same effect on me as my patio shower and drag and drop me back into this world. But try as I might, I just could not shake the feeling of being alienated from the world. Eventually, standing on the balcony with my brother and in response to his asking me if I was okay because I seemed distracted, I told him the whole story of my experience earlier that afternoon.

'A curious experience,' was his initial non-committal response. He always does that when I talk about things that matter to me – yoga, the highs and lows of teaching at a university, my ambivalent feelings about philosophy. Whatever issue I raise, whatever doubt I express, his response is always a mixture of bad puns and a lack of interest that masquerades as the kind of lightness that is supposed to comfort me with the reassurance that he has 'been there' and knows exactly what I am talking about. ('I'm sick of all the meaningfulness,' I once told him. 'I just want to stop thinking, move to the Karoo and run a small hotel.' He responded with, 'Unless you have a formidable pension plan, you would have to think again, or just keep thinking about it.' Then he went on to tell me how for a while he and Cath had spent endless nights wondering how they could possibly afford to sell up and move to the Karoo and run a small business.)

What is so annoying about his responses? I have often wondered. But because we did not see each other that often, I somehow never stayed with the question long enough to really understand what irked me so much. Despite the fact that his defensiveness always confirmed the rift between us – a distance that was not overcome, but rather confirmed every time we met on the shaky middle ground of buns and ketchup – I always tried again, as if hoping for something more or something different. Which is why, in spite of our history, I told him about my experience in the curio shop. And now we are just standing there, leaning with our elbows on the balcony looking down on the kids, occasionally taking a sip of our drinks.

'I've got to go help Cath with something,' John said eventually and, after giving me a brotherly slap on the back, he walked into the house. A good ten minutes later I heard someone behind me and turned around. It was Cath. She placed her glass of wine on the balcony rail and lit a cigarette. *Passing the torch*, I thought to myself. I could just imagine the scene in the kitchen. 'That brother of mine is just weird. You go try. I don't know what to do with the stuff he tells me.'

'How's it going, Cath?' I said, taking a sip of wine.

She turned to look at me without answering, inhaled deeply, breathed out the smoke and flicked the ashes away. Then she took another sip of wine, put the glass back on the railing and, taking another long drag on her cigarette, said, 'I don't know. Guess I'm trying to figure out what I'm unwilling to feel.'

I looked at her. She was smiling mischievously. 'He told you, didn't he?'

'Always does,' she said.

Fucking happy Christians, I thought and said, 'I know what you're going to say.'

'Then I won't say it,' she said and turned away. We both leaned on the balcony rail for a minute or two without saying anything.

'What are you guys talking about?' It was Grace. She was standing behind us.

We both turned around.

'Nothing,' Cath said.

'Everything,' I said, at the same time.

Grace frowned and as children are wont to do, trusted my answer more than her mother's. 'One can't talk about everything, silly.'

'Of course, you can,' I said. 'You just have to keep on talking.'

'But even then,' she laughed, 'you can't talk about *every*thing!' and emphasised the 'every' with a mock gesture of hopelessness.

'Why not?' I pretended to ask innocently, sipping my wine.

'Because there are more things in the world than there are words!' she explained, as if it were the most obvious thing in the world.

'Yeah, but human beings are clever like that,' I jumped in, before Cath could say anything. 'We group things together, so that we don't have to talk about every single *thing*.'

Grace frowned again and look at me quizzically.

'Like all of you,' I said, pointing down at her and with a sweeping hand that included all her friends downstairs. 'We have one word for all of you, precisely so we don't have to talk about each one of you.'

'Oh yeah, and what is that Mr Philosopher?' That was not Grace asking the question. It was distinctively Didi.

'Little whipsters,' I said. 'You're all a bunch of little whipsters.'

Didi didn't break speed for a second. 'Not Lilly,' she said. 'She's too sad. She's always sad. She's too sad to be a whisper.'

'Mmm.' I assumed the position of the Thinker, pretending to think very hard. Then as if I were wondering out loud, I said, 'I wonder if there is a word for a whipster who is not a whipster? Or a whipster who is just going through a phase of not being one?'

'No! Not unless you make one up!' She laughed triumphantly. 'I win! There isn't a word for everything. See! So, you can't talk about everything!'

I rolled my eyes in playful mockery and turned to Cath. 'Where did you find this one? And why is she so clever?'

'I don't know, *Uncle Dodo*. You tell me,' she smiled and flicked her cigarette butt into the flower box in the corner of the balcony.

5

In the Uber on my way home that night, I thought back on the brief exchange I had had with Cath before Grace arrived. I have always liked Cath; at some level I like her more than my brother. It is one of those abiding dilemmas in life that one can love somebody without liking them, which is often precisely the reason why relationships with family can be so tiring. The difference between loving and liking a member of one's family is as common as it is fundamental. And yet, it is a distinction that we rarely acknowledge because we think that loving someone automatically implies liking them and because we think that while we can like a friend without loving them, we cannot love a member of our family without also liking them. When it comes to family, we think loving implies liking. And yet, this is often not the case. Sometimes, from a very early age, a parent may well love a child, but not really like them. Or a child may love a parent, but at some point realise that they do not really like their father or mother. Anyone can conduct a simple thought experiment to gauge the reality of this distinction. Just ask yourself: if this person were not family, would I want to spend time with them as a friend?

I have come to understand that I have this kind of relationship with John. We love but do not really like each other. If it were not for the fact that we are family, I do not think we would have spent any time together. We would certainly not have been friends. And yet, there I was at Grace's birthday party, standing on the balcony, telling him about a very strange and personal experience I had had earlier that day. Why did I do that since I knew how he was going to react; when I knew that he was not going to react as a friend should, but would really just bear with me, the way family do? I think the reason is that we are both deeply uncomfortable with the fact that while we love each other, we do not really like each other. It is a difficult tension to acknowledge and one that is probably impossible to speak out loud, which is why I often try very hard to bridge that difference in conversations like the one we had had earlier that evening. But my brother invariably disappoints. His annoying habit of always responding with a combination of sardonic worldliness and a displaced commitment to being older, and therefore wiser than me, always left me cold.

Perhaps that is why I like Cath more. She has always been aware of the gulf between John and myself and also of the fact that perhaps because of my temperament or intellectual interests, I always assume that it falls on me to resolve the tension between not liking and loving him. I have always had the sense that she intuitively understood that the distinction is real for me; that it is not something I can discuss with my brother; that I constantly try to overcome my dislike of him and that he invariably disappoints. Over the years, Cath and I had unwittingly developed a code that we used in conversations when we both recognised what was happening. It was as if we implicitly acknowledged that, real as the distinction may be, to discuss the difference between liking and loving a member of one's family is a taboo as fundamental as its obliterating inverse, incest.

'I know what you're going to say.'

'Then I won't say it.'

Somehow, these little coded exchanges have always been enough to ease my immediate sense of renewed disappointment. It is as if Cath redeems my brother – which explains why I like her more than him – not because we ever have actual conversations, but because, unlike John, she at least implicitly acknowledges the fact that we probably cannot.

I have often wondered why I am at once so fascinated and troubled by this distinction between loving and not liking a sibling. It is a brutal distinction and yet I am capable of making it and sustaining it as some kind of guiding light in my life, as a fundamental truth that for as long as I can remember has steered me through the minefield of Christmas dinners and Easter weekends. Even though I can never recall when I came to understand and accept the distinction so clearly, I always knew where it came from and how I was capable of making and sustaining it as a simple matter of fact. Cath implicitly understood this, too, because somehow she understood my mother and the way in which my mother had shaped the three brothers' emotional landscapes.

The mathematics of affect
My mother was an extraordinarily intelligent woman who, I became more and more certain as I grew older, was probably abused as a child. Whether the pain I sensed was physical, sexual or psychological, I could never tell because the family history had always been shrouded in secrecy – mostly, I think, because of a sense of shame: the shame of having grown up very poor; the shame of having had to sell their small farm and move to the city; the shame of only surviving as the beneficiaries of apartheid-style labour reserved for whites. It was as if the further they got from their original poverty, the more determined they became to forget about it, so that – and this I only understood much later when I was in my mid-twenties – my parents' entire lives unfolded as one drawn-out act of forgetfulness. Was that forgetfulness always *behind* them and did the level and intensity – even the scope – of their forgetfulness increase as they moved up the ladder of middle-class existence reserved for white Afrikaners? Or was the forgetfulness always *ahead* of them, a goal to aspire to, something that drew them on, a promise that motivated their every action? Was the need to forget produced by their actions, in the wake of their movement – like the white folds of water fanning out behind a speedboat? Or was forgetting an expansive horizon that

beckoned them ever forward towards a world in which they could live without memory and so be inspired by their actions?

Over time I had come to suspect that embedded in this larger movement of forgetfulness was a more personal story of forgetfulness that moved my mother. This personal story never broke the surface of knowing; in part because there were other, larger and more important things to forget and in part because it must have been almost impossible to make sense of a personal experience of shame and guilt (let alone articulate it) in a world where words belonged to men and religion was little more than a ritual devised to protect all God's children from the uncertainty induced in them by the indeterminate meanings of the silences produced by men's words.

From this world, my mother emerged an essentially cold person who was incapable of being loved. Because she could not be loved, she could also not love others and so I was born into a world where the difference between loving and liking members of one's own family was as fundamental as it was stark. My mother liked us, but in retrospect I know that at a very young age I came to understand that she did not love us – not because it was normal for parents and children sometimes to love but not like each other, but because liking other people was all she was ever capable of. In her case it was not a matter of liking some and loving others. It took the three brothers many, many years to uncover this stark impossibility in the memories we had of our mother. To be frank, it did not start out as an attempt to understand her as much as an attempt to understand why we were all so singularly capable of suspending love in the name of other things. Love had never been fundamental to any of our lives. It had never been the bedrock upon which everything else was built. No, there were other more fundamental ideas that we had been raised to believe were more worthy of being honoured and pursued: love of humanity, justice and fairness.

If I think of my mother now – and it has been almost ten years since she died – I think of someone who was more committed to recognising the equality of suffering than the need for empathy. For my mother, everyone suffered equally and because there was such great equality in our suffering, nobody in particular deserved any empathy. When my aunt's husband died, her response was, 'Yes, death comes for us all.' When Grace's older sister Susan experienced a shattering break-up with her first love, my mother commented on the tragedy of first loves and how they invariably left one – *one*, she said, not Susan, *one* – forever changed.

I vividly recall the moment I first understood how this calculus worked – a calculus that kept her, and consequently all her children, from feeling anything. I was about ten and we were having supper. The conversation had turned to our domestic worker, who lived in the tiny maid's quarters at the back of the house and only saw her family over the weekend when she travelled to the township at the other side of the city, where they lived. John – who would go on to become a very successful businessman – had asked how much she earned and when my father had told him, he had quickly worked out that she spent half her weekly wages travelling back and forth to be with her family over the weekend.

'That doesn't add up,' he had said – not in a way that made it seem that he felt sorry for her, but rather by way of expressing his dismay at the fact that things did not add up. It did not make sense for someone to earn that little; it did not add up that she spent almost half her weekly wages travelling back and forth. When he said, 'That doesn't add up', John was really wondering how anyone could live with that contradiction and he was more frustrated by the fact that the contradiction existed than with the fact that someone was living it. I recall not being very surprised by his response. Although I was a couple of years younger than him, his fixation on the mathematics of poverty, the fact that he seemed more frustrated by things not adding up than with feeling sorry for her or asking why she could not get paid a better wage did not surprise me because the domain of feelings had by then already been carefully circumscribed by my mother who responded: 'It may not be much, but at least she has a job. There are thousands of people who don't have jobs and who have to get by with very little or even nothing.' There it was. One did not need to feel sorry for her because she was actually one of the lucky ones; she was fortunate to be able spend half a day's earnings travelling between her family and her place of work. If anyone was deserving of our pity or empathy, it was the thousands of people who were not lucky enough to live such an absurd existence. But then, it was not possible to feel empathy for thousands of people we did not know and so the danger of feeling sorry for anyone was cancelled out by the relativity of everyone's misery.

In my mother's Great Chain of Misery, the domestic worker was below us, just as we were below the thousands of people who were in turn more fortunate than us and so, logically, it made no sense to take pity on her, since she was, much like us, just relatively poor. To take pity on her would be unfair to everyone else who was also relatively poor. In this way, my mother succeeded in making herself and her children believe that in a world tainted by the colour of one's skin, the domestic worker's poverty was just more visible than ours. In a world where there were only poor people, it did not make sense to take pity on any one poor person. It was more important to be fair than to be moved by the suffering of others and to the extent that their suffering had a purpose, it consisted in inspiring us to be more fair.

6

And so, the Imposter made his way into my life somewhere in the crack opened up by the mysterious smile of the man in the curio shop and my dreamy recollection in the Uber on the way home of the conversation I had with my brother and his wife, a conversation that was, in a sense, a mere repetition of childhood conversations and impressions of my mother's inability to love. I went to bed when I got home. Well, not immediately. By now I know better than to go straight to bed after a day as emotionally intense and confusing as the day I had had. So, I did what I usually do on such days. I ran a bath and once I had allowed myself a couple of minutes to simply relax and clear my mind, I reached over to where I had placed my phone on the little table next to the bath, opened my Audible app and allowed myself to be whisked away into the Nordic noir world of detective Sebastian Bergman. After a good 30 minutes, I got out, put on a clean pair of boxer shorts and made myself a last cup of chamomile tea, which I sipped slowly, sitting on the deep deck chair on the patio, waiting for the great calm to rise and hold me.

This usually works. At some point I will feel myself being lifted by the cloud of unknowing and doze off. This is usually when I get up and, without turning on the light, get into bed and very often fall into a deep sleep. But I say *often*, not *always*, because I generally struggle to sleep and even on evenings when I can sense the cloud of unknowing rising in me, a part of me often remains alert and awake, even a little terrified. What if I do not manage to fall asleep? What if I never sleep again? Can one lose the ability to sleep altogether? Is there such an illness or condition? Does one have to be born with it or can one develop it later in life? What if something happens to me or my wife or daughter while I blissfully sleep – will I not forever hate myself for not being awake at the precise moment when tragedy strikes? On nights when this anxious part of me remains beyond the pale of noir detective novels, chamomile tea and the slow drift of forgetfulness, I take a sleeping pill. On really bad nights, even that offers only a temporary fix. The sleeping pill may knock me out, but sometimes only for three or four hours. Then I wake up, confused and violently anxious, as if I were caught napping by some higher force and have to explain why I was sleeping. And did I finish everything I meant to do the previous day? Did I check my diary before I went to bed and was I sure that I had set my alarm for the right time? On those nights, I will eventually fall asleep again, sometimes as late as an hour before the alarm goes off and the following day will be shadowed by an insomniac hangover that leaves me disengaged and alienated from the world.

The night after the strange encounter with the curious man and Grace's birthday party was one of those nights. I had eventually taken a sleeping tablet, but woke up again at 3.00 in the morning. I knew how this was going to play out. Should I send Juliet a text to make sure she is all right and at least eliminate one worry? Perhaps she is also awake. That often happens. In the course of one of our regular telephone conversations I would tell her how, say, the previous Tuesday evening I could not sleep and spent half the night awake and she would tell me that the exact same thing had happened to her; she, too, had been awake on the same night; eventually getting up and making tea, then sitting for two hours at the kitchen table, wondering if she should text me to see if I was awake. She never does because she knows I put my phone off when I go to bed, in part because I am always worried that someone might text me in the middle of the night and wake me up. Juliet, on the other hand, insists on leaving her phone on in case one of her siblings or her father tries to get hold of her in the middle of the night because of some family emergency. This leaves things a little bit awkward between us as far as our insomniac nights go. I often think of texting her to see if she is also awake, but I never do because I know her phone is on and I do not want to wake her in case she is sleeping. It is an insomniac stalemate.

At 3.30 a.m. I got up. I switched my phone on to check for messages. None. Juliet is either asleep or not; she is either lying in bed fast asleep or sitting at the kitchen table, wide awake and wishing she could text me. *Which is it?* I wondered, as I turned on the kitchen light to make tea. It was Schrödinger's cat, of course: I would not know if Juliet was asleep or awake until I lifted the roof of the house – quietly, so as not to wake her if she was asleep – and peered inside. Until I did that, she was both awake and asleep. I took my tea outside and slid into the comfortable deck chair on the patio. The tea was still too hot to drink, so I just held my nose above the cup and allowed the scent of chamomile to drift up into my face. I cannot really say I like either the smell or the taste of chamomile tea. I just drink it because it is supposed to help me relax and sleep. I put the cup down on the little table next to the chair, leaned back and closed my eyes. Why am I always so anxious? What is this thing that happens to me in the dead of the night when I am supposed to be drugged into sleep and yet wake up, terrified by worry, the anxiety of having made wrong decisions, a mild panic attack in the middle of the night? What drives these occurrences? What are they all about? What is this anxiety a sign of; what lurks behind it? What speaks through it and what does it want? What has it been trying to tell me for so long and why have I not listened or understood what it has been saying? *What am I unwilling to feel?*

Suddenly I saw his face again – the man from the curio shop, with his sanguine smile, his almost peculiar complacency and apparent ability to embrace the mundane incompleteness of life. I recalled the way he served me, attentively, as if I really mattered, and then the comment about my niece's birthday and his perplexingly strange question. I realised that, without being consciously aware of it, I had remained in conversation with him throughout the day. The answer to his question came with the kind of clarity only known to those who suffer the madness of insomnia: *I am an Imposter. I am always anxious because I constantly worry that I am about to get caught out.*

7

'It's quite a common thing, you know,' Juliet said when we Skyped that evening. It turned out that she had slept well the previous night. Had I managed to lift the roof of the house quietly, so quietly that the act made no difference whatsoever, I would have seen her as I have so many times before, curled up on her side, with her head slightly tucked in under the duvet. As a result of having had a good night's sleep, she was energised and chatty while I was tired, my head foggy from the insomnia hangover that I just could not shake.

'Anxiety or feeling like an imposter?'

'Both,' she said. From the video frame I could tell that she was sitting at the kitchen table. In the left-hand corner of the frame was a supper plate with some leftovers.

'Is that bobotie I see?'

'Yip.' She adjusted the video angle.

'No,' I said. 'It was perfect the way you had it. Now I can only see half your face.' Somewhere at the frayed edges of my mind a wicked pun circled, something about someone who had a stroke and lost half their face, no stroke of luck and so on, but I did not have the mental energy to pull it together.

Once we could see each other clearly again, she continued. 'I think you and I struggle with insomnia for different reasons. For me, it's a relatively new thing. When I can't sleep, it's because I am overwhelmed with boredom. I worry about my life, about where all the excitement has gone. I worry about the fact that I am bored with my job and that, you know, pension and all that, I will have to stick it out for another ten years. The thought of it . . .'

'You're saying you're so bored you can't sleep?'

'Something like that. Whereas you . . . I think with you it's different. I know you like your job, but I also know you and your anxiety.' A slight pause. Then, 'I actually think I understand something about your anxiety. I think about it a lot. Do you want to talk about it now or are you too tired? We can talk another night if you want.'

I raised an eyebrow and shrugged my shoulders to signal that I was too tired to care either way. 'Let me have it. Maybe it will help me sleep tonight.'

'I think you are too identified with the world, with your job, your colleagues, your students, your teaching – the whole lot.'

'Too identified? What does that mean?'

She did not even think about my question. She had clearly given this a lot of thought. 'It's not that complicated,' she said.

I shuddered. From experience, I know that when Juliet says something is not that complicated, she has given it a lot of thought and managed to distil a very complex issue down to its emotional essence. There would be no holding back now. 'You make the classic mistake of confusing what you do with who you are. All the mystics warn us about this: don't confuse or conflate what you do with who you are.'

'Is that Confusionism?' I asked, trying to defend myself against what would follow.

But after 25 years together, Juliet knows that I deploy jokes and puns as distractions when I do not want to engage emotionally, so she did not even smile. 'In order to feel safe in the world and to feel that we belong, we first need to detach from the world, recognise that we are not the world. There is the world and there is the self and that is an important difference. Life calls for a healthy detachment from it all and detachment means that you do not identify with the world. You need to be more detached from it all, from your work, your relationships with your colleagues and students, your writing – everything.' Before I could say anything, she followed through. 'When you over-identify with things in the world, you become a control freak. You constantly worry that things will get out of control, that you will fail, and that when things get out of control, there will be complete chaos. That's all because you over-identify with the world, but you know what, darling?'

The way she uses the word *darling* is always very reassuring. She does not often use it, but when she does, it is like a soothing balm for the battered soul.

'What?'

'The world is not your responsibility. Do your job as well as you do, care as much as you can, but at the end of the day it is just a job and you cannot succeed on other people's behalf. Sometimes you have to let them fail. You cannot control everything. That is the origin of your anxiety. Somewhere in the back of your mind you know things are not completely under your control and you constantly worry. You worry about what will happen when you let things *not* be under your control and then you worry that letting things *be* and not controlling everything will amount to some kind of failure . . .'

'That I will get caught out for not being in control?'

'Precisely. The Imposter is a good guy,' she said. 'Make peace with him. It's your mind's way of reminding you that you belong in the world; that there is a place for you, but you can only find that place when you stop confusing yourself with the world, when you stop thinking you are responsible for the whole world. You cannot belong in a world that you control. Belonging requires letting go, so that you can find your place, just your own little place in it. Does that make sense?'

There was a long pause. I traced the outline of her face on the screen. Sometimes living apart like this is simply unbearable. She smiled into the screen.

'What are you doing?'

'Tracing your face.'

She smiled. 'Are you okay?'

'No, but I will be.'

'Sure?'

'Not really. How do I do it?'

'Do what – stop being you?' she asked smiling. Then, more seriously, 'Just slow down. Do everything slowly and enjoy what you do. The secret is a combination of slowness and pleasure. Walk slowly, eat slowly, work slowly and enjoy what you do.'

'I'm slowly getting tired of this,' I replied.

'Idiot,' she said. 'Go do something. *Slowly*. And then sleep slowly.'

8

Of course, Juliet was right. I did confuse myself with the world. I did think I needed to control everything and that I was responsible for everything. The anxiety generated by the possibility that I will one day lose control and, as a result, the whole world will descend into total chaos presented as the fear of being unmasked as a fake, an Imposter, someone who could not hold it together, someone who got caught out trying but failing to control the world. Over the next couple of days, following the conversation with Juliet, the Imposter and I lived in an uneasy truce. I began to notice how, at the first sign of consciousness and before I had even opened my eyes, he was already there, reminding me that I had probably overslept, that I had forgotten to do something or prepare something for the day that lay ahead. For the Imposter, every day was a creation at the centre of which lay a fundamental error, a disaster, which was the consequence of neglect, *my* neglect, and the beginning of every day was simply the start of the slow and inexorable disclosure of my guilt. I kept reminding myself of what Juliet had said – *the Imposter is a good guy; he's there to teach you something* – and I learned to stare him in the face; him and the fear that my secret would be revealed; I would be recognised as a fake and my true self – which I had come to believe was little more than an attempt at faking my worth – would be exposed to the world and I would one day finally stand there naked, stripped of everything I had ever invented to make myself visible in the world.

As the Imposter and I became increasingly aware of each other, I started to observe his little morning rituals. How he would splash his face with cold water, rubbing some over his closely shaved head; next, cupping his hand under the tap, he would gulp down several large mouthfuls of water before he rinsed away the remaining taste of decay with mouthwash. After relieving himself, he would walk back into his bedroom, pull the curtains aside and open the windows to let in the fresh morning air before shaking out the duvet, fluffing the pillows and making the bed, after which he would walk into the kitchen to make coffee. A little while later, having eaten some leftovers from the previous night's supper, he would sit on the toilet scanning the daily news on his phone while figuring out some witty comment to make about Donald Trump's latest tweet – which he had written while sitting on his toilet the day before and which the other Imposter would read a day later, sitting on his, impatiently scrolling through the headlines, preparing for the worst.

As I observed his frantic morning routine, the need for a different kind of waking-up ritual slowly emerged. I followed Juliet's advice and started to do everything slowly. I quit smoking and I stopped reading the news on the toilet. And I finally stopped worrying about Trump. That was the big one. I no longer felt responsible for the world he was creating. I started to enjoy waking up slowly and crawling back into bed after having relieved myself, wrapping the warm duvet sensually around my naked body, plugging in my earphones and listening to a morning meditation – sometimes a talk, sometimes soothing music.

Now, when I eventually get up, I pull the curtains of the patio window aside, open the door and walk out into the sun. I split my legs as far apart as I can and stretch my arms out. Leonard da Vinci naked on a patio, basking in the early morning Pretoria sunlight. A Vitruvian starfish, in this world, but not of this world. Then I put on boxer shorts, make myself a cup of coffee and enjoy it basking in the morning sun, watching the crisp morning light play on the leaves of the pot plants.

This morning, about 30 minutes after my original intention to wake up had flickered into a flame, I was listening to a talk on Buddhism, in which the teacher quoted Einstein, who had apparently once said:

> The most important question you can ever ask is if the world is a friendly place. For if we decide that the universe is an unfriendly place, then we will use our technology, our scientific discoveries and our natural resources to achieve safety and power by creating bigger walls to keep out the unfriendliness and bigger weapons to destroy all that which is unfriendly and I believe that we are getting to a place where technology is powerful enough that we may either completely

isolate or destroy ourselves as well in this process. If, on the other hand we decide that the universe is neither friendly nor unfriendly and that God is essentially playing dice with the universe, then we are simply victims to the random toss of the dice and our lives have no real purpose or meaning. But if we decide that the universe is a friendly place, then we will use our technology, our scientific discoveries and our natural resources to create tools and models for understanding that universe. Because power and safety will come through understanding its workings and its motives.

The point the teacher made – and this was the point at which the flicker jumped into a flame – is that it does not matter that Einstein got it wrong in his debate with the quantum physicists. Even if he was wrong about the science, he was still right about the attitude we can choose to adopt to uncertainty. If God is nothing but shorthand for the flow of creative energy, do you choose to trust that this is a friendly flow of energy? Is it only destructive or is it also sometimes nurturing? Do you find generosity in that flow, or only alienation; only struggle or also opportunity; only self-doubt or also belonging?

I looked down at the cup of coffee I was holding. Should I keep adding sugar to my coffee or should I learn to drink it the way I have been told coffee is meant to be drunk, black and bitter? I proudly decided that it was a sign of enlightenment that I do not give a damn how coffee is supposed to be drunk and that I would continue to drink it the way I like it. Juliet would agree. Why turn a perfectly good and pleasurable ritual into a duty? Eventually, I got up and assembled my smoothie (I had also stopped eating leftovers for breakfast). Always the same recipe: one banana, half an avocado, a tablespoon of peanut butter, half a cup of desiccated coconut, half an apple, a handful of dates and half a cup of oats all topped with water and blended in the NutriBullet for exactly one minute. After breakfast, I shaved, showered, got dressed and went to work.

Schrödinger's Cat

9

Maretha, the office administrator, is her usual cheerful self when I walk into the philosophy department's rooms. One has to walk through her office to get to mine – an arrangement I have come to appreciate because it effectively makes her the first line of defence against the endless stream of students who come to me with their queries and complaints, with this or that request, or wanting to hand in a sick note to explain why they missed a test or an examination. Very few of them make it past Maretha and, if one of them does indeed have a problem that requires the attention of the head of department, she makes them wait in her office while she comes to discuss the issue with me. That is the second line of defence. I can often handle the situation or sign the necessary form without actually having to deal with the student in person. It is not that I do not like engaging with students. I do. In fact, I often tell Juliet that teaching is the only thing that still makes my job as an academic worthwhile. If I did not have to teach – if, say, I had one of those research chairs that so many of my colleagues are desperate to get because all that is expected is that one read books and write more books – I would die a silent death. But engaging with students in the lecture hall and dealing with the minutiae of their personal lives are two very different things. I am happy to play my role in the former, but I am grateful that Maretha is the barrier between me and the latter.

Maretha lives quite a distance from the university and chooses to start work at 7.00 in the morning and to leave at 3.30 p.m. – that way she avoids both the morning and late afternoon rush-hour traffic. In order for her to be behind her desk at 7.00 a.m., and because of the distance she has to drive, I am sure she needs to get up at some ridiculous hour, like 4.30 or 5.00 a.m., at the latest. I find that very difficult to imagine. Given how long I need in order to wake up and prepare for the day, how I have come to treasure my early morning meditation, which is often followed by a leisurely walk or cycle to campus, being at the office at 7.00 a.m. would be a nightmare for me.

'Good morning!' she smiles, as I walk in. 'And how are we today?'

'Too early to tell. Ask me in an hour when I'm awake,' I reply and head for the door to my office. As usual, she has already opened the door, switched on the lights and air conditioner, and opened the curtains on the window that has a spectacular view of the city, which I have come to appreciate greatly.

'Oh, silly,' she replies, as if we do not have this same exchange or some variation of it every morning. It is our little routine. I check her cheerfulness by pretending to be grumpy and in that way a balance of forces is sustained – at least in my mind. I walk over to my desk and unpack the documents I had taken home the previous day, ostensibly to read in preparation for two long meetings I have later today. I did not read them and consequently will have to find an hour or so in the course of the day to prepare for both meetings. I take out my packed lunch and the bottle of vegetable juice I made the previous night. On my way back to Maretha's office, I stop briefly to admire the view. It is early October and for the first two weeks of the month the purple flowers of the jacaranda trees all over the city and on campus erupt in bloom. It is quite a magnificent sight. After a minute or two, I walk back through Maretha's office to the kitchen, where I put my lunch and juice in the small fridge.

Back in my office, I sit down behind my desk, open my email program and scan through my inbox, deleting as many emails as I can. Sometimes it seems as if my entire life is little more than a never-ending battle with my inbox. I try never to have more than 70 emails in my inbox, but when the days get busy because I am teaching or have to attend one meeting after another, the number can quite easily jump to two or three hundred in a matter of two days. I look at the top right corner of the email program: 145 and counting. I will have to make time for some serious culling today. But not yet. Culling emails involves serious work and I am not ready for that yet.

'Maretha!'

'Yes?' she replies. She has stopped typing to hear what I need without having to get up just yet.

'I feel like doing something with my authority. Isn't there a form or something that needs to be signed? Preferably something that will determine someone else's fate – an application for admission or a credit transfer or something. Just not anything to do with finances.'

'Nope. Sorry,' she replies and starts typing again. 'You will have to find some real work to do.'

I am not surprised. If there had been something to sign, Maretha would have followed me into the office when I came back from the kitchen. Then she would have stood next to me and meticulously laid out the forms in front of me, one after another, briefly explaining to me what they were, what she has done so far, what I have to approve and where to sign. Since my arrival three years ago, we have developed a very trusting relationship and I suspect she has claimed freedoms with me that she never had with any of my predecessors. And so, every document that is placed in front of me comes with an opinion. 'And this student would like us to recognise the first-year semester course she did at ULT so that she won't have to do our first-year course. Here is the calendar entry and description of the course she did at ULT. I think it's fine. We've approved similar requests before.' Then she waits while I glance at the course description again. I sign the request with my beautiful Montblanc pen (the only thing I ever use it for) and give it back to her before she places the next one in front of me, accompanied by the appropriate suggestion. But not today. No authority to exercise and nothing to sign.

So I start culling emails. The first step is easy. I scroll down through the emails and delete all the ones related to internal marketing or those that advertise some service offered by the university's corporitised wellness programme. The second step is almost as much fun. I scan all the address lines for emails from ResearchGate and Academia.edu. These I only open when I am told that I have reached a new personal milestone (an article I published ten years ago now has twenty reads) or perhaps that another three scholars from across the world have read my most recent article – this morning, it is someone in Puerto Rico, another in China and a third in Pretoria. This is mostly so depressing that I just delete them, milestone and all. It is only with the third step that the real work of actually reading emails, filing attachments and making diary entries begins. After an hour, I have the number of emails down to 83. I am very nearly back to the number that were in my inbox when I left the office the previous day. I lean back in my swivel chair, stretch my arms to release the tension in my back and think of the Red Queen from *Alice in Wonderland*, 'It takes all the running you can do, to keep in the same place.'

I get up and walk back to the kitchen, where I switch on the kettle to make tea. I return to my office, cup in hand, and walk over to the window. I let my gaze wander over the city, taking in the streets of purple and thinking about the nice long walk I will have in the early evening when I head up to the Union Buildings, from where the view of the city is perhaps even better than from my office because it is not framed by a window and one can take in most of the city. I sip my tea and look down onto the campus square directly below my office. The square is usually a buzz of student activities – bands, promotions, stalls of this or that student society signing up new members, the odd group of students playing soccer or throwing a frisbee. But it is the week before examinations begin and all activities have been temporarily suspended, which leaves the square unusually quiet. All I can see is a couple of students walking in the direction of the cafeteria. The deeply comforting smell of the Earl Grey tea rises to my nose as my gaze wanders back until I look straight down below the building to the row of noticeboards and bicycle stands. And that is when I see him.

He is standing right in front of one of the noticeboards, one hand shielding his eyes from the glare of the sun's reflection off the white walls. He is looking up at my office window. *Yes, he is looking straight at me!* For a moment, my heart leaps and I am sure I must have audibly gasped. I put the cup of tea down on the narrow wooden windowsill and lean closer to the window. Is it really him? And how could that possibly be? I pull the slide window open so that I do not have to look through the stained glass. Beyond the windowpane is a strange kind of wire mesh that was apparently installed a couple of years ago after a second person jumped to their death from this floor. Subsequently, wire mesh was installed in front of all windows from the fifteenth floor upwards. When Maretha explained this to me the day I moved into the office, I remember thinking to myself, *What is there about this job they did not tell me? And when I find out, what will prevent me from going down to the fourteenth floor and jumping from there?* Now, I squint through the mesh and look attentively at the young man who is staring back at me. There can be no mistake. It is him. I would recognise him anywhere. Luc and I look at each other. I am looking down at him through the suicide wire while he is looking up at me, one hand shielding his eyes from the glare of the sun's reflection. For the briefest of eternities nothing happens; we are locked frozen in each other's gaze and neither of us move. I am the first to break the spell. I turn around and, bumping against the small conference table behind me and nearly knocking over the vase with the white orchid in it, rush out of my office into Maretha's.

'Everything okay, boss?' I hear her surprised voice follow me.

'Yes,' I say, 'just going out quickly.' I dash through her office and into the small foyer to where the six lifts are. Impatiently, I press the button a number of times in quick succession. Then, as if it would make the suspense of waiting more bearable, I scan the noticeboard next to the lift door while I wait. The most recent addition advertises a public lecture in the library auditorium early this evening. Even I recognise the name of the psychologist who has become famous overnight for her book titled *The Mathematics of Affect* – a phrase that subsequently became very popular in certain circles and which I have noticed popping up in various books and magazines. I press the lift button another three times and pace up and down in front of the doors that will open any second now. I could probably contribute something to the seemingly insatiable desire for novelty in the academy by writing something that sounds equally cool, such as *A Critique of Pure Boredom*. A ping announces the arrival of the lift. The doors open and I walk in. There are two other people in the lift and I quietly sigh with relief when I glance at the panel with the floor numbers on it and see that they are both also going to the ground floor. When the bell pings and the door finally slides open, I am the first one out. It happens to be one of the ten-minute breaks between lectures and the main entrance to the building is congested with students and lecturers trying to get in and out. As if chaos has an instinct for these things, two streams have spontaneously formed, one jamming bodies into the building, the other carrying them out. I squeeze my way through the outward-bound stream and, after what feels like an eternity of squeezing and pretending not to notice the impatient looks from irritable students and colleagues, I break free, turn right and run around the corner of the building towards the noticeboard where I saw Luc.

When I get there, he is gone. I stop, turn around and look across the square at the other noticeboards lined up in rows along the edges of the lawns, but he is nowhere to be seen. The square is as quiet and deserted as it was when I looked down from my office. I look up in the direction of my window. It is easy to identify my office window because it is the only one that has been pushed open. I must be standing in the exact same spot Luc was standing when I saw him and yet there is no trace of him. Still slightly out of breath from running all the way from the building's main entrance, I turn and look around again. *How very odd,* I think to myself. *Did I make it all up? Was I hallucinating? Mistaken? No. I clearly recall Luc standing right here where I am now standing and looking up at me.*

I take my cell phone out of my pocket and dial Maretha's cell phone number. After three rings I hear her familiar voice.

'Maretha, please do me a favour. Stand at your window and look down on the square. I'm supposed to meet somebody here and I saw him from my office window waiting for me, but when I got here, he was gone. I can't see him anywhere. Please see if you can perhaps see him.' After a couple of seconds, I see a faint presence appear at the window next to mine.

'Who am I looking for?' she wants to know.

'Young man, early twenties, about my height, brown jacket, blue jeans,' I reply.

Maretha is quiet for a moment, during which I imagine her to be scanning the square. 'No, I'm sorry,' she says. 'I don't see anyone like that. Just two students over there near the cafeteria and a couple sitting on the lawns next to the bicycle stand . . .' Her voice trails off.

'By the way, where are you?' she wants to know. 'I thought you said you were down there below our office windows where you were supposed to meet him.'

'I am,' I say. 'I'm standing right below my window. Next to the noticeboard. Here!'

I half expect her dreamy voice to respond with an 'Ah yes, now I see you', but she doesn't.

Instead, I hear the slightest tone of impatience in her voice as she says, 'Oh, come now. I don't know what game you're playing, but you're not where you say you are. I'm looking straight down below the window and the only people I can see are those students and none of them look like the one you described.'

'No man, I'm here,' I say. 'I'm waving my arm. Do you see me now?'

'Tsk, tsk,' she replies. 'You're being silly now. I've got to go. There's a student here.' And with that she puts the phone down and the faint figure at my window disappears.

10

I cannot recall a single day over the past five years when I did not think about Luc. In fact, his imaginary presence has come to define every quiet moment of my life. As soon as the ordinary activities of my everyday life slow down and my world comes to a standstill – whether in the course of my early morning or my late afternoon walks, or when I sit on the patio late at night sipping a whisky – the moment my thoughts promise to become mere sensations, Luc steps into the quiet. For instance, I can be taking my late afternoon stroll up the hill to the Union Buildings where there are always hundreds of tourists milling around the big statue of Nelson Mandela, and suddenly Luc will gently steer me away from the crowds towards a quiet, more desolate part of the gardens. Or I would have been headed for that section of the park anyway, only to arrive and find him already sitting on one of the benches, arms folded, legs outstretched, lost in thought or perhaps admiring the view. If something is always on your mind – not because you often think about it, but because it can make itself thought even though all you want is to just sense the world around you – when something has that much power over you, then you know it has become part of the very fabric of your imagination. Over the past five years Luc has become that and, ever since I first became aware of the way he shadows me, I have been wondering why. What does he want from me? Since he always arrives when I am trying my best not to think of anything at all, I have come to the conclusion that it is not so much a matter of me thinking about him, as it is his thinking about me. *But what does he want from me?* How can I get him to stop thinking about me?

Then one day, about two years after I first became aware of his persistent presence in my imagination, I understood. Just a couple of weeks earlier, my late afternoon walk had started off in the opposite direction, away from the hustle and bustle of the Union Buildings gardens, deep into the suburb on the hills above my apartment. Initially, I had found this extremely relaxing. Because I did not know the suburb very well, I could meander aimlessly up and down the streets until I happened to find myself back in the vicinity of my apartment. Of course, that did not last long. I soon got to know the suburb and which route would take me how long to get back to the apartment. But that was not all bad. As a number of routes became more familiar to me, I found that familiarity, too, breeds freedom; not the freedom we sense when we find ourselves overwhelmed by possibilities, but the freedom that comes with predictability, with not having to worry about the unexpected. There is as much freedom in noticing for the first time a well-hidden courtyard garden or peering through a garden gate to see a beautifully restored façade as there is in walking past the same couple sitting on their patio every evening, their chairs at an angle to each other, glasses of wine in their hands. Eventually, I started to raise my hand to wave at them and they invariably returned the gesture. This became part of our routine and, soon after, the freedom of predictability settled in, perhaps as much for them as for me; the freedom of doing something not because you want to or because you are forced to, but simply because it has become a routine. Routines allow the mind to wander. It was on one of those days, when my amiable exchange of gestures with an elderly couple had left me almost dizzy with contentment, that Luc suddenly appeared in my mind's eye again. It was as if the gesture had beckoned him back into my imagination and, along with that, a thought I had not had before: *Luc haunts me because, from the moment I met him, I sensed that he was haunted.*

I had first encountered Luc about seven years earlier when I wrote a novel called *Imitation*. There, in Part Six, he briefly appeared as a young man with a very troubled history. As a teenager, over a number of years (just how many I never decided), he had tried to commit suicide no less than seventeen times – always unsuccessfully, except for the time he nearly succeeded when he had a near-death experience. Ever since that mystical encounter with the afterlife, he had refused to speak a single word. He lived in complete silence and his therapist and his parents were so concerned about this development that they sent him to a world-famous rehabilitation centre for addicts near Lyon, France, where he was temporarily placed under the care of the unconventional physician and psychiatrist, Doctor Cottard. As is to be expected in such a treatment facility, all the patients knew not only each other's business, but also the reason for their business. Who was addicted to what and for how long. How many failed attempts at rehabilitation has this or that one survived? Is so-and-so perhaps a rehab junkie? Could be, because look at so-and-so, who is obviously a group therapy junkie. Much of the daily conversations – between sessions, outside on the massive staircase leading up to the front door, or over late afternoon games of pétanque – consisted of patients updating each other with what they had discovered about other patients. And so it happened that not even a week after his arrival and despite the fact that he had not spoken a single word, everyone had become familiar (or so they thought) with Luc's story and what had brought him to the treatment centre. It soon became common knowledge that at the young age of 24 Luc had already tried to commit suicide 17 times. There was no consensus about his preferred method of suicide; some suggested pills; others, that he had tried to drown himself with a stone around his neck; yet others spoke authoritatively about the day he had borrowed his father's car and drove into the countryside where, in an isolated place in the forest, he climbed onto the roof of the car and threw himself head first to the ground. Yet others told the story of how a desperately sad young man's attempt to gas himself in his parents' garage was interrupted when his unsuspecting parents, who had gone out for the evening, returned home earlier than they had planned. While there may have been a lack of consensus regarding the many different ways in which Luc had tried to end his life, and while the facts – both the true and the false ones – became the currency of conversations that sustained a whole economy of trauma for weeks, there was one indisputable fact that all the stories converged on, namely, that Luc's most recent suicide attempt had very nearly been successful – in fact, he had come so close to killing himself that he had got a brief glimpse of the afterlife. The only reason Luc was still alive, so the story went, was because of the actions of a very determined young doctor who managed to shock him back into existence (the rest of the medical staff had given up and had already started to pull off their rubber gloves and lower their face masks when the young doctor shouted one last time, 'Clear!' and administered the shock that pulled Luc back from the light). Everyone agreed that it was this near-death experience, the fact that Luc came so close but ultimately failed to overdose on his longing for oblivion, which accounted for his silence. The more empathetic patients just shook their heads and said things like, 'So near and yet so far' or 'If I had come that close to the next life I would also have nothing left to say in this life'.

The point is that even by the time *Imitation* was published, I had spent very little time in Luc's company and had paid no attention whatsoever to all the rumours about him. It is not that I was oblivious to the rumours. I just did not know the truth and so decided not to become complicit in perpetuating half-truths. In addition, I must confess that at the time I described his particular condition (if one could call it that), I thought of him as quite a peripheral character. Of course, his refusal to speak to anyone – including Doctor Cottard – and the fact that he spent his days in absolute silence had intrigued me, but there was simply too much happening in the other characters' lives for me to spend time thinking through his singular fascination with silence and death. In hindsight, however, I know that even then his commitment to silence fascinated me more than I realised. Brief as our encounter may have been, I had not realised that in the silence of our occasional communion a bond was forged between us that would follow me like the spectre of a family secret long after I thought I had left the world of *Imitation* behind.

While I did not pay much attention to all the rumours, I did notice something peculiar about the other patients that I promised myself I would one day explore in more detail – their discomfort around Luc. They seemed at once fascinated and unsettled by his refusal to speak. Why were they so fascinated by somebody who refused to speak? And why did it seem to me as if they almost experienced it as a deep betrayal of sorts that someone may have decided never to break their silence? Of whom, or what, would it be a betrayal? As for myself, I must confess that I find the idea that someone could choose to spend their entire life in noble silence, never breaking the surface of shared meaning, deeply intriguing and something I know that a part of me has always yearned for.

On that particular day, two years after I had become aware of the way he shadowed me and just as the elderly couple on the patio started to recede, along with my memory of the fact that we had just exchanged a cordial greeting, I understood that the reason he kept thinking about me was because, ever since we first met, he knew that I, too, was haunted by the possibility of living in eternal silence. I fascinated Luc because he knew that silence fascinated me. Once I got back to my apartment, I took a bottle of water from the fridge and sat down on the patio and breathed in the cool late afternoon air. I pondered my insight. Luc haunted me because he was haunted by silence. *How simple,* I thought and took a long drink of water. And yet it took me nearly five years to understand that the object of my haunting was never Luc the person. It was not him that I constantly thought about and it was not him who constantly thought about me. He was just a vehicle for a haunting that haunted me, a haunting so fundamental that it could not say its name or articulate itself, a haunting that could only express itself in the image of Luc. I was haunted by the possibility of living in eternal silence and in my mind Luc had come to represent that yearning.

I realised that both Luc and I would have to find our way back to the world of language and shared meaning. I stood up and walked into the kitchen to start preparing supper. While absent-mindedly going about the business of putting together a simple pasta and making my usual vegetable juice to take to the office the next day, I mulled over what this would mean for Luc. How does one come back from such a commitment to silence? Does it depend on the reason for the silence, the trauma that plunged one into an addictive fascination with silence? And does that mean that coming back to language would always be equally traumatic? One thing I did know was that in order for me to survive my own longing for that eternal unity with the world that precedes meaning, for me not to get sucked into silence, I would have to find a way to imagine that Luc did eventually find his way back to language. If he is the image of my fascination with silence, his return to the world of language would also be my way of making peace with living in that world. But what would such a journey back to language look like? What would it entail? Where would I even begin to imagine such a journey?

That evening, as I poured the vegetable juice into an airtight bottle, I thought back to the many times the image of Luc had accompanied me on my late afternoon walks and how reassuring it was finally to understand his continued presence in my life. I thought of the long journey that lay ahead for both of us. I screwed on the lid of the juice bottle and put it in the fridge. As I closed the fridge door, I paused, as if lost in a daydream.

The Finger

11

The close encounter with Luc on campus left me disoriented and distracted. Over the previous couple of years I may have come to understand his continued presence in my life, but that did not make it any easier to suddenly be confronted with him in my real life. And yet, there he was. I can still vividly recall seeing him down there in the square, one hand shielding his eyes from the glare of the sun, looking straight up at me. *Did he also see me?* Seeing him standing there looking up at my office, running down to meet him, his sudden disappearance and then – almost more unsettling – Maretha looking down at where I was standing and not seeing me; all of this had left me with a strange sense of vertigo. Over the following two weeks I teach absent-mindedly, stare at the table in front of me during meetings, have restless naps over lunch and barely manage the most basic administrative tasks. Occasionally I walk over to the window and look down onto the square in the hope of seeing Luc again, but every time I return to my desk disappointed.

Every day at exactly 3.30 in the afternoon Maretha appears in my doorway to announce that she is leaving and to wish me a good evening. On a couple of occasions, I happen to look up only to catch her standing there already, looking at me quizzically. She never asks any questions, but I can see that she knows something is amiss. Instead of asking, and in the habit of her generation and its fondness for using the diminutive form of Afrikaans nouns, she leaves every afternoon wishing me a 'good little evening' and locks her office door behind her. Life has, by all accounts, returned to normality, albeit of a very strange kind – as if something quite extraordinary did not happen; as if seeing Luc were all a dream or a fantasy or, at best, the result of two parallel worlds brushing up against each other momentarily, allowing some meaning to bleed across. Did it also happen the other way round? I sometimes wonder. Did something or someone from this world also bleed across into the other word when they briefly collided? Did someone or something from this world also make a ghostly appearance in the other world, leaving some other version of 'me' equally confounded by the event? If so, has that 'me' also been struggling to get their former life back on track again? Who knows? Perhaps what happened to me in this world is quite an ordinary thing in the other world and people there are not at all fazed when it happens. Five days after I formulated this Other World hypothesis in a desperate attempt to explain how I could possibly have seen Luc so that I could get on with my life, something even stranger happens.

On that particular day I get home and unpack the rucksack that I take to work every day, put my empty lunch box and vegetable juice bottle in the sink and my wallet, access card and keys in the woven grass basket on the counter. Then I switch on the radio for company and, while undressing and putting on a comfortable tracksuit, contemplate whether I should go to gym, go for a nice long walk through the suburb or just stretch out on the couch, with my feet up and relax. I cannot make up my mind and decide to postpone the decision until I have brought the washing inside. I hope it will be dry because, although I hung it on the line early that morning before I left for work, I did not roll back the retractable overhead canvas, which means the washing would have got very little sun all day. I did briefly contemplate rolling back the canvas, but the weather was undecided and the thought of coming home to dripping wet (as opposed to possibly damp) laundry did not appeal to me; in addition to which, for security reasons, I never left the canvas retracted for the whole day anyway. If the canvas were rolled back, someone could quite easily climb down onto my patio once they had scaled over the neighbour's garage, whereas if the canvas were stretched out over the patio, it would be very difficult to get in. Not impossible, just very difficult.

Despite the fact that the washing has hung in the shade all day, everything is dry. I take the clothes off the line, fold what needs to be folded and stack everything in three neat piles on the low patio table: one pile for things that need to be ironed, a second for things that do not need to be ironed, such as T-shirts, towels and sheets, and a third pile for socks and underpants. Then I take the washing inside and return to the patio. I unwind the hose and wash the patio floor with the sprayer set to jet stream. Then I roll up the hose and enjoy the fruits of my handiwork. Everything seems fresh and alive, including the pot plants, which often look a bit dishevelled by late afternoon. It never ceases to amaze me how quickly they perk up once I have sprayed them with the sprayer on its gentle mist setting. I decide there is still enough time before sunset to roll the canvas back and allow the remaining sunlight to dry as much of the patio floor as possible. It is only when I reach for the rope to release the canvas so that it can roll back that I notice a slit in the canvas just above the double hook I use to wind the rope around. The slit is about fifteen centimetres long and had obviously been made by someone who had tried from the outside to get to the rope in order to roll back the canvas. This would, of course, be dangerous because, to reach down through the slit in order to unwind the rope that allowed the canvas to roll back, one runs the risk of catching one's arm or hand in the roll-back motion of the canvas before one could pull it out again.

And then I see it: proof of the fact that this is indeed a stupid and dangerous idea. Just as I lock the rolled-back canvas into its final resting place and start to wind the rope around the double hook, something that must have got caught between the canvas and one of the steel pipes that provide the skeleton for the retractable canvas drops at my feet. Not thinking much of it, I continue to wind the rope until it is properly tied. Then I bend down to pick up the object that had fallen at my feet. To my horror, I then see what it is.

A finger. An index finger, by the look of it, neatly severed at the joint closest to the hand.

For a moment I am too horrified to speak or move. Is it perhaps a toy thing, a play-play finger that one of the children who live upstairs accidentally dropped down onto my canvas? Or is it a real finger? I poke at it with my foot (thank goodness I had put my slippers on) and watch it slowly roll over. Then I get down on my haunches to take a better look. It is real, I am shocked to realise. The cut that had severed the finger from the hand was not precise. Quite the opposite. The finger looked quite mangled. Whatever had happened to this finger did not happen on purpose. I look up at the slit that had been cut in the canvas, but cannot see any blood. Then I pull one of the garden chairs closer and, standing on it, push my face right up against the canvas. There it is. Although the whole area around the slit had been thoroughly wiped, I can still make out faint smears of red on the steel pipe next to the cut. Then I see the final and definitive evidence: small blood spatters on the canvas. Small, but definitely there. Some poor schmuck had cut through the canvas, released the rope, got his finger caught between the retracting canvas and the steel pipes with their finely serrated edges and lost his (or her?) finger in the process. Did they get into my apartment? I walk over to the patio door that leads into the lounge and inspect the lock, as well as the windows on either side of the door. I can see no obvious signs of forced entry. I turn back and look up again at the slit canvas and down again at the finger on the ground. Something does not make sense. Even if someone had managed to release the rope and, minus one finger, climbed down onto my patio, and even if they had somehow managed to get into and out of my apartment without leaving any trace of forced entry, how did they get out again? To climb back up and somehow pull the canvas back over the patio leaving the rope neatly wound over the double hook again, would be impossible. Unless this someone is simply a lot more clever than I am. Either way, I decide, something strange happened here while I was at work and I need help to make sense of it. I take my phone out of my pocket and phone my neighbour Marius.

'What's up?' He has been sweeping up leaves on his side of the fence. I often hear him do this after work and I heard the sweeping stop just before he answered the phone.

'I think you should come over. I feel like I just walked onto the stage set for an episode of *Twin Peaks*.'

'Well, that sounds ominous,' he replies. 'What do you mean?'

'Just come over. You'll see.'

'Sure.' The line goes dead and I hear him shout to Barbara, his wife, that he is just popping over to see me. Next, I hear the security gate that leads from his garage into their garden swing open and close again. A couple of seconds later he knocks on the entrance door to the patio. He looks at me quizzically as I open the door, but I just grin and gesture with my head for him to step inside. I close the door behind him and point to the finger on the floor. 'Look what I just found.'

'Jesus!' he says. 'Is that a finger?'

'Indeed,' I answer and for a couple of seconds we just stand there looking at it. The next few minutes are all a bit of a blur. I think when one encounters something that is fundamentally at odds with reality, one can kind of cope with it on one's own. As long as one is alone (as I was when I saw Luc from my office window), one can still entertain the possibility that one is perhaps mistaken; perhaps one had dreamed or hallucinated or simply mistaken one thing for another. But when another person gets involved and confirms that indeed something has happened that is at odds with the laws of the world, the shared sense of facing something weird somehow makes it seem even stranger. In retrospect, I vaguely recall offering my explanation, that someone must have tried (or succeeded) to climb down through the canvas, but Marius instantly dismissed the theory on the grounds that it would have been impossible for anyone to escape and extend the canvas back over the patio again. I also recall one or two Mafia jokes and that Quentin Tarantino got a mention before the conversation eventually drifted back into the mundane reality of logistics.

'What are we going to do with it?' I ask.

'You mean what are *you* going to do with it,' he states emphatically.

'I don't know. What does one do with a severed finger? Scoop it up like dog poo and dispose of it in the garbage, or does one bury it in the garden like a dead pet?'

'Better call the cops,' he says. 'Just now someone comes looking for it and what do you say then? That you never saw a severed finger on your patio?'

'Whoever leaves a finger behind at the scene of the crime is unlikely to come looking for it again,' I reply.

'Who knows?' Marius says. 'All I'm saying is play it safe. Call the cops and let them do what they do.'

'You mean file a missing finger report?'

'Well,' he says, 'how often do you get to show the police a middle finger?'

He gets up from his haunches and grins at me. 'It's an index finger, I'm sure,' I add as he leaves and I hear the security gate open and close again. After another couple of seconds, the sweeping starts up again. *How does he do that?* I wonder.

I call the cops. Since it is not a serious incident of damage to life or property, they will only be able to send someone in about 30 minutes I am told – which ends up being an hour and 30 minutes, during which time I have two double whiskies sitting on the steps that lead into the lounge, alternately looking at and avoiding looking at the finger.

Eventually, the cops arrive. A large woman and a scrawny man. At first only the female cop comes in and asks what is going on. I tell her how I came home to find a finger on the patio floor and point it out to her. I say I did not know what to do with it and so decided that it was better to report the incident and ask them to take it away.

'*Eish*!' she exclaims. 'But whose finger is it?' she asks, also getting down on her haunches and, taking a pen from her top pocket, rolling the finger over again. Since I had previously rolled it over with my slipper, the finger had now rolled full circle and is back in the position in which I found it, fingernail on top.

'Whose finger is it?' I exclaim incredulously and in my slightly befogged whisky brain recall an incident that took place about two weeks earlier. I had ordered a chair – one of those that arrives in a flat box with very little by way of instructions on how to assemble it because the design is apparently so self-evident. Once I had spread out all the parts on the lounge floor, however, I realised that one part was missing. I phoned the suppliers and explained to the man that a central part of the chair was missing. He was sympathetic, but not very helpful. In fact, it sounded as if he had no idea what the chair I had ordered looked like and after several failed attempts to describe to him which part I thought was missing, he asked me to send him a picture of the missing part.

'I don't know whose finger it is or how it got here,' I reply, slightly irritated. 'But I suspect that somebody tried to break in through the canvas – there . . .' and I point to the slit in the canvas top, 'and maybe got his finger cut off on those serrated edges as the canvas retracted. Something like that.'

'*Eish*!' she exclaims again and straightens up. She looks at the slit in the canvas as if to consider the plausibility of my explanation. Then she turns around and in one of the nine official languages I do not understand, shouts something to her colleague, who has been waiting in the car. After a couple of minutes, he appears and with understandable trepidation steps over the doorstep onto the patio. Even though I do not understand the language they are speaking, the voice of authority is clear – hers. She points first to the finger, then to the slit in the canvas and, clearly borrowing my theory without acknowledging its source, explains in the same voice of authority what had obviously happened. When she stopped talking, Scrawny takes a plastic bag from his pocket and bends down to bag the finger.

He has no tools or instruments to do it with, no tweezers or even a pair of gloves, so I am curious to see how he intends to do it. He puts his hand inside the plastic bag, picks up the finger and inverts the bag over the finger. *Like dog poo, after all,* I think. He leaves and the woman turns to me again. She explains that they will be taking it to the laboratory for tests and so on and so forth and that they will get back to me once they knew more. I half expect her to add, 'And in the meanwhile don't leave town without notifying us', but she does not. She just asks me to let them know if I discover anything more. *Anything else?* I think. *Like what? A pinky finger?* I briefly consider asking them if they are not supposed to dust the canvas for additional fingerprints of a possible accomplice or some such detective work, but something in me just gives up.

'Sure, officer,' I say and close the door behind them.

The rest of the evening I am too bewildered by the strangeness of the day to do anything productive. I phone Juliet and we talk about our days. I had not mentioned seeing Luc to her and that evening is still not the right time. So, I tell her about the finger. She is suitably surprised and asks the obvious questions – 'You're pulling my leg, right? What the hell? and 'Whose finger could it be?' But her surprise does not last as long as I hoped it would. Once it is clear that I have told her everything I know, she gets distracted and starts telling me about the frustrations she experienced in the course of her day. After some discussion of domestic affairs, and agreeing on what items to prioritise in the monthly budget, we say goodbye.

I warm up some leftovers and eat listlessly while watching the news. Then I run a bath and allow my body to sink into the water. I do not feel like listening to my audiobook. Detective Bergman will have to wait. I have other things to think about. For a while, I keep thinking about the severed finger, but soon tire of it. There is nothing more to understand about the whole business. Then, as if some mysterious train of associations connected them all – or perhaps because I want to think about something less disturbing and more familiar – I think back, as I so often do, to the day I saw Luc from my office window. As if it were a video, I run the memory of that encounter again, starting with the moment I arrived at the window with my cup of tea in hand and looked down onto the square, and ending with Maretha's shadowy silhouette retreating from the same window. Memories run into thoughts about Luc's silence and his fascination with me, which in turn remind me of something I have often heard referred to as the 'mystic's curse'.

The Mystic's Curse

12

Why would anyone be attracted to the idea of living in utter silence, never to speak a word? It sounds like a complex question about an esoteric desire, which it both is and is not. We get a sense of the complexity of this desire when we recall that the meaning of the term 'mystery' dates back all the way to Pseudo-Dionysius the Areopagite, who was inspired by the Greek word *musterion*. But the original meaning of *musterion* is itself a mystery and so it should come as no surprise that as soon as Dionysius revived it, a battle ensued over its application in the real world. The battle lines emerged between, on the one side, Christian theologians inclined to mysticism, who used it to suggest something of the ineffable nature of God's divine presence, and, on the other side, ecclesiastical authorities and church administrators, defenders of the faith, who used it as a label to contain those who claimed to have experienced this divine presence and who therefore often refused to subject themselves to the 'mere' authority of church administrators. This contestation resulted in one of the most fundamental disputes in Christian theology: can we speak about God or not? Is it an insult to use words to describe Him and is He not much bigger than any word we can invoke to refer to Him? In fact, is He not bigger even than the sentence 'God is bigger than any attempt to talk about him'? Indeed. The paradox did not fail to attract, first, the attention of Ignatius of Antioch, who declared, 'It is better to keep silence and to be, than to talk and not to be' and, later, equally enchanted by the ineffable nature of God but much more given to clever paradoxes, Saint Augustine, who commented, 'God should not be said to be ineffable, because when this is said a statement is made. There results a form of verbal strife in that if the ineffable is what cannot be said, then what is called ineffable cannot be ineffable.'

Long story short, the conflict between mystics and church administrators is as old as the mystery we refer to as 'God'. On the one hand, mystics such of Joan of Arc insisted that their experience of the divine was unmediated and *mysterious*. On the other hand, church administrators knew that their power depended on everyone getting the same message – which proved difficult when it was claimed that the notion of a 'message' insulted the very idea of a God who existed so far beyond our imagination that we could not even think Him, never mind decode so-called messages from him. And so, mystics have always lived a cursed life: so close to the only thing that matters that they cannot talk about it.

But enough about the complexity of the desire to live silently embraced by God. The mystic's curse is a much more ordinary and everyday phenomenon than this reified history of the word 'mystery' suggests. Imagine a man who is going for a long, peaceful walk early one evening. Being by himself, he muses about this and that and, as his thoughts slow down to the point where they become superficial – not superficial in the sense of lacking in substance, but superficial as in light; so light, in fact, that his thoughts become indistinguishable from other sensations, such as the twitter of birds, the smell of someone cooking supper, feeling the evening breeze on his face; superficial, then, in the sense that all sensations and thoughts about sensations have become equally light. He starts imagining a world in which he could spend his days like this: completely devoted to just allowing thoughts to become sensations. He marvels, first at the superficiality of thinking, then at the depth of his desire to live an utterly superficial life. It has never crossed his mind that he could want to live like that, but would it not be the most beautiful thing?

So enchanted is our wanderer by this lightness of thinking that he is almost overcome by a sensation he cannot quite name. It is a singular sensation, a sense of unity with the world. The autumn leaves in the trees are vibrant, the smells immediate, the sounds part of his soul. He looks around him and is taken by the simplicity of it all. He sees an elderly couple on a patio enjoying a glass of wine. He waves at them and they wave back. And so, our wanderer meanders home, enraptured in a blissful state of superficiality. He cannot recall ever thinking of thought as a sensation, and the very idea that thinking is nothing more than a sensation so exalts him that he feels completely at one with the world. As he approaches his garden gate and removes the keys from his pocket, an overweight, middle-aged woman, whom he often sees running up and down the hill in front of his apartment, runs past him, uphill, her face tired with determination. Our wanderer smiles at her and a thought breaks through the surface: *If only you knew how little this matters*. But she mistakes his smile for an invitation to pause and escape her determination.

'God! This is killing me!' she exclaims, panting. 'Why do us woman struggle so much with our weight and you, you men . . .' She pauses to catch her breath. 'All you need is to go for the odd walk and look at you! Is that fair, I ask you!?'

And there it is. Two thousand years of mysterious theology, of contemplating the mystery of the ineffable and the possibility that a life articulated may well be a life misspent, interrupted by the banality of worldly chatter. Our poor wanderer. What is he to do? Should he turn away rudely and preserve his silence, relishing the unity that he refuses to allow this woman to shatter? Should he insist on staying in the mystery of unity, ignore her and reconcile himself to the fact that from that moment onwards he will only get from her rude stares, if anything at all? Or, should he recognise the woman as essentially representing the necessity, even inescapability, of worldly affairs – an emissary of the church fathers who always insisted on controlling the mystic experience? Should he bow to her authority and allow her to convert their encounter into the kind of capital we need in order to live in a world we share with others? Precisely this has always been the mystic's dilemma: do I trade this experience or not? If I do not, I will be cursed as a social outcast. If I do, I suffer the loss of divine intimacy.

Poor Luc. Nobody is meant to survive a near-death experience. A near-death experience is always a death of sorts – there is nothing 'near' about it. How was he meant to know that an encounter with the Godhead would leave him dead to this world, speechless; that in the mystical unity with the Godhead one experiences the original unity of the world, the very unity that has to be shattered in order for there to be language, so that we can communicate with others? Language makes a difference. It differentiates between you and me, this and that; we learn to live in a world broken by the power of language to make differences. One who is afforded a glimpse of the Godhead encounters the original unity of the world that precedes language. They subsequently experience language as a particularly violent shattering of that unity. And yet, when the experience of the mystery is over, it is over; we brace ourselves and speak while we remain conscious of a little pang of pain, the pain of betrayal that accompanies the act of speaking, a pang we recognise as leaving the experience of unity with the world in order to be among people again, regardless of whether they are church authorities or an overweight woman steaming up the hill.

Of course, some people are so enchanted by this experience of the mystery that they choose to spend their entire lives dedicated to its pursuit, their enlightenment. But, for those such as Luc who are suddenly and unexpectedly surprised by the mystical experience, it is very different. Having no recourse to monasteries or the desert life, they know that language betrays us into difference and the jolt they intuit would be necessary in order for them to make differences again seems so extraordinarily violent that they withdraw completely. Eventually, life becomes possible again. But it is always a life shadowed by divine melancholy, calculating the losses generated by naming people and objects as if they were indeed separate things. Luc and our late afternoon wanderer may not know this, but they are both haunted by Ignatius of Antioch's pithy declaration of war on the human condition: 'It is better to keep silence and to be, than to talk and not to be.'

Part II

Arrival

1

I imagine it was late one afternoon when Luc's parents dropped him off at Doctor Cottard's sanatorium. Not quite dusk, but late afternoon. It had been a long drive. They were all tired and it would not be a long, protracted farewell because Luc's parents still had the return journey ahead of them. The man Luc would come to know as Maurice, who seemed to double as a butler as well as Doctor Cottards' right-hand man, had been waiting at the top of the big staircase, his white gloved hands folded one in the other, the very picture of patience and compliance. He was pleased that Luc's parents arrived, almost to the minute, at the time they had told him they would. As the car pulled up and came to a stop at the bottom of the staircase, he initially did not move. He had done this hundreds of times and knew the scene. The parent or friend dropping off the new patient (much to Doctor Cottard's irritation Maurice refused to refer to them as 'clients') would get out of the car, open the passenger door and assist the patient with getting out. Then they would open the boot of the car and take out the patient's luggage and invariably leave it at the bottom of the staircase, as if there were some invisible sign that stated: 'No family or friends beyond this point'. Perhaps it was the fact that Maurice appeared to look like a butler that compelled them to use the beginning of the staircase as the dividing line between their world and the patient's future world. Once they had placed the luggage on the ground, Maurice would slowly descend the staircase and introduce himself. He would explain that he would take the luggage and accompany the new patient to reception. This usually made it clear to both family or friend and patient that this is where they would have to say their goodbyes. Sometimes there were tears, other times – particularly when it was a man dropping off a male friend – a rather brisk embrace and a pat on the back, often, but not always, accompanied by some rhetorical statement of bravado, 'You can do this', 'Make the best of it' or some such. This, Maurice had learned over the years, was often the case when the family member or friend looked utterly exhausted, like a ghost: hollowed-out cheeks, dark rings under the eyes, or red eyes; sometimes, a demeanour that spoke of guilt or irritation with themselves for having put up with their friend or family member's addiction for too long, irritation at what they perceived to be their own failure and the guilt of having failed, yet again. Maurice had seen all the permutations of this moment and so, after his explanation and once he had taken the luggage, he usually let people get on with it.

On this occasion Maurice watches as a tall black man pulls a young white man closer in a tight embrace, kisses the crown of his head and holds him for a long moment. Then, holding Luc at arm's length, he looks him in the eyes and says, 'You will get through this, my son, whatever it is. But you're going to have to go all the way, you're going to have to go right through this, all the way to the other side. We'll be waiting there, but take your time. We will wait, however long it takes.' Then, with the unconscious habit of one who is in shock, he says, as if for the first time, 'You will get through this. Take your time. We will be there.' Then he pulls Luc closer again and holds him tight.

I imagine being Luc, feeling the warmth of his father's love, which is so big that it even embraces the silence that has enveloped him for so many months now. As he relishes the moment, he hears the chatter of birds in the trees and the sound of laughter drifting down from a lounge or games room somewhere inside. For the longest moment he leans into his father's shoulder, his black shoulder under that immaculately starched white, linen shirt. An image flashes before his eyes from when he was very little, perhaps four or five. He had asked his mother why his father's skin was black and what was under it – the same stuff that is under their white skin? Were all people in Nairobi black like his dad? Another image fades across his mind's eye. They are driving somewhere, he and his father, *just the two of them*. He is sitting in the front passenger seat looking at his father, who is concentrating on the road, preparing to overtake the car in front of them. He watches his father's hand on the knob of the gear lever. His father gears down and overtakes the car. Once there is a safe distance between them and the car behind, his father lets the car glide back elegantly onto the right side of the road and gears up again. Luc stretches out and touches his father's hand where it is still resting on the gear knob. He traces a line on the black skin, from the knuckles, over his father's wrist all the way to his elbow. His father turns to him smiling, white teeth flashing from under his cap. And now he feels those same arms around him, hugging him closely, gently rubbing his back. Luc opens his eyes, but he sees nothing in particular; his attention is unfocused and diffused through the sounds of chattering and laughing and the feeling of a slight late afternoon breeze on his face. It's all one, even the butler with the gloved hand is only one of the sounds around him. And all the sounds come to him at the same time. All is sound; sound is the world.

Then his father lets him go and Luc walks over to his mother. She looks distressed. She bends over and kisses him on the cheek. 'Be good my son. We'll talk soon.'

A little bit of love, Maurice thinks. *Probably as much as she is capable of.*

Then Luc turns around and walks up to Maurice, who picks up one of the suitcases and together they walk up the massive staircase, where a number of other patients are either sitting on the stairs smoking or half leaning against the balustrade, idly chatting or just looking out over the expansive gardens. When they get to the top, Maurice walks straight through the front door, but Luc stops and without putting his suitcase down, half turns to look back at his parents. He waves at them with his free hand. Everything is still the same; nothing has changed from the moment he walked up the staircase to the moment when he arrived at the top and turned around. The only difference is that the balance of the world had shifted; he is now closer to the sound of human laughter and further away from the chatter of birds, but not even that affects the balance of silence that surrounds him. He closes his eyes. There is the sound of his breathing. It is always just closer to him than the other sounds.

First Session with the Emperor

2

Luc had woken up with a profound sense that all the furniture in the room was in the wrong place and with an urgent feeling that everything had to be rearranged. The bed should be against the other wall and not under the window; the cupboard faced the wrong way, so that when the doors were left slightly ajar, they blocked the way to the bathroom and to the basin – well, he could not do much about the basin. The basin was where it was and the very fact that it could not move was probably the reason why everything else could only be in the wrong place. Everything had to find its place in relation to something that could not be moved. Still, he could try. He decided that as soon as he had settled in a bit more, he would ask permission to rearrange the furniture or, who knows, maybe he would just do it one day without asking anybody's permission. It was his room after all – at least for the time being. Either way, it could not stay like this. It just felt wrong.

His first night had been a restless one. It had taken him a long time to fall asleep and it was not only because of the furniture. He felt displaced and restless and he feared that he might not be able to sleep at all. Can one forget how to sleep? Is sleep something that one can become good or bad at? But he did eventually doze off, even though he woke up a couple of times – twice? three times? – to see a figure he dreamily decided must be a night nurse of sorts glide quietly across the room, briefly looking down on him, as if to make sure that he was not just pretending to sleep. Luc had waited until he could hear that the man had straightened up, turned around and started back towards the door again before he opened his eyes. Yes, it was indeed as if he glided. Either he was taking very small steps, or he just had disproportionately short legs. Luc had not seen the man since his arrival and so could not decide, but one thing he could be sure of was that the man made absolutely no sound when he walked. *His shoes don't make a sound. What is he wearing? Some kind of slipper? Would he be walking around in his socks? But why?* When he woke up that first morning, the feeling of disorientation and displacement had not left him.

As Luc would discover over the next six weeks, Doctor Cottard – or 'the Emperor', as many of his patients referred to him – had a rather unconventional approach to the treatment of addictions. Some of the patients were not at all convinced by his methods, or rather the beliefs that underpinned them, and Luc would soon realise that there was much discussion about the efficacy of their sessions with him and whether they were getting their money's worth. It was in order to protect new patients from these stories – or at least to give them an opportunity to form their own opinion – that Doctor Cottard insisted on seeing all new arrivals the day after they arrived.

I have always imagined Doctor Cottard a rather jolly, burly kind of chap. It is true that he is from one of France's oldest aristocratic families and renowned all over the world for his unconventional approach to the treatment of addictions. But his idiosyncratic approach to rehabilitation is only the professional reflection of his idiosyncratic dress code (he favours colourful waistcoats and is hardly ever seen without a spotted bow tie, mostly black with dots that match the colour of his waistcoat), which, in turn, is but the outward appearance of an inner idiosyncrasy, an irreverent levity with which he conducts himself, both socially and in the treatment of his clients. His unconventional approach to the treatment of addictions can best be summarised by a number of deeply held convictions: in modern societies everyone is an addict – in fact, an individual can only survive in modern society by being addicted to something, whether drugs, shopping, exercise, coffee or whatever the case may be; the only meaningful difference between, say, someone who is addicted to coffee and another person who is addicted to heroin is the fact that addiction to caffeine is a socially useful addiction, whereas the heroin addict is rendered quite useless to society by their addiction; in the third instance, Doctor Cottard maintains that what all addictions have in common is a fascination with repetition, with repeating the same action over and over again. Addicts, he believes, live in a trance, and consequently, what is required of an individual to be cured of their addiction is – and here he always displayed an almost childlike pleasure in conforming to his reputation for irreverence – to 'snap out of it'! But not everyone could simply 'snap out of it', either because sadness had become fundamental to their existence, or because they feared getting swept away by the impermanence of the world the moment they became unfettered from their addiction, or perhaps because the trance of addiction was actually a trance of misunderstanding, a trance the individual entered when they encountered the question about the meaning of life at a particular point in their lives, when all the answers that used to satisfy them had simply run out of currency. Yes, the answers that family, upbringing, education and tradition provide to the question 'What does it all mean?' can wear out, much like coins or paper money that have been in circulation for too long and at some point lose their distinctiveness. When that happens, they become useless to us; 'They've lost their purchase,' we say. And so, Doctor Cottard had come to believe that sometimes an addict resists 'snapping out of it' simply because they are buying time. Over the years he had worked out that with such clients his levity and irreverence have no purchase and that they require a different approach, something more quiet and compassionate. It was only through quiet compassion that such a client would come to see the value of a new currency, that they would open themselves to the possibility that a different answer to the age-old question about the meaning of life is not only possible, but also plausible. In such cases, Doctor Cottard did not hesitate to introduce his clients to his final core belief; namely, the reincarnation of the soul. Yes, Doctor Cottard believed that it was through reincarnation that the individual soul burns off any residue of the previous life's failures to snap out of the fascination with repetition that shadows all addictions. So, while it was true that he hoped an addicted individual – even the ones who were reduced to beggars after their life savings had been devalued and reduced to utter disbelief – would at some point snap out of it, he also recognised that snapping out of it may require more than one lifetime.

This more patient, understanding and compassionate face of Doctor Cottard made it particularly difficult to simply dismiss him as an idiosyncratic buffoon who fumbled his way through other people's sorrow. Despite appearances, he was also capable of a quiet and measured engagement with some clients, particularly the ones who remained entranced in the dead end of understanding. Clients who were in a trance of sadness needed his levity while those who had spent all their understanding, needed his compassion. It was almost as if he allowed the nature of his conduct to be determined by how he was perceived by a client and that was precisely the reason he insisted on meeting new arrivals before their perception of him could be influenced by the gossip about him that circulated among the clients at the sanatorium.

And so, on the morning of Luc's first session, Doctor Cottard is standing at the window with his back to the door when Luc arrives. He has studied Luc's file carefully and the case intrigues him. He has noted the obvious record of failed suicide attempts and brooded for a long time over the reference to Luc's near-death experience, subsequent to which the young man had not uttered a single word. If such a commitment to silence were to be understood as an addiction, it would be a singular addiction, indeed. And yet, given Luc's repeated attempts at taking his own life and his commitment to silence, Doctor Cottard felt that his central belief that everyone was addicted to something was validated and he instinctively knew that he would have to be very gentle with Luc. Too much difference and Luc would simply recoil and never discard the blanket of silence he had wrapped around himself. He hears Luc sit down. There is a long silence. Then, without turning around to face Luc, Doctor Cottard says, 'Subtle is the body, Luc.'

A greeting? A statement? Luc frowns. It is a comforting voice; slightly raspy, but calm, knowing and unhurried. The man who is standing at the window with his back turned to him is rather short and plump and is dressed in a long-sleeve shirt, black pants and a waistcoat of a strikingly deep emerald green, hands folded behind his back. There is nothing strained or forced about his body language or in the way he is dressed. He exudes ease. Luc waits for him to say something more, but he does not. The silence of things waiting to be said slowly gives way to a silence that knows no waiting, a silence that deepens until it gently engulfs him, so that *it*, and not time, becomes the measure of the moment.

Feeling his whole being relax into the silence between him and Doctor Cottard – a deeply comforting silence in which there seems to be no expectation that either of them should say anything – Luc lets his eyes wander away from Doctor Cottard to the left, across the bookshelves, the dark wood desk in front of him, the deep red carpet at his feet, the grey-white of the walls, shadows that play lightly in the morning sun, shifting as he looks at them, the strange green of the spherical paperweight on the desk and the calendar underneath it. Colours. So many colours. Luc closes his eyes and allows all the sounds to carry him away to the centre of the world, where nothing makes a difference: the chattering of the birds in the trees outside the window; the faint sounds of kitchen activity floating up from somewhere below them, which add a brass-like quality to an otherwise pastoral symphony of chatter; dim voices and the whisper of a slight breeze outside in the tree tops; his own breathing, which as always seems to conduct the symphony of the world, so that not a single sound ever seems out of place. There is no difference between the sounds that are expected and those that are not. Sitting here is forever. Silence is eternal and yet there is never silence, just a stream of sounds that float through his mind, as if he is not even there.

And yet, he can hear silence if he allows his mind to slip through the sounds. That is where it is. *There.* In the split second when the breeze subsides and the rustle of leaves calms down; when, at the same moment, there is also a lull in the chatter of the birds and a collective pause in the kitchen below. *There.* Silence becomes audible when the whole world briefly pauses to recollect itself like an eddy behind a rock. When all the different pauses coincide, the majestic silence that gives birth to sound itself becomes audible.

He opens his eyes. Doctor Cottard has sat down across the desk from him, when or for how long Luc has no idea, but he is sitting there, calmly, the ankle of one leg resting on the knee of the other, his arms placed on the elegantly curved wooden sides of the chair on either side of his body. Luc now sees the bow tie, black with emerald green dots that match the waistcoat. Doctor Cottard smiles broadly as he says to Luc, 'Nice to meet you, Luc. I am Doctor Cottrad, head of this . . .' he hesitates for a second, 'centre or institute. Some call it a rehabilitation centre, others a sanatorium. Doesn't really matter. You may also hear the other clients refer to me as "the Emperor",' that broad grin again, 'I don't know where that one comes from but there it is. I'll be working with you for the duration of your stay. You and I will have a total of three sessions while you are here and, of course, in between there will be all the other activities. This will be explained to you after our session today. Ajna will show you the whole centre and provide you with a schedule of your daily activities. If you have any questions, please ask . . . well, communicate to her in some way. She oversees pretty much everything.'

He pauses for a couple of seconds and then continues. 'I know about the silence, Luc. There is no expectation that you speak to me, okay?'

Luc nods.

'So,' and with that, Doctor Cottard sits up and moves closer to the desk, resting both arms on its top, one hand placed over the other. 'Do you know what all of us here have in common, Luc?' He does not wait for an answer. 'Yes, when I say all of us, I mean all of us, myself included. I also used to struggle with an addiction. But . . .' and he seems slightly self-conscious as he adjusts his bow tie, 'that was a long time ago. Then I inherited a lot of money and started this centre to help others such as yourself not necessarily to overcome addiction – that, only you can do – but to assist you in understanding something about it. The *why* or the *how*. Let's just say, I will try to assist you in understanding the kind of thinking that makes addiction possible. It sounds complicated I know, but it's not'. He pauses for a couple of seconds and then continues, 'There are people here who are addicted to substances – heroin, cocaine, alcohol and so on – but also people who are addicted to sex and a whole range of less conscious addictions – self-loathing, self-doubt, obsessive thinking. In your case – silence seems to be the thing that has a grip on you. Is that necessarily a bad thing? I don't know. We will know more once we understand it in relation to your near-death experience and what got you to that point.' There is a long pause. Luc avoids Doctor Cottard's gentle but penetrating gaze. Eventually the doctor speaks again. 'Let's start with your repeated suicide attempts. Have you ever thought much about repetition, Luc?' The words flow through Luc's mind as if they are of no concern to him; the sound of words that make sense, but a sense that is somehow unrelated to him. Like the rustling of leaves in the trees outside, the light murmur of voices in the passage and the comforting sounds that float up from the kitchen below.

'What is it about repetition that so fascinates us Luc? Have you ever thought of that?' Without waiting for any response, Doctor Cottard continues. 'Repetition. It is what all addicts have in common, a compulsion to repeat – a pattern, taking a substance, repeating this or that. All addicts are addicted to repetition – the rest, the substance, the patterns or whatever, is just what is being repeated, but that is not really the issue. The issue is: why repeat? What is it about repetition itself? If our primary addiction is to repetition, I always think our task is to understand that addiction. Because once we do, the other addiction – to substance, behaviour patterns and so on – will go away. It strikes me, Luc, that your fascination with silence is perhaps also driven by a fascination with repetition.'

Again, a long pause. All the other sounds have faded into the background. All Luc is aware of now is the sound of his own breathing.

Doctor Cottard seems unperturbed by Luc's lack of response. 'A wise man once said that repetition is symptomatic of an inability to experience pleasure – often pleasures that are frowned upon or not permitted by society. If we have a desire for such a pleasure and it cannot be satisfied, we create a repetitive pattern involving something that gives us some pleasure. So, instead of satisfying the one desire, we repeat the bit of satisfaction we get from another. In that sense addictions are really devised to help us forget a desire or a pleasure that remains unsatisfied. Formulated the other way round, somebody who is fully capable of experiencing pleasure, of feeling good about himself, of feeling at home in the world – and who experiences that as a good and pleasurable thing – such a person will not be intrigued by repetition and consequently never become addicted. I think this is an important insight, although I also think it's only half the story. The addict's problem is not simply pleasure or the inability to experience pleasure. The problem is deeper. For what does pleasure permit us to feel?' Again, a rhetorical question into the silence. Doctor Cottard takes one leg off the other and leans in on the desk, arms crossed. 'To experience pleasure is to experience a sense of belonging in the world. Pleasure is the gateway to belonging. To experience pleasure means feeling part of the world – I belong in it, I exist and I have a right to be here. If I do not think that I belong or that I have the right to exist, I will invent an action that I will repeat over and over again because it gives me a quick-fix sensation of belonging in the world. This action gives me a false sense of belonging. And because it is false, it doesn't last and because it doesn't last, it has to be repeated again and again. Does any of this make sense, Luc?'

Luc allows all of this to wash over him. It is as if he recognises every word Doctor Cottard says, as if he already knows all of this. There is nothing new in what he is hearing – it all seems so very familiar and yet, it is as if he is hearing it from behind a veil, as if none of it actually enters his mind. He hears the words, recognises their meaning, recognises the familiarity of their meaning, but then the meaning dissolves again, drifts off like the faint traces of campfire smoke into the night. All that remains behind are the ashy remains of meaning, the sound of the words, the sounds that come and go.

'Put it this way,' Doctor Cottard says, 'the addict is like a hamster on a wheel, repeating the same action over and over again in an attempt to get out there in the world. Two parallel worlds: the one inside the cage, the other next to it, but outside the cage. He doesn't realise that running will not get him there; that only opening the mind and body to the experience of pleasure can open the door to the wider world. He doesn't realise that he needs to find the portal to take him to the other world and that pleasure is the portal to belonging.' He pauses again and leans back in his chair. 'So, Luc. This is the question before us. I am less interested in why you think you do not or cannot belong in the world. What I am interested in is reminding you that you already belong in the world. I think of our three sessions as, shall we say, three exercises in remembrance. Somewhere deep inside you, you know that you belong in the world. It is my task to make you trust what you already know. To do that, I will be working with your subtle body, not your physical body.' He continues as if the distinction is the most obvious thing in the world. 'Some people also refer to the physical body as the gross body, but I don't like the word "gross".' He pauses and smiles. 'It may well be that I dislike the term "gross body" because I am somewhat . . . shall we say, aware of the fact that I have been overindulging in our chef's culinary exuberance over the last couple of months, but let's just say the "physical body" is a more elegant term than the notion of a gross body,' – and here he pauses to make a gesture with his right hand, little circles that get smaller and smaller as they rise up in the air until the very idea of a physical body evaporates in the unspoken phrase – 'but that is neither here nor there. The subtle body, on the other hand, is in a sense more real. It is what some refer to as our energy body, our spiritual body. That is the body I will be working with.'

And now the familiarity with what Doctor Cottard has been saying is gone. These are strange words that Luc has never encountered before. Unlike the other words the doctor spoke earlier, the notion of a subtle or spiritual body does not even briefly convey meaning. It just arises and disappears again into the silence it came from.

'Today, I want to talk to you about your arrival in the world, your soul's arrival; this soul that at the same time does and does not belong to you. Our entire life is given to us in how and where we arrive. It is the ground zero of our quest for belonging and that is where we will start. Yes, Luc, I am talking about rebirth or reincarnation. They're two different things, but let's, for the moment, assume they're the same thing. Every birth is an arrival. And every arrival is a return. The only question is this: are you ready to accept what that means?'

Luc looks up from the spherical paperweight his eyes had been resting on in an attempt to avoid making eye contact with Doctor Cottard. He looks up and for the first time really looks at the doctor's face. It is an ordinary face. There is something simultaneously gentle and stern about it. *Emperor.* The word floats into his mind and drifts off again without leaving any trace behind. For a couple of seconds Luc just stares at Doctor Cottard. And who would not? To be told with such gentle confidence that you have been here before, that what you think of as your life and your soul is actually not yours, does not belong to you, that it is actually the other way round and that you belong to your soul and that 'your' life is living itself through you – to be told all this by someone who does not seem to know a trace of self-doubt is quite a thing. Even more so for Luc. What a statement to throw at a young man with a history of seventeen failed suicide attempts, who so nearly succeeded the last time that he briefly got a glimpse of the afterlife – which now, if anything Doctor Cottard is saying is to make sense, is not the *after*life but the *before* life, a world that precedes this life, the world he came from and to which he very nearly succeeded in returning.

I cannot imagine what is going through Luc's mind as he sits there lost in the unity of all sounds. The best I can do is to speculate that in the moment when Doctor Cottard in a very matter-of-fact way presented him with a truth that will eventually turn his life around, Luc was protected by the fact that in his trance of fascination with the majesty of an original silence, nothing is ever truly unexpected because nothing is expected. Unity with the world knows no time and, as a result, nothing can arrive out of time. Is it a mere coincidence that a young man who had been to, and returned from, the very threshold between this life and the life after would, in the process of recovering from that terrifying experience, encounter a therapist who stated with such simple conviction that the soul keeps returning to this world until it is purified? I do not think so.

Short History of a Long Fable I

3

In the popular imagination, the fable about the reincarnation of the soul is associated with India and the Far East. But this is a convenient mythology and just another example of how, over the past 2 000 years, Western civilisation has dedicated much time and effort to cleaning up its act – adopting the children it likes and disavowing the ones it does not; kidnapping writing, geometry and the origins of philosophy, while leaving on the steps of the Orphanage of Amnesia a basket full of abandoned responsibilities: the consequences of slavery, colonialism and, yes, its own long-standing fascination with the reincarnation of the soul. Like any parent who is handing over the reins of the family business, the West constantly revises its last will and testament to include those children it will allow to inherit its name, while disinheriting those who have shamed it in the past or threaten to do so in the future.

Reincarnation, or some version of it, has been one of these problem children. As a doctrine, it represents a belief that is as universal as the idea that actions have consequences or that gods exist whose true nature recedes further and further into silence with every attempt we make to articulate who they are or explain to ourselves why they only sometimes give us what we want. At bottom, all religions are human attempts at working out the relationship between the Great Mystery and the fact that actions have consequences. We can perhaps formulate this more succinctly and say that the Mystery consists of trying to understand the relationship between silence and consequence. One of the ways in which we have tried to connect the two is through the notion of 'karma'.

We tend to think of karma as shorthand for 'consequence' when, in fact, it means the exact opposite: action. Similarly, karma or action initially had nothing to do with reincarnation. In the Vedas, the foundational Sanskrit scriptures of Hinduism, it is assumed that the Great Creator, or Brahman, is an orderly mind and that creation is therefore equally orderly and imbued with intelligence. Every individual owes compliance to this divine order of things. But the kind of compliance intended here should not be confused with the kind we associate with having to sacrifice our free will in order to conform. No, compliance simply means that one has to know and act in accordance with one's place in the divinely ordained order of things. In the Vedas, life is seen as a harmonious, ordered whole and when the individual gets it wrong and acts in a manner contrary to this order, a specific action is needed to restore that balance: *that* action is karma, and in the past it usually assumed the form of a sacrifice performed by a Vedic priest, with the aim of righting the balance. In other words, the initial meaning of karma was neutral and simply referred to the action needed to restore order and harmony.

Over time, however, the notion of karma as a corrective action acquired moral overtones and soon it was said that if a son does his duty (or acts in accordance with his place in the world), blessings will come to his ancestors and living family. But if he behaves badly, things will go horribly wrong for them. At this point, karma came to be understood not only in terms of actions, but also in terms of consequences: individuals can create karma, much like circles of consequences that ripple out in order to cause harm or bring about future benefits. So prominent did this conception of karma-as-consequence become that it was soon believed that the effect of one's bad actions could actually cancel out the consequences of one's good actions. From here, it was a small step to invoke karma to provide an answer to two of the most enduring questions that have haunted the human imagination: why are some people born ugly or poor and why are others born pretty or wealthy? Suddenly, there was a plausible answer: being ugly or pretty, rich or poor, was simply one of those ripple effects that played itself out in an individual's life. We are constantly reaping the good and bad consequences of all actions that ripple through us – both our own actions and those of the people whose lives affect ours. Being part of a whole network of people and actions, all our actions reverberate as consequences throughout the network. But the causality is not single and direct (son refuses to pick up garbage, so father loses his job; or son refuses to pick up dog poo and steps in it on his way home). Rather, every cause is singular, but multiplies infinitely throughout the network, creating resonances and consequences throughout it in such a complex way that we cannot possible keep track of them. Good actions may cause good consequences and we may reap the benefit; bad actions may generate adverse consequences, some of which may return to us. So, we become who we are through our deeds. Our deeds become us, or, karma makes and unmakes us.

It did not take very long for this earthly notion of actions and consequences considered as one great tangle of resonances to invoke the Great Mystery and to proclaim that we would need more than one lifetime to work through the consequences of actions that affect us. And so, a specific understanding of the immortality of the soul entered the stage of Indian history, according to which one may reincarnate many times to work through the ripple of consequences of one's own and others' actions. That it was initially assumed to always be the same soul that returns is clear from a famous analogy in the *Bhagavad Gita*, in which reincarnation is explained by means of a distinction between actor and costume. We (the souls) are the actors, who remain the same and every time we return to perform on the stage of life, we do so wearing different costumes (bodies). Over time, the analogy of the 'actor' who returns in a different 'costume' with every reincarnation would appear and disappear from the stage of Hinduism like, well, a freelance actor. Sometimes, he was barely visible; at other times, he played an important role and, at yet other times, he just waited in the wings or only put in a cameo appearance.

Then, onto the stage walked the most famous actor in this theatre of Indian history, Buddha himself, an actor who turned out to be more of a scriptwriter who intensely disliked actors. Though deeply influenced by the ideas of karma that had been doing the rounds for hundreds of years, he shocked his audience by promptly declaring that there is no difference between actor and costume, between a true and a dressed-up self. With one fell swoop, the bottom of karmic theory dropped out and the idea of an actor who constantly returns to work through his karma exited stage left. Instead of thinking of the human being as an actor who keeps returning dressed in a different body, Buddha suggested we think of the 'self' as no more than a 'constellation' of elements orbiting planet Void. These elements were the physical elements acknowledged by tradition (earth, fire, wind, water and space), to which he added another five – physical body, sensation, perception, disposition and consciousness. We can understand our nature and the way we exist by observing these elements, their nature and the way their gravitational pull determines how they orbit one another. In so doing, we discover interesting things, such as the extent to which our sensory perceptions affect our thinking patterns, our feelings and emotions. All these things mutually influence one another. So, here is the crux: the physical and mental elements are not just the costume behind which the fixed 'self' is concealed or not just the costume the actor wears. The implication of all this is pretty profound because it is no longer the individual self who creates karma; rather, karma is the effect of the specific way in which the configuration or constellation of elements plays out in any given moment.

Because we need to survive in the world, we like to imagine this operational 'self' as a real self, a fixed self that continues to exist over time and whose existence is grounded by the permanence of things. We imagine ourselves looking at reality and observing how everything is connected. We go for a long, quiet walk through the suburbs, wave at a couple we regularly see sitting on the veranda drinking wine and, because of all these continuities, we assume that the 'self' who set out walking is the same 'self' who returns home; or that the 'self' who waved at the couple yesterday is the same 'self' who waved at them today. But that is no more than an operational fiction, a necessary story we tell ourselves in order to get through the day. And necessary it is. What would happen to the world if a man who signed a contract in the morning later that same day acted contrary to the contract because, according to Buddha, the evening constellation of his 'self' was different from the one who signed the contract that morning? And what kind of marital infidelities and betrayals of friendship could not be justified on the basis of such an operational sense of self!

The problem, Buddha reminded us, is not that there is no fixed self; the problem is that we act as if there were one. We take the operational self to be our real self, to be fixed. What we need to do is to constantly remind ourselves that the 'self' does not exist outside the whole network of interconnectedness of which it is an ever-changing product, which, in turn, produces the network and so on. The 'self' is not so different from that other mysterious force we call 'gravity': it holds the whole lot together, but does not exist outside of all the things that it holds together. This, explained Buddha, is the point of meditation, which is nothing but an exercise in becoming gravity. It is the subtle art of allowing the 'self' to dissolve back into the constellation of interactions that produce it. By the same token, enlightenment does not mean finding the true Self. It simply means sustaining the dissolution of the self in the network of constellations that produce the fiction of a 'self'. The longer you can sustain that, the more enlightened you are and the experience of being nothing more than sustained gravity is called Nirvana. Indeed, Nirvana – that much maligned figure of our displaced longing for Being – is nothing more than the subtle ability to sustain being gravity.

But what, then, of reincarnation? Since we started to ponder this question a few pages ago, it has lived an entire life – mostly in the background, like a faithful servant, who comes and goes when we do not observe her, always hovering in the background, appearing not to listen, not to be present, but always there, waiting to clean up after the guests have left, perhaps once they have finished their conversation or when they get tired of the exchange of ideas. We know the scene: the wine is finished, the ashtrays overflowing with cigarette butts, the air thick with misunderstandings that will eventually just drift out through the window, opened by the dutiful servant to air the room. But that need not be the fate of our question. We can allow it to reincarnate into another passage and to allow it the time and space it needs to wear out its own karma.

If we do indeed return, if we do have past and future lives, how do we account for this continuity? If there is no fixed self, who can be said to have lived before and who will return again in future? Does not the very idea of a return imply continuity, which in turn implies a Self that exists continuously? Consider Luc: if Doctor Cottard wants him to believe that his arrival in the world is a *return* to the world, then surely Doctor Cottard is assuming the existence of some fixed 'self' or 'soul' that has made the return journey?

Having dismissed all the actors from his play, having presented us with a script in which actors and costumes are united in and through their actions, Buddha introduced a distinction between eternalists, fatalists and his own proposed 'middle way'. Eternalist believe in life eternal, a fixed Self who keeps returning to this life, over and over. This is reincarnation. Fatalists believe that death is death. It is a full stop. Like this one: . It interrupts our life sentence and that is the end of it. Between reincarnation and nihilism, Buddha posed a third way: rebirth – not the return to life of a constant Self, but rather the continuation of something like a stream of consciousness. Yes, but how do we conceive the 'quantum' of life that physically comes to embody the continuation of such a stream of consciousness? The Yogacarins proposed a solution that essentially amounted to positing the Buddhist equivalent of the unconscious, which they called *alayavijnana*, or 'storehouse consciousness'. We may well become unconscious for a while, or die and be reborn, but latently present at an unconscious level is a storehouse of all the karmic traces and dispositions that make us who we are. It was through the notion of this 'storehouse of traces' that the Yogacarins explained our remembrance of things past, which enable transmigration from one life to the next.

And so the actor who was temporarily left unemployed by Buddha found employment again with the Yogacarins, albeit in a diminished role – no longer the lead actor or star of the show, but in a support role as a constellation of imprints that hangs around at the edges of our consciousness. When an individual does re-enter the stage of life, he or she brings a constellation of imprints from their previous life, which are never enough, or so complete that one can say: 'Hey, look! There's Peter again!' No, even if we could wipe off all that stage make-up and strip him of his costume, it would never simply be Peter Again. It is not the embodiment of Peter we encounter, but something far more subtle; a *subtle* Peter, an imprint of the previous Peter. To this subtle Peter we are bound to respond with mixed feelings, a combination of the familiar and the uncanny: 'Have we met before?' or 'You remind me of my friend Paul'. What we recognise in that moment is not Peter or the body we associate with the name 'Peter', but rather the return of aspects or parts of Peter's subtle body, an impression of Peter. Yes, if Peter and I knew each other in a previous life and we generated karma, we will intuitively recognise each other again in this life, not as 'me' and 'Peter', but as a vaguely familiar storehouse of imprints. And this is indeed how the relationship between the gross and subtle body is to be understood: when our 'stream of consciousness' or 'soul' returns in a new body, it brings with it a quantum or imprint of lived experiences that makes up its subtle body, in which is stored all that was experienced and gathered during past incarnations.

Short History of a Long Fable II

4

We tend to think of this fable as an exotic story about things that are completely foreign to the Western imagination. But this is not the case – as is clearly demonstrated by one eternalist version of the myth of reincarnation that had a particularly vibrant and long life in the West. We have come to treat this myth a bit like a bastard son, as if it were the illegitimate offspring of a husband and servant, a bastard idea that, because of its mixed origin, could never quite aspire to the throne. But the belief in the return of the soul is as universal as, well, the notion that a bastard son cannot inherit the throne. Among the Greek philosophers there are, of course, the usual suspects, such as Pythagoras and Plato, who believed in some version of what Buddha called 'eternalism' or the reincarnation of a constant Self, but I want to remember that other bastard child here, the one whose teachings (and reincarnation in England, centuries later) resulted in his being declared a heretic and his teachings, anathema.

Church Father, Origen of Alexandria (*c.*184–*c.*253), was widely regarded as one of the most influential Christian theologians of his time. The core element of his teaching was the pre-existence of souls. According to Origen, God created a great number of souls before he created the world. At first, all these souls devoted their entire existence to loving God, but as time went by, some of them got bored. By the time He created the material world, for their punishment, those who had become very bored with a life of complete devotion became demons; those who had become only a little bit bored became humans and those who had become the least bored became angels. Although our bodies were created as vehicles for our souls *after* their fall away from God, no human soul can exist without a body. More importantly – and this is what matters for our little fable – human souls keep returning to the world in order to work at re-establishing the original relationship of full-time devotion to God.

The doctrine of the reincarnation of the soul spread so fast among early Christians that Emperor Justinian I (c.482–565) felt compelled to suppress it. In 543 he condemned Origen as a heretic and ordered his writings to be burnt and in 553 the Second Council of Constantinople declared the Christian scholar's teachings on the pre-existence of the soul anathema – a 'thing devoted to evil' – in a pompous decree (a genre by that time perfected by both emperor and pope), which stated: 'If any one says or believes, that human souls pre-existed, i.e., were once mere spirits, and holy, that having become weary of divine contemplation, they were brought into a worse condition; and that, because they cooled down as to the love of God, they were therefore called in Greek . . . souls; and were sent down to inhabit bodies, as a punishment; let him be anathema.'

Alas, bastard children always have a way of returning home just in time to ruin Christmas dinner and this one is no exception. In seventeenth-century England – just as Western powers set out in all seriousness to enslave the rest of the world to One Truth – the teachings of Origen returned as Origen*ism*, a doctrine particularly associated with Cambridge theologians. There, in 1647, a lively debate erupted, with one of the theologians so taken by Origen's teachings that he summarised the Church Father's theology in six tenets or 'dogmata', of which the second, third and fifth are relevant here. While the second tenet meekly states that the souls of human beings do pre-exist, tenet three goes on to declare that through their fault and negligence souls appear as inhabitants of earth, clothed with terrestrial bodies, while tenet five holds out the promise that after a long period of time the damned shall be delivered from their torments so that they can try their fortunes again in such regions of the world as their nature sees fit for their needs.

From the opposition bench of theologians it was argued that the notion of the pre-existence of the soul was not suitable for

Christians and, in fact, incompatible with Christianity, while those who found themselves somewhat caught in the headlights saw no obvious incompatibility between revealed truth and Origen's doctrine because the latter at least solved the problem of why there is evil in the world. According to them, if souls pre-existed their incarnation in human form and these souls committed the original sin of falling out of love with God, then sin was pre-human and reincarnation demonstrated God's mercy in giving fallen souls a chance at redeeming themselves. As far as the origin of sin was concerned, Origenism let both God and human beings off the hook because clearly neither had anything to do with it.

But the more bureaucratically minded theologians – let us call them the Delegation from the Third Floor – could not even get that far. For them, Origen's whole doctrine was an administrative and logistical nightmare. 'How on earth,' they declared, waving the doctrine in the air as if it were nothing but a form that had somehow managed to make its way through the system without being filled out in triplicate, 'how on earth could one be expected to believe that a soul who is destined to return to this world just so happened to be ready at the precise moment of coitus? And what about the problem of finding the perfect match between a body waiting for its soul and the appropriate soul to fill it with? Who is overseeing this logistical nightmare,' they demanded to know and why had they not been informed of this plan? If nobody from the Third Floor would be there to oversee the implementation of this plan – to simply assume that everything would be hunky-dory and the right soul would arrive at the right bed at precisely the right moment of ecstasy, to leave all of this to chance – they argued, implied a miracle of such magnitude that one may as well believe that everything was created out of nothing.

The revolt led by the Delegation from the Third Floor gained momentum and soon the logistics seem insurmountable: those who thought reincarnation more ridiculous than a virgin birth argued that if it were true that our souls kept returning to work through their karma, why then can we not recall anything of our previous lives? To this, those who found the idea of a virgin birth more ridiculous than reincarnation replied that to say reincarnation cannot be true because I cannot recall a past life is like arguing that I could not possibly have been four years old because I cannot recall being that age. On the contrary, they argued, we can, through regression and other techniques, recall being that age and, similarly, even remember previous lives. The impressions of past experience that lie dormant in our subliminal selves are never lost. What we call 'memory' is nothing more than the awakening and rising of latent impressions from the storehouse of imprints above the threshold of consciousness. There have been many yogis who could not only remember their own past lives, but also those of others, and do not forget (and with this they played a trump as irrefutable as any eyewitness account of the immaculate conception), it is said that Buddha himself remembered 500 of his previous births.

As for the other logistical matter, the issue of exactly *where* – in what context, what situation and to what parents – a soul returns, the doctrine, they insisted, is pretty clear: the soul chooses those conditions for its reincarnation that will be most propitious for realising its destiny and for enabling it to learn in this life what it needs to learn. Parents are nothing but the channels through which the migrating souls receive their material forms. Parents do not create souls because as mere human beings they do not have the power to create (in the divine sense of the word). They can only provide the suitable environment necessary for manufacturing a gross physical body into which the soul will arrive with its tendencies and desires in order to do the work of this life.

I can think of at least one example that proves the veracity of both these counter-arguments to the logistical complaints raised by the Delegation from the Third Floor (that souls can remember their past and that they choose for their reincarnation the parents who will be most propitious for the realisation of their destiny). Consider a character called Luc. He was first born – or so I thought – in a novel called *Imitation* (which I now realise was simply one of his earlier rebirths). There, in Part Six, he lived out his life according to the karma created for him and by him. I do not know what became of him in the world of *Imitation* because I had to leave him behind at the end of Part Six in order to pay attention to some of the other characters in Part Seven. What I do know is that he – or some impression of him – subsequently reincarnated into a second novel, titled *Subtle Gravity*. What I also cannot know (simply because there are so many different viewpoints on the matter) is whether it is Luc's soul in its entirety that reincarnated into *Subtle Gravity* or just some storehouse impression or an aspect of him. Is the Luc I have been following and spying on in the preceding pages Luc Again, or just an impression of the previous Luc?

Of his previous life in *Imitation* I recall that he battled with an addiction to silence and oblivion and, as far as I knew then, this battle was left unresolved. The fact that he is here again in *Subtle Gravity* can mean only one thing: he did not resolve his addiction and therefore some version of him has returned in order to work through his karma. So, the Luc of *Subtle Gravity*, who recollected important aspects of his life in *Imitation*, is perfect proof of the fact that we can indeed recall important aspects of our previous lives. But he is also proof of the second important point of the doctrine; namely, that the soul carefully chooses the circumstances of its reincarnation. Luc chose *Subtle Gravity* as the scene of his reincarnation (and not, say, a novel called *Elephants Are Also Animals* by a young Ethiopian writer), and me as the author or parent who will guide him through this life. This novel, and not *Elephants Are Also Animals*, was simply the most favourable circumstance in which he could be reborn to continue the work of purification. Considered together, it must be acknowledged that never before has there been such irrefutable proof of the doctrine of reincarnation!

There is a sacred synergy in all this. Luc and I both struggle with the seduction of divine unity and silence and I can only resist the temptation of eternal silence and make my peace with language by understanding how he might have returned from silence to existence. It is because of such synergies that souls choose the parents of their next life: parent and child have karma and they have to work it out together. So, yes, I am his author/parent but more than that, Luc and I have karma. For those who are still sceptical and unconvinced of the truth of these claims, all I can say is: *Be patient. The proof will be revealed before this story is out.* In the meanwhile, looking back over the preceding pages, I feel I have discharged my duties as a parent rather well. Have I not put him in touch again with somebody who can assist him in overcoming the addiction that so haunted him in *Imitation*? Is Doctor Cottard not sitting right there in front of Luc at this precise moment that I am working through our karma, hands folded across his somewhat protruding belly, assessing Luc's subtle body and comforting him with the reassuring statement, 'Every birth is an arrival. And every arrival is a return. The only question is this: are you ready to accept what that means?'

5

Doctor Cottard does not wait for an answer from Luc. Experience has taught him that he can expect any number of responses. Some clients respond with condescending dismissal ('I'm not into all that New Age nonsense'), others with incredulity ('Is that not just some Oriental thing?' or 'I may not be religious, and I certainly am not a Christian but the whole reincarnation thing seems a bit far-fetched to me'). Some display curiosity ('I've often wondered what to make of reincarnation. It's not that I think it impossible or untrue, I just don't know . . . yes, as I said, I just don't know what to make of it'). Only a small minority immediately get excited, either because they have been long-time believers in the reincarnation of the soul, or because they long ago tentatively accepted the idea but have not yet found someone who could help them integrate the belief into their lives and consequently see in Doctor Cottard just such a person.

Those whom Doctor Cottard had over the years come to think of as the curious and the believers initially always seemed a little tired, even defeated: 'Well, I can tell you one thing. *This* soul has been round the block a couple of times' or 'I feel so old, almost like I've never had a youth, as if I was born old' or, more emphatically, 'I feel cheated of an ordinary life – why did I have to know that this is not just my life? Because, if I didn't have to live with this burden of knowing that I am just passing through the world again, then I, too, could have lived my life as if it were my own. I could have been young and reckless and lived my youth as if I were immortal, keen and excited to see what will become of me and my life, what awaits me.' For Doctor Cottard, these were of course the most productive responses, although, given the way he worked with the subtle body, it did not actually matter whether or not a patient believed in the reincarnation of the soul.

Doctor Cottard had always been curious to know how, why, or at what point the curious and the believers had come to embrace belief in the reincarnation of the soul when they lived in a society that mostly dismissed the idea as foreign and strange. Some simply said that they had somehow always just known it to be true; others that they knew from a young age. Occasionally, they would confess to having had some experience (often a near-death experience) that had led them to believe that there is some part of them that has lived a previous life and that they are back again in order to work through some unresolved lesson or resolve some aspect of their 'journey' (they seldom used the word 'karma'). Some of them – most recently, a woman called Sheena – speak with great urgency about what it means to recognise the return of the self. 'I was born old,' Sheena had said, leaning forward in her chair, knees wide apart, her elbows on her knees (a posture that seemed quite manly in contrast with the floral print dress she was wearing) 'and my entire life has been an attempt to forget everything so that I could work out or remember: why this time? What is incomplete? What lesson or insight eluded me in my previous life? How do I recognise it in this life, so that I can get it right and learn what I need to learn?'

Doctor Cottard had learnt that he could only pose the question he just posed to Luc and then allow the patient to respond in whatever way they needed to. Nonetheless, to the 'non-believers' he had to offer a rudimentary explanation of the difference between the gross and the subtle body, so that they would understand why he was not going to try and convince them of anything or explain to them the physical dangers and consequences of their addictions. Nor was he interested in guilt or shame. Since he would not be engaging with the gross body, but directing his attention at the client's subtle body, it did not really matter what they thought of what he said. Those who were receptive to his approach would find their subtle body receptive in ways they would only understand much later.

The subtle body always knows more than we do. It knows where we come from and where we are going or where we need to go. It knows what we need, not what we think we want. It also knows that we always get what we need and when we seem at a loss for direction, meaning or purpose, it is often simply because we are imposing on our life a story about who we are and where we are going that is at odds with where the subtle body knows we are going. When we experience life as meaningless or without purpose, it is symptomatic of our personal will or intention being out of sync with what the subtle body knows we need. To put it differently: the experience of life as meaningless and lacking in purpose is a consequence of the fact that the story we have been telling ourselves about our lives has run out of steam before we have acquired the wisdom to listen to the journey that the subtle body always knew we were on. The 'tiredness' of the 'old soul' who feels cheated of their youth, and exhausted by the recognition that the meaning of their soul's existence derives from a story much larger than life, is an example of what is means to be out of sync with the subtle body.

The second thing Doctor Cottard knew to expect from this first encounter with his clients is that, regardless of whether he was dealing with a believer or a non-believer, they would instantly jump to the vexed question of 'Did my soul choose the situation it reincarnated into?' The idea that our soul chooses its parents is not an easy one to accept. It goes against the grain of everything many of us have been taught to believe. But that probably explains why it is almost invariably one of the first questions Doctor Cottard's clients ask (even those who just hypothetically play along). It is as if they sense in that very possibility a glimmer of hope; things could not have been different from the way they turned out because their ancient soul had chosen the starting point. It is as if in the mere possibility of having chosen the circumstances of the soul's arrival they already intuit what they will only later understand with clarity; namely, if you chose the circumstances of your arrival, it is impossible for life to be meaningless; to find life 'meaningless' means that your actions have lost sight of the intention that marked your arrival. For Doctor Cottard, it does not matter what his clients believe. They do not need to share his commitment to the healing powers of the subtle body. As far as he is concerned, if a person's karma brought them to his facility, then he, Doctor Cottard, is just one more variable in the endless chain of causes and effects propelling the individual through life. They would not be here if he were not part of their journey.

Knowing that Luc was not going to ask any questions, Doctor Cottard simply proceeds as if Luc did ask a question. He walks across the floor to the desk and sits down across from Luc. In what is perhaps a stereotypical gesture, he moves close enough to the desk that he can place his elbows on its smooth, dark, wood surface and with the fingers of his two hands spread, corresponding fingertips pressed against each other, says: 'Every soul that arrives in the world wants to belong. That is our primary instinct, Luc. Let's call it the inherent goodness of the soul; the soul accepts itself as good in itself and sets out to find people who will recognise that goodness. The soul knows it can only exist in relation to others and in the world. If we arrive in a world in which we are loved and accepted and our thirst for fulfilment is mirrored by those responsible for our safety in the world – they listen to us, care for us and mirror our basic goodness back to us – we have an early sense of belonging and of feeling safe in the world. We will accept that the world we live in is a generous place.'

The sounds of the world fade into the background. 'In a world where we know we belong, and in which we sense the generosity of the universe, we will also believe we have a right to exist, a right to occupy the world, to take up space and that we have a right to everything we need in order to support our existence – food, safety, security and so on. Belonging, kindness, generosity and a sense of belonging – these are powerful forces, Luc. It is not difficult to identify someone who arrived in the world like that, their quiet self-assurance; their subtle, unassuming confidence; how they don't judge, not themselves nor others, because what does being right or wrong have to do with one's essential goodness?' Here, Doctor Cottard pauses for a couple of seconds, allowing Luc time to absorb everything he has just said.

'But,' he continues, 'they are the lucky ones. The world, our civilisation' – he makes a sweeping gesture that includes the rehabilitation centre and the whole world beyond it – 'our world has forgotten this simple truth, with the result that, at some level, most people who walk around out there do not trust – they may know and assert it very loudly – but they don't really trust that they have a right to exist. Such trust, in the deepest sense of the word, is the prerogative of those for whom the universe is a generous place. One could even say that it's a matter of inverse proportionality: the louder the person who claims everything in the world for himself, his family or his society, the deeper that person's mistrust of the fact that he actually has a right to exist. Such a person cannot simply accept their existence as a fact because that would mean recognising that he belongs in the world, along with everyone else who has the same claim to what they need in order to exist. But we've drifted . . .'

Doctor Cottard reaches across the desk and pours himself a glass of water from a jug. Then he pushes the jug and another glass in Luc's direction, making it clear that the young man should feel free to help himself. Doctor Cottard takes a deep drink of water, places the glass back on a silver-plated coaster next to his desk calendar and, once more adjusting the black and emerald green bow tie, continues. 'Let's just say that souls who arrive in the world and find their basic goodness mirrored back to them are the lucky ones. Most of us have to live our lives backwards; we have to reverse engineer our goodness back to the moment of arrival in order to recognise and make peace with the fact that our basic goodness was not mirrored back to us when we needed it to be. Our original intuition that we have a right to exist was not affirmed and, as a consequence, we have been living with a terrible sense of anxiety, of not being in control of our lives, of being fake people who will one day get caught out for pretending to be something we're not. The only solution is to go back, as it were, to the moment of arrival and imagine it differently. Not that re-imagining our arrival is a quick fix. Don't get me wrong. This is not psychotherapy or hypnotherapy. There is no dreaming ourselves back to the origin in order to fix things. It's not as if I will somehow dream you back to the origin and when you wake up your goodness will be restored. It doesn't work that way. Instead, for me it is rather a case of enabling you to recognise your arrival for what it was meant to have been and allowing that recognition to play itself out in the awakening of your subtle body. Does any of that make sense, Luc – what we're going to try to do here – to restage your arrival?'

Every sound that arrives in the world already belongs to the world. Doctor Cottard's words are so many sounds that arrive as if for the first time. They should be new and make a difference, but they do not. It is hard for Luc to distinguish them from the other sounds that have been drifting through his head for the longest time – as if his head were nothing more than a node where sounds converge, link, de-link, form temporary relations, connect – only to disconnect again – and keep passing through the world beyond him. He senses in his heart a longing to hang on to the sounds of Doctor Cottard's words, to soak them up, eat them, retain them and digest them; to allow them to acquire the weight of meaning that will allow them to sink into his soul and change him. But they do not. They, too, drift aimlessly through his mind just like all the other sounds – soft voices from elsewhere in the building; birds in the trees; in the far-off distance, a jet plane soaring overhead and, for the last ten minutes or so, far down the corridor, a new sound that has joined the ensemble – the sound of a vacuum cleaner, the soft, pulsating rhythm of the machine being pushed and pulled, pushed and pulled across the thick carpeted corridors.

How long is this reverie going to sustain him? Doctor Cottard wonders to himself, while he watches Luc sitting there, lost in a trance, beyond anyone's reach, lost in a silence so captivating, so absolute that it is almost unimaginable that he will ever find his way back. *What is it going to take?* Doctor Cottard thinks. Then he stands up. 'We're done for today, Luc,' he says and as he walks around the table to make his way to the door, his body half turning to make sure Luc is also getting up and following him, he adds, 'If any of this makes sense, Luc, just ask yourself, what keeps you from wanting to belong? Whose permission are you waiting for? Nobody can give you permission to live.'

6

Luc feels slightly dizzy when he closes the door to Doctor Cottard's office. He is at a loss and briefly contemplates returning to his room until he is called for whatever activity they have lined up for him next – or who knows, maybe he will be lucky and they will leave him alone until lunchtime. But the thought of being alone in his room does not appeal to him. Neither does he want to be with other people. After aimlessly walking through some of the corridors, now turning right, now turning left, he finds himself back in the reception area. He walks out the front door into the late morning sun. How long has it been since he arrived and turned around on exactly this spot to wave his parents farewell – two days? Three? He cannot recall. His memory of the immediate past seems to have fallen prey to the dizziness he experienced after leaving Doctor Cottard's office. Everything seems vague and timeless. He walks out onto the top of the elaborate staircase, with its decorative balustrade, where some of the other patients are sitting or standing around in small groups – some smoking, others hanging over the balustrade, staring into the distance. Luc does not smoke and neither does he feel like company. And so, he walks halfway down the stairs, where he sits down, hoping that the way in which he avoids making eye contact with anyone makes it clear that he is not interested in making conversation. He stretches out on the steps and closes his eyes, allowing his face to soak up the warm late morning sun.

He must have dozed off because at some point he wakes up with a start, pushes himself up on his hands and looks up in the direction of the front door. Everyone else has gone inside. He tries to recall from the schedule Ajna had given him on the first day whether she had scheduled anything for him on the day after his first session with the Emperor (even she calls him that), but nothing comes to mind. He still feels slightly dizzy. How long was he gone for?

Only then does he notice a thin girl whom he has not seen before. She is strikingly beautiful, but thin; so beautiful and so thin that he is sure he would have remembered her if she had been at breakfast that morning. She is sitting at the top of the stairs, just to the left of the front door, with her knees pulled up, smoking a cigarette. She is looking at him intently. When she sees him looking at her, she blushes slightly, looks away, and takes another drag of her cigarette. Then, avoiding his gaze, she flicks the cigarette butt over the balustrade, gets up and walks back inside. Luc lies down again. So what if he has forgotten whatever he was meant to do after his session with Doctor Cottard? What is the worst that could happen? The sudden realisation that he is in a place where he is supposed to be looked after and that it may well be expected of him to make the odd mistake relaxes him. His gaze drifts upwards to the window on the top floor where he discerns two faces through a window looking down at him. He thinks he recognises Doctor Cottard, but cannot be sure, and the other face is obscured by the thin white lace curtain. Then the hand holding it drops the curtain and both faces recede back into the room.

Luc Falls through His Own Arsehole

7

After a week or so, Luc had got used to the strange rhythm of the centre: breakfast; one or two group sessions, where he usually just sat and allowed the sound of the other patients' life stories and struggles to wash over him or through him; artistic activities, such as drumming (which he enjoyed) and painting (which he found boring). The previous night, he had struggled to fall asleep and tossed and turned, first onto his right side, then onto his left side, worrying the whole time about what others were thinking of him – if Doctor Cottard had meant it when he said that he did not expect Luc to speak, worried that at some point everyone would lose patience with him and just shake him by the shoulders until he was forced to let go of the one thing that made sense in his life: this sense of quiet belonging in a world that only he understood. Eventually, he felt his breath slowing down and the tiredness take over, along with the realisation that it was pointless to worry about things he could not control. What did it matter what others thought of him and what did it matter if Doctor Cottard's patience sooner or later ran out? What did other people's disappointment have to do with him? With that reassuring thought washing over him, Luc eventually fell into a deep sleep.

But his sleep was as restless as the troubled wakefulness that had preceded it. He had a dream. In the dream, he found himself on a chair in the middle of his room at the treatment centre, except that the room had been stripped of all the furniture, including the basin. The curtains were drawn and the room well lit, even though there was no lamp anywhere and no light above his head. *It is as if the room is lit from inside,* he thought while he looked around him. He tried to get up from the chair, but could not. He looked down at his legs and arms, but he was not tied to the chair. He tried again to stand up and felt only an immense powerlessness, an incapacity to make his body do what he commanded it to do. He leaned over and looked under the chair for what might be holding him down again his will. And that was when he saw them: a tangle of roots, some charcoal grey, others a luminous green, sprouting forth from an invisible place in his body through the chair and into the ground beneath him. He grabbed the chair on either side and tried to lift it up with him, but the chair would not move either. After repeated failed attempts to stand up, he eventually gave up. *This is not my fault,* he thought. *Not my fault.*

In the morning, when he opens his eyes, he is sitting on the edge of his bed. Confused, he looks around. All the furniture is back where it is supposed to be, albeit it still, to his mind, in the wrong place. The morning sun is streaming through the curtains, which he must have forgotten to close the previous night. He looks down at his crotch. A half erection is straining against his boxer shorts. Nothing strange about that. Then he lifts his arms and legs and stands up. Nothing unusual there either. For a couple of seconds he is almost pushed down again onto the bed by the sheer weight of the strange dream, but he bends over, puts on his slippers and walks across the vibrant red carpet to the bathroom where he relieves himself before turning on the shower. After a long shower, he walks back into the room, the towel, which matches the red of the carpet, wrapped around his waist. As he crosses the room on his way to the cupboard, he catches sight of his own reflection in the full-length mirror.

Every soul that arrives in the world wants to belong. That is our primary instinct, Luc. Let's call it the inherent goodness of the soul.

He turns and faces the mirror, drops the towel and looks at his own reflection. He looks at his toes and wiggles them slightly. He has never had a problem with his toes. They seem fine. His feet are perhaps a bit too long and narrow, but that is preferable to feet that are wide and flat. His gaze glides over his ankles to his calves. Now, they could do with some work. He never wears shorts because he is self-conscious about how thin his calves are. They create the impression that he has thin legs. What makes them look even thinner is the fact that his thighs somehow seem right. He looks at his scrotum and penis. His scrotum is hanging helplessly at the mercy of gravity. Compared to the size of the scrotum, his penis seems disproportionately small. But that is because of the last minute of cold water he ended his shower with. He always does that because he finds it invigorating, but a cold shower comes at a cost and, right now, he is looking at that cost. His only comfort is that his penis gets surprisingly large when it is erect. The first time he slept with a girl, she could not hide her surprise at how big his erection got compared to how small it was when she unexpectedly unzipped his pants and slipped her hand into his underpants. His eyes moved up to his navel. *Navel gazing.* A phrase like any other sound that suddenly crosses his mind like the sound of Doctor Cottard's voice, his reassuring, matter-of-fact statements floating across Luc's mind like images cast on the wall by a Japanese spinning lamp.

In a world where we know we belong, and in which we sense the generosity of the universe, we will also believe that we have a right to exist, a right to occupy the world, to take up space and that we have a right to everything we need in order to support our existence . . . These are powerful forces, Luc.

His eyes linger for a moment on the thin line of pubic hair that fades away just under his navel. He does not have any more hair than that, for which he is grateful. He has often heard other boys talk about how they shave their chests to look like the clean-shaven men in movies, but he will never have to do that. He may grow more hair as he gets older and that would be okay. Just as long as it is not too much. Too much hair and a man looks like an ape. Not to mention hair on a man's back. His eyes gently meander up to his chest and come to rest on his pecs. Sometimes he wishes he had more pronounced pecs. It would make him look less like a boy and more like a man.

He looks at his eyes with his eyes and, once again, it strikes him that the one eye is slightly higher than the other. Just slightly. Once or twice, he had asked his mother if this was true and why it was so. But she would not concede. She said he had perfect eyes and there was nothing wrong with him. Of course, that is what she would say.

Most of us have to live our lives backwards; we have to reverse engineer our goodness back to the moment of arrival in order to recognise and make peace with the fact that our basic goodness was not mirrored back to us when we needed it to be.

He looks at his forehead and his hair. Not bad. Not wildly attractive, but also not ugly. He turns around and looks back at himself over his shoulder. Thank God he does not have hair on his back – the whole ape thing really upsets him. He kicks the red towel aside and turns his back to the mirror. Then he spreads his legs as far apart as he can and drops his torso down between his legs. The roots from his dream – that is where they sprouted from, but he realises, with some relief, there is no trace of them now. Other images of thoughts float across the wall of his mind as he hangs there, head down between his legs. *Is this defying gravity or just allowing it to have its way with me?* If one willingly jumps off the roof of a building, fully intending to die, can one still be said to be 'falling', or even that one is at the mercy of gravity, that we cannot 'beat' gravity? At what point does working with the forces of gravity in order to achieve a certain end amount to overcoming gravity? Like now, this moment, when he has dropped his torso down between his legs to look at himself upside down in the mirror.

What a strange sight. One face and one arsehole. An arsehole with a face. Or is it the face of an arsehole?

A strange image floats across the wall of his imagination – one he had never imagined before. In a world in which he was really supple, fantastically supple, he could go all the way around and stick his head up his own arse and just keep crawling, elbowing and crawling deeper and deeper into himself, just crawl right through his own arse. At some point his legs would have to follow and what would happen then? Would he eventually turn inside out, invert completely? And what would that look like? A small ball of inverted arse, rolling round on the floor?

You're going to have to go all the way, you're going to have to go right through this, all the way to the other side.

Is this what his father meant? That he was going to have to crawl all the way up his own arse, all the way, crawl right through to the other side. Pop inside out. Is that what was required to become a new person, to invert himself, turn himself inside out? Is that what it will take to survive this moment, this place? And what about the roots in his dream? If he could crawl all the way through himself, would he at some point encounter the roots – and what would that mean?

Luc straightens up, slightly dazed by the strange image of his inverted self. He picks up the towel and walks over to the wardrobe and looks at his pile of jeans and T-shirts. *What to wear?*

There is still an hour before breakfast. He will have to think of something to do. He puts on a pair of jeans and a T-shirt. He lifts his right arm and sniffs at the sleeve of his T-shirt. He cannot smell himself because his mother made sure that all his clothes were washed and clean.

A little bit of love.

The smell of bacon and eggs drifts up from the floor below, mingled with the dim sound of chatter from the other patients on the outside staircase and the birds chirping from the other side of the garden.

Harvesters I

8

The second time I see Luc is just as unexpected and unsettling as the first. It had been an exhausting day at work, meeting after meeting after meeting and in between a seemingly endless queue of students who needed things from me – information about course admissions, minimum requirements, prerequisites for this or that course. Maretha had dealt with most of them because, in between the meetings and dealing with the various students' requests, I also had to teach a class. Teaching usually inspires me and wakes me up from my administrative slumber. On a good day, it reminds me why I entered the world of academia in the first place – something one easily forgets in an age when the university has basically become just another corporation, with performance measure plans and wellness programmes for the sick and faint-hearted. I, in turn, measure the wellness of the university by counting the number of emails I get inviting me to workshops on how to handle anger in the workplace, how to resist feelings of helplessness, how to foster healthy (that is, productive) human relations in the workplace and so on. I am never certain about the diagnostic values of these emails: if I get five of them on any given day, does that mean the institution is really in a bad way, that some urgent interventions in our lives are necessary to get it to work well again? Or do the emails simply mean the university is really *well* because, at some level, it is being run as a wellness centre for the fortunate few who get paid to think?

I wish I still had left in me sufficient optimism about the future of the university to say that all of this makes me sick. But it does not. It just leaves me empty, devoid of any feeling. The university is just a place where I spend a significant part of every day in the company of people whose interactions in the passages and tearoom are shadowed by memories of the days when we felt like the guardians of traditions of knowledge, when the university felt more like a church than, well, even a church did; a church of non-believers, who found their love of belonging to a community of believers mirrored by the quests of their colleagues and by students. If the church was always the home of knowing, the university was the church of unknowing, of the unknown. But those days are long gone. It is as if the university's bottom has fallen out, so that it is no longer essentially different from, say, a filling station or a late-night convenience store or a pet shop. This petrification has taken all the desire to write out of me. I no longer feel like I have anything to say. Besides, what is the point of saying something (presuming that in this age of information clutter somebody will even notice that you've said something) if it is just going to be converted into metadata that will be used to statistically validate claims about the reputation of the university? Universities have become Ponzi schemes: they exist in order to become famous for existing.

On this particular day, it is late afternoon by the time I finish doing everything that cannot wait until tomorrow. All my colleagues have already left, their offices locked, the passage deserted, the students gone for the day. Even the lifts are empty and I go all the way down to the ground floor by myself. In the entrance hall, I wave at the security guard and notice a group of three students hanging around near the door, one leaning against the wall, all three of them chatting distractedly while they scroll up and down on their phones. It has been a couple of weeks since the day I pushed my way through the throng of students in order to get to the front door because I was certain I had seen Luc standing below my window, looking up at my office. I sometimes still think of that day, but the memory is fading – not into forgetting, but rather because it is slowly being encroached upon and engulfed by doubt, alternative explanations and, fuelling both, a melancholy sense of incredulity. When I get to my bicycle, I remorsefully recall the days when I used to smoke and how, on a day such as this when I felt tired and grumpy, I would smoke a cigarette while I pushed my bicycle to the main gate. Smoking always seemed to take the edge off. But then a time came when I realised that instead of alleviating my stress and anxiety, smoking made it worse.

When I reach the shopping mall where I want to get things for supper and perhaps a couple of beers, I decide on the spur of the moment to treat myself and order take-aways when I get home. Uber Eats has become the new god of the harvest. I lock my bicycle against the stand in front of the curio shop and walk over to Harvesters, thinking that I will order supper while I drink a beer and track the delivery on my phone, so that I arrive at my apartment at the same time.

On the way to Harvesters, I pass Dreyer, the only white parking marshall who works in this parking lot. Because this is quite an upmarket shopping centre, Dreyer and his colleagues are not referred to as mere 'car guards', but wear formal-looking, security-guard-style uniforms with the words 'Parking Marshall' printed on the back. They spend their days guiding motorists in and out of parking bays. How on earth did we ever manage to park our cars before there were parking marshalls? My usual irritation with the poverty of a system that can produce such a thing as a 'car guard' is no defence against Dreyer because he has only one proper arm. The other one is no more than a stump, with strange, contorted, little fingers. After months of watching him and having the odd, casual conversation, I have become familiar with his particular marshalling technique: he uses his long arm to attract the attention of drivers as they drive into the parking lot and to point in the direction of the nearest available parking bay, but when they leave and have to reverse out of the parking bay again, he uses the little arm, with which he makes frantic circles to signal whether they must keep reversing or stop and wait for a car to pass. *Quite clever,* I thought. He does not even need the little arm to make the cars stop reversing. He can just stand there. Nobody is going to run over a (white) properly dressed parking marshall with one little arm.

On this occasion, I can see he is warming up for a bit of small talk as I approach, but I do not feel like it. But there is no way of avoiding him, without seeming rude, so I resign myself to a couple of minutes of small talk with him. As I get closer, I suddenly recall that I actually do have a genuine question I have been meaning to ask him for quite some time that I keep forgetting about. The long islands that separate the rows of parking bays are lined with the most eerily beautiful trees I have ever seen. Talk, stark and thorny. They have long, spindly branches, with smaller branches studded with thorns, instead of leaves, sticking out in all directions. But the most striking feature about them is their colour. The whole tree – trunk, branches and all – is luminous green, an eerie, slightly unreal green that lends the entire parking lot the look and feel of a surrealist painting. On days when I am particularly aware of them, I often walk around them, almost as if to avoid some kind of spell that they will cast on me if I get too close, unable to shake the feeling that something is not real. They make the entire parking lot and complex feel as if something were out of place.

'Hey, Dreyer! How're you doing?' I ask, as he limps up to me (there is also something wrong with one of his legs, but I've never been able to work out what).

'Who knows?' he says in his usual friendly way, the stump making little circles in the air.

'Tell me, Dreyer,' I continue, 'what are these trees called?'

'They're fever trees,' he says.

'It is the strangest green,' I say and walk past him right up to the nearest one.

He comes up behind me and says, 'I know. Weird, hey? And the really weird thing about them is the green stuff. When you rub the trunk with your hand, it comes off. Look . . .' he says, stepping closer to the tree. He rubs one of the luminous green trunks with the hand of his normal arm. He turns around to show me his hand, which is covered with a thin film of green powder. 'But not to worry. You just rub your hands like so . . .' and he rubs his hand on his uniform, 'and then it comes off again.'

'Ha!' I say and imitate him, first rubbing the trunk and then wiping the green powder off on my pants. 'It's a very strange business,' I say, but as I turn around, he has already walked off. A woman in a big SUV has just put her car in reverse. The red lights are on and Dreyer has positioned himself carefully between her and the incoming cars, his little arm frantically waving to indicate that she should wait until a car had passed. Then he waves her out, collecting the coins she holds out to him in a long, bejewelled hand that lazily droops out the window. *We all find a way to make it work,* I think to myself, as I head for Harvesters.

I slide into one of the booths on the veranda and stretch out in the fading sun, allowing the rush hour traffic in the background to wash over me. The owner's cat comes up to me, no doubt sensing that I am extremely allergic to cats, and tries to jump on my lap. I brush it off. Then a friendly waitress appears and offers to bring a menu while she wipes down the table, but I tell her I am just there for a glass of their homebrewed beer. A couple of minutes later, she reappears, puts a coaster down in front of me and with a cheerful 'Enjoy!' turns around and disappears inside again. From where I am sitting, I can see most of the L-shaped shopping centre. In the right-hand corner in front of me is the grocery store and then, one next to the other, all the way to the end, where the entrance to the parking lot is, the barber, curio shop and coffee shop. The coffee shop is at the end of the row, from where the row of shops continues at a ninety-degree angle in the other direction, so that I cannot see any of them. I have worked out that the area extending from the barber to the coffee shop is Dreyer's territory. I watch him go about his business, welcoming cars, ushering them into parking bays and carefully signalling them out again. I used to wonder how he does not go mad with boredom until one day he told me about the blind woman who also works the parking lot. She sells imitation pashmina scarfs, a whole stack of which she carries draped over her shoulders and arms. She lives in Soshanguve, which she once explained to me, is 'three taxis away from here'. It takes her almost two hours to get here and two hours back home again, every day, and she has been earning her living in this way for thirteen years. After Dreyer told me her story, I felt guilty about the fact that I did not know how they coped with the monotony of it all. Suddenly, *not* being bored seemed like a luxury.

    I order my supper and check the time of delivery. There is ample time to finish my beer, perhaps even have a second one. I watch a tourist bus park on the pavement just outside the main entrance. A stream of tourists half stumble off the bus, stretch their legs and walk over to the coffee shop. From having watched so many of these buses stop at the centre, I know that they would usually head straight for the curio shop, but today they are too late. They will have to make do with pancakes and coffee. Maybe it's Aunt Pashmina's lucky day. If they have not managed to satisfy their desire for Afro-kitsch at the row of hawkers' tables at the Union Buildings, they may well buy some of her scarves. 'Look at this nice pashmina scarf I bought near the Mandela statue!' I can feel the alcohol feeding my grumpiness and realise that I should probably just call it quits and go home. I look at my phone: the food is thirteen minutes away. If I leave now and push my bicycle the last two blocks up the road, I will get there more or less at the same time. I leave money for the beer, reach over to take my rucksack from where I had placed it on the bench opposite me, and that is when I see him. Luc is standing with his back half turned to me, half facing the window of the curio shop. If he were not standing at an angle, I would not have given him a second look because he looks just like any other young tourist that has wandered away from the main group to look at what is on display next door. But, at this angle, I can just see enough of his profile to recognise him. I put my glass down slowly, as if any quick movement would alert him to my presence and make him disappear again. I sit down and lift my sunglasses so that I can see more clearly.

It *is* him, no doubt about it. But how? He appears to be looking at the craft on display in the shop window, but even from where I am sitting, I can tell that he is not interested in any of it. Then he starts to stroll up and down in front of the window, as if lost in thought, and the thing that strikes me most is his strange gait; it is heavy, as if he somehow finds it difficult to walk.

What the fuck? I think to myself, paralysed with indecision. Instinctively, I know that if I make any quick movement or try to approach him to get a closer look, the same thing that happened the first time is likely to happen again. He will somehow disappear before I get to him. With my heart pounding, I watch him as he slowly walks up and down outside the curio shop, hands in his pockets, glancing now at the crafts on display, then around him, as if to see who may be watching him. I decide to take the risk. Without taking my eyes off him, I pull my rucksack closer, shove my cell phone in my pocket and slowly step out of the booth. As I straighten up and slide my bag onto my back, so that I can walk faster, I glance in the direction of the coffee shop. All the tourists are huddled deep in conversation around their little tables. I look through the glass door of Harvesters to see if anyone is about to leave, but I see only the waitress. She catches my eye and signals that she will bring the bill. I point to the money on the table and look back to where Luc's outline has started to fade into the early evening shadows in the passage that I know from experience will soon be flooded by lights that automatically come on after dark. I start to walk in his direction, not taking my eyes off him for a second. And that is when it happens. As I step down off the patio onto the tar surface of the parking lot, Luc sticks his face right into the window of the curio shop – no, not *into*, but *through*. As if the shop window were nothing but a translucent pane of water, he sticks his face through the window and I watch as, in a matter of seconds, the rest of his body follows – first his right arm, then his head, followed by his torso, both legs and, finally, his left hand. I stop abruptly as if I have walked into a solid wall. For an eternity I just stand there and stare at the window of the curio shop. At some point the sound of chatting tourists starts to drift into my head again. In my pocket I hear the faint sound of an alarm bell announcing that the delivery man will arrive at my apartment in seven minutes. I reach into my pocket and switch the alarm off. Then I walk over to where I had seen Luc standing. I hesitate for a couple of seconds, but then put my hand out and carefully press my right palm against the window. The glass is cold and hard to the touch. An ordinary window. I pull my hand back and turn away.

As I turn around, I notice the old woman who sells scarves. She is looking in the direction of the tourists, but who knows – perhaps she saw something? I walk over to her.

'Excuse me, Mama,' I say.

She turns around and looks in my direction. 'Yes, *buti*? I have nice scarves. Lovely for the winter coming. Look . . .' and she starts to slide the pile of scarves off her shoulder.

'No, thank you, Mama. I don't need a scarf. I bought two last week, remember?'

I had bought two scarves from her the previous week and put them in my cupboard to take home to my wife and daughter the next time I went home. From what I could tell, they were of good quality. Today, I am slightly annoyed by her response. She always greets me with the exact same enthusiasm and sales pitch. Does she not recognise me and can she not remember that I bought two scarves from her just a couple of days ago?

'I'm looking for my friend, Mama. He was standing just there by the window two minutes ago. Did you see him?'

'No, *buti*,' she says, clearly disappointed. And then more emphatically, 'I stand here all the time. *Eish*, nobody standing there. I know all these people,' she says, sweeping her arm over the parking lot, including the tour bus with its passengers.

'Are you sure?'

'Yes, *buti*. You don't want a scarf? Look, nice one. Nice . . .' she says and again starts untangling one from the pile of scarves draped over her arm.

'Thanks, Mama. Next time,' I say and walk over to my bicycle. I push it past the coffee shop, where the tourists are eating, drinking and chatting, as if it were just an ordinary day. As I leave them behind and turn up the road to my apartment, I realise that my world will never be the same again.

9

After two weeks, Luc and Thin Smoking Girl (that's how he had come to think of her before he heard her referred to as Angèle) had forged a strange sort of companionship, perhaps even a friendship. Luc had still not said a word since his arrival at the centre, but that did not seem to bother Angèle, who was happy to do all the talking. They began avoiding mingling with other patients and started spending all their time together, either on a bench at the far end of the garden or in the rose garden, which was connected to the main building through a simple wooden walkway with a rustic yet elegant roof made of interwoven vines. Luc and Angèle never made formal arrangements to meet, but over time they came to trust that whenever they were both free, they would find the other in one of their two favourite places. In the beginning, Angèle often talked about her school days. She had gone to a girls-only private school and she had much to say about the kind of violence only girls at that age seem to be capable of. Boys beat each other up, she would say, but girls find ways to systematically destroy your soul. And then there was the obscene wealth. Angèle did not come from a wealthy family and her parents had to use all their savings to send her to a school with an excellent academic reputation. Most of the other children came from well-established wealthy families and Angèle soon realised that with wealth and status came a pecking order that was as immutable as if it were created by God himself. This pecking order was displayed and affirmed after every vacation when the girls returned to school and compared notes, photographs and mementos – a venerable carnival of riches that, for those less privileged such as Angèle, amounted to little more than a carnage of every delicate relationship, alliance of trust and tentative loyalties they had managed to forge in the months leading up to the school vacation. Eventually, Angèle withdrew into herself. First, she stopped talking to the other girls. Then she stopped eating. She faded away, at first, into her private world and then, eventually, very nearly from the world.

'I get it now,' she said one day as she and Luc were sitting on a bench just inside the walkway connecting the rose garden with the main building, a soft drizzle sifting down on the world around them. She had just lit a cigarette and was sitting with her knees drawn up to her chest, taking the first deep drag. 'It was all out of control; the whole world was out of control. I couldn't control my life sufficiently to fit in and I couldn't control what others thought of me. Everything felt out of control. There was nothing left for me to do but to control the one thing that only I could control, so I stopped eating.' She paused and took another drag of her cigarette. She sighed as she exhaled, carefully placing the half-smoked cigarette under her shoe and twisting it into the ground. Then she picked up the butt and put it in her pocket. She leaned back and said, 'Funny how knowing all that doesn't make it any easier to eat. I just can't stand the idea of putting food in my mouth. Why would I? I think I've forgotten how to be hungry.'

Luc listened, nodding every now and then. He allowed the words and images invoked by Angèle's description of school, the violence of friendships and what in her case appeared to be a friendship with violence, to flow through his mind, where they mixed with images from his own life that presented a similar combination of suffering and abundance. In these images he clearly saw his school friend Stan, the son of a diplomat in Paris, and the memories conjured up by Stan's stories of privilege and loneliness set against the backdrop of the exotic places he grew up in: Budapest, Moscow, São Paulo.

It did not take long for Luc to start developing feelings for Angèle that went beyond friendship. And, as his attraction to Angèle increased, so did the flutter of butterflies in his stomach every time he thought of her or saw her sitting on the bench waiting for him. But love and desire evoked painful memories in him, memories that, in part, accounted for his presence in the rehabilitation centre. Mixed with his feelings for Angèle was a sense of terror, of being terrified of getting that close to anyone again. And yet, Angèle stirred something in him, a longing to escape this overwhelming sense of unity with life, a desire to be just himself and not the whole world, so that he could perhaps love her and be one with the world in a different way. If anything, the desire for Angèle stirred in him a longing for things to be different. The evening of the day Luc realised for the first time that he had started to feel something more for Angèle, he was lying on his bed with his eyes wide open, staring at the ceiling, his heart racing with anxiety. The reason for his anxiety had everything to do with the painful journey through which he discovered why having a penis is very different from having an ear or a nose.

Luc's Scrotum

10

Unlike having an ear, the meaning of having a penis is never given to a man. If only more women knew how long it takes a man to work out the meaning of his penis, the scrotum – the whole apparatus – and that no man is born with an understanding of why he has a penis or what having one is supposed to mean. Knowing and trusting that the penis allows him to negotiate his place in the world with the same ease with which he uses his hand to open doors or his eyes to look through windows, *that* knowledge only comes at the end of a long, hard struggle. Some men – and a great many women – have always known and understood this. From the lowliest dishwasher in the dingy Chinese restaurant I pass on my way home to the Queen of England herself, many, many men and women have always understood that the power of patriarchy is founded upon the void, a big I-don't-know-what-penis-means. Yes, patriarchy was erected on this uncertainty. In fact, patriarchy is a monument to men's ignorance; it is the system men invented to buy themselves a little time while they try to figure out what having a penis means. And there are basically two kinds of women: on the one hand, those who think that patriarchy exists because men know what it means to have a penis and, on the other hand, those who know that patriarchy exists precisely because men do not know what it means.

Let us agree that in addition to configuring the body in terms of body *parts*, we can also configure it in terms of *zones*, notably those zones that are erogenous and those that are not. Just which zones we deem to be erogenous is subject to the logic of the exception, to the little quirks of individual desire, memories of childhood and our morbid fascination with death (including the death of desire), but generally we can say that the erogenous zones – the feet, the ears, the sexual organs, nipples and so on – have a kind of meaning that the non-erogenous zones, such as the knee, the calf, the elbow and the nostrils, do not have. Of course, this does not apply to very young children for whom it is all much of a muchness when it comes to which part of the body gives them pleasure. It seems that self-consciousness comes at a cost: the more heightened our self-awareness, the more body parts we lose to the erotic until, that is, self-awareness comes full circle and we become eroticised children again. But until that day, we have what we may call a special relationship with the erogenous zones, precisely because, being what they are, we consider them windows to the world. As such, they demand to be made sense of in a way that non-erogenous zones such as the nostril or the elbow generally do not. Erogenous zones are special because it is through them that the soul not only experiences, but also communicates with the world. It is through our senses that we experience the pleasure of belonging in the world and it is because of their power to communicate our souls to the world that erogenous zones are imbued with the kind of mythical power they have: they fascinate us because through them our fascination with the world finds its deepest and most fleeting expression in the pleasure of belonging.

But this is not a grand history of the human house and its erotic windows. These are really just a couple of casual remarks on the way to explaining why Luc would be lying there on his bed in his orange boxer shorts. He had returned to his room after walking Angèle to hers and, after taking a shower (abstaining this time from finishing with a cold shower), he put on his shorts and lay down on his bed. Even though he is thinking of Angèle and feeling the stirring of sexual arousal, he is not touching himself. He is simply lying there, like so many young men at his age, observing with a look of bemusement the power of his throbbing erection to make his pants move up and down.

Through a peculiar series of circumstances, Luc had come to understand something about the meaning of his penis that most men spend many years figuring out, something we can perhaps call the grand-narrative-of-becoming-penis. In this grand narrative, the penis starts out as a *thing* that becomes a *myth* before it becomes just a *thing* again. It sounds simple and in a sense it is. But the important thing about the journey from thing to myth and back to thing again is that it also represents a man's journey through the world. At a very young age, the penis is a thing of some special importance to the boy – it is just a thing, but he already senses it is somehow slightly different from his elbow because he somehow understands that the penis is an erogenous zone, a window to the world. But what kind of window is it? As the boy grows into a man, this is the question that will occupy him for the duration of the prolonged mythological phase. And while he tries to figure out an answer to the question of what it means to have a penis, he erects a whole world to defend himself against having to admit that he does not yet know. The third phase – of which the revolutionary slogan may well be 'Back to the thing itself!' – has a redemptive quality about it. A man now realises that he is just another human being and that while his penis offers a window onto the world, the house has many other windows. To put it bluntly: he realises that the penis is just another window. It is not the front door.

Luc arrived at the third phase of manhood prematurely. He was not yet ready for it. Or perhaps he was ready for it, but found himself in a world that lacked the generosity to allow him to be ready for it. Whichever way we look at it, Luc was out of sync with the world in a subtle yet very important way and it was this being-out-of-sync that lay at the origin of the suicide attempt that resulted in the near-death experience, which ended with him being committed to Doctor Cottard's facility, where he now lies on his bed, watching himself throb and relishing the sheer enjoyment of feeling life pulsing through his body, wave after wave, without any desire to have the waves crash on the shore. As often happens during moments such as this, he recalls the series of events that brought him to this point. And, as always, it is the same three scenes that float across his mind like figures cast on the wall by a Japanese spinning lamp. To some degree, all three memories embarrass him, but this somehow never bothers him because the embarrassment always finds forgiveness in the waves of warm energy that ripple through his body.

In the first scene – in which an old villager is waving a stick above his head while he is chasing a white mountain goat – Luc is eighteen and still a virgin. His friend Stan's parents have gone away for the weekend and Stan decided to invite all his friends over for a party on the Saturday evening. It is late and everyone has had too much to drink. Lucy has been flirting with Luc all evening and he is getting so excited that it is hard to contain himself. Just before midnight, they find a room at the far end of the house. There, they lie down on the bed where they kiss passionately for a while. She removes Luc's shirt and he gently unbuttons her bright orange blouse, kissing his way down her gradually exposed cleavage. By the time he undoes her bra and her breasts slip into his hands, he is almost beyond himself with excitement. They remove their pants and he eases himself down on top of her, rubbing his erection first against her belly and then lower down until he slips in between her legs. Lucy throws her hands wide open (which annoys Luc a little bit because he would rather she grabbed his buttocks), but he is getting lost in the world between her breasts and soon forgets about his buttocks. As he enters her, she groans with delight, 'Oh God! I just love men's cocks!'

The peculiar construction of her groan aside – what other kind of cocks could she be referring to, women's cocks, plastic cocks? – in that moment, Luc feels a shudder of numbness, starting from his head, slowly seeping down his chest, and leaving only numb limbs in its wake. His nipples lose their sensitivity, then his shoulders, his belly and, eventually, his penis. Embarrassed and confused about the sudden and inexplicable dissipation of his sexual energy, he withdraws. Sitting on the side of the bed, he shakes his head and mumbles something of an apology.

'What's wrong, Luc?' Lucy asks, pulling her legs up and covering her breasts with her blouse.

'I think I had too much to drink,' he mumbles, pulling his pants up and reaching for his shirt. And so the scene ends – not for our two young lovers, but for us, because the rest is well known and predictable. Luc skulks out of the room and leaves Lucy behind. She falls back on the bed in frustration. Both spend the rest of the night drinking too much and avoiding eye contact. Over the next couple of weeks, they are awkward in each other's company. Once or twice, one of them will try to ease the tension with a joke about how silly people get when they have had too much to drink and so on and so on.

Poor, embarrassed Luc. What happened? Well, the problem was not Lucy or the alcohol. Even Luc knew that because by the time he entered her he was so hard he could have exploded. But then she exclaimed, 'Oh God! I just love men's cocks!' and this exclamation, far from exciting Luc, emasculated him. Instead of spurring him on with the fantasy that he represented all men and their cocks, that in Lucy's eyes he was the very embodiment of the manly cock, instead of allowing himself to become Cock of All Ages, he went limp. It is tempting to think that he lost his erection because of the weight of expectation (what kind of man gets excited by the idea that when he makes love to a woman he is representing all men?). But it is more complicated than that and to understand why, we have to return to the grand narrative of the penis becoming thing-myth-thing.

There is a glorious moment when young boys discover the power of their erections, a moment whose beauty derives from the fact that it is pre-mythological, in the sense that the penis is not yet invested with the weight of history and patriarchy. It is a purely physical moment, devoid of any meaning. One of the first things a boy does in this moment is to test the power of his erection against the force of gravity. He hangs a towel over his erection to see who wins; charmed by the fact that his erection defies the combined force of gravity and the weight of the towel, he tries a damp towel. And still his body wins. After that, he tries a bigger towel and an even bigger one. Instead of using a damp towel, he now uses a wet towel, and so it goes on, until eventually gravity wins. At that point, the boy comes to understand something about the pre-mythological limits of his sexual power. It is a pre-mythological moment because in that moment he is not concerned with the meaning of his penis or his masculinity. His penis is just a muscle and he is testing its power against gravity. But, later, his body becomes the battleground of history and slowly the penis as pre-mythological muscle becomes the stuff of mythology, a sword every young man is trained to wield on the battleground of the sexes. Once a boy's penis enters the mythological phase, every move he makes on the chess board of gender politics is made on behalf of all men. His penis is no longer his own; instead, it is what makes 'a man' of him, what makes him belong to the category of 'man'. And so, the individual stops simply being 'Luc' and instead becomes 'a man', one of many pawn pieces in a game in which the rules precede him and the meaning of every move is predetermined.

Luc was a latecomer to this game of gender chess. Sure, he had been aware of the game and of his place in it, but because he was still a virgin he mistakenly believed that his penis belonged to him alone, so that when he entered Lucy he thought it was *him* who was entering her, not all men. For Luc, nothing could have been more disappointing in that moment than to be reduced to Cock of All Ages, to find himself representing Cock. Small wonder, then, that all life would drain out of him and that he would go limp with . . . with what? Expectation? Did he go limp because he felt he was not worthy or man enough to represent all men? No, that was not it. Luc went numb with anonymity. Lucy's moan reduced him, Luc, to 'a man' and mythologised his cock into something that no longer belonged only to him. When Lucy moaned 'Oh God! I just love men's cocks!' she draped the big sopping wet towel of masculinity over Luc's penis and the gravity of history won.

The second scene that floats across the wall of Luc's memory – the same old villager is now being chased by someone who appears to be his landlord (perhaps because the old man allowed the white mountain goat to escape) – restored his faith in himself, if in a somewhat unexpected and comical way. His adoptive father, Doctor Obiwan Ojuok – whom his mother had met and married in Nairobi when she worked there for a non-governmental organisation – was the Kenyan ambassador to Paris. And so, from a young age, Luc had socialised with the children of other diplomats. With the exception of Stan, son of the South African ambassador, Luc despised the company of the other diplomats' children. They struck him as spoiled brats, who only ever spoke about the countries they had grown up in, their interactions carefully regulated by the pecking order of whose parents had been deployed to the most prestigious embassies in the world, and their lavish gifts and invitations nothing less than carefully constructed gestures of competitiveness and humiliation. But Stan was different. His real name was Svad – a name he hated and would never forgive his parents for inflicting on him, which explains why he insisted on being called Stan. He was serious and fun at the same time, courageous in an unassuming way, which probably had something to do with the fact that he had been paralysed from the waist down since the age of eleven as the result of a rugby injury at school.

On the Saturday morning that would be etched in Luc's memory as the second image in the long, troubled story of his sexual awakening, he was at Stan's house and they were watching reruns of *Star Wars* – Stan in his wheelchair to one side, Luc lying on a couch at an angle, both with an ample supply of soft drinks and popcorn, engrossed in the action.

> *Threepio:* Did you hear that? They've shut down the main reactor. We'll be destroyed for sure. This is madness!
> *Threepio:* We're doomed!
> *Threepio:* There'll be no escape for the Princess this time.

Threepio: What's that?
Threepio: I should have known better than to trust the logic of a half-sized thermocapsulary dehousing assister . . .
Luke: Hurry up! Come with me! What are you waiting for?! Get in gear!
Threepio: Artoo! Artoo-Detoo, where are you?
Threepio: At last! Where have you been?
Threepio: They're heading in this direction. What are we going to do? We'll be sent to the spice mines of Kessel or smashed into who knows what!
Threepio: Wait a minute, where are you going?

Out of the blue, Luc suddenly felt overwhelmed by an urge to tell Stan about the night with Lucy. Trying to sound as casual as possible, he said, 'Stan, can I tell you something?'

'Yip,' Stan said, without reaching for the remote control.

Vader: Where are those transmissions you intercepted?
Rebel officer: We intercepted no transmissions. Aaah . . . This is a consular ship. We're on a diplomatic mission.
Vader: If this is a consular ship . . . where is the Ambassador?
Vader: Commander, tear this ship apart until you've found those plans and bring me the Ambassador. I want her alive!

'Can we pause for a second?' asked Luc.

Stan picked up the remote and paused the movie. 'What's up?'

And so, Luc told his friend the whole story, from beginning to end, slightly self-conscious about the fact that he was sharing his embarrassment with the one friend who would never know what it feels like to enter a woman. Luc insisted that he was probably too drunk, but somewhere in the back of his head there was a nagging feeling that it was not the alcohol. And yet, he couldn't quite place his finger on it.

When Luc finished telling his story, Stan was quiet for a while. He did not laugh or joke about it. He just sat there, playing with the knob of his wheelchair's driving controls. When he eventually did respond, it was not at all what Luc had expected. 'Are you sure it works?'

'Am I sure what works?'

'Your erection. Can you do it?'

'Of course, I can do it. What kind of question is that?'

'Then show me.'

'Show you what?'

'That it works.'

Luc was completely taken aback. 'Are you fucking serious?'

It was only when he sat up abruptly and looked at Stan that he realised the conversation was no longer about him and his misadventure with Lucy. The conversation was always going to be about Stan, who looked self-conscious and sad, as vulnerable as Luc had ever seen him.

'Indulge a cripple,' Stan said and, before Luc could say anything, his friend added, 'You know how often I think about everything I am missing out on. I will never be able to experience your embarrassment, not in the same way. And I constantly hear the other boys at school talk. They think that because I'm a cripple I'm also deaf, but I hear them talk.' And here he blushed before he went on. 'They talk about masturbating together. Standing in a circle and taking turns to call out the names of the girls they like. The one who comes first wins.'

On the screen, Vader remained frozen mid-menace.

Luc was taken aback. But the sudden urgency and vulnerability of his friend left him speechless. He knew what Stan was referring to. He had also heard the boys talk like that, but they had never invited him to join them. If they did invite him, what would he do? There was little doubt in his mind that he would decline and, in the process, further alienate himself from the rest of the boys in his class. And yet, he understood Stan's desire to be part of a circle of young men his own age, playfully celebrating their masculinity together.

'Can't I just go and rent you a porn movie? I'll watch it with you.'

'Not the same,' Stan said. 'I've watched many of those. They don't do much for me.'

At that moment Luc realised that Stan was perfectly serious and that there was no way out of it. 'What, here?'

'My parents are out for the day. The cook is only coming in at 5.00 p.m. We're completely alone.'

Luc lay back on the couch. This was the most unimaginable outcome of his confession. 'Let me just make sure. You want me to lie here and masturbate while you watch?'

'Yes.'

From the immediacy and clarity of his response, Luc could tell that Stan had thought about this for a long time and that he had just been waiting for the right moment to ask. There was no escaping his request. How to say no to the request for male bonding from a paraplegic friend in a wheelchair? Luc settled down on the couch, took his shoes off, pulled his pants down over his knees and closed his eyes.

Lucy has aged into a mature and seductive young cabaret performer. The spotlight hovers on a barely visible split in the stage curtain, which is the same orange of the blouse she had worn that fateful night. After a couple of seconds, two hands appear from behind the curtain. They slowly separate the curtains and her face appears, made up to resemble a cat with big, black eyes, whiskers and a beauty spot on her left cheek. As she pulls the curtains wider apart, the rest of her head appears. Luc notices that she is also wearing a set of bunny ears on her head. Nervous giggles ripple through the audience, as she looks first left, then right, wiggles her nose and steps through the split in the curtain, completely naked, apart from her high-heels and the whip in her left hand, which she cracks loudly once – a cue for the musicians to start playing. For the first couple of minutes, she merely strides up and down the audience, snarls at the men who laugh and jeer at her, cracking her whip every now and then. Then she walks over to the piano on the side of the stage. She places the whip on top of it, puts her right knee on the piano stool and, smiling naughtily at the audience, wiggles her buttocks. The men in the audience start clapping their hands to encourage her. First in slow unison, then faster and faster: clap . . . clap . . . clap . . . clap, clap, clap, clap, clap, clap-clap-clap-clap . . .

'That's enough.'

Luc opened his eyes. 'What?'

'That's enough, thanks. You can put it away now.'

For a moment Luc was lost. Was this really happening? It was broad daylight on a Saturday morning. He was lying on the couch in Stan's TV room – Vader was still frozen on the screen mid-command – with his warm erection in his hands, dying to ejaculate. 'But I'm not done,' he said.

'It's not about you,' Stan said. 'I've experienced what I needed to. Thanks.'

Luc lay back and sighed. He closed his eyes again. Lucy is still standing at the piano, one knee on the piano stool, one of the bunny ears slightly drooping to one side. The music has stopped, the audience is quiet, and Lucy is looking straight at him with a combination of confusion and expectation. She needs direction, he knows, but he can no longer give her any.

He opened his eyes, pulled his pants up and put his hands behind his back. There was a moment of quiet between Luc and Stan. Perhaps even slight embarrassment. Then, to break the silence, Luc said, 'And what exactly did you experience?'

'That it's just a limb. Like any other.'

'The cock?'

'Yes,' answered Stan. 'It's just a limb – like an arm or a leg. A thing. You can make it do whatever you want, but there really is nothing special about it, is there? You can make it go up and down, just like you can wave your arm. I tend to desire these things because I am incapable of what I saw you do just now. But the right woman will come along for me, too. Until then, I'm sure I'll miss out on a lot of fun, but that's about it, isn't it? Fun?' And with that, he pressed the play button again.

> *Trooper:* There she is! Set for stun!
> *Trooper:* She'll be all right. Inform Lord Vader we have a prisoner.
> *Threepio:* Hey, you're not permitted in there. It's restricted. You'll be deactivated for sure.
> *Threepio:* Don't call me a mindless philosopher, you overweight glob of grease! Now come out before somebody sees you.
> *Threepio:* Secret mission? What plans? What are you talking about? I'm not getting in there!
> *Threepio:* I'm going to regret this.
> *Chief pilot:* There goes another one.
> *Captain:* Hold your fire. There are no life forms. It must have been short-circuited.
> *Threepio:* That's funny, the damage doesn't look as bad from out here.

Oh, if only Luc understood how the strange incident with Stan had, in many ways, saved him. Sure, it was a little bit embarrassing, but he forgot all about that the moment Lucy strutted over to the piano. Then, when Stan stopped him, he was strangely frustrated at having his fantasy interrupted – despite the slight awkwardness of indulging his fantasy in the presence of a friend. Sad and comical as the situation may have been, the real sadness is that Luc did not realise one very important thing: by calling his cock 'just another limb', a *thing*, and by comparing it to an arm that one can wave up and down at will, Stan had peeled away all the layers of masculine mythology that Lucy had draped over his penis that night, the weight of history and myth that had weighted down his soul ever since. By dismissing his cock as 'just another limb', Stan had reduced it to just another thing, and thus returned Luc's penis to him. Yes, it took his friend who was singularly incapable of the pleasure he was witnessing to understand that pleasures of the body are one's own and that Luc's pleasure did not represent the pleasure of all men.

In the third scene that the Japanese spinning lamp of history casts on the wall of Luc's memory, a woman is chasing the landlord (who is chasing the old villager, who is chasing the white mountain goat) with a big soup spoon held ominously over her head. It is a couple of weeks after the Saturday he spent as Stan's house and Luc finds himself again poised over Lucy's naked body. This time they are outdoors. They have gone for a picnic at a remote spot next to the river. It is a late Sunday afternoon. They have not encountered anyone else the whole morning and feel perfectly secluded and private. They have had their meal. Now, they are lying on their backs, looking at the clouds and talking about inconsequential things, the calming sound of the river reassuring them that while everything changes, much stays the same. They start to kiss, at first hesitantly and then with increasing passion. Again, there is a rush of excitement in Luc's body, his erection that pops out of his pants when Lucy unzips him, and the promise of infinite pleasure that spills out of her blouse. He finds himself once more on top of her, fully stretched out, his hands next to her head on the grass. Between them, a look of recognition. They have been here before and they both acknowledge the fact. Is this going to be the consummation of their mutual attraction, of the desire that had drawn them together ever since they first set eyes on each other? Luc enters Lucy and she closes her eyes, her hands falling wide open on the grass beside her. She bends her head back and moans: 'Oh God! I just . . .' but she does not get to complete her sentence. Luc gently places his right hand over her mouth. He stops thrusting and she opens her eyes and looks at him. He puts his finger across her lips and says: 'Shh. It's just me. It's just me.'

He can tell from the look in her eyes that she knows exactly what he is saying and why. He removes his finger from her lips and, supported by his hands next to her head, kisses her body all the way down, between the cleavage, circling her nipples with his tongue, as he thrusts deeper into her. He watches as she slowly relaxes and drifts off into oblivion while the waves pick him up and carry him forward, a ceaseless swelling that seems to defy gravity itself.

I wish I could just leave Luc and Lucy there for a little while, nestling in the comfort of their shared intimacy. I wish we could draw the curtain, block the sun and allow them some privacy. But history is less gracious. History is impatient, always surging ahead, welling up from behind us like a wave rushing towards the shore. We can ride the wave and enjoy the feeling of getting carried away while clinging to the fantasy that we somehow remain in control. But the waves of history always come crashing down, for they, too, are at the mercy of gravity, a pull that is as enigmatic as it is relentless. We can ride a wave and feel on top of the world for a brief second, but a wave is just a wave. It is destined to fulfil its rhythm.

And so it happened that a week or so after the day in the park, it came to Luc's attention that Lucy was telling everyone that he had forced himself on her; that they had indeed made love, but she had not consented to it. Luc was astounded. Recalling the look of recognition in her eyes and the gentle rhythm they shared right up to the moment of climax, when they both released in unison, he could not believe what he was being told. So he phoned her. Perhaps the rumour was no more than the audible moan of a small circle of boys who were jealous of the fact that he managed to do more than just fantasise about having sex with Lucy (which most of them did). Luc and Lucy talked awkwardly for a while. Then he asked her if the rumours he had been hearing were true and she confirmed that they were.

'But how is this possible?' he asked incredulously. 'You did not once say "no" or "stop" or indicate that you were not consenting. How can you tell people that I forced myself onto you?'

There was a pause. Then she said: 'I didn't want intimacy Luc. I just wanted sex.' The clarity with which she spoke was terrifying. 'When you put your finger over my lips, you silenced me. If you had allowed me to say what I wanted to say, you would have realised that I did not want intimacy. You forced your intimacy on me and violated my need for nameless sex.'

And there it is; the cusp of the wave just before it breaks. At the precise moment when Luc, having demythologised his cock and claimed it back as his own, recognised it as a limb with no more signifying power than an elbow or a knee, at the precise moment when he entered Lucy as one man and not as Cock of all Ages, she passed him going in the opposite direction, longing to dissolve her desire in the comforting myth that to fuck one man was to fuck the very idea of masculinity.

Needless to say, the repercussions of Lucy's accusation reverberated through the diplomatic community in Paris. Stan was a great source of comfort, but ultimately the claims of forced sexual intercourse could only be resolved through a complicated arrangement between Luc and Lucy's parents, a therapist and a non-disclosure agreement between the two families' lawyers. Luc would take longer to recover from what he perceived as a fundamental betrayal, a betrayal that had left him with the indelible impression that pleasure is not the gateway to the world, that he had no right to feel, that it is not through pleasure that we discover what it means to belong and that the world was therefore not a safe place. And so, a couple of weeks after the formal end of proceedings, he decided that recovery was not possible and attempted again to take his own life. Unlike the many times before, he very nearly succeeded. In fact, there was a short while when he did die and encountered the Godhead. For a brief moment, he was suspended between this life and the next – this world of promises, and another vision of a world of plenitude and fullness, of unity with everything, which comforted him and made him feel at home, as if he did, after all, belong in the world. It was that experience of belonging that haunted him when he came to, when he found himself back in the world where he felt he did not and could never belong. He remained committed to the only belonging he knew and could trust: the unity with the Godhead, a unity he intuitively knew would be betrayed and shattered the moment he spoke about it. Luc emerged from the tragic comedy of pleasure and betrayal with a commitment never to speak again. And he did not. So concerned were his parents by his state of mind and the fact that since his return from the hospital he had not said a single word to anyone that they eventually agreed that he needed professional intervention. And so, late one Friday afternoon, they dropped him off at Doctor Cottard's famous institution. His father ruffled his hair and said something like, 'Go all the way, my son. We'll be waiting for you' while his mother – well, all he can remember of saying goodbye to her was the familiar smell of her perfume and how much fuller her body felt in comparison with Lucy's.

11

And now, like the lone survivor of a shipwreck, Luc is lying on his bed, mulling over the scenes that brought him to this moment. He sees Angèle again, wickedly and irreverently sticking her finger in her mouth to demonstrate how she felt about the nurse who sat with her every time she had a meal. Luc smiles and closes his eyes. The three images of his encounters with Lucy and Stan flicker in and out of focus in his mind like little patches of light and shadow under a tree in the late afternoon sun. He is dispassionately detached from all three scenes. None of them mean anything to him now. They are just images. For the first time since that fateful Sunday afternoon with Lucy, he discerns how the warm energy that wells up from the ground of his being dissolves the anxiety associated with his memories. His testicles glow with tension, sending the warmth of excitement up his spine, slowly pulsating through his erection like gentle waves lapping at the shores of his broken soul.

To experience pleasure is to experience a sense of belonging in the world. Pleasure is the gateway to belonging. He closes his eyes and watches the thoughts gently emerge from the cloud of unknowing.

This is my being. This is what life feels like, a flux of change and movement. The entire world is pulsating through me.

Part III

Detachment

Harvesters II

1

For about a week after I watched Luc disappear through the window of the curio shop, I manage to carry on with my life as if nothing extraordinary had happened. I make jokes with Maretha when I get to the office, sign what needs to be signed, attend meetings and teach my classes. At noon I walk over to the student cafeteria to buy lunch, which I eat sitting on one of the benches in the sun or I take it up to the kitchen, where I put the food on a plate and warm it in the microwave before taking it to my office, where I eat while listening to relaxing YouTube tracks. Sometimes, I eat standing at the window, from where I can look down at the place where I saw Luc the first time.

It is not that I am making a concerted effort to live my life as if nothing extraordinary has happened. On the contrary. Since the evening I saw Luc walk through the shop window, it is as if I have been living in two realities simultaneously. On the one hand, there is the ordinary world in which I cycle to and from work every day, often stopping to buy things for supper at the supermarket two doors down from the curio shop. On the other hand, there is a very different world in which inexplicable things happen and the laws of physics do not seem to apply. The confusing and disconcerting thing is how this second, strange reality seamlessly blends with my ordinary reality. Often, when I walk past the curio shop, the disconcertingly content shopkeeper smiles his mysterious smile and waves at me, before looking down again to continue with whatever he is doing. Sometimes, when I know he is not looking, I gently slide my hand across the windowpane as I walk past – no, *through* the place where Luc had stood before he disappeared. *This is the place where my two realities coincide,* I often think to myself, but not even that realisation can dispel the unsettling feeling of living in a world that consists of two realities, both of which I feel equally alienated from. Below the surface of my everyday behaviour, the seed of otherworldliness (or is it worldlessness?) has taken hold and is slowly eating away at me, almost as if it were drawing sustenance from my soul. I can feel how it erodes the spontaneity of my laughter, how it chisels away at my lightness, leaving me with the sensation that what has seeded inside of me is a void that I cannot account for, much less explain. It is as if I have been impregnated with the inexplicable and it will come to terms with me as and when it sees fit. There is seemingly nothing I can do to speed up this process.

Sometimes I think of Sigourney Weaver and imagine that I have become host to an alien creature that has nothing to do with me and would not recognise me or care for me the moment it was born. At some fundamental level, my spirit has given up on the expectation that the world should conform to my expectations of it. My soul has resigned itself to the fact that it has been outwitted by a phenomenon that is so carelessly far beyond the laws of physics that it makes no sense attempting to understand it. How does one make sense of being invaded by an alien race of superior intelligence when they simply refuse to communicate? It is that sort of thing. On the evening when Luc walked through the shop window, an alien creature crawled right into my solar plexus – the third propeller, as I explained it to Grace that day next to the pool, the pit of my stomach, at exactly the place we touch when we say, 'I feel queasy' or 'It makes me sick to my stomach' – where it now burrows until such time as . . . as what? Until I am ready? Until it is ready?

After about two weeks, I can feel that I am struggling to hold it together. I start to become forgetful. I find my thoughts drifting away mid-sentence. In classes I catch myself repeating jokes I had made the week before and in meetings I start to feel like a placeholder for the real me. I also notice that Maretha is getting worried about me.

At first, her early morning 'How are you?' starts to sound like a real question and not just a greeting. Then I notice that she starts to ask me the same question again two or three times in the course of the day. I always just say, 'I'm fine, thanks', but I know she is not buying it. Then, one day, with the diplomacy that is a combined product of her age and of having worked for so many stern and authoritative bosses before me, she says, 'You look tired. Remember you asked Jason to take the next two weeks' lectures for you? Everything is under control here. Why don't you take a couple of days off? Stay at home, or if you don't want to take leave, just work from home for a couple of days.' And before I can respond, she adds, 'If there's anything we need here, I'll phone you.'

It is as if I have been fighting unseen forces that are dragging me down a bottomless pit of quicksand, only at the last moment, with the sand already up to my chin, to find an outstretched hand ready to pull me out. Why has it not crossed my mind to do just that? Of course, I had asked Jason to take two weeks' worth of lectures for me because he knows more about Buddhism than I do. The fact that I have forgotten that I had asked him and somehow in the back of my mind assumed that I would be able to teach the next cycle of lectures coming up, without registering that I had not done any preparation for it, is the last straw. I realise that I had better take some time off before I make a real blunder.

After Maretha leaves my office, I sit with my feet on the desk for a while, contemplating how to do this. *Shall I take leave or just work from home?* I decide that if I am going to take a break, I want a clean break. I fill in the online leave application for five days' leave and pack all my personal belongings in my rucksack. I fetch my juice bottle from the kitchen and, along with the leftovers from lunch, pack it in my bag, followed by my wallet, access card, house keys and headphones. Just before I leave the office, I check my email one last time, just in case there is anything I have to do before I leave and, to my great satisfaction, see that my leave has already been approved. I stop at Maretha's desk and tell her that she is right and that I have not been feeling well. I say I have taken her advice and I will be back the following week. She just smiles knowingly – obviously pleased with her powers of observation – and says she hopes I make a quick recovery. *Recovery? From what?* I think, but just thank her for her care and leave.

The decision to take some time off is a good one. I get home at about 3.00 p.m., after having stopped to buy a bottle of whisky and picking up some groceries for supper. I place the shopping on the counter and walk out to the patio, stripping off my clothes as I go. Standing naked under the retractable canvas cover, I unwind the hosepipe, turn the water on full blast and, holding the head of the shower above my head, allow the water to stream down my face. I direct the forceful stream of water all over my body – specifically at all the 'propellers'. Invigorated, I close the tap and, with a towel wrapped around my waist, go into the kitchen where I pour myself a stiff whisky, topped with lots of ice cubes and a little water. *Day drinking,* I think. *So, this is what it has come to.* I walk back out to the patio again and slump down in the easy deck chair. I put my feet on the table, take a deep sip of the whisky and instantly feel how it relaxes my body and mind. *What an unspeakable relief.* Before I can take a second sip, my phone rings from somewhere inside. I cannot even remember putting it down and for a brief moment consider not answering it. Then I decide it may be Maretha, stand up and walk over to where my pants are lying on the floor. I fish the phone out of my pocket and look at the screen. Unknown number. *Shall I just leave it?* Slightly irritated, I opt for the peace of mind I would have once I had dealt with whatever it was. Perhaps it is just a call centre.

It is the policewoman. I instantly recognise her voice and realise that I had completely forgotten about the finger. After we have exchanged the obligatory pleasantries, she informs me that they have been unable to identify the person to whom the finger belonged. They had sent it away for DNA analysis and ran the results through all their databases, but came up with nothing. As far as the police were concerned, she adds, this was the end of the investigation until somebody came forward or I provided them with more information. Just that. I thank her and end the call. How funny, I had completely forgotten about the finger episode. In the strange worlds I now simultaneously inhabit, the case of the lost finger occupies a very insignificant place.

I slump down again in my patio chair and take another deep sip of my whisky. I pick up the phone and phone Juliet. She is still at work and sounds distracted. We chat for a couple of minutes, but there is no intimacy in our conversation. Just two tired people at the end of a hard day's work, talking on the phone. I tell her about the phone call from the police, but she also had to be reminded about the finger episode and so does not have much to say in response to the feedback from the police. I am partly to blame for the recent lack of intimacy in our conversations because I have not told her about the things that have been occupying my mind – the strange man at the curio shop and the even stranger remark he had made about Grace's birthday, nor the two occasions when I had seen Luc. Juliet knows when something important is happening in my life precisely because I do not talk about it. I am the kind of person who likes to withdraw and think things through and only once I have an answer do I share it with her. I have always been like that and she has always been the exact opposite. The moment she is confronted by a problem or a situation she does not understand, she starts talking about it – to me, her friends, her siblings. In the first ten years of our married life this often led to arguments. She accused me of not trusting her sufficiently to work out the problem with her, and I accused her of talking issues to death and not giving me sufficient head space when I needed to think things through. 'Why not just trust that that's what people are there for – to help you figure things out? No, Mr Philosopher has to resolve it for himself and then, only then, will he deign to share his thoughts with us mere mortals. Don't you understand that this is precisely how men have made such a mess of the world?'

She knows how it annoys me when she makes me represent all men in the world, as if my way of acting in the world is typical of the way all men act in the world and as if, by not sharing my thoughts with her, I am by implication responsible for global warming. In the beginning I used to fall for that and argue back. Then I learnt that it was pointless and Juliet and I accepted that we deal with things differently. I may take longer to seek my partner's advice on something, but I will do so when I am ready.

We chat on the phone for a couple of minutes. She is envious of the fact that I have been able to take five days' leave and wishes she could do the same. I feel sorry for her. She does work incredibly hard, much harder than me, I often think. We agree to have a decent chat again over the weekend when we could Facetime or Skype while we make supper and have a long-distance supper together. Then we say goodbye and I am lost again in my own strange worlds. I take the last sip of whisky and, leaning my head back against the chair, contemplate how best to make use of these five days to get my head back in the game again.

2

After a second whisky, and largely as a result of the failed conversation with Juliet, I start to understand the full extent of my dilemma. I simply cannot continue to live with this solid void in my gut. This is not one of those times when I should withdraw into myself and think things through on my own until I understand what is going on. On two occasions now, what should be patently impossible had turned out to be perfectly possible. But not even the appearance and reappearance of Luc in my world is the kind of incident that would compel me to act contrary to my nature, to entrust my experiences and what I had witnessed to someone else and, together with them, work out what had happened. But am I not already at the point that I need to discuss this with Juliet? Would she believe me? I very much doubt it. Would I believe someone who told me that they recently saw a character they had created in a novel appear at work and subsequently saw him walk straight through the windowpane of a curio shop? Would I believe such a tale? If I have to be honest, I would not.

And so, I realise, after a third whisky, as much as this case requires of me to act differently from the way I usually do when I am trying to understand something, the facts of the case are so strange that I have no choice but to act as I always do. This one I would have to work through on my own – not by choice, but by necessity. And that is when I realise that there is only one other way forward, one way of processing and overcoming this feeling of being hollowed out from the inside by an eeriness that I will never understand, and that is to return to the shopping centre. I have to return in the late afternoon when the shops have closed, and sit and wait at Harvesters and watch the curio shop. There was something so specific about the way Luc walked through that particular windowpane that I am certain that whatever had happened would happen again. It is not much to work with, but who knows? If I did this every night while I was on leave and nothing like what I had previously witnessed happened again, then I must, over time, let go of what I had witnessed and relegate it to the realm of a strange anomaly of sorts. Of course, that would not be easy because I had not for one second doubted the truth of what I had witnessed that evening. On the other hand, if I went back and it happened again, it would mean that the strangeness was *real* and I would have more to work with. What I would do with that knowledge is not clear to me, but at least I would be able to think of it as a pattern or series of events and, as such, as the kind of phenomenon that conforms to some of the known laws of the universe. As I sit there, I realise that, strange as it may sound, I would prefer the second outcome. One would think the first option would make more sense, but there is something comforting in patterns and series – even if it involves patterns of the impossible or a series of improbable events. At the end of the day, a pattern is still a pattern and a series is still a series. Even if the event itself defies the laws of this universe, its recurrence as a pattern or a series would somehow make it obedient to some laws of the universe and therein would lie at least the potential of comprehending how it could be possible. I decide to implement my decision that same evening.

I have not yet had supper and can feel that the whisky had taken a bit of a toll on my energy levels. I will have to eat something very soon. I get up and throw some snacks in my rucksack, carefully wrap the bottle of whisky in a kitchen towel, along with a glass and a small bag of ice cubes. I put on a sweater, a dark green one that would allow me to blend into the fever tree environment. Then I mount the night lamp on my bicycle and open the electronic gate.

Outside, it is fresh and chilly. The streets are relatively quiet because it is the middle of the week. I get onto the bicycle and start riding in the direction of the shopping centre – all along the pavement because I am slightly lightheaded and do not trust myself to cycle on the road. It is after nine when I get to the centre. All the shops, including the coffee shop and Harvesters, are closed. It is quiet and desolate, but there is nothing strange about that. It is to be expected. Harvesters is a suburban pub and closes early on week nights. On Friday and Saturday nights, they get bands to come and perform and then they stay open until the small hours of the morning. I briefly calculate how my five days' leave would play out in terms of the shopping centre's rhythm. My vacation starts the next day, a Tuesday, which means I basically have six nights of quiet to conduct my investigation. Given how busy the place is on Friday and Saturday nights, nothing would happen then. After that, I would have the Sunday and the following Monday. That would have to suffice.

When I get to Harvesters, I lean my bicycle against the railings and since I am the only one around and I am going to be sitting right there I do not bother to lock it. I sit down in the booth on the veranda where Jason and I had first met and he told me that he used to be one of my students. Since that day we have got to know each other well and often go out for drinks. He went on to register for a postgraduate degree and, from what his supervisor tells me, is doing well – so well in fact that a number of lecturers in the department have offered him the opportunity to take some of their lectures. I open the rucksack and take out the snacks and whisky. I am suddenly starving. I pour myself a drink and add a whole handful of ice cubes, seeing that I have forgotten to bring water. Then I get stuck in to the dried meat and crackers. From where I am sitting, I have a good view of the curio shop window, but the veranda is so dark that I doubt anyone who looks in my direction will be able to see me. Once the first hunger panic has been satisfied, I lean back in my seat. Now I just have to wait. I suddenly become aware of a presence at my feet. When I look down, I see that it is the same cat I saw last time. It is certainly not a wild cat. On the contrary, it looks domesticated and well cared for. I reach down and pull at the tag around its neck. Engraved on it is a phone number. I decide to leave it at that. Perhaps it belongs to the pub's owners and the cat has learned to follow them here. I am not going to make friends with it, however, given my extreme allergy to cats, so I gently push it away with my feet. It keeps coming back and at one point even rubs itself against my foot, purring with pleasure. Eventually, it gets the message and slinks off into the night. I open a packet of peanuts and raisins, sip on my whisky and, with my head supported on my right hand, stare at the curio shop window. But nothing happens.

 It is just before midnight when I wake up with a start. I must have dozed off. *Too much whisky and strangeness,* I think. *Not a good combination.* I rub my face and look around. Everything is still where it is meant to be, including my bicycle. I pack the whisky and remaining food in my bag, put the sweater on and cycle back home, where I make myself a hearty meal of fried egg, bacon and smashed avocado on toast. I eat standing at the kitchen counter because I am too tired to dish up and sit down in the lounge. Once I have finished eating, I put the dishes in the sink, switch off the kitchen light and collapse on my bed. I fall asleep before I can even wonder whether I am going to struggle to sleep.

The second and third nights nothing happened either. On both nights, I eventually fell asleep; on the third night, even with the cat curled up at my feet. If it had been any closer, my eyes would have exploded with an itchy rash and within a matter of minutes be so swollen that I would not be able to see. I left feeling quite dejected on the fourth night, knowing that Friday and Saturday nights were going to be very busy and therefore not worth the effort. I would have to try again on Sunday evening. I packed up my things and went home. It was a restless, insomniac night, the kind of night one ends up so anxious about not falling asleep that one cannot fall asleep. But knowing that I did not have to get up early; in fact, that I could sleep as late as I wanted to, anxiety did not set in and I eventually fell asleep.

And so, when I woke up this morning, I made myself a big mug of coffee, which I am now enjoying on my deck chair on the patio, basking in the early morning sunlight. What should I do with my time over the next two days until I can assume my post at Harvesters again on Sunday evening? I have no urgent work to do and I do not feel like reading. Over the past week I have, on a couple of occasions, tried to immerse myself in novels at night, but have found it almost impossible. How can I focus on one activity in this world when I am trying to figure out how to live in two worlds at the same time? Even Detective Bergman could not capture my imagination sufficiently to escape from my world. It may well be time for binge movie watching. For a long time now, I have wanted to do all three *Lord of Rings* or all three instalments of *The Matrix* or *Star Wars* back to back. This is my chance. But which one? I decide on *Star Wars*, drop Juliet a WhatsApp voice note informing her of how I plan to spend my Friday and suggest that we have our planned supper Skype early tonight or, if she is too tired, on Saturday.

I order an Uber to the nearest shopping mall, where there is a DVD store, take out the original *Star Wars* trilogy, and walk around the mall for a while. I buy a pair of pants and two shirts, which I had been planning to do for a long time, but not being a very conscientious consumer, I have somehow never got round to it. I go home and spend the rest of the day cleaning my apartment. Mid-afternoon I get a voice note from Juliet saying that tonight will not work for her for a long Skype supper because she is only going to get home at about 7.00 p.m. She would, however, like to briefly chat and say hello, at about 7.30. She sounds tired. I know that tone in her voice. She is absolutely exhausted from a week of teaching and either rehearsing various student productions or attending them and giving the students and her colleagues feedback. She sometimes starts teaching at 8.00 in the morning and works right through the day, including lunch, to only finish at 6.00 or 7.00 in the evening. I do not know how she does it, but I can tell from her voice that it has been one of those days and that she will be in bed by 8.00 p.m. Not to be deterred or allowing my plans to be derailed, I prepare supper, and by late afternoon, I settle in to *Star Wars* with a big bowl of popcorn next to me and two cold beers on the bedside table. Not long into the first instalment, I get to my favourite scene:

Trooper: There she is! Set for stun!
Trooper: She'll be all right. Inform Lord Vader we have a prisoner.
Threepio: Hey, you're not permitted in there. It's restricted. You'll be deactivated for sure.
Threepio: Don't call me a mindless philosopher, you overweight glob of grease! Now come out before somebody sees you.
Threepio: Secret mission? What plans? What are you talking about? I'm not getting in there!
Threepio: I'm going to regret this.

Chief pilot: There goes another one.
Captain: Hold your fire. There are no life forms. It must have been short-circuited.
Threepio: That's funny, the damage doesn't look as bad from out here.

'Don't call me a mindless philosopher, you overweight glob of grease!' How funny. I stop, rewind and watch the same sequence again. Then the phone rings and I see Juliet's name come up on the screen. Much earlier than she said she would phone. I pause the film and answer: 'Don't call me a mindless philosopher, you overweight glob of grease!'

'No! You didn't, did you?'

'Of course I did. Did you think I was joking?'

'You're too old to binge on *Star Wars*, darling.'

'There is no age restriction on *Star Wars*.'

'Mmm. Glad to hear you're having fun. Wish I could say the same, but I am so exhausted. Just got home.'

And then she goes on to describe precisely the kind of day I thought she had had and how she plans to be in bed by 8.00 p.m. 'The only relaxing thing in my world,' she says wistfully, 'is that I am so over the whole Friday night thing, the compunction to go out and socialise. I'm so over that whole carry-on, know what I mean? Nothing will give me greater pleasure tonight than to get into bed with a book, which is actually exactly what I'm going to do after supper.'

It is on the tip of my tongue to tell her how much I would rather be at home and in bed with her at 8.00, cuddling up with books and taking turns every now and then to get up to make tea or get snacks from the pantry, but I realise it would just add sadness to her exhaustion and spoil her evening. We say goodbye and I return to *Star Wars*.

3

I do not return to Harvesters on Sunday evening. I feel too despairing. The whole idea of planning to watch a miracle occur twice seems impossible and so I just watch more TV, order more take-aways and go to bed early. Which, in retrospect, was the right decision because it finally happens when I return on the Monday evening.

The cat seems to have worked out that we will never be friends and I have worked out that it is better to have a substantial supper at home before I come to Harvesters than to spend the night snacking with my whisky and then having a big supper when I get home. This way, I know that I will not run out of energy and fall asleep at my post. I arrive fresh, rested and relaxed. A part of me even looks forward to going back to work the next day. Sometime over the weekend, a gentle resolve had taken shape in my mind. If nothing happens tonight, I will put it all behind me, try my best to forget about it and get on with my life. It is still relatively early when I arrive at the shopping centre. Harvesters has closed for the day and so have all the other shops, except for the coffee shop, where I can still see a small number of people at the outside tables finishing their meals. The coffee shop would soon close, too. I slide into the booth facing the curio shop, my rucksack next to me. Then I take out the whisky bottle, water, ice and glass. Glass in hand, I check my phone messages and emails. I even respond to one or two work-related emails while I sip my very weak and watered-down whisky.

They must have arrived while I was busy on my phone. I only see them when I glance up from my phone to look in the direction of the curio shop. Two men and a woman are standing in front of the curio shop window, in exactly the same place Luc had stood the previous time. One of the men is unmistakably Luc, the other is slightly older and looks a bit more worn. The woman has a shock of what must surely be artificially coloured red hair. Both Luc and the other man are standing with their hands in their pockets, the woman equally casual with her arms crossed behind her back. I put the phone down and hold my breath. They look so ordinary. If I did not immediately recognise Luc, I would have thought they were the last of the tourists, taking a stroll through the complex before they leave. But there is definitely something suspicious about their behaviour. As if by agreement, the other man is facing the window, making a concerted effort to look very interested in the crafts on display while Luc and the woman pretend to be having a conversation. But I can see they are just feigning it while they are actually scanning the passage and parking lot for potential witnesses. At one point, the woman walks away from Luc and stops to inspect the inside of the next two shops – the barber and the supermarket. Not strange behaviour in itself, except that I notice how she walks with the same somewhat heavy gait Luc had the previous time I saw him here. *As if walking is something she intentionally has to focus on, as if it requires effort,* I think to myself.

She returns to the others and she and Luc exchange a few more words. The other man, who had been looking intently at the display of crafts, turns to them as if to join their conversation, but only briefly. He suddenly turns away from them and, without looking back and with the same ease as Luc the previous time, walks straight through the window of the curio shop. Then it all happens within seconds. Luc and the woman also turn towards the shop window. Luc politely allows the woman to go first and she, too, walks through the window. Then he follows and, all of a sudden, it is over. They are gone and I am once again left alone, sitting on the Harvesters veranda, as if it were just another ordinary night. This time, I throw all caution to the wind. I slip out of the booth and run across the parking lot to the window. When I get there, I stop, breathing heavily from the run and the excitement, my mind racing. I have a small window of opportunity to figure this out. Whatever allowed them to do what they just did may still be available to me. I walk up to the window and tap it with my finger. It seems perfectly ordinary. Perhaps it is about intention. Perhaps I just need to believe that I, too, can walk through the window and if I do it with conviction I, too, will succeed. I take a deep breath and walk straight up to the window with every intention to follow Luc and the others wherever they have gone.

Bang!

I cannot say I walked into the glass because my body does not even get there. The moment I tried to step through the window, my foot encountered all the resistance of the known laws of physics. I stand back and press my hand against the glass. Solid, as it should be. Nothing out of the ordinary in this universe. Disappointed, I stand back. One last time, I walk up to the windowpane and gently pulling my sweater sleeve over my right hand wipe the glass window as if to remove every trace of my failed intention. Then I walk back to my table. I gather my things, pack them in my bag and cycle home. I feel simultaneously vindicated and defeated: vindicated because I now know beyond any shadow of doubt that I did not imagine Luc when I saw him from my office window or when I saw him walking through the shop window that first time. But I also feel defeated because, as comforting as this may be, the fact that I am not mad does not mean the world is not. On the contrary, I now know that I am alone in a very, very strange world.

Second Session with the Emperor

4

There is a hesitant knock on the door. Doctor Cottard stands up from behind his desk, walks to the door and opens it. When he sees Luc, he stands aside and allows him to enter. Then he closes the door again. They sit down, he on his side of the desk, Luc across from him. For a couple of seconds, while Luc looks around the room to familiarise himself again with his surroundings, Doctor Cottard studies the young man's posture. There is a subtle difference, an almost imperceptible shift in his posture. Luc seems more confident, as if, for the first time since they met, he is physically occupying the space he inhabits. When Luc's eyes return to him, Doctor Cottard smiles and says, 'Remember our agreement, Luc. You are not expected to speak. Not here, not in this room, not anywhere if you don't feel like it. You can speak when you are ready to. Agreed?'

Luc's eyes drop from Doctor Cottard's face to the black bow tie with orange dots, slightly darker than the orange of his waistcoat, but none of this registers because Luc senses the arrival of the image that always pulls him to the centre of the universe; there, where everything is equidistant from him, where every sound, loud or soft, travels through him without any meaning. But some sounds are higher or lower than others. He briefly closes his eyes in order to work out if the distance of the sound is in any way related to its proximity to him. But there does not seem to be a correlation. Then the old image flashes through his mind. Again. He allows the image to well up in him, as it often does. Yes, this image does not disclose itself or slowly emerge from behind the cloud of unknowing in the way all other images do. This one is different. It wells up from below. He always feels the surge before he sees the image, and the surge is a clear indication that the image is about to arrive, to reveal itself. Along with the revelation comes the feeling of his soul gasping for life and, suddenly, the understanding that life is not – perhaps never was – confined to his soul. Instead, his soul is the expression of life itself; it does not belong to him, but merely expresses itself through him. Luc takes a deep breath and allows the surge to carry him away, down a tunnel, faster than the speed of light, even faster than the speed of thought, and, even as it does, he wonders again, as he does every time, *Where am I going and what is happening? Is this a wormhole? Am I on my way to another universe, a parallel world where I will finally recognise myself?* These thoughts flash through his mind as Luc hurtles down the tunnel. The wormhole twists and curves, but he never loses speed; he just keeps hurtling, neither up nor down, but along, sideways and through, through everything faster than the speed of thinking. And then, suddenly, from one split second to the next, it is all over. He is spewed out the end of the tunnel into a big, black void of utter silence where nothing moves. He hangs in the middle of deep, dark space, equidistant from everything in the universe in a silence that is pitch black. In front of him there is a vast circle of light; not clear or crisp, more like a circle of frayed light as pitch black inside as the void that surrounds it.

I'm at the source.
This is the origin of everything.
Suspended, weightless, motionless, thoughtless Luc.
This is God's head. I am in God's head.

Who could know how long Luc spent inside God's head the first time this image found him? How long he hung there, suspended in the void, staring at the big circle, marvelling at the simplicity of everything. He understood everything; all was given to him, nothing remained hidden. How long did he spend in that sublime moment of weightlessness, in which all of existence flowed through him as if he were pure mind? What does it mean to ask about the duration of an experience that lasted all eternity, an experience that took him back to the origin of all things, before anything happened, before anything was? And what does it mean to ask what it means?

'. . . of belonging and that the world is a generous place, do you remember that, Luc?' Luc blinks and focuses on the face in front of him. Doctor Cottard smiles slightly. *How strange,* he thinks. Luc is the first person he has ever come across who somehow manages to be at once absolutely present and absolutely absent. *Where does this young man go when he is so absolutely present?* he wonders. He knows that Luc has not heard a thing he has said since they sat down, but he continues as if it does not matter because, in a sense, it does not. What matters is not the physical Luc – the ears, eyes and mind that receive information. What matters is that Luc gets the subtle message – and, clearly, he is. *There is real iridescence possible here,* Doctor Cottard thinks to himself before continuing.

'The returning soul is, in a way, goodness incarnate. And the goodness of the soul drives us to want to establish relations with the goodness of other souls because the soul intuits that we are social creatures, that we need relationships with others, and one way of establishing those relationships is for us to mirror our basic goodness back to one another. So, the obvious question is this: what happens if my basic goodness is not mirrored back to me? Is that not the biggest and most fundamental question of them all, Luc – what happens when, at a very young age, our basic goodness is not mirrored back to us by someone we love?'

He pauses for a second, then continues, 'Would you agree?'

Luc does not move. He is looking at Doctor Cottard, who can see that he is listening to every word. He is not going to ask Luc to respond in any way. The moment is too delicate. He moves his chair forward and takes up his habitual position, with his elbows on the desk, fingertips touching to form two half spheres, before he continues. 'Thing is, Luc, when the basic act of mirroring does not take place to make us feel loved, wanted and as if we belong in the world, the result is a profound sense of self-doubt; doubt becomes our most fundamental moving force. Of course, all of us know self-doubt – we must doubt ourselves; it is a sign of a healthy mind and a mature personality. But for the person whose basic goodness was never mirrored back to them, self-doubt becomes as fundamental as a sense of belonging would have been. So, we have a situation where an innately good person arrives in the world, intuitively sets out to forge relations with the goodness of other souls but, because his or her basic goodness is not confirmed in them, they become fundamentally detached from the world and others. Instead of attachment, there is detachment; instead of belonging, there is self-doubt: do I have a right to exist; do I belong; am I worthy of love, and so on. But, and here's the catch, Luc . . .' and with this Doctor Cottard leans back in his chair and, placing his right ankle on his left knee (which, given his somewhat protruding belly, always requires a bit of an effort), continues, 'the need to relate, to establish relations with the world outside us can never be repressed or denied; it never goes away. The self-doubting person continues to seek out attachments that will make him feel that he belongs and so the person who was not allowed or encouraged to relate to others and who did not feel unconditional love and a sense of belonging, ultimately ends up attaching himself to things and actions that will give him at least a temporary sense of belonging. And so, the basic building block of what will become the addictive mindset is put in place. Addictions are really just attachments to things and actions that will confirm that you are loved and that you have a right to exist, but constantly fail to give you what you truly need. And because they cannot but fail to give us what we really need, we have to keep trying and repeating the same action again and again. Addiction, Luc, is driven by a beautiful and profoundly correct impulse. It is driven by the need to connect, to exist in relation to something other than the self. It is just not a lasting or real solution. As I always say, addiction is the wrong answer to the right question. Does that make sense, Luc?'

It is that summer day when his father rolled back the roof of the car and his mother allowed him to sit in front next to his dad. He knew that the man next to him was not his real father (his parents were always very open about this), but he has always insisted on calling him Dad. He looks at his father's hand on the gear knob, the black hand resting there gently, ready to move it into the next gear at just the right moment. He stretches out his hand and traces a line over his father's hand – from where his fingers curl around the gear knob all the way across the top of his hand to where his father's watch interrupts the flow of sensation. 'Luc! Don't do that!' His mother's voice from the back. 'You're distracting your father. He has to concentrate. What – do you want to kill us all!? This is the last time!' His father withdraws his hand from the gear knob and places both hands on the steering wheel. He looks down at Luc and winks.

'. . . so, we have arrived in the world. If we felt loved, we formed healthy attachments. If not, we became detached from the world at a very young age and tried to correct this detachment by attaching to things that would give us what we instinctively always knew we needed. But the detached individual is a lonely soul, always at the mercy of self-doubt: am I good enough; do I have the right to be here? Over time, the self-doubt will become quite a monster of a thing. The tendency to doubt ourselves at such a fundamental level eventually grows into the belief that one is an Imposter, a fake person. We constantly live with the fear of getting caught out, revealed for pretending to be something we are not. And how do we assure ourselves that we are not an Imposter? By adopting the same strategy we deployed when we first started to feel haunted by self-doubt: the repetition of actions and patterns that, because they briefly give us a sense of belonging, also briefly make us feel real. But it's not all bad news, Luc. I believe that to become aware of feeling like an Imposter is to recognise that one's coping strategies have run out of credibility. It is the beginning of a long journey back home, back to the origin, back to the moment when the soul arrived in the world, hungry to be recognised for being essentially good. To feel like an Imposter is a good thing because it means that one understands that something other than being an Imposter is possible, something that preceded it. Ironically, to feel like an Imposter means recognising the pull of that original moment and a desire to go back all the way to the first unsatisfied desire, which gave birth to self-doubt and the mask this doubt would eventually come to wear – namely, the face of an Imposter. Which brings us to the vexed questions of guilt and forgiveness. Shall we go on Luc, or have you had enough? Do you want to stop?'

Doctor Cottard watches as Luc gets up from his chair. Without gesturing or indicating that he is asking for permission, he walks over to the big, soft leather couch and lies down. He does not turn his back on Doctor Cottard, but stretches out full length. Because he is slightly too long for the couch, he puts his feet on the arm rest at the end of the couch. He folds his hands behind his head and turns his head slightly to look at Doctor Cottard.

'"What if, what if, what if?" we always ask ourselves, don't we Luc? *What if* I were more loved; *what if* I were more affirmed when I arrived in the world? *What if* I were born there and not here, then and not now? *What if* I had different parents or different siblings? *What if* we were rich and not poor, or poor and not rich? Don't we all do that? And, invariably, after the *what if* follows the big *Then*: *then* I would have been this or that, or not this or that. *Then* I would not have been addicted to this or that – and so we go on, endlessly impersonating other lives in order not to take responsibility for our own. Most people accept it as true when I tell them that addiction is a way of loving oneself into existence and that addicts do this because they were not loved into existence when it mattered most. That's in a sense the easy bit. And it naturally raises the question of guilt and blame. All of us blame our parents and we want them to acknowledge their part in who we have become. Since I started this centre I have yet to come across somebody who has not asked me that very question: what if I were born into better circumstances, would I still have had this addiction? I have worked out that, in effect, what people want to know is this: how many (and which) past variables would need to have been different in order for me *not* to be here in the way that I am? It's an idle game, of course; change one variable and who knows what the consequences may be? A change may be as small as a flap of a butterfly's wings, but the consequences may be incalculable. You see, Luc, what people who play this What If game do not realise is that they are effectively recalculating their lives in terms of karma: they're trying to understand the consequences, variables and conditions for any given state of affairs as the result of past actions and conditions. And there is nothing wrong with playing that game, as long as we don't think we can master it or fully understand all the variables at play or the final outcome of making even one insignificant change to the infinite set of variables and conditions that have made us who we are. But I'm getting distracted now. Just know that What If is a karma game and if karma teaches us anything it is that we cannot understand, much less control, the game. So, we can ask the What If question, but we cannot even begin to imagine an answer.'

Doctor Cottard gets up from behind his desk and walks over to the window, where he stands for a moment, his hands folded behind his back. After a couple of seconds, he turns around and looks at Luc, who appears to be sleeping. But he is not asleep. *It's the deep rest of remembrance,* Doctor Cottard thinks before he walks over to one of the easy chairs across from the couch and sits down.

'Remember how in the first session I told you that our souls are returning souls? Well, they also choose the conditions they return into. Our souls know what work lies ahead and they know what condition or situation they must be born into to facilitate the journey they need to go on in order to do that work. In that sense, Luc, parents are no more and no less than the principal parts of the environment the individual reincarnates into, just one more variable in the complete set that will usher the soul along its path. The returning soul will – and here language gets a bit difficult – but let's just say the returning soul will involuntarily choose or unconsciously be drawn to suitable parents and will be born of them. Can you see what happens to blame and guilt in this picture, Luc? You cannot blame your parents for the life you were born into, for the situation in which your soul was or was not mirrored in recognition of its basic goodness – not if our souls seek out the situation that will facilitate what they know they have to learn. In that sense, even for those whose essential goodness was never affirmed, the original situation was never a curse, but always a blessing. Yes, Luc, the origin is always blessed and there is never anything to forgive. From this it follows that if the original scene of one's birth was blessed – and therefore beyond guilt and forgiveness – then every situation is blessed in the sense that it contains the possibility for the realisation of your true self. Can you see where I am going with this? It is neither the *will* of God nor the *fault* of our parents that we become who we are. Each child and each soul is responsible for shaping itself according to the conditions of its karma. It is our past karma or actions and the infinite consequences and implications of those that return to us in order to make us and shape us.'

Doctor Cottard stops talking. They remain there in silence for a good couple of minutes, Luc lying on the couch breathing deeply and completely at rest, Doctor Cottard watching him. Eventually, Luc opens his eyes, sighs deeply and stretches. Then he gets up from the couch. *He suddenly looks immensely tired,* Doctor Cottard thinks. *It's time to stop.* He walks over to Luc and, placing his hand on the young man's shoulders, looks him in the eyes and says: 'Where you are going, Luc, is neither God's will nor your own. The secret is to exercise your will in such a way that you know it coincides with the Divine Will – and believe me, when you make the right decisions, you always know that they are right because you will sense the coincidence.'

Then Doctor Cottard smiles that broad, generous smile of his. He ruffles Luc's hair and says, 'Enough of all this. Go and enjoy the rest of the day. Go and find Angèle and go for a walk. Do something pleasurable.'

Luc looks at Doctor Cottard. *The self-conscious iridescence of love becoming aware of itself,* Doctor Cottard thinks, then nudges

Luc with his head in the direction of the door. 'Now go.' He returns to his desk and sits down. When he looks up, Luc has gone, opening and closing the door behind him without making a sound.

Luc Has a Gut Feeling

5

After the session with Doctor Cottard, Luc is not in the mood for company. He feels confused and unsettled and spends most of the day strolling aimlessly through the rehabilitation centre's vast grounds. He thinks a lot about everything Doctor Cottard had said to him that morning. More than that, he keeps contemplating the manner in which Doctor Cottard spoke to him. There is indeed something imperial in his demeanour – his quiet confidence, the matter of fact way in which he speaks so authoritatively about the most unexpected things, such as repetition, reincarnation, belonging and addiction, the original loss of attachment, the resulting detachment from the world, and the way in which addictions fulfil an original desire to belong, to be held and loved as if one belonged. Dr Cottard had spoken about these things as if he were presenting an uncontested truth, as if he were merely relaying the truth. Yes, that was it – he spoke as if the truth were speaking through him, as if he were simply a spokesperson for the truth, a conduit even, and precisely because of this, his authority was unassailable. No wonder he had acquired the nickname of Emperor.

What threw Luc off balance in that morning's session was Doctor Cottard's almost brutal dismissal of the What If game as both necessary and futile. He had acknowledged that it is necessary that we sometimes wonder *What if* because in that way we become conscious of the karma we are living out; to ask 'What if' is to conduct a thought experiment of sorts: we identify and isolate one variable in the infinite network of variables that structure our lives and then we attempt to trace what difference it would have made if that one variable could be or had been replaced with another. In that way, we understand something about the forces that have shaped and continue to shape our lives. But he had also made it clear that the What If game is futile precisely because the network of variables that constitutes our lives is infinite, and nobody, not even a buddha, can fully comprehend the whole network and the consequences of how different it would be with or without one or other variable.

In Luc's imagination he immediately conjures up one such variable. *What if* he had left the house five minutes later that morning a few years ago? Then he would not have met Lucy at the bus stop (she had also overslept and, like him, missed the earlier bus, which is how they got talking) and they would not have become friends at school. Remove that one variable – 'meeting Lucy' – from the network of interconnected variables and try to imagine all the consequences and all the different permutations that his life could have assumed! It is not possible, Luc realises, as he approaches the pond at the far end of the garden. He does not come here often, but today just the idea of sitting next to a pool of water already has a calming effect on him. He sits down and looks over the water's surface, the great flat leaves of what he assumes must be a water lily of sorts spread out across it like stepping stones, just waiting for someone to come along and skip across the water, lightly moving from one leaf to the next.

And then there is the connection between the What If game and the impossibility of blame and forgiveness. Did he, Luc – or his soul, or whatever it is that keeps returning again and again – really choose to be born to the parents he knows? Was that his soul's decision? Did it purposefully choose to return to this world and to these parents because the context of their lives would provide him with the necessary starting point to experience what he needed in order for his soul to . . . to what? Purify itself? Resolve all its issues? Do souls have issues? Are souls nothing but a constellation of issues that live through one life after another, trying to burn off as many impurities as possible in the same way that a space rocket burns fuel on its gravity-defying way into the sky? And, if that is the case, then everything that has happened in his life up to this point has had something necessary about it, including meeting Lucy at the bus stop and the subsequent embarrassing sexual experiences with her and Stan. And what about the experience he had when he came so close to dying? What was that vision of a big, burning circle of light and the dark silence around it that promised such an eternal sense of knowing and belonging? Did his soul think – do souls think? – this life was over and start its journey home, only to be shocked back into this world again by the doctor who would not give up? And was his refusal to give up and the way he shocked Luc's soul back into this life also part of necessity?

Luc suddenly feels dizzy. It is all too much to contemplate. He feels caged and frustrated. He gathers a handful of small pebbles and stands up. He tries to throw one pebble onto each of the big, flat lily leaves. Most of them completely miss the leaves and of those that do fall on a leaf, only one remains perfectly poised in the indentation in the middle of the leaf. The others roll over the edge into the water or slip through unseen slits in the leaves and disappear into the deep, dark calm of the pond.

That night, after supper, Luc tries to watch TV in an attempt to distract himself from the questions and thoughts that have continued to haunt him throughout the day after he returned from the pond. He is the only person in the TV room and eventually gets up and switches the TV off. He is still troubled, restless. He goes to the kitchen and makes himself a cup of coffee. On the way out, he passes two of the other patients standing in the entrance having a conversation. They nod as he passes, but they do not attempt to elicit any response from him other than the nod they receive in return. Luc walks through the great front door and sits down on the top step of the staircase. He thinks about the interaction he has just had with the other patients. In their world, language exists; the world fragments into things and differences, which make language possible. In that world nobody is ever at the centre of the universe;

everyone has agreed to their place and all they are really trying to work out is how to survive and how to limit their responsibility to what impacts on their lives. But in Luc's world everything remains in sacred unity – days, and the time that marks the passing of each day, are indistinguishable from the timeless universe in which it feels to Luc as if he lives equidistant from everything, regardless of where he may find himself or where he goes. And it is exactly because of the fact that he lives equidistant from everything else that he feels strangely responsible for all the suffering in the world. There is no suffering that is not his.

Luc brings the mug to his lips, but the coffee is still too hot to drink. He puts the mug down next to him, stretches out on the cold marble step and looks up into the clear night sky. *The secret is to exercise your will in such a way that you know it coincides with the Divine Will – and believe me, when you make the right decisions, you always know that they are right because you will sense the coincidence.*

There was something urgent in the way Doctor Cottard had said that, as if he were passing on a coded message to Luc across the divide between the world of language and the world of unity. Can anything cross that divide? Surely, any message sent from the world of language to the world of unity would dissolve along the way, like a spaceship that was never built for travelling at the speed of light being pushed to break that barrier, only to dissolve into impossibility at the very moment it reached the speed of light? Surely, the same would happen in this case? Any message from the world of language to the world of unity can only disappear in the black hole of differences that exists somewhere in the space between the two worlds. Surely, such a message would get sucked into a destiny it was never meant to contain?

Luc suddenly and unexpectedly feels a surge of anger. That is why he is here. This whole process of 'rehabilitation' is devised to send him from one world to another, to force him, or at the very least to urge him or nudge him, to cross over from the world of unity into the world of difference. That is what this is all about – he can see it all so clearly now! They are forcing him to give up the vision of the ring of light and the experience of knowing and belonging he experienced at the Source: *that* knowing, *that* understanding, *that* utter and everlasting peace. They want him to 'move on'; in other words, to come back. But when he even briefly tries to imagine what 'coming back' means, it feels as if his soul is being ripped apart. There is no leaving this silence. If they force him to leave, he will implode long before he 'comes back' because crossing from one world to the other is impossible.

What is he going to do? Spend the rest of his life here? The whole business of this morning's session, the Emperor's attempt to seduce him – yes, that is what it was, he tried to seduce Luc into surrendering the comfort of his silence by making him believe that whatever decision he makes (if one could even call it a decision) would be the correct decision when he recognises that it coincides with God's will. But what does that mean? What if he chooses to stay where he is? Would that also be God's will?

Then a thought breaks the surface, a thought so terrifying that it could only be true: he has to burn the whole fucking place down. Tonight. That will put an end to it. His parents will have to come and take him home and leave him alone. Yes, that is what he must do. He must burn down this infernal halfway house for the undecided. He, Luc, is not undecided. He knows what he wants. He has the right to act and burn the place down and that is what he wants to do. *That* is his will. Let *that* coincide with the Divine Will!

6

Luc is huddled over the pile of wood he has gathered. From having been on school camps, he can recall the rudimentary elements necessary to start a fire with limited means – that is, without all the artificial fuel, sticks and newspaper that people nowadays use to start a fire. He has carefully assembled a pile of dried grass and stacked a pile of twigs and kindling on top of the grass. Then, on top of that he has placed a small pyramid of thicker pieces of wood and branches he gathered from the woods beyond the gazebo, near the elegant wooden walkway. It was a big pile and it had taken him the better part of two hours to gather all the wood and to stack it in such a way that it would readily ignite while still leaving enough space between the layers of grass, kindling and wood to allow for air to circulate and fuel the fire. The whole construction nearly came up to his shoulders. It was going to be a big one. He had realised that it would be impossible to set the centre itself on fire from the outside. Instead, he had decided that if he started a fire on the far side of the garden, a fire as ferocious as his intention, it would easily run along the dry winter trees all the way to the gazebo. It would destroy the gazebo and, from there, run along the dried grapevine walkway connecting the gazebo with the wooden veranda on the side of the rehabilitation centre. Next to the veranda, there is a wooden store that may or may not catch fire and that is as far as the fire will go. How far it goes will determine the extent of the damage he will manage to cause and whether he will have sufficient reason to phone his parents to come and fetch him. Either way, he will have made his point.

    Luc reaches into his pocket for the box of matches he had taken from the kitchen when he returned his empty coffee mug. He goes down on his haunches, takes out the first match and strikes it. He holds the little flame to the dried grass, but a gentle waft of air blows out the flame before the grass can take. He strikes a second match, but this one dies before he even gets it close to the grass. He takes a third match from the box and just as he is about to strike it, he hears the unmistakable sound of a presence in the woods to his left. He ducks behind the stack of wood and peers around the edge of it in the direction of the sound. At first, he cannot see anyone. But then he sees her. It is Angèle. She has just emerged from behind the gazebo and is about to enter the forest. *What is she doing up so late?* he wonders. *What is she up to? Where is she going? Is she running away? Does she perhaps need his help?* He hesitates and recedes behind the stack of wood. He bends over, hands on his knees, the box of matches still clutched tightly in his right hand. He drops his head. Now he is not sure what to do. He feels almost dizzy with inertia. He clearly has two choices, both of which are true, although he will have to choose between them. He has to make a decision and he has to decide quickly because there is not much time. On the one hand, he could start the fire and then run after Angèle. But then he would not have the pleasure of watching the fire catch and spread through the trees and to the gazebo, all the way to the main building. What would the point be of intentionally starting a fire but not watching that intention spread in order to consume the world it was designed to destroy? The fire would seem like an afterthought to the real action, which would be to catch up with Angèle. He decides against it. The fire he has in mind cannot be rushed and he needs to be a witness to its destruction. It cannot be a prelude to some other decision of greater ethical significance because that is what the fire will be reduced to: an accidental action, a preliminary action, something to get out of the way so that he can run off and pursue an action of true ethical significance.

He straightens up. The late evening fog has lifted. So has the confusion in his mind. He realises that he was momentarily paralysed by what appeared to be two irreconcilable choices, to start the fire and stay to watch it, or to forget about his plan and follow Angèle. But this need not be the choice. He can run after Angèle tonight in case she needs his help and perhaps come back later, or even the next night, to start the fire. What he does know with certainty is that the fire has to be a free-standing event – it cannot be an epilogue to another event, particularly if the ethical significance of the other event is such that *not* to honour it and to stay and light his fire would only make his own plan seem insignificant at best and selfish at worst. He decides that he will come back, either later tonight or another evening. If later tonight the ferocious fire of his determination to protect his world has subsided, he will wait for it to flare up again on another night. *What matters most*, he thought, *is that the decision has been made.* When exactly he gets to execute it is less important.

He crawls around the stack of wood and looks in the direction Angèle had gone. He cannot see anyone. He stands up and starts running towards the place where she must have entered the forest. Once he gets there, he stops and momentarily does not know which direction to go. Which way would she have gone? To the right, if she planned to follow the driveway all the way back to the main gate; straight ahead, if she thought of going to the main gate, but wanted to avoid the driveway in case anybody came looking for her; and to the left, if she wanted to avoid the main entrance altogether. In that case, she would make her way through the woods until she got to the far end of the estate and there climb over the fence and make her way to the road that leads to Dijon. Three ways in front of him and he has to choose one. He chooses to go straight and starts running until he reaches a point beyond which he is certain Angèle could not have gone further than him. *She had only a couple of minutes' head start,* he thinks. *She cannot possibly have run further than this.* He stops. Bent over, with his hands on his knees, he takes a couple of deep, controlled breaths, in and out. Then he gets up and starts running again, this time to the left, brushing the low-hanging, dry winter branches out of the way and pausing every now and then to listen for Angèle's footsteps.

7

After half an hour of running towards the western end of the estate, Luc gives up. He has clearly made the wrong choice. Worse, of the three choices he had, he chose two wrong ones. Angèle was obviously less concerned than he thought about someone noticing her absence and driving out towards the main gate in search of her. He circles back and after another twenty minutes of half running through the low-hanging branches of the forest, reaches the centre's meticulously kept lawn again, about a hundred metres away from his pile of wood. He slowly walks back to the scene of his future crime. He is exhausted. The decision to start the fire, followed by nearly two hours of wood gathering and stacking and then running through the forest has taken it out of him. He suddenly feels more tired than he has ever felt before. Back at his stack of wood, he lies down. He has to recollect himself before he decides what to do next. Would it still make sense to start his fire now? There is nothing left in him to make him believe that it would still make sense. And yet. He closes his eyes briefly to contemplate the possibility. He is overwhelmed by the reality of facing yet another decision. He is too tired for that. The fire will have to wait.

He must have dozed off because when he comes to, the moon has risen high above the forest and is hanging quietly over the garden, gently bathing the whole estate in pale blue light. Luc gets up. He slowly starts dismantling the pile of twigs and branches. The bigger pieces he throws in all directions into the forest. The twigs he manages to bundle together in his arms and distribute about ten metres into the forest. As a final act of obliterating any evidence of his failed intention, he kicks the remaining pieces of grass and twigs in all directions until there is no obvious sign of any attempt to start a fire. Once he is convinced that he has not left behind anything that will attract undue attention and raise the kind of suspicion that may prevent him from trying a second time, he starts walking across the lawn back in the direction of the main building. He knows the front door is never locked and at this time of the night nobody will be awake except for the two night nurses stationed on each floor. He is about to ascend the staircase to the second floor where his room is when he thinks, *What if Angèle had changed her mind and returned while he was asleep? What if she did not go through with her plan, whatever it may have been?* Perhaps he should check her room, in case she has come back. He quietly walks down the passage towards her room. He knows he will have to pass one of the night stations and at this time of the night the nurse will surely be nosy about any attempt to visit Angèle. He slowly approaches the night station and is relieved to see nobody behind the counter. The nurse must have gone for a walk or a smoke break, or perhaps she went to the kitchen to make coffee. He strains his ears to listen, but the only sounds he hears come from the small radio on the counter next to the vase of yellow flowers. He picks up his pace and heads for Angèle's room. Then he sees her. The nurse is fast asleep in her chair. Her body has lost the battle with gravity and has sagged halfway down the chair, her head lolling, her mouth inelegantly open. She is snoring softly. He sneaks past her and, without knocking, quietly pushes open the door with Angèle's name on it. His eyes require a couple of seconds to adjust to the darkness, but then his heart leaps. Angèle is in her bed, curled up, with the blanket pulled up over her head. Luc tiptoes over to the bed, afraid of waking her, if she is asleep. When he gets to the bed, he instinctively bends down, even though he is determined not to wake her. Angèle suddenly turns on her side and pulls the blanket off her. She is wide awake. At first, she looks startled to find someone in her room, but then she recognises him. She pushes herself up and flings her arms around him and starts to sob uncontrollably. Luc sits down on the bed next to her and, taking her in his arms, pulls her closer to him and gently strokes her hair.

'Oh, Luc – I don't know what happened. It just happened, but I don't know why. I can see it all so clearly, but I don't know why I did it.' She continues to sob and Luc strokes her hair. 'I think I killed a lot of people tonight, Luc . . . a lot. Oh my God, I don't know what got into me. They came, one after the other, the cars, I mean. I just couldn't take it any longer, Luc. I ran out of the main gate and out onto the road. When I reached the highway, I sat down in the middle of the road. I don't know why. I just, I just wanted to die. I sat down and pulled my legs up and put my head between my knees and waited. There were so many, Luc, and I just wanted them to run me over. The cars came, but they kept swerving – I suppose to miss me . . . and then they all crashed into the ditch along the side of the road. There were so many of them, Luc. I think at least three.' By now Angèle's sobbing had become so uncontrollable that she literally had to snatch the words from the pauses between one gasp for air and the next. 'Then . . . then . . . then . . . I . . . I . . . decided . . . I did not . . . not want to . . . die anymore and I . . . and I ran all the way back. Oh Luc, it . . . it . . . it is all . . . all . . . m-m-my fault. What . . . what did I d-do?'

Luc pulls her even closer to him and strokes her head, then all the way down her bony back, gently massaging every vertebra of her spine. How anybody this thin could run that far and back again, he does not know. After a while, she looks up. She is shaken and clearly distraught. She has stopped sobbing and her breathing has calmed. 'Luc, sometimes I just don't know. I just don't know,' she whispers, before dropping her head onto his shoulder. He brings her head closer to his and smells her hair. The words find him before he can do anything to stop them. 'I know. I know,' he says.

He rests his head against hers and closes his eyes. *What if I had not planned on starting that fire tonight?*

Harvesters III

8

I have given up on my disbelief because it had started to wear me down. There is never going to be a way to explain how I could have witnessed three people walk through a shop window and disappear from sight or how, immediately after their disappearance from this world, I rushed to the same window and found it as solid and impenetrable as any other glass pane. It is not to be comprehended and for a while I lived my life in a suspended state of disbelief in which I believed neither the truth of my old world nor the new one that had revealed itself to me. My life continued much as it had, but along a track somewhere in the middle of these two worlds. It is difficult to believe that you exist and that the things you do make sense when everything is overshadowed by the fact that you have witnessed something you cannot explain. You have to believe it because you witnessed it – in my case, on more than one occasion – but because you cannot comprehend it, you end up disbelieving what you believe to be true. As a result, my every encounter with a student or colleague, every meeting, is overshadowed by a sense of unreality. A voice inside me keeps asking, *What makes you think this world is more real than the impossible world in which people walk through shop windows?* I suddenly have a constant companion who accompanies me to every meeting, who sits in on every consultation and takes part in every conversation with students and colleagues.

This companion reminds me a bit of the Imposter I had to deal with for some time, a voice that made me believe I was faking it, that the life I lived, which I thought was real, was in fact not real; that there was another reality more real than the one I was living and that as long as I chose to live in this world, I was nothing more than an Imposter who would one day get caught out. This Imposter went everywhere with me, silently observing me in every encounter, without saying anything, even though I knew he was constantly trying to get me to ask, *Is this encounter real? Is this world more real for being explicable and is the other world any less real for being inexplicable?*

And so, the idea of domesticating the impossible has emerged as the only way forward. I have to collapse the distinction between my possible and impossible worlds; I somehow have to bring the impossible home until it becomes just another part of my ordinary life. This intuitively feels like the right way to go about things, but how on earth does one domesticate the impossible into possibility, the extraordinary into the ordinary? How does one collapse the difference?

For a while, I considered the obvious way of doing this – to tell Juliet everything. But the problem is that in the end everything leads back to Luc. Juliet knows Luc is a character from my novel *Imitation*, so how can I possibly tell her that I had seen him on campus one day, and then subsequently on two other occasions when I saw, first just him, and then him and two other people walk through a window? She just would not believe me. Nobody would. I knew what would happen. Imagine, for example, I decided to tell my neighbour Marius everything. I would call him over again one day when I heard him sweeping leaves and he would say, 'Yo! What's up?'

And I would reply, 'Come over. I would like to tell you something.'

Once he replied with the predictable, 'What? You want to show me a finger again?' and I said, 'No, but I can fill you in on what the police have managed to find out' and so on, he would come over and we would sit in the deck chairs. I would take a deep breath before I started to tell him everything. Now, until the moment before I started to tell him the whole story, we would inhabit the same universe and live in the same world, in which we considered each other sane, mature, intelligent men, who have an amicable relationship as neighbours. Then, eventually I would get to the point where I had to explain who Luc was and the moment I uttered the phrase 'a character from my previous novel', the moment we got over the first round of banter – 'You're having me on' and 'No, I'm not', '*Eish*, man, is this some weird kind of game?' and so on – the moment he realised that I was being truthful and that I insisted in all seriousness on the truth of what I was telling him, the world we had until then shared would split off and another, second world would be created: an abyss would open between the world in which Marius (and the me he thought he knew) lives, and the world in which I (and the Marius I had hoped would believe me) live. From that moment onwards, he would live in a world inhabited by himself and a spectre of me (the me he thought he knew) and I would continue to live in my world with a spectre of Marius (the one who could not follow me into my new world). Gradually, we would become estranged from each other, conscious of the fact that from now on we each live in our own world. Long before I would even get to the two episodes when I saw first Luc and then Luc and two companions walk through the window, Marius would have stood up and gone home and I would be left alone on my side of the wall listening to him sweeping leaves. *How does he do that?*

 No, telling somebody else, whether Marius from next door or Juliet, would always risk the danger of ending the same way. Instead of domesticating the impossible world that I had been introduced to and unifying it with my familiar world, I would achieve nothing more than to replicate the number of worlds I have to contend with: the multiple worlds Marius and I live in, the multiple worlds Juliet and I live in and so on. No, if domesticating the impossible meant telling them what I have experienced so far, then witnessing was not the solution. I would have to do this without involving a witness.

 And so, I conclude that the only other solution is to repeat the occurrence of the impossible so many times that it would eventually become an ordinary part of my life. The secret, I decide, lies not in witnessing, but in repetition. I have to go back in the evening and watch the strangers walk through the window again and again until it becomes a commonplace in my life – in fact, until it becomes such an ordinary thing that I may, one evening in the distant future, sit there, notice them walk through the window and return to the book I am reading. At that point, I decide, when it would be of no consequence whether I am there or not there, watching them walk through the window or ignoring them while they do it, my two worlds would be reconciled again. I would no longer experience this strange sense of living in a world relative to another. My two worlds would finally be unified. That was my personal Unified Theory of Relativity.

And so I started to live a strange double life. By day, the self-doubting philosopher, who gets on with the ordinary business of life, who exchanges banter with Maretha every morning when he arrives at work and spends his days administering a department, holding meetings and teaching classes and, by night, the stalker of strangers from another world, who disappear through the window of a curio shop in a quiet shopping centre.

Every night, I return to Harvesters. I make myself comfortable (I even started to take a cushion because the pub stores its cushions inside at night), some snacks and something to drink. Some nights the strangers arrive and other nights they do not. When they do, it is always the same, as if they, too, are committed to repeating the same action over and over again. Even though it is not always the same people and even though Luc is not always among them, all of them always walk with the same heavy gait – as if walking requires not just attention, but *intention*, and they behave as if they had been trained for the moment. There are always three of them and the only constant is one woman who is always present and behaves a bit like a tour guide. I soon gave her the name Anya because she looked like an Anya to me. She would always keep watch and, when the three of them stopped behaving like tourists who are window-shopping and eventually stopped in front of the curio shop window, she would be the one to keep looking out for potential witnesses while the other two continued to look at the crafts on display inside the shop. Eventually, after one more quick glance around, she would turn to them and nod and the first one would disappear through the window, followed shortly after by the second.

At first, I thought the obvious thing would be to film them on my cell phone. But that did not work. The distance was too great and there was insufficient light to even register an image on my screen from such a distance. Feeling, nonetheless, the need to somehow record what I was witnessing, I took a sketchbook with me. On the first couple of nights, I made some sketches of the shop window. Then, over the next few weeks, the strangers made four more appearances and I sketched as best I could what I witnessed. If they did not see anyone – and there was never anyone but me, huddled in the darkness of the booth – Anya would give them the go-ahead nod. Then the first would walk through the windowpane, followed by the second and, eventually, by Anya herself.

The truth of my personal Unified Theory of Relativity was soon established. Things started to become as predictable as most things in life – so much so, in fact, that soon, even while watching them go through their motions, I would start thinking about other things. *When do they arrive? Where do they arrive? Is there some other time of the day or night when they suddenly emerge from inside the window to walk out into this world, or do they arrive somewhere else? How does it work? Does the shopkeeper with the mysterious smile have anything to do with this? Is this whole business the source of his mysterious ways? And could this explain how he knew things about me that I had never told him?* As my theory predicted, the bafflingly impossible gradually mutated into the weird and later, the predictable – never quite crossing the line into the possible, but nonetheless becoming so predictable that what I was witnessing lost the eerie sense of being impossible. This led to the formulation of the first axiom of my Unified Theory of Relativity: possibility = impossibility × predictability. Gradually, the Imposter who accompanied me throughout the day and whispered in my ear,

'How do you know this moment is real?' faded into the background and my daily existence assumed its former status of being not quite as real as it used to be, but real enough for me to live in it without that terrible feeling of inhabiting two different worlds simultaneously, not understanding the one and feeling like a fake in the other.

I realise that I have managed to restore some semblance of normality and balance again when, one fine Saturday morning, I walk past the curio shop and pause just long enough in front of the window to see if I can see the shopkeeper, who many months ago asked me, 'What are you unwilling to feel?' And, indeed, there he is, serving a customer, smiling his dreamy smile of contentment. He had grown a beard in the meanwhile, but other than that the shop seems pretty much the same, even though I knew what might happen there later that same evening. Even that knowledge suddenly no longer feels like a secret. I turn away from the window and walk past the parking marshall, Dreyer, who is hanging around looking bored. 'How're you doing, friend?' he asks, as I walked past.

'Don't ask, don't tell,' I grin and head for the exit.

Luc's Heart Goes Out

9

The week following her failed suicide attempt, Luc and Angèle purposefully avoided each other. Like two students who drank too much at a party and found themselves in bed, only to realise that one of them was too drunk to have sex and, having to abort the whole enterprise, avoided each other afterwards, Luc and Angèle had crossed a line that night, a line they knew existed between them and that I know Luc had fantasised about crossing. I am less sure that Angèle wanted to cross the thin line between friendship and intimacy. I do not think she was ready for it yet. She was too self-conscious about her body, too certain that she was too fat to be loved. In short, I think she was too caught in a reverie of self-loathing to be receptive to love. So, she avoided Luc. Not in any extreme kind of way – it was not as if she did not greet him or walked the other way when she saw him approaching or anything like that. She just no longer headed for the rose garden or the gazebo between therapy sessions and they did not spend hours sitting together on one of the benches in the garden. She kept to the staircase at the entrance and socialised with the other patients, smoking cigarettes between sessions.

Angèle avoided Luc, in part, because she was embarrassed – not about the fact that she had attempted suicide, but because she had failed. Macabre as it may seem, when she woke up the next morning and even before the full realisation of the suffering she had caused others hit her, she had the thought that both she and Luc were such amateurs when it came to suicide. *Such amateurs* – that is the phrase that crossed her mind. A wicked, sardonic, dark thought that made her open her eyes and sit up in bed, only to be hit by the full recollection of what had happened the previous night. Yes, she had walked all the way to the edge of the forest, turned right, which she knew would eventually lead her to the driveway leading from the main road to the sanatorium; and, yes, she did think of hitch-hiking to Dijon, where she had vague (and, she now realised, childish) fantasies about starting a new life on her own, unencumbered by her past. She had seen a poster of Dijon on the wall of the night nurse's station and it seemed like a friendly place, with generous people who would not expect anything more of her than she was willing to give. But then, by the time she had reached the road, the thought of continuing her life elsewhere, the same life riddled with the same paradoxes and subtle mutations of self-loathing, overcame her. That was when she walked into the middle of the road and sat down, pulled her knees up, folded her arms around her knees and, with her head burrowed between her arms, waited for the inevitable impact. When the headlights of the first car swept over her, she braced herself and thought, *This is it!* But the car swerved and ended up crashing into a ditch off to her left. The next car, which must have been close to the first, swerved off to the right and similarly crashed into the ditch. It was only after the third car also swerved to avoid her – and, like the other two cars, crashed into the ditch – that the full impact of her actions, or rather her inaction, hit her. It was a terrible moment of absolute choices. *What if she helped them? What if she just ran away?* She had only a couple of seconds to make a decision but *what if* she made the wrong decision? If she helped them, the consequence may be that all would be revealed, and she would go to jail. On the other hand, if she left them there, somebody might die. In the end, Angèle decided, quite rationally, that if three cars followed so close to one another, then another car would probably come soon. Probability dissolved uncertainty and she ran back to the rehabilitation centre, sneaked in through the back door and, touching her way back against the wall, slipped past the night nurse's station, back to her room and into her bed, where she pulled the blanket over her head. She lay there for what felt like an eternity when she heard somebody open the door.

It is the night nurse, she thought. She had been caught out! The nurse was going to ask her where she had been and she would not be able to lie. She would have to say what had happened and the next morning, when the accidents would be in the news, that would be the end of it. Finally: suicide by consequence. But it was not the night nurse. It was Luc. She did not know what he knew or why he came in just at that moment. *What had he witnessed? What did he know?* She did not know and she did not care. All that mattered was the way he sat down next to her on the bed and pulled her close to him; how she sat up and leaned into his arms sobbing, wiping her tears on his green T-shirt, half confessing that she had done something terrible, only to feel his hand caress her hair and her back, a warmth of love and acceptance she had never experienced before. And then the most extraordinary thing happened. As he stroked her hair, Luc spoke for the first time since she had known him. 'I know. I know,' he said.

After so many weeks of having to endure and make sense of his strange silence and his silent perseverance, she heard his voice for the first time. And it was an ordinary voice. Perhaps a bit hoarse, but steady nonetheless. The knowing that his voice articulated was audible in the articulation itself. They sat like that for a long time. When her heart stopped racing and her breath became regular, deep and calm, he gently helped her back under the covers. She looked up at him and he smiled down at her. 'Sleep now. Tomorrow you can tell me everything.'

But she would not. Not the next day and also not over the next couple of days. Their fleeting intimacy came to an unexpected end because Angèle could not decide how much to tell Luc about what had happened that night. He must have been able to piece it all together, she had realised, because the story of the accidents was all over the news. For some or other reason, three cars had crashed into ditches on either side of the road just outside the famous sanatorium. One driver died at the scene and two were rushed to the nearest hospital, where another died shortly after. Two dead. Of course, the obvious suspicion was that somebody from the sanatorium may have had something to do with the accidents and two detectives showed up, presumably to meet and talk with Doctor Cottard. But he must have reassured them that none of his staff or clients could have had anything to do with the accident because the detectives did not return.

Angèle did not tell Luc what had happened that night because she did not know him well enough to be absolutely certain that he would not betray her. There was that. But probably more important was the fact that in the back of her mind she remained haunted by the wicked and bizarre thought she had woken up with the following morning: *Amateur. You can't even kill yourself.* She recognised the thought and where it came from. It was a version of a deeper thought that had haunted her for as long as she could remember: *You cannot get anything right; you always fail at things; you fail because you're not in control. Learn to control all the variables in life and you will succeed. As long as you fail to control all the variables, you will fail at everything you do.* Yes, in Angèle's callous world of self-loathing, she experienced her own failure more intensely than the fact that she had been responsible for the death of two other people. It was as if their lives and deaths could not penetrate her shield of protective self-doubt. It was not that she did not care or did not experience sadness about the consequences of her actions. Rather, it was as if what she knew she needed to feel – remorse, guilt, sadness, regret – had to take their place in line. She was processing her emotions one at a time, careful to remain in control of what she allowed herself to feel. And the morning after that disastrous night, the first thought in line was that she felt like a failure.

For Luc's part, he noticed that Angèle was avoiding him and he did not mind. On the contrary, he was grateful because he, too, needed space. It did not require much of an imagination to work out that Angèle somehow had something to do with the accident reported in the news and, yes, he was horrified by that fact. But they did not know each other that well and, if he were in her shoes, he would probably also want to avoid the one person who knew about his culpability. And yet he was drawn to her because, when he closed his eyes, he could still smell her hair and feel her thin body under his hand as he caressed her. But he also knew that, given her mysterious involvement in the bizarre accident, it was the wrong moment to pursue intimacy with her. She had too much on her plate. She would signal when she was ready. All he had left of that night was the green T-shirt, the front of which had been soaked with her tears, but now only carried the faint smell of her perfume. He kept it in his drawer and when he really missed her or missed the moment they had shared, he took it out and held it to his nose and drew in the fading smell of her tenderness.

As for the words that had so unexpectedly left his mouth, he was surprised by how uneventful this huge but ultimately strangely insignificant leap was. He did not have to force himself to speak, but neither did he feel that he had betrayed himself by speaking. The unity of the world was not shattered, as he had expected it would be, and nothing was betrayed. Saying those words was as easy as breathing out and the words were as light as air – so light, in fact, that they seemed to have the quality of sounds produced by nothing. As he folded Angèle into his arms, the thought crossed his mind that whether one speaks or not makes no difference. Silence is haunted by language and speaking is haunted by silence. Language makes differences, this he knew and resisted for such a long time because the kind of belonging he experienced in his encounter with the Godhead did not care for differences. *No, that's not right,* he corrected himself. It is not as if divine belonging did not care for differences. There is nothing careless about recognising and staying with the origin of all things – if anything, divine belonging *is* care, the ultimate care. The origin takes care of the world; it is the world's caretaker and care *is* compassion. No wonder, then, he realised, as he recalled Angèle's breath slowing down until her head had relaxed into him, that in a moment that called for true compassion, a moment that required of him to recognise and take up his place in this world, something deep inside of him knew what was needed to make a difference.

10

I imagine it was only two weeks later that Luc and Angèle found themselves sitting together again on the bench in the gazebo. Neither of them referred to the night of the accidents or the intimate moment they had shared. That night had been so exceptional and both of them had been so reluctant to speak about it that the only way forward was to return to the beginning of their friendship and to get to know each other again, as if from scratch, by sharing simple thoughts about the centre, Doctor Cottard and some of the other patients.

'Do you believe all this stuff Cottard is selling us about reincarnation and whatnot?' asked Angèle.

'I'm not sure,' Luc said. 'I'm still trying to decide. I'm inclined to say it makes sense, somehow, but I don't know why or how.'

'"Subtle is the body, Angèle." I mean, what the fuck? The drama of it all. Did he do that to you too? Stand by the window and let you sit there for all eternity, making you feel like you had walked into the wrong room and then the . . .' – at this point her voice dropped to imitate Doctor Cottard's deep, soothing voice, '"Subtle is the body." I mean, really. What is the man on?'

Luc felt a pang of disappointment. He remembered the day well and how disjointed he had felt sitting there, Doctor Cottard's voice just one more sound drifting through his head, along with the twitter of the birds and the sounds drifting up from the kitchen. At some level, he must have thought he was special; that Doctor

Cottard was addressing this one person alone, with a statement only intended for him, Luc, and that he had prepared a special kind of treatment for Luc that involved everything he had said during the two sessions they had had so far, about reincarnation, parents and forgiveness. What a fool he had been. That is obviously Doctor Cottard's technique. Everyone gets the same treatment. Along with the pang of disappointment, Luc could also sense relief. It felt good to be just another person. Nothing special, nothing extraordinary. Just another lost soul. But was he lost? He remained quiet for a while and reflected on everything that had happened since his arrival. There had indeed been subtle shifts in his mood and the way he felt about himself and his life – even he could recognise that. He could not name these shifts or what they amounted to, but he could feel them in his body. He could sense that somehow these shifts were related to the sessions with Doctor Cottard, but he could not explain just how. 'I think there is something to it,' he repeated softly, as he stretched out his legs and looked at the ground in front of him.

'I don't buy it. It's just too easy. I won't even go into how you possibly explain to a child who has been abused by his or her parents, or who grew up in extreme poverty and misery and whatnot that it's all karma, that their soul knew what it was looking for. It just shifts the blame away from parents and society back onto the poor soul and that is fucked up. First, you get screwed over and then you're told you were looking for it. What annoys me even more is the holier-than-thou dismissal of blame and forgiveness. I realised that this morning when my parents came through for family therapy. Did you know they were here? No? Well, probably a good thing. Anyway, I got it out of my system this morning.'

"'I said to them that I had felt unloved for as long as I could remember – which, of course, did not go down well. Mother cried and Father just shook his head in disbelief. 'How is that possible?' he asked. 'How many times did I not tell you that I love you unconditionally?' Such a difficult thing, Luc, this thing of unconditional love. People think that when they say, 'I love you unconditionally' it means you can never doubt their love, question the limits of their capacity to love or even suggest to them that as long as they do not love themselves, they have no right to make such a statement. It's almost as if people use the phrase in order to absolve everyone from doing the really difficult work of love. Know what I mean?'

Luc did not look at her. He was staring at the ground in front of him, hands in his pockets, nodding thoughtfully.

'I said I knew they loved me, at some level, but it's almost as if I couldn't trust their love; as if it weren't real.'

'Eventually,' Angèle said to Luc – and by this point she could tell from the irregularity of his breathing that he knew exactly what she was talking about – 'I got angry, really angry at them. Madame Beliveau always encourages me to get angry; she says it's a healthy emotion – did your parents ever tell you anger is a healthy emotion? Anyway, that's when I told them that I thought they were both too fucked up by their own parents to love a child, never mind love it unconditionally. They didn't take that well either. They both started to cry and I kind of felt sorry for them. But it was so good to express that anger! And you know what? It did make me think. Afterwards in my room, I thought: I am right. Their love, as well intentioned and well meaning as it may have been, was always a dry love. Their love was never tangible like a summer rain or even like winter snow; it was dry like a desert wind. In that instant when I told them their love was never *real*, I understood that people who are themselves damaged cannot love anything but their own damage. They spend their lives parenting themselves, trying to grow up, to leave the damage behind. In the process they get married, have children and buy dogs and so on and yes, they try their best to love all of that, but they cannot bring themselves to make their love *real*, not because they are inadequate or unworthy people, but because love only becomes real when you leave your self behind. But they can't. Their damage is their first-born. I may be an only child, but I have always had an invisible sibling to contend with. What I got was a dry love, like rain that is not wet, or snow that is not cold, or a winter sun that does not warm the skin. Fuck it,' Angèle said and lit another cigarette. She offered Luc one, more out of habit than anything else because she knew he did not smoke. 'I think what I worked out this morning is that a love rooted in one's own damage is a conceptual kind of love: it looks like rain, it has the appearance of snow and it feels like sun, but it is neither wet, cold or warm. You can't feel a dry love.'

I wish I could say that these words meant something to Luc, that he suddenly turned his head to Angèle and said, 'I know what you mean.' But he did not. Other than the irregularity of his breathing and the occasional nod, he gave no sign of companionship nor of understanding. He heard everything she said, but at the same time it was as if someone was talking to him from the other side of the world, a world he no longer lived in and from which he had become estranged. After a while, he realised that she was waiting for him to say something. He had to say something – comfort her, agree with her, affirm her anger. But he could not. What Doctor Cottard had said about blame and forgiveness suddenly made even more sense to him than before. Or perhaps it just made sense to him for the first time. Doctor Cottard was right, he suddenly understood. And he no longer had a choice about what to believe and what not. He could no longer just let the indecision be, or wait for it to resolve who he was and what he believed in. Something inside him had decided while he was listening to Angèle raging on about her parents. Somewhere inside himself, he suddenly knew. But still, Angèle needed him to say something. He thought back to what she had said. All the beautiful metaphors she had used to describe love by its opposite – a rain that is not wet; a snow that is not cold. Yes, it is indeed a strange kind of love that makes one feel so desolate – dry rain, warm snow. He breathed out, a long, slow breath that made him feel as if he had sunk into the bench.

Then he said: 'What about air, the air we breathe; the air that surrounds us and connects us to the world; the unseen cement that holds it all together? What about space? Can air and space be metaphors for empty love? Your love is like solid air, as heavy as air? Your love is an empty space, a solid void?'

It was her turn to say nothing and so they just sat there. It was nearly time for lunch. They would soon have to start walking back. Then, as if she suddenly remembered something, Angèle turned to him and said, 'Have you heard about the lightweights and the heavyweights?'

Luc thought for a second and said, 'Of course. You call somebody a lightweight when . . .'

'No, not that. I mean here at the centre. Have you heard them talk about lightweights and heavyweights?'

Luc did not have to think for too long. Because he had kept silent for so long, nobody spoke to him and he had generally not been interested in their conversations either. He would be the last person anyone would share a secret with. 'No.'

'Ha!' Angèle said and pulled out another cigarette, her hands shaking slightly with excitement. She lit it, took a drag and turned to Luc, one leg half bent and folded flat on the bench between them. 'It's like this. Those who buy the whole incarnation story are called the lightweights; those who don't are called heavyweights. You, my friend,' she said and took another drag of her cigarette, 'are apparently a lightweight. I'm a heavyweight.'

'And, is that a good thing?' Luc asked.

'What, to be a lightweight?'

'Yes.'

'Fuck knows,' she said. And now she looked at him with an expression on her face he had never seen before, the expression of someone who is privy to a secret they are not supposed to even know exists as a secret and who relishes the moment of breaking the prohibition. 'But I know it has something to do with the portal.'

'What portal?' he asked.

Angèle rolled her eyes in mock despair. 'Christ, Luc. You really have been living with your head up your arse. Have you not heard about the portal?'

'What portal?' he repeated, and even he could hear the urgency in his voice.

Part IV

Attachment

Harvesters IV

1

I could measure the degree of normality my life had assumed again by the fact that I decided one night that I was ready to discuss the whole strange business with Juliet. The time had come. I had worked through Luc's appearance in my life and the strange disappearance of people through the curio shop window as much as I could on my own. I had reached the limits of my understanding and it was time to take a leap of faith, to tell Juliet everything and to hear what she had to say about it all. Of course, there was the risk that in doing so our worlds could split off from each other and I could be left alone in this world while she went on to live in another world inhabited by herself and the spectre of me (the 'me' she would remember from the days 'before he got all weird'). But that was a risk I had to take. It was unavoidable.

So, one night I packed my rucksack with the usual sketchbook, a bottle of whisky, some food and a small cushion to sit on and went to the shopping centre an hour earlier than I usually did, so that Juliet and I would have enough time to talk. It was not going to be easy and we would need time. Earlier that evening I had texted her and we had agreed on a time when I would phone.

She answers after the second ring. 'Hello, darling,' I say.

'Hello, yourself,' she says.

I can tell by the sounds in the background that I am on speakerphone and she is making supper. 'What are you making for supper?'

'Ah, nothing interesting. The grilled tofu thing André taught us.'

We chat a bit about our days, work, and the drought in her part of the country. I jot down a couple of items she reminds me to add to the monthly budget. We will get paid later that evening and over time I have become the one to work out the monthly budget – which had become a bit more complicated since we were now running two households. Then I take the plunge.

'You won't believe who I saw the other day.'

She thinks for a couple of seconds. 'Your old high-school flame. What's her name again? Didn't you say she also lives in Pretoria now?'

'Yes, she does, but no, not her,' and before Juliet can say anything, I continue. 'You won't guess, so I may as well tell you.'

'Well, what a fun person you are,' she says. 'Anyway, I'm all ears.'

I hear her sit down and pour a glass of wine. I am no longer on speakerphone, which is a relief. I look at my watch. I have been rushing the conversation because we need time to talk before they come – if they do. 'Luc,' I say, as if it were the most ordinary thing in the world.

Silence. A sip of wine. 'Luc? As in *Luc* Luc?'

'Yip,' I reply and take a deep sip of whisky. This is going to be tricky.

'Um, that's unexpected,' she says, 'but also not. You always had a special relationship with him . . .' and then, almost as an afterthought, 'or what you thought of him. But what do you mean you *saw* him? And where did you see him?'

'From my office. I was standing at the window looking down on the square and saw him standing down there looking up at my office. I could swear he was looking straight at me.'

'He knows where you work? A bit odd, don't you think? And, what did you do?'

'Well, I ran down . . . I mean, I ran out of the office and took the lift down and ran around to where I knew he'd be standing, but when I got there he was gone.'

'And you're sure it was him?'
'Positive.'
'Did anyone else see him?'

The philosopher in me got slightly irate. 'Well, I'm sure lots of people saw him, but if they didn't know it was him, they wouldn't realise they were seeing him – that it was Luc, I mean.'

'Don't get irritated now,' she says. 'This is all very strange, so just bear with me.'

'Sorry.'

'So, what did you do?'

'It was all very strange. I phoned Maretha from where I was standing and asked her to look down over the square. I described to her what Luc was wearing, but she could not see him. It was like he had just disappeared. What was even weirder was that she could not see me either – even though I was standing right there where he had been, looking back up at our office windows.'

'So, she was standing in the exact same place?'

'Well, more or less. She was in her office . . .'

'Sure, but that's just two or three metres away. And she was looking down at you standing exactly where Luc had been standing when you saw him, but she couldn't see you?'

'Yip.'

There is a long silence. I sip more whisky and hear Juliet top up her wine.

'And did you see him again after that?'

This was going better than I had expected, so I plucked up my courage and continued. 'Yip, and here's where it gets really weird. Remember that shopping centre with the Harvesters place where we went for tapas a few times when you last came to visit?'

'Yes – nice place. Lots of those fever trees in the parking lot. I loved their luminous green. A bit Dali, I thought.'

'Well, I'm sitting there now.'

'At this time of the evening? I thought you said they close early on weekday evenings.'

'They do. I am here to see if Luc will come again. I've seen him here a few times. First, on his own and then a couple of nights later with two other people.' I can hear Juliet wants to say something, but I cannot let her interrupt me now, so I just pretend not to notice and keep talking. 'It's a bit odd. They came and stood around in front of that curio shop window, remember the one where they sell of that touristy Afro-kitsch? Well, they looked around to see if anyone was watching them and then, one by one, they walked right through the window and disappeared into the shop.'

'They what? Oh, come on!'

'Yip. They walked right through the windowpane into the shop and disappeared. It is the weirdest thing. I've been coming back night after night to watch them do it and to try and make sense of it, but I can't really say that I have.'

There is a long silence. Juliet is processing what I have told her. I have no idea what to expect and so I just wait. I hear her sip on her wine and I take small sips of whisky. After what feels like an eternity, she says, 'Remember a while ago when I said you should get out more?'

'Yes.'

'Well, this is not what I meant.'

'I know,' I say and, in a lame attempt to emulate her humour, 'but this is better than watching TV.'

'I believe you,' she says. 'I mean, about Luc.'

The relief is instant and deeply comforting. *There will be no splitting off of our worlds after all,* I think. *We will remain together in this world.*

'But I do need to figure it out,' she adds. There is the background noise again of a chair scraping on the floor and I hear her lift a pot lid, stirring something and putting the lid back on.

'Are you sitting down again?' I ask.

'Yes, had to,' she says and continues. 'You know what? I think you going there to watch him appear and disappear like that, night after night, is your way of letting him go. I think you've started to let go of him.'

'Just disappear, not appear,' I correct her.

'What do you mean?'

'I don't know how or where they appear, but it's not here. Unless that happens at some other time of the night. It is possible, I suppose. I just haven't given it much thought.'

'So, here's the question,' she says and pauses for a second, presumably to find the right words. 'What will you do when he stops showing up?'

'I don't know. I can't think that far ahead. I first need to figure out what this is and how it works.'

'Have you tried it?'

'What, walking through the window?'

'Yes. That would be one way of eliminating some of the options.'

'Yes, I did. After the first time I saw them do it.'

'And?'

'Well, I didn't walk into another universe, if that's what you're hoping for. Just slap bang into the glass.'

There is a long silence, interrupted only by the sound of us sipping our drinks.

'What you drinking?' I ask.

'I think you need a witness,' she says, after a while. 'I think you should try again, but with somebody watching you when you do it.'

I think about her suggestion for a couple of seconds. 'I kind of get what you're saying,' I say, 'but also not. Having someone witness me trying to follow them through the windowpane makes sense somehow, but I don't know why.'

'Well,' she says, 'there are two options – either you will walk through the window or you won't. Maybe the outcome depends on whether somebody is observing you. Life is like that. When we suffer, we want somebody to witness our suffering and when we're happy, we want to share our happiness. Having a witness somehow makes things more real. When our suffering or our happiness is not witnessed by someone else, it often doesn't feel quite as real. It's as if the act of being witnessed when we suffer or experience happiness makes the experience real. That sort of thing. Maybe this is one of those cases. If you don't have a witness and you walk into the window, well, that's one thing. But maybe you will only be able to follow them when someone observes you trying.'

What Juliet is saying suddenly makes more than just intuitive sense. 'I think you're onto something.'

'Always am. So, what are you going to do tonight? Just sit there and wait for them?'

'I might as well,' I reply. 'I'm here now.'

Third Session with the Emperor, in which Luc Makes a Demand

2

They are sitting across from each other at the desk. Doctor Cottard, dressed in a white long-sleeve shirt and an indigo waistcoat, but without a bow tie today, is gently swaying from right to left in his swivel chair, fingertips pressed against each other, contemplating how to proceed. Luc had arrived for his session and, as if it were the most ordinary thing in the world, said, 'Good morning, Doctor Cottard' as he entered the room.

Doctor Cottard had heard that Luc had broken his silence. For a couple of days, it was all everyone at the centre talked about. But he paid no attention to the stories and did not show any surprise when other clients mentioned it in their sessions. He subsequently heard Luc's voice a couple of times – in the corridor outside his office, in the dining room and sometimes even drifting up to his window from the great staircase leading up to the main entrance below. He had intended to start this session in the same way as the previous two, talking and talking, pretending that he did not know that for Luc something fundamental had shifted. He had decided to wait for Luc to indicate that he was ready to speak. But Luc had surprised him with this greeting, and had then said nothing more. Now, Doctor Cottard is contemplating whether he should simply keep talking or ask Luc a direct question to make it clear that he knows that Luc is able to share his thoughts with him. He decides to proceed as usual.

'That's how we got to the idea that addiction is the wrong answer to the right question, Luc. Remember that? A soul that arrives in the world whose inherent goodness is not affirmed will find itself detached from other people and suffer perpetual and extreme self-doubt. The soul knows that it has to form attachments and, if the attachment to others doesn't work, the person will form attachments to other objects, things, and actions in an attempt to fulfil his unsatisfied need for belonging. Addictions, or to be more precise, *satisfying* our addictions, does indeed give us a momentary sense of belonging and of living in relation to something outside of us. But it is not a healthy attachment. It is, as I said, a fleeting attachment and offers us at best a quick-fix sense of what it would feel like to belong. Because it is a quick fix, it cannot but leave us disappointed when it wears off and so we have to repeat the same action again and again in order to sustain the temporary attachment and our momentary sense of belonging.'

Doctor Cottard waits for a couple of seconds to see if Luc wants to say something, but the young man just looks at him thoughtfully. Doctor Cottard decides to take one step closer to getting Luc to participate in the conversation. He briefly raises his right hand as if to adjust his bow tie, but then, as if remembering he is not wearing one, his hand stops halfway and slowly returns to the arm rest.

'Luc, I know that something fundamental has happened to you since we last met. I've heard your voice, out there in the corridor and sometimes . . . down there,' he waves lazily in the direction of the window. 'This is our last session, but because you have not said anything in any of our sessions – which is, of course, fine, as I told you the first time – but today is different. I would like to know if anything of what I have been saying makes any sense to you. Did anything I told you have . . . shall we say, purchase? Do you want to give me some idea or shall I just continue with my train of thought?'

Luc nods. Doctor Cottard is slightly perplexed, if only for a second. Then he continues, 'Very well then. The solution or the way forward, as I see it, consists in systematically replacing our wrong answers or flawed attachments with nurturing ones, doing what makes you feel loved and what makes you feel good about your body; doing things that are meaningful in themselves and not because they serve a purpose; to become conscious of the world around you, to enjoy the company of others and being in the world. While we *cannot* consciously create nurturing attachments, we *can* consciously make an effort to be open to them and to enjoy them when they offer themselves and start making us feel good about ourselves. That is the most important thing: to allow oneself to feel what is nurturing about nurturing attachments, to own and enjoy being nurtured.'

Doctor Cottard stops, a smile on his face. 'I'm sorry – I was getting a bit carried away there, wasn't I? Looks like you want to say something?'

'What is the portal?' Luc asks, 'and where does it lead to?'

If Doctor Cottard is surprised by the question, he does not show it. Instead, he simply asks, 'How do you know about it?'

'Angèle told me.'

Doctor Cottard reflects for a long moment. Then, with a slight hesitation in his voice, 'And what exactly did she tell you?'

'Not much. She doesn't seem to know much about it, just that people sometimes go through it and that it leads to another world . . . or something like that.'

Doctor Cottard leans back in his chair and, realising that this is going to be what the conversation is about, adjusts the collar of his shirt where the bow tie would normally have been and replies, 'Indeed, it does and before you ask what it is all about, I'll tell you. It is part of the therapeutic process but, shall we say . . . an aspect of therapy that only some people need. Not everyone needs what the portal has to offer. The reason you don't know about it and the reason I haven't discussed it with you is because, in my opinion, you don't need it. The portal is only for the heavy-hearted, not the light-hearted. I send the heavy-hearted there . . .'

'The heavyweights?'

'Uh, yes. I've heard of them being referred to in that way, but that's a name some of the people here have come up with, in the same way they refer to me as the Emperor.'

Before Luc can hide his surprise, Doctor Cottard waves dismissively. 'It's fine. I know about all these nicknames. It doesn't really matter what we call them, but I prefer to think of them as heavy-hearted . . .'

'And light-hearted.'

'Precisely. Let me put it like this. Addiction, or the infatuation with repetition, the reverie of longing, or whatever you want to call it, is a longing for permanence. Because the addict does not have a deep sense of belonging, he or she feels at sea – nobody to hold them, to anchor them in life. But this inability to belong also assumes a different form – namely, a longing for the constant flux of life to stop; a longing for permanence, for *being* rather than *becoming*. So, the most difficult thing any addict has to resolve is this attachment to permanence, to being. The way forward is to embrace impermanence. But here it gets tricky because it is not uncommon for somebody who is beginning to truly embrace the impermanence of everything to initially be almost overwhelmed by a sense of loss and to experience a profound sense of mourning. And this mourning is particularly challenging to work through because it has two dimensions. On the one hand, there is the loss of permanence; we mourn the loss of permanence, being and stability. But then, once that has passed, another mourning arises from the realisation that we have missed so many beautiful moments of impermanence because we tried to convert them into permanence, into being. Mourning is the recognition of how much we have lost through our pursuit of permanence and how much of it is now irretrievably lost. Do you follow what I am saying, Luc?'

'Yes. I think so. But I still don't see what any of that has to do with the portal.'

'The way I have come to think of it is that there are two kinds of people here. There are those who stay attached to the loss and who cannot escape the mourning; they seem forever caught in a reverie of mourning. Melancholy souls. I think of them as the heavy-hearted. Then there are those – and I think you are one of them – who have already started to let go, not just of the loss, but also of mourning the loss – the light-hearted.'

They sit in silence for a while. There is a slight frown on Luc's face as he thinks through Doctor Cottard's explanation.

'Which brings us to the question of why some people find it so very difficult to let go of the loss and of mourning the loss.'

'Fear?' asks Luc.

'Yes, perhaps. But fear of what?'

Luc shakes his head and, when he does not say anything, Doctor Cottard continues. 'I think of the original experience of detachment, when our goodness is not mirrored back to us, as a trauma, a very early experience of trauma. By trauma, I simply mean any experience that exceeds the mind's capacity to process what happens – it can be anything from abuse to radical neglect, but also something less obviously traumatic, such as a mystical or near-death experience. All these experiences exceed our ability to make sense of them and are, in that sense, traumatic.'

Doctor Cottard waits a little while to allow the last statement to sink in, to let Luc process the full extent of what he has said, so that he, too, can understand why his parents brought him to the centre. Then he continues. 'You see, Luc, what trauma does, apart from confronting us with the incomprehensible, is that it rends us from the world and makes us feel utterly alone; it deprives us of any sense of trust and, consequently, of belonging. Overcoming trauma is all about finding our way back into the world, learning to trust the world and to find a way back to experiencing belonging.'

Luc nods.

'But – here's the catch. For a person who was traumatised as a young child – and most of the clients here were abused or neglected in some way and to varying degrees – the trauma over time comes to function as . . . how shall I put this? It comes to function as a foundation in their life. Much like the belief in, say, God or rationality functioned for so many centuries as foundational to our concept of what it means to be human, so too can trauma come to function as foundational in the lives of those who have experienced it. The traumatised person comes to believe that his or her very existence is founded on trauma, that it defines them. It gives them a sense of identity . . .'

'So, what's the catch then?'

'Imagine that trauma has been the foundation of your life for a very long time and one of the effects has been that it has made you feel terribly alone in the world, as if you did not belong. Well, what do you think is going to happen when that person's trauma promises to get resolved and they get a glimpse of life after trauma? I can tell you. The moment you help them overcome the trauma, you start taking away their foundation and without that foundation they sense an even greater loneliness. Overcoming trauma means letting go of what has become foundational to their life and reintroduces again the trauma of loss. The long and short of it, Luc, is that many people struggle to overcome trauma because they get to a point when they cannot bear another loss – not even the loss of their trauma.'

'And those are the heavy-hearted?'

'Precisely.'

'And the light-hearted?'

'The light-hearted somehow manage to understand that overcoming trauma is not unlike a leap of faith. That is what is so light about it, or them. They realise that they have to let go of that foundation, of trauma as their companion, and learn to trust that belonging, *real* belonging is possible after that loss. They understand that although overcoming trauma is a kind of loss, it is a loss that may just for the first time release them into belonging.'

'I see,' says Luc. He thinks for a moment and then asks, 'But what do the heavy-hearted learn by going through the portal? What is on the other side? Where do they go? Do they automatically come back light-hearted?'

Doctor Cottard leans back in his chair and places his hands on the arm rests. 'I never tell them. I think if I did, it wouldn't work. All I tell them is that it is safe to go through the portal, that Ajna will accompany them and that they will learn something very valuable in the process. Then, when they get back, we have a – call it a debriefing, if you wish – of their experience. For some people, it really does help, but, alas, not everyone. Some return completely and instantly changed, others not at all or only much later when it is impossible to tell if the portal experience contributed anything to their recovery.'

'I want to go,' says Luc.

'Do you think you need to?' asks Doctor Cottard.

'Yes, I do. I'm not sure why. I can see why you may think I don't need to go, but from the moment Angèle told me about the portal, I wanted to go, quite desperately. The whole idea seems to resonate very deeply with . . .' Luc stops and his sentence trails off into silence.

'With what, Luc?'

'I'm not sure. There's a yearning. I *yearn* to go. There is a yearning that pulls me, draws me on. The yearning seems to come from the portal. It's suddenly as if my yearning has a place, a name it emanates from. It's the same yearning that used to be so diffused, pulling and pulling at me from all directions . . . but I could never tell where it was pulling from. But now it has a place. It seems to me as if the yearning comes from the portal. It is from the portal that I am drawn and I do not know what I am being drawn to or why, except that it is as if . . . yes . . . as if it yearns for me. Does that make any sense?'

'It does. It does indeed,' says Doctor Cottard. He leans forward in his chair. He reaches for a small green button next to his desk calendar and, as he presses it, says, 'I'll ask Ajna. I don't know when she and Maurice are planning their next outing through the portal, but one of them will accompany you. I'll leave it up to them to make the arrangements.'

Luc Crosses Over

3

The first thing that strikes Luc as he puts his foot down is a sense of heaviness. Doctor Cottard and Ajna had both warned him about this and it is indeed a very strange sensation. As he takes his first step, he realises that it is almost as if he has to work twice as hard to lift his feet when he walks.

'Remember what I told you, Luc,' Ajna says. 'There is significantly more gravity in this world, which makes it hard for us to walk. But it gets easier after a couple of hours. One gets used to it. You'll see.'

'Where are we?' asks Luc, as he looks around.

'As in . . . where in the universe are we or . . .'

'No, not that. I get what Doctor Cottard told me – there is a portal from our world to this one and we will never know exactly where we are and all that. I meant where are we . . . in this world . . . what is this place?'

'There is much about all of it that we do not understand,' says Ajna, 'and to be frank, I don't always know how much Doctor Cottard himself knows. He's only ever been here once or twice. That somehow persuaded him that it would be a good idea to send some of his clients over every now and then. How he decides who does and who does not come, I don't know.'

Ajna turns to Luc. 'I'm surprised he sent you. You somehow don't fit the typical picture . . . but then again, who am I to say? My job is just to accompany whoever he sends and you're lucky today. It's just you and me. Or shall I say, I'm the lucky one? Sometimes there are four or five and then it's hard work for me . . . like herding cats. Let's go that way,' she says and points in the direction of the entrance to the alley they are standing in.

They start walking. Luc says, 'I meant, where are we? What kind of place is this? It looks like a big school or university campus. Is that what it is?'

'Yes, indeed,' replies Ajna. 'It is a university campus and I have come to know it quite well. Not to spoil anything for you, but there are some old buildings that look very much like some of the old buildings in our world, and then there are also some newer ones that will look . . . I suppose, weird to you, different, the design not quite like anything you've seen before. I always find them just a bit *off*, as if somebody had told the architect what the building should look like, without showing him any drawings.'

Luc stops, turns around again and looks back in the direction they had come from. 'So, this is where we come and go from? Isn't it a bit dangerous – to just arrive? What if people see us? Has that ever happened?'

'No,' Ajna says, 'nobody ever comes here. This alley is closed off on that end, so it's no longer used as a thoroughfare. In all the times I've come here, I've never seen anyone in this alley – not around the entrance or where we came from. It seems to be a bit of a dead end.'

'And is it the only place?' Luc wanted to say, 'Is this the only portal?' but it just sounded too strange.

'No. As far as we know, there are two. There is this one and there's another one off campus. Back home, there is only one, though. Don't ask me why; it's just one of those things we've figured out – or haven't figured out, depending on how you look at it. There may well be more portals on both sides, but we haven't found them. I don't know about Doctor Cottard, but I haven't really made an effort to find them. *What's the point?* I ask myself. As long as you know you can come and go, what does it matter how many options you have? Somehow, we always arrive through this one though. But then we can choose whether to go back through it or through the other one. Took us quite a while to figure that out, but now it runs like clockwork. We come, we walk around, and then we go back, here or there. We plan things so that we always go back through the other one. Keeps things more interesting.'

'So, that's it? Luc asks incredulously. 'We get here, we walk around and then we go back. Is that it?'

'Pretty much,' replies Ajna, as they approach the entrance to the alley. 'Except *you* walk around and then we go back. Think of me as a glorified tour guide. It's my job to get you here, but how you spend the day is entirely up to you.'

'Aha,' says Luc. 'Sounds riveting. Am I allowed to leave campus and explore the city?'

'In principle, yes,' replies Ajna, 'but there's a good reason why we can't. They've got a thing called biomatrix at the gate . . .'

'Biomatrix?' Luc asks.

'Yes, it's a gadget that you put your finger on. It scans your fingerprint and lets you in. If it doesn't know your fingerprint, you can't get in or out.'

'I have so many questions,' says Luc, as he briefly stops to take in the sprawling campus in front of them. The gravity is also taking its toll on him. Even this short walk has significantly tired him. 'So, what do you do while I walk about?'

'I'll tell you now. Let me just finish explaining. So, we can either go back through this portal, or the other one in town, but if we want to use the other one, which we always try to do, we have to time our visit to coincide with a public event on campus. When there's a public event, they disable the biomatrix at the gate to allow members of the public on campus. And that's the gap we can use to enter or leave the campus . . .'

'. . . to leave through the other portal if we want to?'

'Precisely. And today is one of those days, so actually . . . It's up to you.'

Luc is still looking at the vast campus grounds. He whistles. 'Impressive! This place is huge!'

'I know,' replies Ajna. 'Come on, let's go,' she says and sets off again. Luc notices that she has clearly mastered the art of walking effortlessly in this world. There is almost no trace in her gait of what he still experiences as a struggle with the earth with every step he takes. 'Which is why it's not so bad to spend the whole day here. There's lots to see. Now, what I usually do – and tell me if this is okay with you – I leave you alone to roam the campus. I think of it as a day off. No work and no worries, so I just spend the day in that coffee shop over there . . .' – she points to a terrace with tables and colourful umbrellas – 'reading this riveting book I found in the lounge yesterday. *Elephants Are Also Animals* – such a ridiculous title, I thought I may as well give it a go. Anyway, then later we meet up again, around six or so. There's a public lecture early this evening – at five, if I remember correctly.' She starts to fumble in her pockets. 'That's why I chose today. Wait, let me see. It's here somewhere. Ah, here it is. This is the pamphlet I took last time I came.'

Luc takes it from her hand and reads it out loud. '"The Mathematics of Affect", a public lecture, blah, blah . . . Professor Steinway from Harvard University . . . library auditorium . . .'

'The mathematics of affect?' he asks, as he hands the pamphlet back to Ajna. 'As in . . . what is the square root of happiness?'

Ajna puts the pamphlet back in her pocket and lifting her book in her other hand, makes a defensive gesture and says, 'Don't ask me – I just work here.'

She turns around and starts walking in the direction of the cafe. 'So, go and do your thing. You've got as much time as you like and – oh, by the way, you don't have to attend the lecture if you don't want to. Nobody is checking. It's not like that. If you want to miss the lecture and go back earlier, that's also fine, but just bear in mind that if we want to go back through the other portal, we will have to wait until about eight before we can use it. Too many people around before then.'

'Thanks,' says Luc. 'Let me see what there is to see. The walking is slowly getting easier, but it's going to take me a while to stop feeling like a fool. And who knows – maybe I'll learn how to calculate the precise degree of my future happiness.'

He spends the first two hours exploring the campus and it is exactly as Ajna had described. Some of the buildings look very familiar, built in a style that he knows very well, while some of the more recent buildings look – how did she put it? – slightly strange, not completely alien, just a bit *off*. As he rounds a corner, he finds himself right in front of what is clearly the highest building on campus. He had not intended to walk there, but as he finds himself in front of it, he realises that he had been drawn to it because it is one of those slightly off buildings. Shielding his eyes protectively from the glare of the sun reflected off its white surface, he counts the number of storeys. Twenty in total. Each window has a little canopy extending over it, presumably to provide some protection against the sun. His eyes come to rest on the top six storeys, where the windows are covered with a strange wire mesh, which makes that section of the building look a bit like a chicken coop. *A strange design, indeed,* he thinks, as he drops his hands, turns away from the building and walks in the direction of what appears to be the library. Casually, as if he were just another student wandering around, Luc stops and looks around the foyer, his hands in his pockets. On the walls there are artworks that he does not find attractive at all, lots of posters announcing future events and even one big colourful poster advertising the public lecture 'The Mathematics of Affect', accompanied by a picture of the professor herself, looking surprisingly serious. As Luc turns away to leave the building, he sees a sign indicating the direction of the library auditorium and he makes a mental note, just in case he later decides to attend the lecture. He spends the rest of the day walking aimlessly around the campus, self-conscious about the fact that people often do not look him in the eye, but inadvertently drop their gaze to his legs, as if trying to understand why he seems to find it so hard to walk. But Ajna is right – it does get easier and, by late afternoon, he is much less self-conscious about it and fewer people seem to notice anything out of the ordinary about his gait.

It is almost 5.00 p.m. when he makes his way back to the part of the campus where Ajna has spent the day. He has decided not to attend the lecture after all. He is famished because he has not eaten anything since they arrived and has had only a couple of mouthfuls of water from the public water fountains. *How does Ajna pay for her food, then?* he wonders, as he approaches the cafe, where he immediately notices her, deeply immersed in her book. She looks up when she realises somebody is standing next to her table. When she sees it is him, she closes the book and pushes it to one side, next to an empty plate, with the knife and fork neatly placed across it and a cup half filled with coffee.

'And so?' she asks, trying to look interested.

'You first,' he says, as he sits down. 'Are elephants animals or not?'

'That remains to be seen,' she says, pulling the coffee cup closer. 'I anticipate a plot twist towards the end. How's the walking? Got used to people staring at you?'

'Eventually,' he replies. 'It was a strangely uneventful day. I somehow expected more.'

'Yes, I know what you mean,' she says and takes a sip of her coffee. 'It's like that for everyone the first time. Gravity seems to be the main attraction.'

'Tell me about it. Walking is like extra hard work here. Feels like I walked a hundred miles today.' His conversation with Doctor Cottard flashes through his mind. *Is this what it feels like for the heavy-hearted?* he wonders. *All the time?*

'Well, in a sense you did. If that is how hard your muscles needed to work, then you did walk a hundred miles. Tiredness is a function of gravity, not distance travelled.'

'Are you saying there's a mathematical way of calculating my tiredness?'

'Yes, and maybe it's part of that funky new discipline called the Mathematics of Affect.'

'Oh, right. Anyway, I'm hungry and I want to go home. By the way, how do you pay for stuff here?'

'That, my dear friend, is my secret. Now, do you want to go to the lecture or shall we wait for the gates to open and take a stroll over to the other portal?' She glances at her watch. 'Actually, the gates will be open already.'

'What a question,' he says. 'Let's go. Twenty minutes you said?'

'Give or take.'

'Another fifty miles,' he says. 'I don't think we have to worry about waiting until it's dark. It will be dark by the time we get there. My legs are numb.'

Harvesters V

4

Jason agreed to meet me at Harvesters, despite the lateness of the hour. He reminded me that it is a weekday and the place will be closed, and even suggested an alternative place a few blocks down the road, closer to the city centre. But I explained that I need to discuss something with him in private, so Harvesters is perfect, precisely because we can sit outside on the patio, even though the place is closed. I promised to bring some whisky and specifically chose a Wednesday evening because, for some reason, I have never seen the strangers there on a Wednesday. Over time, they have appeared on every other weeknight on at least one occasion, except on a Wednesday.

I had decided to follow Juliet's advice and have my attempt to walk through the window witnessed by somebody to see if that would make a difference. Jason, a mature and intelligent postgraduate student with an abiding fascination with everything absurd, seems the best person for the job. For a brief while before I phoned him, I wondered if it would not be simpler to have him join me on a night when the strangers did appear and to let him see for himself what was going on. That way I would not have to explain as much. But I resisted the temptation to make it easier for myself. What I had witnessed over the past couple of weeks was my secret. It felt like private knowledge and although I did not mind sharing the *knowledge* with someone else, sharing the *experience* with them before I had managed to make more progress in figuring out what was going on, seemed wrong.

An hour after I had phoned him, we are sitting at the table where I always sit. This time, I am sitting facing the back wall, so that he can see the shop window. I take out my usual array of snacks – peanuts and raisins, gluten-free crackers and cheese, some olives and cold meats – and pour us each a whisky. We had just sat down when the cat came slinking around the corner, rubbed itself against my leg, gently purring. Then it went out into the night again. *About time you got the message,* I thought. After some icebreakers about the progress Jason has been making with his dissertation and some of my regular and well-worn complaints about the burdens of being an academic administrator, I decide to edge closer to the real reason for the meeting.

'So, what is the most absurd thing you've ever experienced?' I ask, casually eating a handful of peanuts and raisins.

He seems to have thought about this before because he does not hesitate. 'The final philosophy exam last year . . .'

'That was absurd?'

'Not the exam,' he says, 'what happened the week before.'

'And what was that?' I ask, reaching for my phone. I had forgotten to put it on vibrate.

'I had my wisdom teeth pulled.'

'Oh – and what was so absurd about that?' I ask absent-mindedly while I struggle with the phone. I am of the generation who cannot see the sense in upgrading to the latest model of cell phone as long as the one I have still works perfectly fine, but the only thing that really irritates me about my ancient iPhone S5 is that it has a tiny red button on the side that one has to slide up to put the phone on vibrate. It's tricky to get to and I always have to use the nail of my little finger to switch it on and off.

When I eventually succeed and look up again, Jason is sipping his whisky, peering at me over the edge of his glass. 'They obviously pulled yours a long time ago,' he says.

I get it and feel a red glow in my face. 'Fucking millennials,' I say. 'Too clever for your own good.' I take a deep breath and in a more serious tone, continue. 'I invited you here because I want to share something with you and also ask you a small favour.' Then, for the second time in as many days, I recount the uncanny story of Luc, where he comes from and where I have seen him. Without taking a break or giving Jason an opportunity to speak, I plunge straight into an account of the window disappearances that I have been coming here to witness night after night. I point over my shoulder in the direction of the curio shop window. 'Right there, through that window.'

Jason keeps looking at the window and back at me again, obviously perplexed. I eventually conclude with, 'Well, there it is. That's all I have, but I am serious about it and I need your help going forward.'

Jason tries to play it cool and says, 'This beats any of the absurdities I've come across in Kierkegaard, Camus and all of them. Wow, man! This is like Kafka meets Murakami.'

'I know,' I say, even though I do not agree with the Kafka reference because none of what has happened to me over the past couple of weeks seems absurd to me in that sense, but Murakami, yes, for sure. A world perpetually poised on the knife's edge of the ordinary and the surreal.

'So, why am I here?' asks Jason and pours himself another whisky.

He holds the bottle over my glass, but I place my hand firmly over the top. 'No, not for me, thanks. I've got to keep a clear head.' He frowns, but does not insist. 'I'll tell you why in a moment. Besides, there is not much left and you're going to need it while you wait for me.'

'You mean it gets weirder?'

'Well, perhaps not for you, but for me. We've reached the part where I ask you a favour. On two separate occasions, I have tried to follow Luc and the others through the window to see how it works and where they go, but both times I walked slap-bang into the window. There was nothing unusual there, nothing extraordinary about the glass. Just an ordinary windowpane. The second time I tried with such confidence I'm surprised I didn't break the thing. Anyhow, last night when I discussed the whole business with my wife, Juliet – remember her? I think you met her briefly here one night when we came for tapas and your band was playing?'

'Oh yes, I did. Remember her well.'

'Any case, last night when I told her everything that I just told you, she came up with a fascinating idea. She suggested that I get someone to witness my attempt to follow the strangers. She reckons that it is possible that I would be able to follow them if somebody witnessed me doing so. She thinks it's all about being watched, that being observed in the moment will make all the difference.'

'Ooh!' laughs Jason, 'and just for good measure he throws Schrödinger's cat among Murakami's pigeons!'

'Yes – something like that,' I admit, laughing at his clever summary of the situation.

'I like it,' he says, taking another sip of whisky. 'Observing you negotiate whether the window is there or not, dead or alive, who knows until you walk into it. I like it a lot. One day when I'm grown up, I want to marry a woman like your wife.'

'Anyway, so here we are,' I say and lean back on my bench. 'Are you up for it?'

'Up for it? Hell, yes!' he says and holds up the bottle of whisky for a mock inspection. 'But if you break through to the other side, just don't take too long because this won't last very long,' and then, before I could say anything further, his eyes light up with mischief. 'Tell you what – if that window is indeed a door to another world, then I want to ask that you take your phone with you and, when you get there, phone or text me. Let's see if signal can help us resolve Schrödinger's dilemma.' He feigns drifting off into deep and profound scientific thinking. 'By the way, has anyone ever thought of putting a mic on the cat or a video camera in the box? That way, surely, we can tell whether its dead or alive?' Then he resumes his normal voice and continues. 'If you don't have signal, you can email the phone company when you get back and complain, like, "Hey guys, I did some intergalactic travel the other day and when I got there, I had no signal. What's up? Don't you have any imagination? You should be out there erecting those shitty little cell phone masts on the other side even *before* customers need them. It's called customer service. Build the masts and they will phone."'

'Nobody quotes that movie anymore, you know. Not even your millennial irony can save that line from itself. But back to business. If it works and I am away for God knows how long, what will you do?'

'I don't know,' he says, looking puzzled. 'Depends on how long God-knows-how-long is. If it's days, then you're on your own. I'm not sitting here that long. I think,' and he lifts up the bottle of whisky for another mock inspection, 'there's enough here to keep me entertained for a little while. But, in that case, my boy,' again, the mock gesture, this time looking at his watch, 'curfew is 11.00 p.m.'

'Good,' I reply, smiling inwardly at his cheeky charm. 'Then I don't have to worry about you being bored out here. Anyway, don't you have some shitty little app on your phone with some shitty little video game to play? I don't know, kill somebody for fun?'

'Of course, I do,' he says, 'let me show you,' and he starts flicking his finger over the phone screen. 'I think I may have just the right one for the occasion.'

'Thanks, but no thanks,' I reply and start getting up. 'Right now, my life already feels like a video game. I don't need inception and I certainly don't need an app to escape my world.'

'App-arently not,' he says, the finger still flicking over the screen. Then he stops, looks up and says, 'Shit, that was dreadful. Sorry,' looks down at his screen again and continues scrolling. I get up and stand next to the table.

'Okay, put down the toys now. You can play again later. We have work to do, so pay attention.'

5

The first thing I notice as I put my foot down is the lightness of my step. It is almost as if I am walking on air cushions, as if my step is somehow cushioned from touching the ground. So unusual is the feeling that for a while I struggle to find and maintain my balance and make sense of walking not quite on air, but with far less effort than I am used to. I take a couple of steps and while I walk up and down, I search my mind for an image or a memory that will allow me to make sense of what I am experiencing to explain to Juliet what this feels like. The first image that comes to mind is as unexpected and ridiculous as it is appropriate.

A couple of years ago, before I took up my current position and Juliet and I started commuting, our friend Margot came to visit from London. She had brought with her a pair of what she called 'moon shoes' because they were cushioned with some kind of spring mechanism in the soles, so that when you walked around it literally felt as if you were walking on the moon, or at least with the same kind of clumsy weightlessness so familiar to everyone who has watched footage of the moon landing. The evening got a bit out of hand because after she demonstrated the gravity-defying power of her moon shoes, we insisted on having a turn. Out came the wine and, several moon landings later, we declared her moon shoes the best invention ever and she left two days later, promising to send us each a pair when she got back to London. The moon shoes never arrived, but to this day the memory of that evening still makes us laugh when we talk about Margot and her lightness of spirit. Explaining to Juliet what I am experiencing by comparing it to wearing moon shoes would certainly be the best way of conveying to her something of what it feels like walking around in the room I unexpectedly find myself in.

After walking up and down a while and gradually getting more confident in maintaining a dignified balance and stride, I start exploring the room. It dawns on me that the room is in fact very familiar to me. It is a spacious office, with a desk against the left-hand wall and a big window in the opposite wall, in front of which white curtains gently sway in the breeze. I know this room and I also know that, even without checking, I will be able to describe quite precisely the view from that window. If I were to push the curtains aside, I would look down on a massive staircase below, where a number of people (whom some refer to as patients and others as clients) would be sitting or lying sprawled across the steps in the sun; some of them smoking, others idly chatting. Further to my left and situated in the middle of the expansive gardens, I would be able to see a gazebo with two benches on either side of a table and beyond that, somewhat further off towards the edge of the garden, just where it starts to fade into the surrounding forest, I would see a rose garden, also with two benches across from each other on either side of a baroque fountain and, connecting the rose garden to the main building, a curving wooden walkway under a canopy of interwoven vine leaves. For a brief moment, I contemplate walking over to the window to give myself the pleasure of confirming that I am correct about all the details, but before I can move, I hear somebody open the door. A man enters. He has the erect posture and the restrained demeanour of a butler. I do not recognise him at all and for a moment I am at a complete loss for words. But he does not seem to be surprised to see me or at all fazed by my presence in the room – on the contrary, it almost appears as if he has been expecting my arrival. *He did not accidentally walk into the room*, I realise, *he came in because he was expecting me.* And, indeed, he walks up to me and stretches out his right hand. 'Good day, Sir. My name is Maurice and I've been asked to welcome you.' I shake his hand, but before I can offer a greeting in return, a cold shiver runs down my spine. Maurice is missing the index finger on his right hand, which makes for a very, very creepy handshake. I press his hand briefly and withdraw mine as soon as I can without seeming rude.

Maurice smiles. 'Please wait here,' he says. Then he turns around and walks out the door again, only to return a couple of seconds later, pushing a room service trolley, on which is a tea set and a plate of neatly arranged biscuits. 'Doctor Cottard will be with you soon,' he says and with a slight, old-fashioned bow, he leaves the room and gently pulls the door shut after him.

I walk over to the trolley and take a biscuit. I bite into it and savour the taste. A biscuit is a biscuit is a biscuit. I walk over to the window, push the curtains aside and look down on the staircase below. Just as I imagined, except there is no one there – no patients sitting around smoking or lying across the stairs chatting. It is quiet and deserted. Not a soul in sight. I turn my head to the left and look out over the expansive gardens, into the distance, where I expect to see the gazebo. But it is not there either. I crane my neck slightly to look further towards the edge of the gardens. There is also no rose garden or curved wooden walkway. A strange feeling starts to creep into my stomach, not unlike the solid void I first experienced after I had seen the strangers walk through the window the first time. But before the feeling can take hold properly, I hear the door behind me open a second time and I turn around.

A man enters, whom I presume must be Doctor Cottard. But if this is Doctor Cottard, he looks very different from the Doctor Cottard who lived and worked in the sanatorium I described in *Imitation*. My Doctor Cottard was a bit of an eccentric buffoon: short, invariably wearing a colourful waistcoat over a pot belly, a pointy moustache and a dotted bow tie. Although undoubtedly clever and very good at what he does, I always found his appearance deceptive. He was one of the world's most famous clinical therapists specialising in the treatment of addictions, but he looked more like a country bumpkin and had what some would no doubt have dismissed condescendingly as a raucous and uncivilised manner. For instance, when he laughed, he would rub his hands together, as if he were soaping them, expressing his delight in a way that many people thought should be a little bit more restrained coming from an eminent doctor such as himself.

But the man who just entered the office where my Doctor Cottard treated his patients and who introduces himself to me as 'Doctor

Cottard', is a very different person. He is slim and of medium height, has a gentle manner and is dressed in a way that I can only describe as elegant. He is wearing simple black pants, spotless black shoes and an immaculately pressed white shirt. His black hair is neatly combed back and his skin has an almost unnaturally healthy glow. His eyes are calm and penetrating, but without being invasive in any way. He does not walk up to me like Maurice did, nor does he make any effort to welcome me or shake my hand or any such niceties. Instead, he smiles, walks over to the trolley, pours himself a cup of tea (no milk or sugar, I notice), walks over to his side of the desk, where he places the cup slightly to the right of his writing pad. He sits down, crosses his legs and folds his arms in his lap.

'So, you've managed it?' he says and looks at me with that calm and penetrating gaze.

'I suppose I have,' I say, trying to keep my cool, even though my heart is pounding in my chest. Imitating his measured behaviour, I, too, pour myself a cup of tea and drop a slice of lemon in it. I take my cup and walk back to his desk, where I sit down across from him. Placing the cup on the desk, I also cross my legs, but resist the temptation of also folding my hands. *Too much*, I think and instead place them on the arm rests and smile.

'So, what do you think?' he asks.

'Of what?'

He makes a gesture that sweeps across the world, making it clear that he is referring to everything.

'Well,' I say, 'I haven't had much time to look around, but everything seems about right, except . . .' He frowns quizzically. 'Except that some things seem – how to put this?' I suddenly find myself stuck, trying to articulate a thought I have had, but have not yet attempted to articulate. I am still trying to match word to thought when he completes my sentence.

'Slightly *off*?" he says and takes a sip of tea.

'Yes. That's it. Slightly off.'

'Tell me more,' he says, a faint smile playing on his sensual lips.

'Well, the building is pretty much as I imagined.'

'As it would be,' he says 'It's oh-so-old European that one can hardly make a mistake imagining it. A chateau is a chateau is a chateau.'

'I suppose so. The same goes for the decor, the furniture, the staircase and the gardens.' He nods. 'I suppose that takes care of the obvious,' I conclude.

He is still nodding, almost as if lost in thought, his head bowed over the cup he is holding in his hands, deeply inhaling the fragrance of the tea.

'But the gazebo and rose garden are missing,' I say, pointing in the general direction of the garden, where I imagined them to be.

'No, they're not,' he says. 'They never existed.' Then, looking up from his tea, 'That would be one of those *off* moments.'

'I see,' I say. 'Pity about that. They were always quite important to me. I spent a lot of time there with Luc and the gazebo was also one of his and Angèle's favourite meeting places.' Then, as if repeating the memory would make it more real, 'They always met there.'

'Ah yes,' he says. 'Angèle. She stayed here much longer than we all anticipated. I think something developed between her and Luc, a love of sorts. But given the circumstances, it was destined not to last.' He continues wistfully, 'I often see that here. It is at once quite touching and somewhat tragic.' Then, as if snapping out of a reverie, 'But Luc. We will have to talk about him. And you. And then, of course, about you and him. But before we get there, I need to know what you are doing here. Why did you come? And what do you hope to find here?'

'I'm not sure,' I answer as plainly and honestly as I can. 'I've been following Luc. I suppose once I saw him disappear through the window, there was no going back.'

'Interesting that you managed to figure out how to use it. Ajna tells me it's slightly different on that side.'

'Well, actually that was my wife's idea. If it weren't for her, I would still be thinking I was going mad.'

That faint smile again. 'But that doesn't answer my question. What did you expect to find when you followed Luc through the portal?'

I shift uncomfortably in my chair. 'Well, for starters, I suppose Luc himself. I'm intrigued by the fact that he actually exists. I'm not quite sure what to make of that. Beyond that, I suppose I will find either nothing or everything.'

'Typical philosopher,' he says, putting the cup and saucer down on his desk and leaning back in his chair, hands locked behind his head. 'Always wanting answers, but you cannot decide whether you expect nothing or everything.'

'How do you know that I'm a philosopher?' I ask.

'Oh, I know quite a bit about you, but only what you yourself have told me.'

'What I've told you?' I can hear the sharp rise in my voice.

'Yes. You're a philosopher. But you're also a novelist. I'm not familiar with your philosophical writings. In fact, I haven't made any effort to get hold of any of those because I know better than to expect to find you there – who you are and what you're really looking for. But when I discovered that you had written a novel, I knew that would be the place to look. So, yes. I know about your novel *Imitation* and I've read it.'

I don't know how to respond. There is too much in what Doctor Cottard has just said to find a possible way in. But he does not seem perturbed by my reaction – or the lack of it. He obviously knew how I was going to react. He leans forward, takes another sip of tea, leans back in his chair again and, with his fingers pressed against each other to form two perfect spherical halves, calmly continues.

'We'll come back to that in a while. Let me just say that I tried my best to prevent Luc from going to your world. For me, the use of the portal is part of a therapeutic process and I didn't think he needed that particular experience. Turns out I was wrong. The moment he found out about it, there was no stopping him. So I allowed him to go. What were the odds of your seeing him? Quite incredible. And now, here you are. Expecting everything and nothing.' He pauses for a moment and, in the silence, I realise that he does not fully understand everything either. Then, as if he can read my mind, he continues. 'I intuit a connection between his going there and you coming here, but I must be honest, I don't quite see it. Do you?'

'No,' I reply. 'No idea.'

'Well, let's try to work it out. I'll tell you what I know. But be warned, there are bound to be a couple of surprises. My interest in your world was piqued when – and Luc and Ajna do not know this – I sent Maurice to follow them. Every time Luc crossed over, Maurice went too, to see what he did and where he went, whom he met and so on. I needed to know what Luc found the moment he found it because that would explain to me why he wanted to go when I didn't think he needed to and, after all, I am responsible for his healing. So, on one of these occasions, Luc lay down on one of the campus lawns to take a nap – which he always seems to do – and Maurice used the opportunity to explore the campus on his own. Eventually, he walked into the library and noticed a gathering of sorts in the auditorium. Curious to find out what it was all about, he entered the venue, only to discover a man sitting on the front bench reading from a book. He quickly realised he had walked into a book launch. So, he listened for a while and was about to leave when the man started to read a passage from a novel that not only described this place,' Doctor Cottard makes a sweeping gesture to include everything around him, the office, the chateau, the vast grounds and the whole world beyond it, 'but also named me, yes *me*, "Doctor Cottard" and, hold on to your seat, a young patient called "Luc", whom the author described as being in the grips of a fascination with death and silence. It was your book launch. Remember the event?'

'Mine?' I ask incredulously.

'Yes. Didn't you have a book launch of your novel in the library auditorium one day? Remember?'

I am so taken aback that all I can say is, 'Yes . . . But how?'

'This is what we are trying to work out. How indeed? Now, can you see why you piqued my interest? *Who is this man?* I asked myself. *And how does he know all this?* Problem was Maurice couldn't buy a copy of *Imitation* that day because he did not have the right money. So, the next time he went over, I gave him some of the money Ajna had managed to get and asked him to bring back a copy of the novel. There were none for sale in the campus bookshop and, after trying various other bookshops in town, he still could not find a copy. You don't seem to be very popular. It's almost impossible to get hold of your novel. Did you know that? How many copies have you actually sold?'

My embarrassment is greater than my curiosity and I cannot stop myself from firing back, 'Well, it's a literary novel, not the sort of thing you buy at the airport. You have to order it from a bookshop. But the publisher is quite good like that. Once you've ordered it, you get it in two or three days.'

He waves his hand impatiently. 'Whatever. Point is Maurice couldn't find a copy anywhere, so we had to make another plan. He could not order a copy because they would want an address or phone number and so on and so on. So, he proposed something quite drastic. The next time he crossed over, he would follow you home to see where you live and then, on the next visit, he would wait for you to go to work and . . . and . . .' For the first time, Doctor Cottard looks slightly uncomfortable and at a loss for words. 'He, um, broke into your apartment. We assumed you would have one or two extra copies there and he would simply take one of those. And, indeed, he saw a few in your study . . .'

'The finger!' I exclaim before I can help myself.

Doctor Cottard smiles, with a combination of bemusement and embarrassment. 'Yes, indeed. He said something about a canvas that he had to roll up from the outside to get in and then roll out again once he was out. I can't remember the details of how it happened, but somehow his finger got caught in something somewhere. It sounds like a dangerous contraption that roll-up canvas of yours. You'd better be careful.'

'It's only dangerous if you break in,' I respond defensively. 'It would be difficult to injure yourself if you roll it back from the inside.' I am surprised by how willing I am to defend myself and the patio canvas roof from his accusations, even though it is not even my property.

Again, that dismissive wave of the hand. 'Whatever. I'm sorry for him, but that was not the first time he has injured himself. He can be quite a careless traveller, our Maurice. Point is he managed to bring back a copy of your novel.'

I have a thousand questions to ask. So many, in fact, that for a moment it is impossible to identify and articulate any one of them. That sometimes happens. You have so many questions to ask about something that it is impossible to prioritise them sufficiently, to acknowledge one as more important than the others, or to find a way in, so that you just sit there, imagining them, feeling them whirl around in your head and experiencing their clamour as if they were a swarm of bees in your head. Somewhere in the midst of my indecision, I detect in myself the pathetic need for affirmation, to know what Doctor Cottard thought of my novel. I want evidence of the fact that he had read and liked it. More than that, I want to hear him make at least one reference to a particular scene, paragraph or character that he enjoyed to prove that he had actually read it. And, above all, I want to hear that he recommended it to all his friends. Then a thought barges through the swarm of bees: *How ridiculous! Here I am, sitting in a parallel universe talking to someone who sent an intergalactic butler to steal a copy of my novel from my apartment, who, having lost a finger in the process, brought it back here, where the man now sitting across from me confesses that I had managed to accurately describe his world, and all I want to know is, 'Was it any good?!'*

As if he could read my mind, Doctor Cottard continues. 'Quite a remarkable novel. The picture of you on the back cover was taken quite a while ago, wasn't it? I almost didn't recognise you. Be that as it may, I must confess, I am not familiar with Kundera's novels, so I don't know the one you engaged with – what's it called again, *Immorality*?'

'*Immortality*,' I correct him.

'Ah yes, *Immortality*, that's right.' He seems to get lost in thought for a couple of seconds before he says, 'Sounds like a fascinating read.' Then he looks straight at me and says, 'I was very impressed by the accuracy with which you described all this,' again, that sweeping gesture. I feel dizzy. This is simply too much to take in. It suddenly feels to me as if there are multiple worlds – never mind the questions – in my mind and they are all bleeding across into one another. I lean forward and clasp my head with both hands. I hear Doctor Cottard stand up and walk around the desk. There is the sound of him picking up my empty teacup and walking over to the trolley. When I look up again, he has placed a full cup of tea in front of me, with two biscuits on either side of the cup. 'I added some sugar,' he says. 'Eat something. And then, let's take it from the beginning, shall we?'

6

'Two questions, really,' Doctor Cottard says, as he walks around the desk back to his chair. 'How are such identical worlds possible, and yet, when you travel from one to the other, you find that they are not identical, but slightly different, just *off*? And the second question,' he says, as he sits down to assume the leaning-back-in-the-chair-hands-interlocked-behind-the-head posture, 'how did you know about this world when you wrote *Imitation* and how did you get your descriptions so right – particularly Luc and his struggles? That is the question that intrigues me. I imagine you may be more perplexed by the first question, although . . . although . . . the fact that you are here indicates that you are also looking for answers to the second question. So, let's start with the obvious. Two worlds with an interconnecting portal. How is that possible?'

I lean back in the chair. Again, I have to make a concerted effort not to also clasp my hands behind my head. Instead, I place them on the arm rests and wait for him to continue. The rationality he has introduced to the conversation suddenly calms me down. This is much better. I can work at this pace.

'Schrödinger's cat,' he says. 'Are you familiar with it?'

I try to disguise my ignorance with a nod that ideally should simultaneously indicate yes and no. When he lifts his eyebrows, I say, 'Sort of. I've tried a couple of times, but I've never been able to quite understand it.'

'Well, that can take days,' he says, 'and we don't have days. I'll keep it simple.' He pauses, reflecting on exactly what the best point of entry would be into what even I know is a very difficult subject. 'Let's start with one of the most important scientific discoveries of all time, that electrons are both particles and waves; both a thing and not-a-thing. It took scientists a good while to accept this and the initial confusion was perfectly understandable. So much so that in 1906 J.J. Thomson received the Nobel Prize for proving that electrons are particles, and 30 years later his son, George, was awarded the Nobel Prize for proving that electrons are waves. Can you imagine that? Both father and son were right, although they lived in two completely different worlds – in the one, electrons were considered things and in the other, waves. *How often does that happen?* you may well ask. Anyway, turns out an electron is both a thing and not-a-thing, both a particle and a wave. So, here's the problem that scientists soon had to deal with. Although the electron is both particle and wave, no experiment can demonstrate that, or *how* it can behave as both particle *and* wave. Experiments designed to detect particles will detect particles; experiments designed to detect waves will detect waves, which means – and this was the cat Heisenberg threw among the pigeons, which caused such great uncertainty – it means that reality is created by the observer. The act of observation determines what we see. If we design an experiment in order to detect things, we will detect things, and if we design one to demonstrate the wave-like nature of electrons, we will see non-things and waves. How to explain this was the obvious question for many, many years. Over time, various hypotheses emerged, but they all more or less accepted the same basic premise; as far as the electron itself is concerned, one state of existence – existing as a thing – must somehow be superimposed over another state of existence – as a wave – right until the moment that we look. Strange kind of compromise, I know, but there it is. Scientists decided that what is weird about the quantum world is that the electron is both a thing and not-a-thing until the moment we look, and, depending on what we want to see, we see a thing or a not-thing, a particle or a wave. Long and the short of it is that this became known as the Copenhagen interpretation of the world of the small. But then along came Schrödinger, who wanted to reveal the flaw in assuming that one state of affairs can exist superimposed over another until looked at. He invited his fellow scientists to imagine a cat inside a box. Also inside the box is a mechanism that will kill the cat if it is triggered and there is a 50/50 chance that, once we close the box, the mechanism may be triggered. So, he asked: For as long as the box is closed and, given the 50/50 chance that the mechanism will be triggered and kill the cat, is the cat dead or alive for those of us who live and think outside the box? Well, the good folk from Copenhagen would have to say that the only way to describe the situation in the box is to say that the cat exists in two states – life and death – superimposed upon each other, until we open the box and look, or that only looking will reveal whether the cat is dead or alive. Until we look inside the box, the cat is a dead-alive cat – much like the electron *is* and *is not* a thing. So, and this is the point of Schrödinger's little thought experiment, if we want to accept that electrons are and are not things, we must also be willing to accept that, until we look, the cat is both dead and alive. Schrödinger's cat outraged many scientists, who responded by arguing that the cat is perfectly capable of deciding for itself whether it is dead or alive and that it had nothing to do with us, to which yet others replied that while this may or may not be the case, we would not know whether the cat is capable of deciding anything for itself until we know whether it is dead or alive – and so it went on and on.'

Throughout Doctor Cottard's lucid and simple explanation, I had been dunking the biscuits in my tea and nibling away at them. He was right, the sugar helped to clear the dizziness from my head. I think of the two questions we had started with and a vague understanding begins to form in the back of my head, like clouds gathering on the horizon. There is the promise of possible rain in the air.

'An elegant solution to this back and forth about the living-dead cat came from a young graduate student at Princeton university, Hugh Everett, who basically said everyone was right. In one reality, he said, the electron is a thing, but in another reality it is not, and which one becomes our reality is the result of looking; so, yes, the act of observation does create our reality – one in which the electron is either a particle or a wave – but, and this was his groundbreaking insight, the act of observation, as much as it creates one reality, doesn't destroy the other. The act of observation just cuts the tie that binds the two alternative realities together, allowing them to go their separate ways. The two realities will drift apart, the one containing an observer who sees a dead cat, the other an observer who sees a live cat. Whereas the Copenhagen folk effectively argued that both states are in a sense *unreal* until we look and through the act of looking, we create our reality, Everett argued that both states are *real* and all that the act of observation does is to separate the two realities from each other. The tie that binds can be dissolved at a glance.'

By this time, the clouds in my head had become heavy with rain as they drifted across the sky in my direction. Doctor Cottard's explanation was as comforting as it was unsettling and so I ventured a stab at the only weakness I could sense. 'Okay, I get it. So, there are many worlds. But since we are constantly looking at the world, that must surely mean that every split-second reality splits off into different worlds . . . so, since there are, what, seven billion people in the world looking at the world . . .'

'Don't get too hung up about the whole looking business,' he interrupts. 'It's not about looking. The quantum world constantly splits in order to realise every possible world. Yes, Everett argued that anything that is possible does in fact happen, but not necessarily in one world. All possibilities are realised in realities or worlds that continuously split off in order for those possibilities to be realised in another world . . .'

'All possibilities?'

'Yes. There are about, oh, 10 to the power of 100 copies of you and me in as many worlds, all slightly different from us and each having realised a different possibility. And we keep multiplying. In some of these worlds the geo-political balance of power shifted from ancient China to Africa, which then colonised backward Europe, the pyramids never get built, and so on,' and there is that dismissive wave of the hand again.

After the sweeping gesture that always includes the sanatorium and the whole world beyond it, this must be his second favourite gesture in what appears to be a very limited repertoire, I think, as if containing him with an insult like that would make his unsettling explanation of the universe easier to cope with. *My imagined Doctor Cottard may have been a bit off, but he had a much broader range of gestures. It's almost as if the real Cottard lacks imagination.*

'While most people find it a very strange, even counter-intuitive or incomprehensible idea, the many worlds explanation is much closer to common sense than we realise. We approach something of its explanatory power every time we play the What If game with our lives, or even with one day. Take you, for instance. Earlier, you said you saw Luc one day. Well, you didn't say where you saw him, but let's say it was in a shopping complex you sometimes stop at on your way home after work. Well, *what if* you had gone to a different supermarket that particular day, or if you went there an hour earlier or an hour later? Would you still be here today? Most likely not. Now, imagine a world in which you did go to the same supermarket and another in which you didn't and there you have it, just one instance of the endless splitting off of possibilities, each of which is realised. All Everett asked of us was to not just imagine *what if* I did or didn't do this or that, but to imagine a universe in which every *what if* possibility is actually realised.'

As Doctor Cottard speaks, I try to keep a straight face and not to show any of the disquiet I am experiencing as he talks. *One world in which Luc did burn a part of the property down because he did it the night after Angèle's failed suicide attempt and another world in which he did not and . . . that's why the sanatorium did not temporarily close, and we can still be sitting here?*

But Doctor Cottard has not noticed and, as if suddenly catching himself drifting off the topic, he interrupts himself. 'Of course, this creates its own peculiar set of paradoxes and unanswerable questions because if the universe is as finite as the general theory of relativity suggests, then the universe cannot contain an infinite number of worlds, unless, of course,' a faint smile, 'there is a world in which that problem has already been solved. So yes, many uncertainties remain, but here we are.'

'So, are you saying my world, the world in which I live and work, the world in which I saw Luc and those other strangers, that world is parallel to this one?'

'Well, technically, they're not parallel. The mathematics suggests that the many worlds don't run parallel, but rather at right angles to one another. Worlds branch off perpendicular to each other, sideways – like branches of a tree, a fractal of worlds, if you wish – which also means that to travel from one world to another involves time travel and a lot of other complicated things that needn't detain us here because our time is limited and because, quite frankly, there's much of it that I don't understand. Let's just say, your world is perpendicular to this one and they are connected with a portal, which you have now discovered.'

I had seen this coming. Before I can say anything, he continues with a slightly melancholy expression on his face. 'Funny thing is that, as far as I know, back in your world, scientists still argue which is correct, the Copenhagen or the many worlds interpretation of uncertainty. And yet, here you are, experiencing the truth of the many worlds hypothesis, living it. You now have the answer to that question, but the problem is that once you return to your world, you will have no proof of it. You will not be able to prove that many worlds exist just because you've been to another world and that, I must warn you, is going to be very difficult. You will have seen a greater, perhaps an absolute, objective truth that you will not be able to explain to anyone, other than by saying, "But I've seen it." It is a particular kind of curse, I must warn you, this thing of having seen the truth, but not being able to articulate it. In another register, it is a dilemma all mystics who have encountered the Godhead struggle with and, if I remember correctly, it's sometimes referred to as the mystic's curse – don't know if you've heard of that?'

My mouth is too dry to speak. Any attempt to say something now would only come out like the pathetic croaking of a strange intergalactic frog. I must retain my composure. Everything is at stake here and I must protect what I know. I close my eyes for a brief moment because I sense that nauseating void that I first experienced after I had witnessed Luc walk through the curio shop window, the experience of a solid void in my gut, which haunted me for so many weeks while I tried to figure out what was going on.

When I open my eyes, Doctor Cottard is looking at me with those deep, calm and penetrating eyes. 'So, you see, the answer to the first question of how these two worlds exist is, in a sense, the easy one to answer. The two worlds can be explained. What we don't yet understand is how travel between one world and another is possible, how the portals come into existence – why and for how long. This we do not know, but as far as we are concerned – I mean you and me – the more difficult and, dare I say, urgent question is how did you manage to describe this world so accurately in your novel without ever having been here? Now *that* is an intriguing question. What is your relationship with our world and would the answer to that question perhaps allow us to answer some of the other questions? What do you think?'

I shake my head. 'I don't have any words right now. It's all a bit much for me.'

He stands up, unexpectedly and decisively. 'Yes, I can see you're tired. You still have some time before you have to return. Technically, there is no reason why you cannot stay longer, but we have quite a rigorous schedule here and I am seeing a number of clients later this afternoon and early this evening. Why don't you go for a walk in the garden? Let all of this sink in and then we can meet again, say,' he glances at his watch, 'in an hour? We can have lunch outside. I'll ask Maurice to set up a table under the trees in the garden, where it's nice and cool. Yes?'

7

We sit down to an immaculately set table, with a white tablecloth, white plates, silver cutlery and crystal glasses. Maurice is nowhere to be seen. Instead, next to the table is a service trolley, similar to the one he pushed into the study shortly after my arrival, with a couple of dishes covered with silver domes. Doctor Cottard gestures to the dishes and says, 'Please help yourself.'

I am starving, so I get up, lift the three domes and put them to one side. I do not know what I expected, but I am somewhat disappointed: chicken, broccoli and salad. I dish up for myself and sit down while Doctor Cottard pours us each a glass of wine. Then he puts the bottle down, gestures to my plate and says, 'Please go ahead. I'll have some just now.' I start eating, and after a couple of perfectly normal mouthfuls of chicken, broccoli and salad, he says, 'So, we have the second question to deal with.' His tone is calm and wandering, as if he is thinking aloud. 'What is the relationship between your world and this one; what enabled or inspired you to visualise this world so accurately in your novel and what is the nature of the relationship between you and Luc? Because, let's face it, it's no simple coincidence that someone you wrote about in *Imitation* discovers a portal to the world in which the author lives – no, not just his world, but his actual place of work – and you see him there, then see him disappear through a portal and then figure out how to use the portal yourself to come to the world he lives in. There are just too many – I don't like the word "coincidences" – let's just say, it's all just too synchronous. How is all of this possible and what does it mean?'

'I have no idea,' I say, chewing my food slowly, absent-mindedly staring at the table in front of me, half listening to Doctor Cottard and half thinking about the series of coincidences he has just listed. It is indeed a fascinating series of events. It borders on the miraculous, which I suppose is why he prefers the word "synchronous". Somewhere in myself, I, too, believe that there must be a logic or an explanation for it all, but neither Doctor Cottard nor I seem to have any idea where to begin to work it out. I feel his eyes on me, but I need some time to think and do not want to be rushed into anything. There is just too much at stake.

I remember how I reacted when I first saw Luc disappear through the curio shop window and how for days afterwards – no, weeks – I could not reconcile the world I was living in with a world in which something like that was possible. I recall how the idea of living in two worlds at the same time, but feeling equally alienated from both, made me feel sick to my stomach, a sick feeling that I subsequently could only describe as an experience of carrying a solid void around in my gut. And now I have managed to follow Luc back to where he comes from and I am having lunch with somebody who should be able to give me all the answers I am looking for. And yet, this same person does not seem to know much more than I do – not about Luc and me anyway. 'I don't understand any of it,' I say, eventually.

'Well, perhaps we will find the answer to this difficult second question as we get to know each other better in the limited time we have at our disposal. Maybe it's one of those answers that can only be arrived at by talking through what we know, clearing the residues, as it were, until the answer reveals itself. So, perhaps

I could start by telling you what we have worked out about the portals – yes, portals,' he says, emphasising the plural. 'This is not the first one I have discovered and used. They seem to open all the time, in different places, leading to different worlds. Each time I – or more correctly *we* – discover one and start exploring it, we try to understand something about the why; why do portals sometimes appear? And why at a particular moment and place? Why do they open between this and one other particular world? Why that world and not another? Sadly, we have not yet managed to answer all these questions. Every time we think we're close to an answer, a portal opens up at a time or in a place so unexpected that its existence completely invalidates what we thought we had understood. Part of the complication is that, as with any scientific phenomenon, there are many people working on various hypotheses. I am just one person involved in the investigations. When this particular portal came into existence, I was terribly excited because, well, let's just say that because I own the sanatorium, I have . . . um . . . certain liberties to explore the meaning of this particular portal pretty much as I see fit.' He pauses and takes a sip of his wine. After he stops talking, a slight frown lingers on his forehead, as if the very repetition of the questions about the existence of the portals reminds him of every disappointment he has experienced so far. 'That said,' he continues, while he gets up and walks over to the trolley, 'this is a particularly interesting case because it does seem to confirm one of the hypotheses that we have been working with . . .'

'Are you going to tell me who this "we" is?' I ask, placing my knife and fork across my empty plate and pushing it aside.

'All in good time,' he replies. 'We'll get there.' He dishes up for himself. Then he carefully replaces the silver domes back on the serving dishes. He walks back to his chair, sits down and carefully unfolds a white serviette, which he tucks into his collar. 'According to this hypothesis, portals open between two worlds when in both worlds there are at least two persons who will benefit in a meaningful way from its existence.' He cuts a piece of chicken, stacks it with broccoli and puts it in his mouth, chews thoughtfully for a while and then continues. 'I know it sounds a bit iffy, but it is almost as if a portal comes into existence when there is a mutual yearning between two people in both worlds. What we don't know is how that yearning manages to stretch across worlds, how it can connect people, or how the yearning can have a physical effect, or even why and under what conditions some mutual yearnings generate portals and others not and so on. As I've said, it's just a hypothesis and like all hypotheses it generates more questions than answers. Except,' he says, wielding his fork like a little magic wand, 'except in this case we seem to have something that may well confirm that hypothesis.'

'And that would be?'

'Your novel, the one Maurice brought back. When I read it, I immediately realised that the hypothesis is perhaps closer to the truth than we had thought. There is just too much synchronicity at play here for it to be a simple matter of coincidence. It can be no simple coincidence that Luc demanded to use this portal, even though in my estimation as a therapist he had no need for it and consequently would not necessarily benefit from the experience your world has to offer. And yet, he insisted. That's our first clue. Our second clue comes from your novel. Your extraordinary ability to imagine this world without ever having been here, your allusion to Luc and his repeated struggle with an unusual addiction – I must tell you, the accuracy was quite staggering. Eventually, when I added it all up, it struck me that the hypothesis may well be true and that in this case, at least, the portal came into existence through your and Luc's mutual yearning – to, or what for, I do not yet know. Perhaps to resolve something? If so, just what that may be, I do not understand. Do you have any idea?'

'Well, as a character in the novel, Luc was very close to my heart. I did not spend much time describing his life or how he ended up here. I'm not sure why I spent so little time with him. What does matter is why he was so close to me and *that* is something I intuitively understood. Come to think of it, it may well be precisely because I felt so close to him that I did not spend much time writing about him. In my mind, Luc and I share a fascination with mysticism and silence – admittedly for different reasons and as a result of very different circumstances. His refusal to speak moved me deeply and at some level resonated with a yearning I've had for as long as I can remember and that is to live in utter silence – noble silence, if you wish – to live before language, despite language. I don't know if such a life is possible or if it's just a romantic fantasy, but what I do know is that it's a very deep yearning. It is quite possible that I did not spend much time writing about Luc's commitment to silence because frankly I cannot make sense of my own – even though, as I've said, he and I arrived at that commitment in very different ways. I guess what I'm saying is that I like this hypothesis you mention. There is an intuitive truth to the whole idea of a yearning portal. Does the hypothesis have a name?'

'Indeed. Unsurprisingly, it is called the Yearning Hypothesis.'

We sit in silence for what feels like a couple of minutes. He finishes his food while I look around. The moment feels timeless. Doctor Cottard and I are both aware that I will have to return soon and that we still have much to talk about and yet there seems to be no rush, possibly, I think, because I could always return for another visit if the questions we are grappling with today remain unresolved, but possibly also because once a conversation turns to the primacy of and the longing for that which precedes language, it is only to be expected that silence will gradually assert that primacy and roll over the conversation like a blanket of mist over a mountain peak, slowly enveloping it until everything is hidden. My gaze wanders over the sanatorium grounds. It is uncanny how similar the garden is to the way I had imagined it. The vast, expansive and well-kept lawns gradually become less and less manicured as they get closer to the forest; the dense forest beyond which I know lies the main road that leads to Dijon; the road in the middle of which Angèle sat down in a blue dress one night, legs pulled up to her chest, head tucked between her knees, fully intent on being killed by the first car that would . . .

My thoughts are interrupted by Doctor Cottard, who suddenly seems to have an idea. 'One can, of course, also approach the answer to the second question based on what we've learned from answering the first.' Without waiting for my consent or to see if I have a different idea, he continues. 'Now, we know at least one thing. Our Seers of Subtle Gravity have discovered that there is an absolute . . .'

'Your what?'

For a brief moment, Doctor Cottard seems slightly irritated by my interruption. Then he regains his composure. 'Oh yes, I forget. I'll have to start there. This is the "we" you asked about before.' *My Cottard would never use air quotes.* 'Now, where to begin?' Unlike earlier, when he seemed to struggle to find an easy way to explain the complexities of Schrödinger's cat, only to come up with a perfectly simple explanation, this time he genuinely seems to be struggling to find a way into the complexity facing him. *What can possibly be more difficult to explain than the physics of the many worlds hypothesis?* I wonder.

He begins, at first hesitantly, but then with increasing confidence. 'As in your world, we recognise that there are two . . . um . . . shall we call them *fields* of gravity, two kinds of gravity. There is the gravity that weighs down the physical body, Newton's gravity, and then there is the gravity that impacts the subtle body . . .'

'The subtle body?' I ask.

'Yes,' he replies. 'Have you not heard the phrase?'

'Subtle body – as in "the subtle body problem"?' The joke is either lost on him or he does not care much for jokes. Now that I think of it, I have not seen him laugh since I arrived. I suddenly miss my imagined Doctor Cottard, with his clumsy, hand-rubbing guffaw and the way he sometimes doubled over with pure joy when he found something truly delightful. Such a jolly man, my Cottard. The real one is so serious.

'When your physical body gets sick, you go to a medical doctor. Invariably, in your world, anyhow, people are mostly either dismissive or ignorant of the subtle body – or, as it is also known, the spiritual body. Of course, some people and cultures in your world are more open to it and actually practise the subtle arts of healing – acupuncture, homeopathy, reiki, kinesiology and so on. The subtle body is also what people have in mind when they refer to your aura and the chakras or energy centres in the body that generate your aura. Now . . .' he continues – not despite, but I am sure *because* of the fact that he could see I wanted to interrupt him – 'in your world, the subtle body and subtle arts are very undervalued, even dismissed, at worst as inconsequential, weird, hippie stuff or, at best, relegated to that part of the world, a kind of geography of the imagination – India, China, where people "still"' – again with the air quotes – 'believe in the so-called primitive, hocus-pocus healing arts and the reincarnation of the soul because they have not been initiated into the wonders of Western medicine. Yes? Get what I'm saying?'

I know he does not want me to say anything, so I just let him speak.

'Long and short of it is that depending on whether one is talking about the physical or the subtle body, there are two different kinds of gravity at play. On the one hand, there is the gravity of Newton's imagination, which weighs down everything physical, from apples to airplanes. If you jump out of a window, you will fall like a ripe apple. It's all perfectly regular, law-like and predictable and there is no way of escaping its pull except, of course, by means of devices specifically designed to defy gravity, such as rockets and space shuttles. Here we think of that kind as fallen gravity. But then there's also the gravity that weighs down the soul or the subtle body – what we call subtle gravity. As a form of gravity, a force, it is even more mysterious than fallen gravity. To be fair, though, what they have in common is that in neither case does the word "gravity" actually explain anything. If you think about it, the word "gravity" is just a name given to a predictable reaction in the world. But what is it? What is fallen gravity? I'll tell you – it's just a name for a force that we can predict and calculate but which we do not understand. The same goes for subtle gravity. We know there is a force that weighs down on the subtle body; we become aware of it when it becomes visible in the melancholy and sadness that weighs somebody down. Much like fallen gravity, subtle gravity only becomes visible as an effect or a force that acts in the world, but what it is in itself, that we do not know.' Here, Doctor Cottard pauses as if for dramatic effect and holds up his two hands in a gesture of balanced scales. He drops the one hand. 'There is fallen gravity. We don't really know what it is, but we recognise it at work when we see things fall and we call that force gravity.' Then he drops the other hand. 'And then there is subtle gravity. Another mysterious force, which we also don't understand but recognise when we see it at work – for instance, when a person is weighed down by sadness or melancholy, by a fascination with death and impossibility. When a person's spiritual body is weighed down like that, we recognise subtle gravity at work. As a force, subtle gravity may be just as mysterious as fallen gravity, but there are two important differences between them. In the first place, the effect exerted on the spiritual body by subtle gravity is far less predictable than the effect fallen gravity has on our physical body. We may not understand what fallen gravity is, but we can with near perfection predict and calculate the magnetic force it exerts on physical bodies. That is not the case with subtle gravity. We are all subject to it, that much we know, but apparently some people more so than others. You get people who completely succumb to its pull while others seem to live quite happily with it or even manage to work with it, turning it into a driving force that allows them to be free – or if not free, then at least they see it as something to work with, to manipulate for the purposes of their own healing and transformation. But in order to do that, you have to know, really *know* that you are not at the mercy of subtle gravity in quite the same way that you are at the mercy of fallen gravity. From what I know of your world, it takes most people there a lifetime to even learn to distinguish between the two forms of gravity. But here in our world we place much more emphasis on the reality of subtle gravity and that,' the sentence has the ring of a final, concluding statement, an impression confirmed by the fact that Doctor Cottard lifts his wine glass and holds it in the air in a mock toast, '*that* is why I am here and that is what all this is about,' and again that sweeping gesture that reduces the entire world to his domain. 'My job is to get people to embrace the power of subtle gravity, to let them see, feel and understand the difference between the two forms of gravity because once they do, they can start manipulating subtle gravity and escape what they think – what they *think* – is the inescapable and inexorable pull of subtle gravity. Simply put, they are here to learn that subtle gravity can be manipulated in a way that fallen gravity cannot.'

The light of understanding suddenly floods my mind. My world, the world that had become so confusing to live in because it had been torn asunder and divided against me by a series of inexplicable events, suddenly promises to be unified by the obvious. 'So, when I see them at the portal . . .'

'It is because I send them there,' and before I can ask why, Doctor Cottard continues. 'How does one go about making people aware of the difference between fallen and subtle gravity, so that they can eventually embrace the extent to which they can exert control over subtle gravity? This question troubled me for many years after I had opened this centre. Over the years, I tried many strategies and techniques, but they always returned me to the same conclusion: you cannot get people to understand the nature of subtle gravity and the extent to which it is within their power to manipulate it if they cannot first become aware of what inescapable gravity feels like, the inescapable force that fallen gravity exerts on them every day. Think about it. Who among us can say that we are aware of the force that fallen gravity exerts on us every day? No one. We live our entire lives subject to the power of fallen gravity; it is at work in everything we do, touch, every step we take, everything we pick up and put down, and yet we are never conscious of the role it plays in making all of that possible; that it is gravity that determines every one of those actions – how we execute them, what is possible and what is impossible and so on. In order to become aware of gravity, we have to temporarily escape the world, say, by spending a couple of hours in a NASA zero-gravity simulator. For a short while after you emerge from the simulator, you feel gravity and *really* experience its force. Luc's arrival here was an event of particular significance for me in finding a way to give ordinary people that experience. Not long after his arrival, the portal appeared – and just how that happened and how we discovered it is quite an amusing story, but that will have to wait for another day. Let's just say that I visited your world once – no wait, twice; yes, twice in the beginning – and when I noticed the magnitude of gravity there, I immediately realised that this could be my NASA simulator, a place to send my clients, so that they could *really* feel fallen gravity again. And it truly is a big difference. You will see when you return. For my clients, their return to this world is invariably accompanied by a sense of relief, even release.'

He pauses briefly, shrugs his shoulders and continues with an almost apologetic tone. 'Yes, it really is as simple as that. I send them to your world, the heavy-hearted – or, as I've heard some people here refer to them, the heavyweights – the ones who think they have no choice, the ones who have not yet understood the difference between physical and subtle gravity and who consequently do not understand that they have some control over their destiny precisely because they can manipulate subtle gravity. I send them over to your world and when they step back into this world, they suddenly become aware of just how weak our fallen gravity is. They feel a sense of lightness, of what it means to let go and to walk on air and that, *that* is what I want them to experience – that it is possible to walk on air, to be light-hearted, to be a lightweight.'

I put my finger in the air like a schoolboy who has a question, but so does he, as if to indicate *just a second, I'm almost done.* 'Everybody has the capacity to be light-hearted. Some find their own way there and don't have to experience what the portal offers, but others have to physically experience or manifest what being heavy-hearted feels like and, upon their return, feel like a lightweight before they can start embracing the possibility of becoming light-hearted. So, in a sense, I send them to your world not so that they can learn anything about it, but so that upon their return to this world, they can, for the first time, experience how to truly live in their own world.'

The question I have been wanting to ask is still foremost in my mind, but for a moment I am so overwhelmed by the beauty of the therapy Doctor Cottard has developed and how poetic it all is, that I cannot bring myself to ask it. 'That is a thing of beauty,' I say.

He nods knowingly and smiles. 'Thank you. I like to think I've had some successes with it, but it is difficult to tell because – well, as you know, it is not the only form of therapy we offer here.'

'So, who is the "we" you talked about earlier when you said *we* are working on a number of hypotheses. You mentioned Seers of Gravity or something?'

'Oh yes, the Seers of Subtle Gravity. Well, of all the questions we've been grappling with, this is the easy one. This world, *our* world, is not ruled over by politicians, as your world still is. It took Ajna and Maurice a number of rather extended visits to understand just how devalued subtle energy still is in your world. In our world, the really influential people are the Seers and when I say they are influential, I mean it quite literally. Our world is governed, albeit indirectly, as I will shortly explain, by those we call the Seers of Subtle Gravity.'

'Wow! That's a bit far out.' The words escape before I can stop myself. So far, I have managed to play it cool. I kept my cool through the many worlds explanation and the introduction of the Yearning Hypothesis as an explanation for the existence of the portals; I even managed to restrain myself from asking questions when Doctor Cottard introduced the subtle body and the healing role its discovery may have played in Luc's recovery. Throughout it all, I managed to retain a sense of *Well, I'm not that surprised*. But a world ruled over by Seers of Subtle Gravity? That has caught me off guard and the best recovery I can make is, 'What are they? Like priests?'

He smiles. 'No. Well . . . let's say they are individuals who have mastered every single one of the known arts of reading and treating the subtle body.'

'And, in this world, these are the people who make the important decisions?' I ask.

'Indeed,' he replies. 'As I said, they are like your politicians.'

'Well,' I say, folding my arms across my chest in a mock gesture of decisiveness. 'I'm not sure I want to live in a world where the national budget is managed by a kinesiologist.'

And there it is. For the first time, Doctor Cottard bursts out in uncontrolled laughter. 'Very funny,' he says. But then he quickly recovers his seriousness. 'It's not like that. Of course, we have politicians who do what only politicians can do, but each of them, from the most insignificant all the way up to the president, is always accompanied by their own personal Seer.'

'So more like a personal trainer, then?' I smile broadly. This is fun.

'No. More like a spiritual adviser. The job of the Seer is to constantly balance the politician's subtle body before and during every process of important decision-making. The Seer reads their subtle body to make sure that they are, well, you would probably say in the right frame of mind to make the decision, but it's really a matter of their being in the right frame of body to make the decision.'

'That is very impressive,' I say and this time I mean it.

'Here's an example,' he says. 'Are you familiar with the chakra system?'

My heart skips a beat. *How did he know?* For a moment, I am torn between pleading absolute ignorance and gushing forth about the wonders and wisdom of the ancient understanding of the human being as a unified body-mind-soul with a great many chakras or energy centres, very often reduced to the seven big ones. I feel an almost uncontrollable urge to confess and to come out with it all, to tell Doctor Cottard that I have been working on a novel in which I imagine Luc gradually releasing his fascination with death and repetition by tracing his awakening from the first through the seventh chakra. But I realise that I cannot possibly share that with Doctor Cottard yet. It's too early. We have not even begun to understand the relationship between Luc and myself, what brought him to my world and me to his world. And besides, what if I am getting it wrong this time? In *Imitation* I may have done a passably good job of imagining this sanatorium and Luc's reason for being here. Sure, as Doctor Cottard has pointed out, I was a bit off here and there, but by and large I seemed to have got it right. But what if in *Subtle Gravity* I am not just a bit off, but completely off about his recovery? It is simply too early for this conversation, I decide and, feigning ignorance, reply, 'You mean the theory that the human body is driven by seven energy propellers?'

'Propellers?'

'Yes,' I reply. 'That's how I always think about chakras. They're like propellers of an aeroplane and they all have to work in order for us to fly; ideally they have to be synchronised, otherwise . . .'

'We crash?'

'Yes, sort of,' I say sheepishly, suddenly aware of how childish my analogy is.

'Well, that's a bit dramatic. I don't know about propellers,' he says, 'and it's not just a theory. We're dealing with almost 5 000 years of spiritual practice here. But, that aside, you seem to have a vague understanding of the importance of chakras. Let's just say that chakras are the interface between body and mind. Each chakra is connected with a fundamental psychological and spiritual need. The first chakra is located in the perineum and is associated with being grounded in the world, trusting that you have a right to exist and that you have a right to whatever you need in order to survive in the world. The second chakra, roughly situated in the genital area, is associated with sexuality, emotions and our ability to feel, while the third chakra, in the solar plexus, is the locus of our personal power and our capacity to express our will. The fourth chakra is located in the sternum,' and Doctor Cottard briefly puts his hand on his heart and for a split second I cannot help but think he is about to pledge allegiance to something, 'and is related to our ability to express love and compassion. The fifth or throat chakra is all about communication and finding your voice while the sixth, which is often referred to as the third eye, is the source of our imagination and intuition – or in some people who have a particularly well-developed sixth chakra, it can even amount to a degree of clairvoyance. Then, of course, there is the seventh chakra, located at the crown of the head and associated with knowledge, understanding, transcendent consciousness and all that. Chakra spiritual practice is all about making sure that . . . as you put it, each propeller works properly or that they are well balanced.'

'And by "balanced", you mean?'

'Well, at an obvious level, it means being neither deficient nor in excess. In order to strike a balance in any chakra, we need to understand and satisfy the psychological need associated with it. Take, for instance, the first chakra, the so-called root chakra. It is, in a sense, the most fundamental because it is associated with our most fundamental need – to know that we have a right to be, to exist in the world. If your first chakra is balanced, you will believe you have the right to exist and that you have a right to whatever you need to sustain that existence – the stuff necessary to live: food, water, shelter and so on. But, and this is why the Seers play such an important role in our world, to recognise that you have a right to exist means also recognising that other people similarly have the right to exist, and to recognise that I have a right to whatever I need in order to sustain my existence also means that they have the same right. Having a balanced first chakra means accepting that I cannot have everything . . .'

'So, what you're saying is that the Seer . . . well, actually, yes, I understand what you're saying about the right to exist and limitations and so on and I get how this all relates to the first chakra, to the sense of being grounded in the world, and I can well imagine that we all need an adviser to help us, as you say, balance the chakras and satisfy the spiritual and psychological needs associated with each, but how does this relate to what Seers do for politicians?'

'Well,' Doctor Cottard responds, leaning back in his chair, 'isn't the classic definition of politics that it is all about who gets what?' But before I can confirm the truth of that undergraduate truism, he continues. 'We want our politicians to make the right decisions, don't we? And by right decisions, I mean decisions grounded in the recognition that while as an individual he or she has a right to exist, so does everyone else. And just as he or she has the right to what they need in order to sustain their own existence, so does everyone else. The first chakra is the ground zero of every political decision because at bottom, as I said, every political decision comes down to who gets what. In our world we do not want politicians to make decisions grounded in an excessive or deficient first chakra, so the job of the Seer is to make sure that when politicians make decisions that directly impact who gets what, their first chakra is neither deficient nor excessive, but well balanced.'

'Wow,' I say, realising that I sound as impressed as I am. 'That redefines the entire meaning of politics and justice and, well everything . . .'

'Indeed, it does, and to understand the profound impact of prioritising the subtle body as we do, just imagine our world by adding the word "subtle" as an adjective to, well, everything – subtle politics, subtle justice . . .'

'Subtle democracy,' I add wistfully.

'Precisely,' says Doctor Cottard and, clearly inspired by the fact that I have not displayed any of the condescending attitudes toward the subtle that is so typical of the world I come from, continues. 'The third chakra is also an instructive one. In making decisions, all politicians exercise their will. Now, the trick is to make sure that this does not simply come down to politicians imposing their will on the people. You want to make sure that their will coincides with . . .'

'Yes, the will of the people. We also have that one.'

'No, that's just democracy. In subtle democracy the trick is to get the politician's will to coincide with the Divine Will . . .'

'The Divine Will! Are you kidding me? Here we are, two people from neighbouring worlds having figured out how to fold space and time in order to have lunch together and you're still talking about Divine Will?'

But Doctor Cottard does not miss a beat. He is clearly well prepared for this one. 'I see your scepticism,' he says, 'and it's because you still think of Divine Will in terms of the old religious categories of predestination, God having a plan and all that.' There is some truth in this but before I can say anything, he continues. 'But it's not like that. I'm not talking about a force up there planning what happens down here. That's the wrong image. You need a new image. Think of everything, the whole universe as well as the collective and individual consciousnesses in it, as one big unfolding or blossoming flower. There is always direction in the unfolding, although not the kind of direction that we can think of in terms of the old image, of up and down or right and left. The direction is simply fruition, the whole big totality coming to blossom and every individual, by being part of the whole, plays a part in that blooming. So, ideally, every action of every individual, every decision they make, should contribute to or coincide with the blossoming of everything. That, and that alone, is what I mean by the Divine Will. Does my individual decision coincide with this coming to fruition of the world? Does it contribute to or detract from that blossoming?' He pauses, slightly absorbed by what appears to be his own frustration with explaining something that should not need much explanation. Then, almost as if he is giving up trying to make it any easier, he says, 'It's really not that complicated. The universe is one big fractal . . . like a head of broccoli. Did you know that technically the broccoli we eat is a flower? Well, each one of us is no more than a small floret or broccoli flower bud and whatever we do must be done in such a way that it coincides with the blooming of the whole head – which may not be unrelated to what the mystics have in mind when they talk about the Godhead.'

I suddenly feel immensely tired. This is all very intense and I need to rest soon or at least talk about more ordinary things for a while. It is as if my mind had been waiting for that little bit of recognition. 'Do you grow your own vegetables?' I ask.

'Yes, in fact, we do. Including broccoli.' A smile. 'And herbs. Would you like to see the vegetable and herb gardens?'

'Yes, don't mind if I do – if only because it never crossed my mind to imagine a vegetable garden here.'

'Ah, but that may be because you were thinking about all the big questions when you wrote about us . . . but, indeed, you are right. Where is the vegetable garden in all of this?' Then, as if we had not been sidetracked at all, he continues. 'We can't possibly supply every individual in the world with a Seer, but we can make sure that every individual who makes important decisions on behalf of everyone else has one – at least, at that level, there will be some synergy between where the universe is going and where any individual's decision will take us, a synergy between our will and the Divine Will. And that's the job of the Seer. As in the case of the first chakra, the Seer will make sure that the third chakra of the politician who is expressing his or her will is neither excessive nor deficient, but well balanced and that they don't err on the side of oppressing us with a glorified vision of the Divine Will or their own. People can get carried away in both directions, as you know. An excessive third chakra will cause an individual to believe that he understands the laws of history and that he can therefore determine his own future, while a deficient third chakra will let an individual think those laws are imposed on us and that there is not much to do about it all . . .'

'There it is,' I say softly, almost to myself. 'Subtle democracy.'

'Precisely. Based on subtle justice. And this place,' that gesture again, 'is where I do my bit to fix those individuals who don't have Seers to assist them, which is most people, but these are people who perhaps need a more serious intervention.'

There is a long silence between us. Then a question causes a slight surge of energy in my body. 'And how does this bring us any closer to understanding how I could have seen your world so clearly when I wrote *Imitation*?'

His smile speaks of quiet satisfaction. Somewhere in the course of our conversation, he has clearly begun to understand the answer to that question and the thought that he may have an answer dispels the last trace of tiredness from my body. I sit up and say, 'You know, don't you?'

'Yes, I think I do,' he says. Then, cautiously, but with quiet confidence, he adds, 'Perhaps it's not that complicated. It seems to me that you simply intuited this world. Remember what I said about the sixth chakra, the so-called third eye, which is associated with intuition, imagination and in some instances even with clairvoyance?' I nod. 'Well, you clearly have a very well-developed sixth chakra, which allowed you to see – as in *really* see, in the sense of *intuit* – our world. You thought you were imagining it and, in a sense, you were because intuition is the eye of the imagination. But it's also more than that, more than imagination. Sometimes acts of the imagination are not just about making things up. Sometimes when we think we are just making things up, that act of imagining is actually spurred by our intuition, and intuition, as the word suggests, amounts to a kind of seeing into the future or into a different place before it happens or before we get there. I think this is what happened. You intuited this world in the profound sense of intuition as an act of clairvoyance. Through an act of imagination, you portrayed it as you saw it – and, by seeing it, I mean quite literally that you, well, as I said, intuited it . . .'

'Yes, yes, I get it,' I say, almost impatiently. What he is saying is so obviously true that I feel slightly bored by the explanation. *How is that possible?*

'When you wrote the novel, you drew a lot from your own memories, but you also added lots of detail to those memories – elaborations, as it were. For instance, for your setting you remembered a beautiful old chateau much like this one, but you added a gazebo and a rose garden because – who knows? – perhaps the chateau you remembered had these features or you just thought they should be there.'

I briefly think back to one or two scenes in the novel that took place in the gazebo and rose garden, mostly conversations between Luc and Angéle. It was always so quiet there. No wonder I was drawn to those memories.

'As I've said before, there is much about portals we don't yet understand. It's possible that it was only because of the coming into existence of the portal between our and your world that your sixth chakra could intuit what this world looks like, so there is that added complication now. Just as we answer one question, a portal to another question opens. Point is, you saw or intuited a lot, but you also missed a lot and that is perfectly understandable because you did not really understand the world you wrote about. You thought you were making it all up, not that you were seeing into another world.'

'But how . . .'

'I . . . don't . . . know. It may have something to do with the portal that we're now certain has something to do with you and Luc. These things all seem to be linked, but just how they are linked is what we're trying to figure out. At least we've learned something more now, but to get to you and Luc, we have to refine our question a bit, I think. Let's assume that the Yearning Hypothesis is true. What do you think the mutual yearning could be that caused the portal to come into existence?'

I look past his face in the direction of the great staircase and the main entrance. *Just as I imagined,* I think, *but then again, so typical it does not really require much imagination.* A couple of people are coming out through the door, probably just having concluded a session of sorts. They settle down on the stairs. I recognise a couple of the faces from my evenings at Harvesters, watching them as they disappeared through the curio shop window.

'So, you recognise them?' Doctor Cottard says. Not a question but a simple statement.

'Yes, but not from *Imitation*.'

'I know,' he says. 'All the clients who were here back then have left.'

'Except Luc,' I add.

'Except Luc,' he says.

8

We are sitting in silence, contemplating everything that has been said, when I see Maurice approaching from the side entrance to the main building. *Exactly where Luc's fire was meant to reach the building,* I think and notice again with a pang of disappointment the absence of the gazebo and rose garden, the walkway with its roof of cross-beams entwined with vines that should run all the way from the gazebo to the main building. What if I had written that passage on a different day? Would Luc still have made the same decision not to start the fire? I must find out what really happened that night. I watch Maurice as he walks across the lawn, the ease with which he walks, which, relatively speaking, looks like any other kind of walking in any other world where the person walking is used to the gravity of that world. Doctor Cottard is right about so many things. We are never conscious of the gravity of the world we live in. We only become aware of it in a kind of negative way, by visiting a world with more or less gravity, after which we either struggle to walk when we return or suddenly enjoy the light-hearted feeling of walking as if on air. I can see why Doctor Cottard would send the heavy-hearted to our world. I can well imagine a melancholy soul from this world, one of those people for whom the funniest of jokes always remains tainted by traces of sadness and unfreedom (or too much freedom), arriving in my world and thinking, *Hell, just walking around in the world can be so much more oppressive than*

I am used to, and stepping through the portal back into this world to find a lightness of step, a forgetfulness in their bones and muscles that, if only for a fleeting second, allows them to imagine a thought that has not lived rooted in the same place for as long as they can remember: life is possible. 'I don't send them over to learn something about your world,' Doctor Cottard had said, 'but for them to learn something about their own world when they return.'

Then Maurice is at the table and, as he reaches out to collect our plates, I cannot help noticing how the white glove on his right hand does not quite succeed in covering up the missing finger. Where the finger is meant to be, he has had the glove finger shortened and sewn to the palm of the hand, presumably so that it would not flop about uselessly, drawing attention to the missing finger. *It's the obvious thing to do,* I think, as I watch him stack everything on the trolley. Doctor Cottard thanks him, Maurice bows graciously and starts pushing the trolley back towards the entrance from which he had come. As he walks away, I become aware that I have been lost in thought and that neither Doctor Cottard nor I have said anything for quite some time. *Just thoughts and sounds. This must be what it was like for Luc when he was so enchanted by silence, so caught in that reverie of unity that is the sound of the world. Life as simple, silent awareness. How blissful it must have been for him to just exist in that absolute . . .*

'Not quite a burglar, is he?'

'No,' I reply and inadvertently smile at the thought. 'Most certainly not. In fact, there is something quite comical about imagining him crawling around on my patio's canvas roof, trying to find a way in . . .'

'He's a good man, our Maurice,' replies Doctor Cottard. 'Been with me since the beginning.'

I do not know what to say. The silence that follows is not as comforting as the one that preceded it, but before I can think about it any further, Doctor Cottard stands up. 'I think I have an idea. Come, let's go for a walk. I'll show you the vegetable garden.'

'And the herb garden.'

'Same thing,' he says, as we start walking in the direction of where I had imagined the gazebo to be. We do not speak for a couple of minutes and, as we get to the place where I imagined Luc's fire to have been stacked, I steal of couple of glances around at where I imagined Luc would have got rid of the twigs and branches that night. But there are no traces of any human activity around, not even of the ground he would have had to smooth over with his feet to conceal the evidence of what he had been up to. *How far off am I this time? Will I ever be able to trust my imagination again?*

We walk past the imagined location of the rose garden before Doctor Cottard speaks again. 'I have an audacious idea,' he says, as if it were the most ordinary thing to state and, as he says it, I realise that the statement sounds particularly promising coming from somebody so calmly elegant and controlled. 'If we want to understand the nature of your and Luc's relationship, it is to the origin we have to return – not just the origin of this portal, but perhaps the origin of this world. As soon as I realised this, I remembered something that may well be relevant. It's a long shot, but I think it may well get us there.'

I respond with something that sounds like a combination of a soft sigh and a smile, a little guffaw perhaps, and say, 'I'm open to all possibilities.' It was on the tip of my tongue to add, 'I didn't come all this way . . .' but I caught myself just in time. In the short time that I have come to know the real Doctor Cottard, I have learned to rein in my penchant for silly jokes.

'Our Seers of Subtle Gravity, the old ones, or, as we refer to them, the Austere Ones, have recollected in their particularly intuitive way two important facts about the moment our world split off from the one you live in.'

'Only two?' That one slips out before I can stop myself.

'Well, obviously not only two. They know a lot more, but when I say two, I mean two things about the origin that may point us in the direction of the answer we're looking for. Firstly, there is the exact time of the split and secondly there is the Word that resounded at the Origin of this newly created world.'

'The Word?' I repeat in disbelief. 'The Word at the beginning, as in "Let there be light, and there was light"?'

'Precisely,' he answers without hesitation. 'Just like that, except in our case the Word that announced the beginning of the world was a little more, shall we say, human?'

I stop and turn to him, compelling him to do the same. 'And? If it was not "Let there be light", then what was it?' I ask.

Without the faintest trace of a blush, he says, 'You should have told me you were still a virgin.'

'Excuse me?'

'You should have told me you were still a virgin.'

'What on earth are you talking about?' I feel the blood rushing into my face. 'Are you seriously suggesting to me that I should have . . .'

'The phrase,' he smiles, barely containing himself, 'the phrase at the origin of our world. It was not "Let there be light" but "You should have told me you were still a virgin".' And his smile broadens to a wide, comfortable grin. My blush has bloomed into a full tomato-red face and the best I can do is to laugh with him.

'Very funny,' I say when we eventually stop laughing. We have resumed our leisurely stroll and I attempt to recover from my embarrassment with a question. 'So, you're telling me you live in a world where there was nothing and then somebody said, "You should have told me you were a virgin" and suddenly there was light?'

Doctor Cottard smiles a slightly condescending smile. 'No. That's not it. The Word didn't create the world. And the phrase didn't create the world either. Language doesn't have that power – and, as an aside, it is precisely because it doesn't create the world that some people, mystics and so on, are so seduced by the idea that they can somehow find a way back to the big silence that precedes language, but that's another story.' He pauses briefly, as if to allow the mood of our laughter to find its way back into the conversation again. 'Remember how in the Bible it says in Genesis 1 that God created the heavens and earth; that the earth was formless and empty and the Spirit of God hovered over the waters? Only in the third verse, and *after* the act of creation, does God say, "Let there be light." So, there is an act of creation that precedes the Word or phrase that resounds at the origin.'

'I see,' I say. 'And in this world, what do the Austere Ones tell you? What action preceded the declaration "You should have told me you were still a virgin"?'

I realise the stupidity of the question as I ask it and the blood rushes back into my face again. I gratefully acknowledge from the corner of my eye that Doctor Cottard is not looking at me. He is staring into the distance, but the smile is audible in his voice. 'Now, that is not very difficult to imagine is it?' And then, almost as if he were trying to save me from the embarrassment, he continues. 'The problem is that although we can deduce the obvious, the Seers can't actually see past the Word, or to be more precise, past the phrase at the origin, all the way back to the singularity that gave rise to the phrase. That's the bad news. The good news is that with their well-developed sixth chakras they can intuit the precise date when our world split off from yours, which was shortly after followed by the phrase "You should have told me . . .".'

'Well, that doesn't surprise me,' I chip in. 'Where I come from, they've also managed to get quite close to the exact date of the origin, to the Big Bang that got the whole thing going, although I must say I often think 13.8 billion years ago doesn't quite qualify as a date. We can look back all the way to just after the Big Bang, but we cannot see the actual moment itself.'

'Well, fortunately, we are much closer to our origin, so the Seers can in fact be a lot more precise.'

'And? What have they come up with?'

'They say that our world came into existence on 22 February 1996, at precisely 4.36 a.m.' He hesitates and when he speaks again the slight tension of anticipation in his voice does not escape me. 'Does the date mean anything to you?'

I gasp and this time the blood rushes away from my face. I stop and stare at him in complete disbelief. My whole being feels drawn into a vortex, a singular black hole, where the gravity is so intense that nothing, not even thoughts, can escape. I feel the vortex closing in on me, along with the sensation that there is no escaping the inevitable pull of the conclusion that awaits Doctor Cottard and me.

'That is my birthday,' I stammer, his eyebrows lift with curiosity, 'and Juliet and I met on 22 February 1996.'

'This is beginning to sound promising,' he says and for the first time I sense that he is not always completely in control of his emotions.

Then, as the last drop of blood leaves my face, a single thought is released from the gravitational pull of the black vortex. 'Oh fuck!' I say. I feel my hands. At some point I had put them on my head, where they are now rubbing my hair in a gesture of panic and confusion. I start pacing up and down in front of Doctor Cottard, who has stopped to face me.

'Earlier that evening I met Juliet at a party. She's a dancer and I went to watch a show that everyone was talking about. I can't remember how, but I somehow ended up afterwards at the party organised for the cast and . . . and . . . we got chatting and then we went home together, to my place, and . . . well, we made love.' I stop. I know how this story ends and I know Doctor Cottard knows and that he is just waiting for me to say it. *There is no escaping the pull of this one.*

'And?'

'Well, at first she wouldn't let me enter her, said she wanted to get to know me better first. So, we just fooled around and when I couldn't hold out any longer, I told her that I wanted to come inside her . . .'

'And did you?'

'Yes. And as I entered her, I thought I could feel the tightness of her vagina making it slightly uncomfortable for both of us, but . . .'

The blood was returning to my face again, too fast, too close to another blush, but why not? I have never, ever told anyone this story and here I am sharing it in detail with a man I barely know. 'It just happened,' I say and decide to leave it at that.

'But that is not the end, is it?' he asks with a combination of gentleness and humour.

'No, it isn't. Afterwards, we lay there in silence for a while. I remember at one point turning to her. The memory is so vivid. She was lying on her back and I was on my side, my head supported in my right hand. I was looking down at her. I remember tracing the profile of her face with my finger. Then she turned her head and looked at me and there was something . . . yes, something so immediate when our eyes met that I recall a distinct shudder. I even thought, *Maybe she's the one*. That was when I stroked my thumb across her lips and said, "You should have told me you were still a virgin." Given the timeline, I can well imagine that it would have been around 4.00 or 4.30 in the morning.'

Doctor Cottard and I both know that *that* was the end of the story, but he can see how much it meant for me to be sharing such a private moment with him and he knows that honouring the intimacy between us is more important than understanding the origin of the world.

'And what did she say?' he asks and gently touches my left shoulder with his right hand.

I feel the warmth of his touch. 'Quite strange, I thought at the time,' I say. 'She just smiled and said, "The world is as generous as we want it to be." I never quite understood what she meant,' I add.

Doctor Cottard taps me gently on the shoulder again and says, 'Come on. Let's walk.' After another couple of minutes during which I knew we were thinking along the same lines, he eventually articulates what we have both been thinking. 'Well, I think we have a better idea now of the general *deed* that preceded the *Word*, but more than that, we have at least a couple of possible smaller actions of creation that could have been the precise moment of the split.'

'Indeed,' I say.

'It could have been any of those moments, either the moment of coitus, or the moment when you thought you broke Juliet's hymen, or perhaps the moment when you looked at each other and sensed something eternal about love because – am I right? – this is the Juliet you went on to marry, isn't it?'

'Yes, indeed,' I agree. 'Twenty-five years ago.'

'Well,' Doctor Cottard says. 'This is fascinating. In your world scientists can look back roughly 13 billion years to when the world was but a fraction of a second old, but not earlier than that, not beyond that point. In the same way, our Seers have intuited that our world must also have started with a Big Bang of sorts, but little did they know how different our Big Bang was . . .' and he giggles in a way that until that moment I would have thought completely out of character for him. In fact, for very brief moment I get a glimpse of my Doctor Cottard who so delighted everyone with the way he could guffaw with laughter. 'I cannot wait to tell them.'

It is my turn to smile. 'Good luck with that.'

In the brief silence that follows, I recall the two occasions on which Doctor Cottard had remarked that my time in this world was limited and that soon after our return to the main building he would have to leave me because he had work to do. *How much time do I still have?* I did not want to ask him for fear of breaking the spell of our conversation, but I was suddenly aware of a sense of urgency. There is very little time left and we still have to find an explanation for why I have such a powerful connection to this world and the one person in it that followed me all the way into mine.

'Does all of this explain why I have such a strong connection to this world?' I ask.

'Not quite,' he answers somewhat pensively. 'It explains the fact or the origin of the connection, but not why it should be so enduring, nor why it involves Luc.'

By this time, we have walked all around the edges of the well-kept garden, skirting the periphery of the forest. In the process we circled the chateau and are now walking around the back where, for the first time since I imagined it, I have a new perspective of the building. For some reason, nothing I knew of ever happened behind the chateau and I never once imagined the building from that vantage point, which probably explains why I did not know about the lush vegetable and herb garden that suddenly comes into full view. 'There it is,' Doctor Cottard says, as if presenting the garden for inspection. But my thoughts are elsewhere.

'How old is Luc?'

'Twenty-five this year,' answers Doctor Cottard. 'I know because just the other day I went through his life chart, plotting all his suicide attempts, trying, I suppose, to see if there was a pattern of sorts because if that is the . . .' He stops abruptly and turns to me. He knows what I am asking.

'And do you have children?'

'Yes, we do – a daughter. Juliet fell pregnant that night.'

There is that now familiar squint in his eyes as he asks, 'And how old is she?'

'Twenty-five,' I reply.

'Let me guess – she was born November 1996?'

'Seventeenth,' I reply.

'Well, happy birthday Luc,' he says and a smile as generous and beautiful as I have ever seen spreads across his face. 'You know, of course, what this means, don't you?'

'I'm afraid I do,' I answer, and for good measure I repeat myself with a feeling of something I can only describe as a combination of resignation and immeasurable relief. 'I'm afraid I do.'

'Twins,' he says through his big smile. 'My God, this is getting more and more intriguing.'

'But how can you be so certain?' I ask. 'I mean,' and for a moment I am so confused that I struggle to find words. 'It doesn't make sense,' I state so emphatically that I realise I sound defensive. 'According to the many worlds hypothesis, or as you explained it to me earlier anyhow, when the world splits off, it duplicates everything in it, so in my world there would be me and Juliet and our twins and all of us are supposed to exist in this world, isn't that how it's meant to work? I mean, even if the world did split off in the moment shortly after orgasm or when Juliet and I looked at each other, it's the whole world that splits, not just bits of it. How come one of the twins stayed behind in our world and another grew up in this world, presumably with another version of myself and Juliet?'

'Who, I must tell you, got divorced very soon after Luc was born,' Doctor Cottard says.

'Whatever,' I say, slightly irritably.

'Well, in principle, you are right. But we understand as little about the particularity of splitting worlds as we do about the way in which portals between worlds subsequently come into existence. In this case, you will just have to trust me that there seems to be something immaculate about Luc's conception – conceived in your world, but born into this one,' and then in a meandering, wistful tone, 'born upon a void . . . perhaps that explains why he's constantly hankering after . . .'

'Trust you? Because you see it?' I ask and immediately regret the hint of sarcasm in my voice.

'Precisely,' he says. 'I may not be a Seer, but when I see the truth, I see it. Our Seers can discern the truth on the basis of one or two clues, many without any clues whatsoever; they just see it. I'm not that austere yet, but when I get a couple of clues and I *see* the truth, I know that what I intuit is the truth. And *this* is a truth, as mysterious as it may be that one of the twins could have been conceived in your world, but born into this one. It's as miraculous as . . . well, you know what I'm saying. Either that, or our world split off from yours in the moment shortly after the orgasm, so that the two Juliets ended up with separately fertilised eggs – something like that. Whatever the case, it feels like a truth to me that there is something immaculate about Luc's existence in this world, an origin that cannot be fully comprehended, and that it explains much of his behaviour, his fascination with death and silence that you described in your novel.'

My head is spinning. We have arrived at the fence around the vegetable garden, but as beautiful as it is, it cannot compete with the abundance of thoughts rushing through my mind. 'So, in my world, Juliet gave birth to one of the twins and your Juliet gave birth to the other. Is that what we're saying?'

'Yes, that is the truth,' he says with a quiet certainty that dispels any lingering doubt I have. Gently, he adds, 'How does that make you feel?'

'To be honest, for now, just confused. But in a strange way also quite relieved. It's as if I have just found an answer to a question that has been haunting me for a very long time.'

I turn away from the vegetable garden to face the chateau again. Doctor Cottard also turns around. 'She quite a beauty, isn't she?' he says.

'A chateau is a chateau is a chateau,' I say.

He looks at me. 'I'm concerned about time,' he says. 'I think it's time you met Luc.'

9

Doctor Cottard knocks softly and, after a muffled 'Come in', opens the door and walks into the room, with me following close behind. A young man is sitting with his back to the door, looking at what appears to be a very large computer screen. He is making gestures in the air as if conducting an orchestra while on the screen in front of him corresponding traces appear and disappear. He is somehow drawing figures on the screen without touching it, but the figures do not remain on the screen. Their appearance is somehow related to the movements of his hands, but not their disappearance, which seems to occur quite randomly. Before I can think about how it works, the young man stops gesturing and turns around. The screen goes black instantly. He looks at Doctor Cottard and then at me, before he says, 'Doctor Cottard, what a pleasant surprise.'

He stands up and for a brief second the three of us do not quite know what to do. Then Doctor Cottard says, 'Hello Luc, good to see you too. I have brought a guest.' He turns to me and gestures an introduction. I am speechless. It is without doubt the exact same Luc that I saw on campus and whom I have been following around, the same Luc I witnessed on more than one occasion as he disappeared through the curio shop window. *Nothing off here,* I think as I stretch out my hand. He looks exactly as I always imagined. But before I can say anything, Doctor Cottard tells Luc that I am a close friend who has come to visit and that I would like to talk to him privately, if that is okay with him. Luc frowns, then nods as he shakes my hand. Doctor Cottard unceremoniously turns and leaves the room. He closes the door behind him, leaving Luc and me somewhat uncomfortably facing each other. Luc walks back to his desk, swivels the chair around to face the bed and sits down. He gestures to the bed and I sit down on the edge.

'I don't mean to be rude,' he says, 'but who are you again? And why are you here – I mean, with me? What do you want to talk about? I didn't quite understand what Doctor Cottard meant when he introduced us.'

'Mmm . . . it's quite complex,' I begin and for a moment it seems completely impossible to find a way into the conversation I need to have with him. 'I'm a novelist,' I say somewhat hesitantly.

'Cool,' he replies. 'I like novels, although I haven't read much of late. I've discovered Spacedisk,' he says and points to the screen. 'Do you play?'

'No, I'm afraid not.'

'What kind of novels do you write – detective novels or what?'

'No, more philosophical ones,' I reply. 'I like to use characters – no, "use" is perhaps the wrong word – let's say I like to show how characters live complex philosophical ideas or to explore such ideas through the lives of my characters – if that makes any sense?'

'Oh,' he says. 'What kind of philosophical ideas?'

'Well, in my previous novel, I wrote a lot about addiction. I think it's a fascinating philosophical problem.' I am surprised by my honesty and directness. 'Yes, I suppose that's what it's been for me. A philosophical problem that I explored through the lives of the characters. In that novel,' I hasten to add before I get sidetracked by another question, 'I wrote about this sanatorium and the people in it. I thought Doctor Cottard's approach to the treatment of addiction had interesting philosophical dimensions. In fact, I think of addiction as a profound philosophical problem – not many people realise that . . .'

'This sanatorium? Did you come here to talk to people, interview them and things like that? I don't remember seeing you here before.'

'Well, yes and no,' I answer. 'The last time I didn't really collect a lot of information through interviews. I just imagined what they would tell me if I were to interview them. Same with Doctor Cottard. He didn't really explain to me how he treats people here. He didn't have to because I just kind of imagined how he would, you know, treat people.'

'I see' he says. 'Makes sense. And now you're back. Why? Are you writing a sequel or something and you've run out of ideas? Are you going to interview people this time – is that what you're doing here? Is that what Doctor Cottard meant when he said you would like to speak to me?'

'I suppose so,' I say. This could not be more difficult. 'I mean, yes, I am writing a sequel and there's a very good reason I came . . .' I almost said 'back here', but I don't want to lie to Luc. If he catches me out in one lie, he will not trust me when it comes to the really difficult and improbable answers I will have to give him at some point, ' . . . here. It's always easier to write about people and places you have physically met and visited. The imagination can be very limited and limiting.'

'Well, I don't know what other people have said, but if this is about interviews, then I am not interested. I don't like the . . .'

'No, no, no. Don't worry. It's not about interviews. I'm sorry, I should have immediately clarified that.' I am going to have to give him more, I realise. 'Actually, I already wrote about you in my previous novel. There's a character called Luc.'

'But we have never met,' he says and seems surprised and perplexed at the same time.

'I know.'

'How did you get my name? Did you just make stuff up about me? And if it's a fictional character, what does that have to do with me anyway – I mean with me, the real Luc? Doctor Cottard didn't tell you stuff about me, did he?' He suddenly sounds very suspicious.

'No, don't worry. Back then, I didn't discuss any of this with Doctor Cottard. He was just as surprised as you. And, yes, I made up a lot of stuff. That's what novelists do.'

'So, then . . . I don't understand. What does all this have to do with me, then?' He is beginning to sound just a little bit irritable and probably wants to get back to playing Diskspace.

'You don't need to worry about confidentiality or anything like that. It's all perfectly fine. I've already got more material than I can use. In fact, I'm nearly done. Got about twenty or so pages to go. I just thought since I *am* here, it would be nice to meet you.'

Luc nods, reassured, but still non-committal. 'That's cool. I'd like to read the first one. Where can I get a copy?'

'I know Doctor Cottard has one. Perhaps if you asked him, he'd be willing to lend it to you. In fact, I'm sure he would.'

'Okay, I'll ask him. So, what do you want to talk about? And will anything I say change things you're writing about now? I still don't understand how this is not an interview of sorts.'

For a moment I am very nearly overwhelmed by the desire to confess everything; to tell him about the Luc I wrote about, his trials and tribulations, his fascination with silence and death, and how he fell into a reverie of silence that intrigued me so much that I had to write a second novel, which, for reasons I did not understand at the time, felt as if my own life depended on it; that I decided to write him back into language again and imagine the journey he may have gone on to rediscover his voice after such a long silence. Yes, for a brief moment I want to tell him everything – but not because it would matter to him. No, my reason would be much more selfish. I would want to know if I got it right, in the first novel and again this time. Doctor Cottard had said he was very impressed by how well I imagined this world across the mysterious divide that separates our worlds, but we never spoke about Luc and the reason why he was at the sanatorium. There were more important questions to answer in the short time I had with him. But now I am dying to know if I got it right. All of it. Was Luc as troubled as I imagined him to be? Had he indeed attempted suicide so many times, one of which brought him closer to the Godhead than the human imagination can endure? Did he, as a result of that experience, withdraw behind a veil of silence, and did he embark on a long journey back to language of the kind I was imagining in *Subtle Gravity*?

But I resist the temptation. There are simply too many delicate questions, questions that would require of him to trust a complete stranger before he would be willing to even acknowledge that I had asked the right question. It would take a lifetime of getting him to trust me before I could ask the questions I wanted to ask. As much as this is the perfect opportunity to put my mind at ease about a great many things, it is also an impossible opportunity. I simply cannot do it. Besides, a little voice in the back of my head interjected, *What if you got it wrong last time? What if Luc never went through anything vaguely similar to what you imagined?* Indeed. What if the Luc of my imagination was like the gazebo or the rose garden, one of those things that was slightly off in my imagination? What if, for instance, I imagined him physically quite correct – because, my God, he looks just as I imagined him! – but instead of a fascination with death and silence, it turns out he is a sex addict? What if my sixth chakra was not as finely balanced as Doctor Cottard had suggested and all I ended up doing was creating a character on which I projected a whole lot of my own stuff? What if all those delicate thoughts about our mutual fascination with silence and the Godhead turn out to be nothing more than a feeble excuse that I made up to use him, like a pimp, for my own enrichment? *Don't even go there,* another little voice in my head says. *Don't go there!*

'So, do you want to check something? Because if your Luc is not based on me, what do you need from me?' He is getting visibly impatient now and no longer trying to conceal that he is eager to get back to his game.

'I'm sorry to take up so much of your time, Luc. I know this must be strange, but I will explain everything in a short while. There's a very good reason why I need to ask you some personal questions. Just one or two, if you don't mind. Would you be willing to answer them? As I said, it is not some kind of interview and it's not about gathering material for my novel or anything exploitive like that. Just one or two questions. I'll explain, if you just let me . . .'

'Sure,' he says, a bit more relaxed now that it is becoming clearer what I want and do not want from him. 'Don't worry about my time,' he says, swivelling again to face me and leaning back in his chair. 'I have way too much of it here.'

The thought crosses my mind that his sudden willingness to co-operate is really just about getting rid of me as soon as possible. 'Tell me about your father.'

'Well,' he begins, and I am surprised by the ease and directness of his reply. 'He's not my real father. He's my adoptive father. His name is Doctor Obiwan Ojuok. My mother met him when she worked for some NGO in Nairobi many years ago, after she divorced my real dad. Then they moved to Paris when he became the Kenyan ambassador.'

'Ah, that's very interesting,' I reply. 'And do you know anything about your real father? Did you ever meet him? Did Doctor Ojuok or your mother ever explain to you what happened to him, or why they got divorced?'

'No. She hardly ever speaks about him. Now and then she makes a casual remark about him, mostly quite derogatory. Sounds like he was a bit of a prick. I don't get the impression it was a serious relationship.'

I smile. Thank God for Doctor Cottard's many worlds explanation earlier. In the same way that Europe can invade Africa in one world while in another Africans plant a flag on the beaches of Normandy, one can be a prick in one world and a nice guy in another. 'Do you ever wish you knew him, or that you had met him?'

'Not really,' he says a little dreamily, staring out the window. 'Until very recently, that is. I don't know why, but recently I suddenly felt it may be important to meet him. Don't know where that came from.'

'Recently?'

'Yes, a couple of weeks ago. I think it was maybe because of the therapy process. I don't know. Maybe it triggered some yearning in me. Maybe I always yearned to know him, but just didn't realise it. It's hard to tell.' Then, as if he suddenly feels guilty, he hastens to add, 'I like my dad, though. My stepdad, I mean. He's a cool guy. I used to call him Dad. He insisted. But lately I just call him Obiwan. It's more like we're friends now.'

'But at the same time, you started to miss your real father? Makes sense, I suppose,' I answer and stand up. I walk across the floor to the window. I am going to have to take the plunge. But how? There is no short cut, I realise. I will just have to come out with it and then take it from there. I take a deep breath. 'Luc,' I turn around and look at him. He is looking at me quizzically. 'There is no easy way to say this . . .'

He seems perplexed. 'What's going on? It sounds like you have bad news. Is it about Angèle?'

'No, Luc. It's not about Angèle,' I assure him and immediately regret interrupting him. I should have let him tell me what he is worried I may discover. At least then I would have some certainty about something I either got right or not. My thoughts are interrupted by Luc who seems even more worried now.

'Then what?' he demands.

'Look, there is no easy way to say this.' I walk back to the bed and sit down. I take a deep breath. 'Luc, I'm your father.'

He stares at me for what feels like eternity. I can see the meaning of what I have just said sink into his heart.

'You *what*?'

'Yes. I am your father, Luc.'

He stands up and grabs his head. 'What the hell?' he exclaims. 'What the hell are you talking about?'

'I know this must be upsetting and confusing, Luc, but it is as simple as that. I am your real father.'

'The one my mother divorced all those years ago?'

'Well, yes and no.'

'What the hell does that mean? Yes and no? Either you are, or you are not.' Now it is his turn to start pacing up and down.

'Well, that's where it gets complicated, Luc.'

'No. No! That's not true! That's impossible! My mom told me I mustn't think about him . . . you . . . no, *him* because he would never come to look for me. Does she even know you're here?'

'Is that what she said?'

'Yes. Maybe she was trying to protect me, I don't know!'

'Protect you? From what?'

'The truth?' He sits down again and covers his face with his hands. 'She once told me that it . . . me, I mean, that it happened at some party and it wasn't planned. You got married anyway, but it didn't work out and she divorced him . . . you – no, *him* – shortly after. You didn't seem to care much. Maybe that's what she was trying to protect me from. *You*!'

'Shit. Sorry Luc,' is all I can manage, not quite sure how else I can possibly respond to what he has just said.

We sit in silence for a while – him with his elbows on his knees, head hanging down, and me on the bed, waiting for the right moment to speak again. After a short while, he looks up and asks, 'So, was it like that? Drunk at a party?'

'Not quite. It was after one of her performances. We went back to my place and . . . well, yes, that's when it happened. But you have to believe me, it was quite beautiful. In fact, there was a moment when I thought she was the one. That's why I married her.'

I am not sure if he even hears what I am saying. He just sits there, the original anger or excitement gone. He stares at the floor. 'It's impossible,' he says finally.

I stay quiet for a couple of seconds. Then I decide there is no other way. 'As impossible as a portal that leads from one world to another?'

He immediately looks up at me, his eyes as clear as two dark mountain pools. He squints, as if that will allow him to see better. 'Did the Emperor tell you about that? What did he say?' He continues more defensively. 'And yes, so what? I used the portal and went to the other world a couple of times, but what does that have to do with anything?'

'No, he did not tell me about the portal. He didn't have to. I discovered it all by myself.'

'But how could you?' he asks. 'The thing is in his office and only some people get to use it and even then Ajna . . .'

'Not this one, Luc. I discovered the other one, the one in the other world. The world where I come from. I discovered it quite accidentally . . .'

His eyes widen. 'You're from *that* world?' he asks incredulously. 'But then how can you be . . .'

'Yes, indeed, Luc. I am. And,' he opens his mouth to start speaking, but I am not going lose momentum now, 'I saw you there one day when you came to my university campus. You stood at the bottom of the building I work in and looked all the way up to where I was standing on the sixteenth floor. It was far up – or well, far down for me, but there was no mistaking you. I recognised you immediately. I took the lift down and ran to where you had been standing to meet you, but when I got there, you had already left. And then I saw you again on a number of other occasions when you used the portal at the shopping complex to return here again. That's how I know. I started to wait there and, after many attempts, managed to make it here, too.'

While I was talking, his mouth had dropped open in unselfconscious amazement and by the time I finished he just stared at me in utter disbelief. I waited a couple of seconds for him to absorb it all, not sure if I should continue or if I should give him an opportunity to say something, anything, to convince me that he believed me. Eventually, he sits up again and says, 'Fuck me. So, what are you doing here?'

I have no better reply than a counter-question. 'At first I wasn't sure, Luc. I mean, what were you doing over there? Why did you come to my world? Do you know?'

He shakes his head slowly, as if he needs time to think of a reply. 'No, not really. No, I don't know. In fact, apart from the whole weird experience of the gravity on that side, I was a bit disappointed. It was quite boring.' And then, almost as an afterthought, 'Ajna is not much fun anyway. She spends the whole day reading her book. I mean, what's the point? I don't get it.'

The worst is over.

'Well, Luc,' I say, releasing a deep sigh. 'Now you can begin to understand why I said it's all a bit complicated.'

He just looks at me. I take another deep breath and then I tell him everything I learned from my conversation with Doctor Cottard. I don't even try to explain Schrödinger's cat and how the many worlds hypothesis came about because, given that we both know about the existence of the other world and yet find ourselves sitting across from each other, that much I assume can be assumed. Instead, I start with the night I met Juliet, how we went back to my place and how, according to Doctor Cottard, the most reasonable explanation is that our worlds split at the moment of orgasm, or shortly after, and how inexplicably his sister was born of my Juliet and into my world, and he of the Juliet in this world.

Throughout my explanation, Luc just nods every now and then, but I can tell from his face that none of this is coming as a big surprise to him. I suppose once you have travelled through a portal from one world to another, just about everything invoked in order to explain how that could be possible would sound true in some way. Then I go on to explain the Yearning Hypothesis, how this possibly explains his recent yearning to meet his real father, at which point, his eyes start to fill with tears. I am relieved by the ease with which he is accepting the truth. I can see how my words sink into his soul and as I watch him accept the truth of who I am and of the yearning that had so recently taken hold of him, I feel a deep and tender love for this young man stirring in me. There is something so iridescent about him that for the first time since I have imagined him I recognise in myself a yearning that must have been there all along, a confused kind of yearning, a yearning to be young again, to *be* like him; no, to *be* him, to be *that* iridescent again. We are both fighting to hold back tears when I am suddenly overcome by an immense longing to spend the rest of my life with him, to have him by my side forever, to raise him as the son I never had and to conquer the whole world, father and son, side by side! Would it not be wonderful! After 25 years, father and son reunited from two worlds across an unknown distance in the universe! Nobody would believe me, but then again, I would not need to tell anyone, except Juliet, who I know would accept everything without hesitation. As for anyone else, what business is it of theirs?

I stand up and walk over to the window, turn around and say, 'Doctor Cottard has explained to me about subtle energy, this place, his approach to treating addictions, what you're all learning here, how coming over to my world is one of the ways he teaches people to let go of stuff. He has told me about the heavyweights and the lightweights, or the light-hearted – I forget now which one it is. You know, in my world people don't take subtle energy all that seriously and, in that sense, you've been very privileged, Luc, to grow up in this strange world. And he also explained the importance of the Seers of Subtle Gravity – it's all way ahead of where we are. So, I have an idea.'

I sit down on the edge of the bed again and put my hands on his knees. 'Are you ready?' He nods again and as I begin to speak, even I am surprised by the urgency, excitement, perhaps even a slight hysteria in my voice. 'Why don't you come back with me Luc? Yes! Come back with me to my world, the world I come from and live there with me!'

He opens his mouth to speak, but I hold up my hand to indicate that I cannot be interrupted, not now. 'If I am correct about the journey you've been on since you arrived here, if I am right about it at all – and we will have to talk about all that later because right now I am running out of time, we're running out of time – if I am right about it all, you do not yet realise your importance. You've only begun to discover your power, Luc. Join me, come back with me, so that we can help people in my world to better understand the power of the subtle. With our combined insight, we can, I don't know, create a whole subtle empire and bring order to the world. Think how exciting that could be!'

I can tell from the expression on his face that I have become more excited than I realised and I feel slightly embarrassed about it. He makes another attempt to speak, but my urgency will not be stopped. This time I hold up both hands to make it clear that I am not done yet, that I have one last important card to play in my desperate attempt to persuade him. 'Luc, I don't know how you've come to feel about Doctor Cott – the Emperor, as you call him. I don't know how close you are to him and I also don't know how you feel about going home one of these days, but I can tell you that if you come with me you will not destroy the Emperor. He is a Seer of the Subtle. Believe me when I tell you that if you decided to come with me, he would not be surprised. He would have foreseen it. It is your destiny, Luc! Join me, and together, we can rule my world as father and son! Come with me. It is the only way!'

I may as well have been talking to myself. It is clear that Luc has not really been listening to me at all. He is sitting there, staring at me as if I have gone completely mad. There is a long silence between us. I can sense that we are both immensely relieved. Everything has been articulated, the origin, the yearning and the invitation. All that remains is the decision. And it is his decision. Without looking away, he says, 'I hear what you're saying. And yes, I want to go home now.'

10

My heart leaps. Does he mean it? Does he really want to go home? With me? Home to the world where his life, if not began, at least originated?

'Are you certain?' I ask gently.

'Yes. I want to go home. Please leave me alone now. I need some space. And then I'm going to phone Obiwan to fetch me. I want to go home.'

For a moment I am slightly embarrassed by the way I spoke. I must have sounded so desperate! But then again, I was, was I not? If it were true what Doctor Cottard had said, that a portal between worlds opens as a result of the mutual yearning of two people, how strange is it that, although I never knew I had a son, I still yearned for something only that son could give me; that only he could help me overcome this feeling of living in two worlds at the same time; that I would be united with myself, and myself with the world? And if that is what I really longed for, was it not an entirely selfish hope?

I stand up slowly and stand in front of him where he is still sitting in the chair with his head hanging down between his knees. *He is not even going to look up and say goodbye,* I realise. I briefly think of putting my hand on his head and in that way inviting him to look up. I long to hug him, but the gesture, if not the intention, feels out of place because I suddenly feel haunted by the spectre of selfishness. He may or may not borrow my novel from Doctor Cottard and he may or may not read it. My gut feeling is that he will not and that he will never know the journey I have been on with him; how I have watched over him – yes, like a father – for so many years and how I started to miss him the moment I left him behind in the first novel; how that yearning slowly accumulated over the years until it became so unbearably acute that I went on an extraordinarily long and complicated journey to imagine my way back to him. But mostly, I will never know how much of the Luc standing in front of me corresponds to the Luc of my imagining.

I turn away and walk to the door. With my hand resting on the doorknob, I turn around one last time. He is still sitting exactly as he was when I got up from the bed and I cannot help thinking that he looks defeated and I can understand why. Neither of us knew about the bond that existed between us and yet, here we are. We have both travelled across time and space to the other's world to have this conversation, to recognise in each other a yearning we had never named because we did not and could not recognise it for what it was. And yet, in this very moment, I finally realise what I was after, what had inspired me so many years ago to intuit this sanatorium and its people.

'You're quite iridescent, Luc,' I say. 'Thank you for letting me see that.'

I open the door, walk out and close it behind me again. I walk to the front door in the hope of seeing Doctor Cottard, but the whole place is eerily quiet. Doctor Cottard had not said what his appointment was or with whom or how long he would be busy for. I sense a presence behind me and turn around. It is Maurice.

'It is time to go,' he says. 'Doctor Cottard can unfortunately not be here to say goodbye. He said to wish you a safe journey back and asked me to show you the way.'

'Thank you, Maurice. And please thank Doctor Cottard for his time.'

'He also asked me to make sure you know that once you leave, you will never be able to return here again, nor will any of the patients here ever be able to use the portal to come to your world either.'

'Never? Nobody?' I ask. I am surprised, but also not. Although I had initially thought that I would be able to come here as often as I wanted to, just as they come to my world as often as they like, I already sensed in the urgency of my conversation with Luc a certain finality. I intuited a closure that would make future visits, what? Unnecessary? Superfluous? Pointless? Nonetheless, I cannot stop myself from asking, 'But why?'

'As I believe Doctor Cottard explained to you, there is a lot about portals we do not yet understand even though over the years we have managed to formulate a couple of working hypotheses.'

'Such as the Yearning Hypothesis?'

'Yes. Shall we?' He steps aside and with his left hand extended invites me to start moving in the direction of the staircase that leads to where Doctor Cottard's office is. 'We have to return to the office where you arrived.'

As we start ascending the stairs, he continues. 'The Yearning Hypothesis is very credible because not only does it explain how a portal is created, but also how and when it closes. In line with the hypothesis, we've worked out that in cases where it is abundantly clear that a portal came about as a result of reciprocal yearning, the portal closes again as soon as a fundamental decision has been made. I take it that Luc has decided to stay and you have decided to return. That is the closing decision. The fact that you both made a choice closes off the possibility that the portal represents.'

We carry on going up the stairs in silence. Near the top of the staircase, he sighs the kind of sigh that makes me realise that he has probably had this conversation many, many times before. 'There will, of course, be other split-offs from this world – and yours – a great many, and they will always generate portals but never again this one.'

'I see,' I say, but I do not really see. I am suddenly very tired. I, too, just want to go home.

Then we are in front of Doctor Cottard's office. He pushes the door open and lets me in. 'This is as far as I can go,' he says. 'From this side there cannot be a witness who does not also go through the portal. If somebody tries to witness others go through the portal without intending to follow them, it doesn't work. It may be the other way around in your world, but . . . there it is.' I look at him to say goodbye and catch his smile just before it disappears. 'It's a subtle difference,' he says.

'Thank you, Maurice,' I reply. I should probably shake his hand, but I do not want to leave this world with the reminder that not very long ago I found his index finger on my patio floor. So, I walk into the office and close the door behind me. One last time I walk over to the window where Doctor Cottard so often stands, pushing the curtains slightly aside when he wants to look down on the clients who sit and lie strewn across the elaborate staircase like random pine needles on a dirt road. But outside is as deserted as inside. *How odd,* I think and I walk up and down the length of the office a couple of times, savouring the lightness of my steps. *It's time to let go,* I think. *Time to let go.* I walk up to the full-length mirror against the wall. I stop in front of it and tap its surface with my finger. Tink, tink. Nothing out of the ordinary there. Then I take a step back, draw a deep breath and walk into my own reflection.

11

Jason is exactly where I had left him, deep in concentration, looking at his cell phone screen. How on earth am I going to explain all of this to him? That the portal took me to another world very similar, but slightly off from this one, that I had lengthy conversations with Doctor Cottard and Luc and that I managed to work out why Luc came to this world and who we are to each other? Jason will no doubt have a million questions and I will not know where to start or how to answer because so many of the answers burrow into other answers, which in turn burrow into other answers – an infinite regress of questions and answers that only I can begin to unravel and even I will need a lot of time to do that to any degree that will give me some peace. Will he believe me? Does it matter?

He sees me walking towards him and puts the phone down. A big grin spreads across his face. Well, at least he seems to still be in a good mood. Maybe he will surprise me. Maybe all this strangeness will be much more acceptable to millennials who live in multiple worlds anyway. I begin to relax a little bit. This may be a bit easier than I feared. As I sit down opposite him, he can obviously no longer contain himself. 'Well, that must be just a little embarrassing?' he says. He pulls his glass closer, pushes mine in front of me and proceeds to share out the remainder of the whisky.

'Hell, yes, I need one of those,' I say.

Giggling softly, he drops a couple of ice cubes in our glasses. 'Cheers!' he says, holding his glass mid-air.

I raise my glass and take a sip. 'Well, I don't know if embarrassing is the right word. Perhaps I went a bit over the top at the end, but I think once I've explained things you will agree that . . . phew! It's all a lot more complicated than I think I can explain.'

He bursts out laughing. 'What can be complicated about it? A lecturer invites his student to observe him walk through a window that is actually a "stargate"' – again with the air quotes – 'to another world. No, no, wait! The student *must be there* because the lecturer can't walk through the "stargate" to the other world if he's not observed because it's the witness that has the power to make it real.' Jason touches an imaginary communication device on his left shoulder, bends his head down slightly and says, 'Scottie, at your service, Sir. Ready to beam you up!' Then, before I can say anything, 'And then the lecturer walks slap-bang into the window as any other mortal would and, after standing there for a couple of seconds looking as dazed and embarrassed as any other mortal would, skulks back to the student and calls what happened "com-pli-ca-ted". Oh man, such a pity it was too dark to video. It would have been a sensational YouTube hit. I can just see it – "The Subtle Art of Intergalactic Travel". Ha, ha, ha! Cheers Prof!'

I stare at him in disbelief, but he is unstoppable. 'Tell you what,' and by this time he is laughing so much that he has difficulty getting the words out, 'why don't you do it again and this time I'll follow you to where there is enough light so I can make a video of it? Oh, come on! Immortality beckons!'

'It's too late. The portal has closed,' is all I can manage.

My Iridescence

12

I am completely flummoxed by Jason's reaction. I briefly act the self-deprecating, 'weird' professor, play a bit of the embarrassed space-traveller role, feign some light-hearted disappointment about the limits of the known laws of physics, finish my drink and then abruptly announce that as far as I am concerned the fun is over, that I am very tired and have to go home.

As I push my bicycle out the parking lot and head home, I allow the disappointment space to breathe. How is it possible? My recollection of everything is so vivid – the office I stepped into, Maurice and his missing finger, Doctor Cottard – how different he was from what I had imagined! – the long conversations, the garden, the missing gazebo and Luc. Above all, my conversation with Luc. How could that not have happened? No, in *what world* did that not happen? The phrase suddenly strikes me as particularly apt, but without easing any of my confusion. It is almost as if somebody who has been tortured by the Schrödinger's cat experiment for too long suddenly lifts the lid of the box and proclaims, 'The cat is dead!', only to be asked by someone standing next to him, 'But how do you know?' To which he replies, 'Because I just looked in the box, dummy!' And then to be told, 'No, you didn't. I have been standing right next to you the whole time and I would have noticed if you did.' Is it possible that the moment I stepped into the shop window another world split off from ours – in the one world I passed through the portal and in the other word I did not? But then, how would that account for my presence in this world where, according to Jason, I did not? I suddenly get annoyed with myself.

Rookie error! Why did I not bring back some evidence of my travels – a small stone, a piece of bark, a flower, a herb from the vegetable garden, something, anything? Why did I not have the presence of mind to bring something back to prove, even if only to myself, that I had been there? To prove that I knew this because I had something in my pocket when I got back that was not there when I had left.

As I stop to wait at the traffic light at the busy intersection a block from my apartment, I recall an episode of an action TV series from my childhood. The Invisible Man could become invisible simply by (if I remember correctly) turning a ring on his finger. This allowed him to enter all sorts of heavily guarded places to outwit the crooks and save whoever needed saving. But then one day I found myself perplexed. The Invisible Man had broken into a house, made his way to the top floor, entered the bedroom where the safe was and, knowing that he needed a key to open the safe, instantly worked out (how exactly, I cannot recall) that the key was in the drawer of the bedside table. Although he was still invisible, the camera persuaded the viewer that he walked over to the bedside table and removed the key. Then the key happily jingled through the air all the way to safe, where it unlocked the door and a stack of documents floated all the way to the door, where the Invisible Man suddenly re-appeared holding the folders, with a nonchalant grin on his face. That was when it hit me: Why do his clothes become invisible when he turns the ring, but the key and the folders do not?

Despite my somewhat morose mood, I smile at the memory. It was the rookie error of an invisible script writer, just as my failure to return with even the smallest piece of evidence from Doctor Cottard's world turned out to be the rookie error of an amateur space traveller. I push my bicycle back to my apartment because I need the time to think, or at least to calm down. The confusion would not be clarified that evening, that much I knew. But at least I could wear myself down a little more. One thing was certain as far as I was concerned:

my experience was, beyond any doubt, very real. How science fails to explain it is none of my business and that Jason witnessing me allowed me successfully to pass through the portal, yet did not allow *him* to experience the consequences of that observation as *his* side of the witnessing equation, is a radical uncertainty I cannot get my head around.

When I get home I lean my bicycle against the garage door and, after locking the patio door behind me and drawing the curtains, I make a cup of tea while I run a hot bath. One of two things was going to happen after I had the bath. I was either going to sleep the sleep of the dead or not sleep at all and spend the rest of the night tossing and turning, haunted by Jason's jeering laughter and my own bewildering confusion. By the time I sink into the bath, it is obvious which scenario I have to prepare for. The strange sense of living in two worlds, of being divided in myself and feeling equally alienated from both worlds, the familiar feeling of living with a solid void in my gut, has returned.

By the time I get into bed and turn the bedside light off, the feeling has grown even denser and heavier. I place my hand on my solar plexus and it is as if I can feel the solid void pulsating just beneath my hand. I know why the feeling is back. *It is because now I know with undeniable certainty that at least two different worlds do in fact exist.* Earlier that evening I had first-hand experience of the fact that worlds actually do constantly split off from one another and there was a very real possibility that this is exactly what had happened at the precise moment when I walked into the shop window, but I – the person from the world in which I *did* walk through the window – somehow found himself back in the world in which I did *not* manage to walk through the window. The 'I' that is lying in bed thinking through everything that had happened that night is not the same 'I' that everything had happened to. The only way I can explain this is that I am now out of place, out of world, in the wrong place at the wrong time, or in the wrong world at the right time or just... and as my thoughts start to lose ground to a dark forgetting that had started to roll over me like a mountain mist, I think of Luc. How ironic. It is not a matter of *like father, like son* but rather *like son, like father.* Just as Luc originated in one world but was born into another, and just as his birth in that world was therefore a kind of miraculous conception, so my being in this world, lying here on this bed in a world in which my truth is apparently laughably untrue (which means that I am quite literally *in* this world, but not *of* this world), my existence is now also based on a miraculous conception. Like son, like father. *What have you taught me Luc? Did I need to know this?* As the final clouds of unknowing tumble down into me, a final whisp of a thought streaks through the sky: is this the final revenge of the Imposter – leaving me to make sense of myself as miraculous misconception?

13

Perhaps equally miraculously, I wake up the following morning no longer shadowed by doubt or the ominous presence of the solid void, the menacing presence of the Imposter or any thoughts about what it would mean to go on living in a world I had left the previous evening. Instead of all that, I wake up clear as a bell, knowing exactly what needs to be done. I have to go back to the office where it had all started and complete *Subtle Gravity*. All through my strange experiences and encounters, I had faithfully been plugging away at the novel, leaving a trace of rough sketches and outlined chapter sections in various stages of completion. On days that I could not think or found myself unable to concentrate, I returned to the incomplete sections and wrote them out in full, then editing them until I had a nearly full first draft. I might need the whole day to iron it all out to the end, but it would be quite possible to end the day with a complete first draft.

I get up, have a quick shower, shave and put on a comfortable tracksuit. Then I make myself a cup of coffee, which I drink standing up at the kitchen counter. I pack my bag with a bottle of juice and ample snacks to see me through the whole day. Then I get on my bicycle and ride to campus. I never go to work on Sundays because the place is too deserted and eerily quiet. There is a difference between it being quiet enough to write and being too quiet to write. Once I get to the sixteenth floor, I unlock Maretha's office, then mine, put my bag on the couch where I often nap over lunch, draw open the blinds and even slide open the big window. For a moment, I find myself standing in the exact same place where I stood when I looked down and saw Luc staring up at me, his one hand shielding his eyes from the glaring reflection of the sun off the white surface of the building. So much has happened since that day that it feels like a lifetime ago. *How the world has changed!* I turn around and walk back through Maretha's office to the small staff kitchen where I make myself a cup of tea. I drain the last of the soya milk from the box, toss it in the bin and go back to my office where I sit down behind my desk, enter my password and open the file titled *Subtle Gravity*. How many times have I told myself that I should split the text into four different files, one for each part, because it would be much easier to work with each part that way? But I never have and I know I never will. For some reason, I like working with one big file. It allows me to change, add or delete things anywhere in the text whenever I want to, without the additional task of having to open or maximise another file and doing a word search in each one.

    I scroll down the document, stopping every now and then to read a sentence or a passage, fixing a spelling mistake here, a grammatical error there. *Talk about seeing your life flash before your eyes!* Scenes, snippets of dialogue, long (*too long?*) philosophical meanderings, some easy and playful, others more difficult (*too difficult?*) all float up effortlessly from the bottom of the screen, defying gravity in a way only language can until I get to the setting right at the end which I had prepared in my mind as I cycled in that morning. There is so much I imagined since Juliet suggested that what I needed was a witness, things I have not even noted down yet. But those blanks I will have to fill in later.

In this final scene, Luc has gone to Doctor Cottard's office to say goodbye. His parents have been notified that he is ready to go home, and they would be there in about half an hour. I find the place and I am just about to make him sit down across from Doctor Cottard when I hesitate. The final thought that streaked across my mind the previous night just before I fell asleep is there again: if I am a fundamental misconception, what guarantee do I have that what I have been writing and am about to write are not similarly so? Am I about to get it right (presuming that I have been right so far), or will I be just off? And if I am off, how far off will I be? Is what I have written and what I am about to write a true reflection of what has been happening over there in their world, or is it something that I am just about to make up, an intuition that is just off? In this particular instance, am I about to observe the last minutes of Luc's stay at Doctor Cottard's centre, or am I some kind of Imposter who pretends to write about things he knows nothing about? Is what I am about to write a matter of seeing or believing? I lift my hands off the keyboard and lean back in my chair. Staring at the screen in front of me, I try to comfort myself by recalling Doctor Cottard's surprise at how accurately I had managed to intuit his world and smile at how, when I commented on my accurate description of the chateau that housed the sanatorium, he dismissed that as an inappropriate example of my clairvoyance, 'A chateau is a chateau is a chateau.' Perhaps that is the way to think about it. A novel is a novel is a novel. It is impossible to imagine it wrong. I take a deep breath. My doubts may be thousand-fold, but so are the images now cluttering for expression. I am going to trust the real Doctor Cottard on this one. My doubts start to fade behind the cloud and I feel my confidence returning. I can see how this ends.

14

Luc sits down across the desk from Doctor Cottard, who is rolling a pencil over and over between his hands. He smiles at Luc. 'So, finally ready to leave, are we?'

Luc smiles back and says, 'Yes, indeed.'

'I am curious. Why now?'

Luc shrugs. 'Just feels right, I suppose.'

'Really? Just that?'

Luc seems unperturbed by the directness of the question. After his three sessions with the Emperor, he expects nothing less. 'That and . . . everything changed because of my father's visit. Did you know he wanted me to go back with him?'

'No, I didn't know, but I suspected he would try. But you declined, which also does not surprise me. If you don't mind, I'd like to hear why you think you did.'

'That isn't very difficult. I don't know him and, besides, I love the dad I have in this world. I guess I just needed to know that I had a real father and that he cared enough about me to want to take me away with him. That was enough.'

Doctor Cottard smiles. 'Yes, to take you back to his world with him. Not the usual divorce settlement, is it?'

But Luc is not in the mood for jokes. He seems preoccupied by something he wants to say and appears to be looking for a way to steer the conversation in that direction. Almost as if he is thinking out loud, he says, 'I was worried when I went to bed last night. So much happened yesterday that I thought I wouldn't be able to sleep. But it was weird. I thought that I would either sleep like the dead or not sleep at all, but eventually I did fall asleep. In fact, I can't remember the last time I slept so deeply.'

'I can understand that,' says Doctor Cottard and leans back in his chair, crossing his legs.

'Then, this morning I woke up feeling very different from other days. I sat up in my bed and realised that waking up in the morning is probably the most important moment of the day. How we wake up determines so much of how we will spend the rest of the day. It's as if waking up sets the scene.'

'A wise comment,' says Doctor Cottard. 'But how do you think your father's visit changed the way you wake up? And why? I think I know what you mean, but can you say more about it?'

Luc does not need time to think about it. He has clearly been thinking about this. 'It's the longing, or as he put it, the yearning. He told me about the Yearning Hypothesis and how portals come into existence.'

'Yes, a compelling hypothesis, don't you think? And what do you make of it?'

'I think there's something there. It would certainly explain why I had such an urge to go through the portal to his world, even though you thought I didn't need to.'

'Yes, I now see that too. I'm glad you insisted. But you know the portal is closed now, don't you?'

Luc frowns, more in slight surprise than disappointment. 'Nobody told me, but if yearning creates a portal, I suppose it makes sense that the end of yearning would mean the end of the portal.' Without waiting for Doctor Cottard to confirm his interpretation, he continues. 'After he left my room yesterday, I went for a long walk in the garden. I realised that I had spent my entire life longing for something, something so fundamental that I couldn't give it a name. It seemed too big to be contained by a name. But then he came and after I decided to stay and he left, that longing was suddenly gone. Before, I would wake up every morning and start the day fighting for what I wanted or needed because I thought I had no right to exist. It is as if I've always yearned to exist, as if I yearned for existence itself, as if I couldn't simply take it for granted that I did. I often felt like an imposter who was living somebody's else's life, who borrowed a life that did not belong to him and desperately tried to make it his own. I lived in perpetual fear of being caught out and being named for the imposter that I felt I was. After – or now – somehow after he left or maybe because I decided not to go with him, I now somehow trust the fact that I exist. This is my world and the only justification I need for the fact that I exist is that I was born into it. I think at some point I started to confuse the yearning for my real father with the yearning to exist, but . . .' he hesitates for a moment as if he cannot quite understand what he is saying himself, 'somehow the two are related. All I know is that between my going over to his world a couple of times, even if I did not know that it was his world, and his visit yesterday . . .'

'And your active decision not to go back with him to his world,' interrupts Doctor Cottard.

'Yes, all of that presented me with what I had yearned for and somehow in the process dissolved the yearning itself even though in the end I did not want what I yearned for. Does that make any sense?'

'It makes perfect sense, Luc. Those I think of as the light-hearted know that there is something tugging at the end of our longing, but they also know that life is possible only because we will never understand what is doing the tugging.' A slight shrug of the shoulder. 'The heavy-hearted, on the other hand, think life is impossible as long as they don't know what is tugging at the end of their longing.'

'That's nice,' says Luc. 'This is the first time I really understand the difference between the two.'

'I think you understood it long before you realised that you did, but that doesn't matter now. What matters is that the difference between the light- and heavy-hearted also plays out in a number of other attitudes, such as generosity, gratitude. As far as I am concerned, I realise that somebody is ready to leave this place when they recognise that the world is a generous place, that they do not have to fight for and cling to things in order to feel that they belong. Generous people are attached to people, not things; addicts are attached to things, but seldom to people – something like that.' And then, almost as an afterthought, 'And generosity and gratitude go hand in hand.'

'Gratitude?' asks Luc. 'Why gratitude?'

'It's quite simple. People make the mistake of thinking that gratitude is an attitude that one can or must adopt, as if it is something we can *will*. But it doesn't work like that. Gratitude is rather – how shall I put this? – an expression of something else. If you know, *really* know that you exist, that you have the right to exist and that you are only a small but meaningful part in a whole interconnected web of being – an insignificant part, but still, a meaningful part – if you trust all of that, you also trust that you have a place in the world, in the greater order of things. And when you know *that*, you cannot but express gratitude. No, that's not quite it. Let's rather say, gratitude is simply the expression of trusting existence. Gratitude is life become visible. Now, does that make sense to you?'

Luc smiles slightly mischievously. 'I think I know what you mean. Addiction can be quite a thankless business.'

Doctor Cottard smiles. 'Funny, but yes. When I sense gratitude in someone, I stop worrying about them. After that, it is just a matter of time and they end up . . .' one hand drops to indicate the chair Luc is sitting in, 'sitting right there, telling me they are ready to leave. That is the beginning of a new beginning.'

They sit in silence for a while. Outside, Luc can hear the birds in the trees, the quiet rustling of the wind through the leaves, the soft murmur of people chatting on the staircase below and, somewhere down the passage, a vacuum cleaner approaching and retreating, approaching and retreating. But all sounds now seem distant to Luc. They are no longer his world but, just like everything else, *in* the world. He glances at his watch. 'They will be here soon,' he says.

'Yes. What are you going to do when you get home? What lies ahead for you?'

But it is as if Luc does not hear the question. Instead, he slowly shakes his head as if he is still processing everything Doctor Cottard has said in the last couple of minutes. 'I never realised that I would be considered an addict – that is, until my parents brought me here. And even then, for a long time, I did not understand why I was here.

It took me quite a while to understand that the repeated suicide attempts were also an addiction of sorts – did you not say, when was it, in our first session . . . no, the second – did you not say that repetition is the hallmark of all addictions?'

'I did. To be caught in repetition is to find oneself in a reverie of sorts, mesmerised by the possibility that the repetition of an action can stop the world from moving, from becoming, from changing all the time.'

'Yes, I get that now,' says Luc, 'but in retrospect I don't think *that* was my real addiction. I think the closest I came to being an addict was when I could not imagine ever speaking again, when I just wanted to stay silent. Nothing brings the world to a standstill quite like a refusal to speak. I don't know why, but during those months when I did not speak, I somehow understood one thing: language moves the world. It is in speaking that we have to confront over and over again the original loss of belonging in the world. And I just wanted to stay there. I'm still not sure how I ended up there. I know it had to do with the vision – I mean, the near-death experience and all that. It was after that that I just could not bring myself to speak. And it was the strangest thing. The whole time I was aware of the tension between the world of silence and the world of language. I could hear people talking around me and sometimes even to me and with me, but there was just no way I could speak back. Deep in my gut – here,' and he places his hand on his solar plexus, 'right here, it just felt that to speak would amount to the biggest betrayal imaginable.' His face suddenly lights up. 'It's almost as if there was a gulf between the world of silence and the world of language and between them, a portal of sorts that I was expected to discover and figure out how to use . . .'

'Except nothing in you yearned to find out.'

'Exactly. To me, it was as if the world of silence was light, as light as a feather – a world in which there was not just less, but almost no gravity. And on this side, on the side of language, everything seemed so heavy, weighted down by the betrayal of naming things. Is that a weird use of the word "betrayal"?'

'Not at all. I understand what you're saying. But . . .'

'No, wait. Please let me finish. Eventually, when I did speak – the night with Angèle,' a quick glance at his watch, 'I was very surprised by how light the world of language felt. It was not at all as heavy as I imagined it would be. I learnt something important that night – the worlds of silent unity and language are equally compelling. There is a different gravity in each, but it is not a question of heaviness or lightness. It's a question of which is more compelling.'

'That is an interesting difference. What does that mean to you?'

'It's all about traces. In the world of silence, language is a trace; in the world of language, silence is a trace.'

Doctor Cottard frowns. 'And by trace, you mean?'

'Just that which we are aware of, but which is not there. Both silence and language are haunted by what they cannot do, and what they cannot do is ironically all we want them to do when we find ourselves in one or the other. When we speak, we want language to convey silence, and when we commit ourselves to silence, we want to tell people about it and share the experience with them. For as long I didn't speak, all I heard was language and sounds. Since the night when Angèle – well, one night when she made a difficult decision – all I have been aware of every time I speak is what I am *not* managing to say, what gets lost in the attempt to say something. Similarly, I will never be able to speak about the experience of my silent unity with the world because that was between me and God. Now, when I speak and therefore feel a sense of belonging to the world of other people, I still feel lonely because it feels as if every act of speaking is a betrayal of God.'

'So, what you're saying is?'

'I guess what I'm saying is that there is only betrayal either way. We betray ourselves into existence. Betrayal is the ground of our existence. All yearning is a longing *not* to be a traitor, to remain faithful to being. We tend to think that we exist in the tension between two promises of faithfulness: to be and not to speak, or to speak and not to be. But that is not the case. Existence happens somewhere in the middle; life is indifferent to our betrayal.'

Doctor Cottard is captivated by the expression on Luc's face, which had suddenly changed when he mentioned Angèle. At first it looked like sadness, but then he recognises that it is something very different. It is compassion, an all-encompassing empathy. There is something at once graceful and hard about the expression and Doctor Cottard has seen it many times before when clients come to say goodbye. It is the expression of freedom won through discipline, a hard-won freedom snatched from the jaws of repetition through the discipline of allowing oneself not to be in control. For Doctor Cottard, this expression is always a visible sign of hope. Along with gratitude as an expression of life truly understood, this strange combination of compassion as bounded freedom is, for him, a final sign of recovery, of somebody having made their way back into the world of perpetual change, having understood that boundless freedom can be as destructive as discipline without a purpose. One of the most tempting forms of boundless freedom is a limitless empathy with the suffering of the world. It is tempting to suffer the world, to assume responsibility for carrying the suffering of the whole world on one's shoulders, as if one *were* the world. It is tempting because it is often the easiest way to avoid taking responsibility for one's own suffering. *Not* to identify with the suffering of the world, *not* to be washed away by it, *not* to allow one's own suffering to be absolved by the suffering of the world, *that* is the first sign of somebody who truly empathises with suffering in the world. They no longer empathise in order to be absolved of their own suffering. But this requires discipline and what Doctor Cottard sees on Luc's face is that strange manifestation of compassion as discipline. He has mastered something essential about the art of becoming an incarnated person, somebody who can suffer an embodied life.

'Ah, yes, that night,' remarks Doctor Cottard. 'We never spoke about that.' It is his turn to quickly glance at his watch. 'It may be important that we do. Can we? Don't worry about your parents. If they arrive early, Maurice will look after them.'

Luc hesitates for a second. Then he says, 'Yes, perhaps we should. But would what I say remain confidential?'

'Of course,' replies Doctor Cottard. 'Like other therapists, I take doctor-patient confidentiality very seriously.'

But Luc still looks worried. 'Even if something came out that implicated . . . well, both of us in something that may be construed as wrong, even criminal? Would you be obliged to report me or us to the police?'

There is a faint trace of indignation on Doctor Cottard's face – as if somebody he had thought understood him suddenly revealed how little they understood him. 'You should know by now, Luc, that I do not deal in the currency of judgements, successes and failures. My only interest in cause and effect is to understand the unfolding of karma. The rest – all the judgements and punishments, the noise of reprimands and rewards that may be necessary to sustain life in society – all of that, I happily leave to the police. That is not my domain, so feel free to tell me anything you want.'

And so Luc tells him about the night he had planned to burn the gazebo and the walkway with the vines, all the way to the storeroom; how he had stacked a pile of kindling and wood five feet high and how, just as he sat down on his haunches to light the fire, he saw Angèle walk across the lawn and disappear into the forest; how he had followed her, but failed to find her and how, having decided to postpone the fire to another night, he had looked in on Angèle and comforted her and how, finally, when he least expected it, the words 'I know. I know' tumbled out of his mouth.

Doctor Cottard has been listening carefully, palms pressed against each other, chin resting on his fingertips. When Luc stops, he says, 'I did not know any of this. I did detect a change in you after that day, but I was unsure what to make of it. I knew you would tell me when you were ready. I don't know if you know this, but one of the two people who died that night was an Agnes somebody. I can't recall her surname now. There was a bit of a media frenzy about it because she was far away from home, alone; her husband did not know that she was travelling home that night; said she had been in Switzerland on vacation, but you know what people are like. A story emerged in the tabloid papers that she had not been on vacation, but was returning from a secret rendezvous with her lover, supposedly a well-known novelist who also lives in Paris. Anyway, none of that is interesting. But I understand your concern and, no, there is nothing to report to anyone.'

Luc is visibly relieved.

'Remember what I told you in our second session about karma, Luc. We are all here to live through the causes and effects of an infinite chain or network of causes and effects, some in this life and some in the next life. The story of this Agnes is a good example. She was born, I should imagine, like most of us, in a world she may or may not have felt she adequately understood; perhaps she was content, perhaps not. Perhaps she kept asking herself some version of the same question we all ask ourselves at some point: Why was I born into this world at this particular time, or to these particular parents? Why *this* life? And like anyone else, she lived a novel life, or at least believed she did, as we all do, but failed or did not have the time to understand the consequences of some of her actions and how they would culminate in a certain incident, all of which was beyond her control and, in a very real sense, beyond her understanding. Her death was an example of that. For me, all that matters is understanding, with a certain compassion, something of the intricate network of intentions and consequences that brought Angèle here, which made you and her get along, the circumstances that drove her to the decision to end her life that night and how, instead, this Agnes died as a result of another set – no, a whole network of causes and effects unrelated to Angèle's life, which nonetheless intersected and became part of her life and her decision to drive home that night.'

Luc nods. 'I get that now. When you went on about karma that time, I didn't quite know what to make of it, but the way you describe it now makes perfect sense. It's a strange kind of comfort. Not quite useful, but also not entirely useless.'

Doctor Cottard smiles. Then he glances at his watch. 'I think I heard your parents arrive. Shall we?'

'Sure,' says Luc, as they both stand up. They are halfway to the door when Luc, relaxed and with his hands in his pockets, stops and turns to Doctor Cottard. 'I made the right decision not to go back with my father, I know this. It was the right call. I am happy here. But there is just one thing that I wish for.'

'And what is that?'

'The day he came to my room, he told me that he was working on a novel with a bunch of characters from this place, including me. It was all very strange, I thought, that he could have written about us before any of us discovered the portal and visited each other's worlds. I know the portal is closed now, but I kind of wish there was a way to stay in touch with him. I don't know – maybe to let him know that it doesn't matter whether what he writes is correct or not. Know what I mean?'

'That's a lovely, generous thought, Luc, but I don't think you should worry about him too much. Your father seemed to be a very perceptive man. Come to think of it, I found him quite iridescent. Just like you.'

'Funny you should say that,' answers Luc. 'He also referred to that.'

'What?'

'My iridescence.'

Doctor Cottard opens the door. 'I'm sure you'll find your parents in the lounge.'

15

It is late afternoon by the time I finish writing, lock my office and walk over to the lifts. I will think about when to fill in all the blanks that precede the final scene and perhaps at that point add a final paragraph at the end. *What should I make of Luc's determination that there was indeed a gazebo – that that was where he wanted to start the fire?* The poster that advertised 'The Mathematics of Affect' lecture had been replaced by another poster advertising something trying equally desperately to sound interesting. I get on my bicycle and head home. The worst of rush-hour traffic is over, but I still stop at every intersection to look left and right, even when the light is green for me. When I get to the shopping complex, I turn into the parking lot and chain my bicycle to the railing in front of the supermarket. I have a sudden craving for a slow-roasted leg of lamb, simply prepared with rosemary, garlic and lemon, and with all the usual trimmings, including mint sauce. If I get it in the oven as soon as I get home, it will be ready by the time I have cleaned the apartment and decided what movie to rent. I pay for the groceries and on the way to my bicycle briefly stop in front of the bottle store. I think about it for a second, but then decide against buying a bottle of whisky. I want to savour this quiet sense of completion. When I get to the curio shop, I cannot help stopping. It is closed. Inside, the lights are on and the mysterious shopkeeper is nowhere to be seen. Then Dreyer is suddenly next to me.

'Hey, Dreyer. How's it going?' I say.

'Who knows?' he replies. 'Where have you been? Haven't seen you for a while.'

'Oh, here and there,' I say.

'That's the spirit,' he says, 'keep moving, keep moving' and he limps away, his eyes fixed on a vehicle whose back lights indicate that it is about to start the perilous journey out of its parking bay. I look back at the window and focus intensely on the glass surface. Depth of perception is such a fascinating thing – as is our ocular ability to effortlessly control it. When I focus intently on the window, I can see small stains, the odd fingerprint and thin traces of tears – the only remnants of that afternoon's Civil Servant storm, which I hardly noticed because I was so engrossed in my writing. But when I relax my focus slightly and look right through the glass, the whole display of arts and crafts and everything else that had been marginalised in my field of vision as long as I was focused on the glass flood my visual field again. A knitted cupcake of bright African colours next to several figures made of wire: a man on a bicycle, a woman in mid-stride with a basket on her head, a pile of handmade aprons with prints of the Big Five. When I relax my focus even more and try not to focus at all on the shop and what is inside it, I become aware of an even larger world at the periphery of my vision. In the same way that for someone who can suddenly hear for the first time all the sounds come rushing into view, in the reflection in front of me the scene behind me bursts into life: cars drive by, the spindly branches of the surreal green fever trees reach into the sky, the old woman with the pile of scarves draped over her left arm pauses to wipe the sweat from her forehead and Dreyer, now with his back to me, pilots the car out of its parking bay, his little arm making small circles in the air.

Printed and bound by CPI Group (UK) Ltd, Croydon, CR0 4YY
06/04/2026
14854929-0001